Outstanding praise for Joanne Fluke and the Hannah Swensen mysteries!

CHOCOLATE CREAM PIE MURDER

"Hannah's fans will relish following Hannah's journey as she heals and becomes stronger, surrounded by the love of family and the many familiar, quirky residents of Lake Eden. Many delicious-sounding recipes are woven through the story, and Fluke ends this cozy mystery with another cliff-hanger, which will have readers eagerly awaiting the next installment."
—*Booklist*

CHRISTMAS CAKE MURDER

"This is a lovely, frothy treat, a perfect no-hassle Christmas read."

DOUBLE FUDGE BROWNIE MURDER

"Lively . . . Add the big surprise ending, and fans will be more than satisfied."
—*Publishers Weekly*

Outstanding praise for Laura Levine and the Jaine Austen mysteries!

DEATH OF A NEIGHBORHOOD SCROOGE

"This is a thoroughly enjoyable cozy with just the right balance of crime, humor, and holiday spirit."
—*Publishers Weekly* (Starred Review)

MURDER HAS NINE LIVES

"Another expertly conceived whodunit."
—*Fresh Fiction*

Books by Joanne Fluke

Hannah Swensen Mysteries

CHOCOLATE CHIP COOKIE MURDER
STRAWBERRY SHORTCAKE MURDER
BLUEBERRY MUFFIN MURDER
LEMON MERINGUE PIE MURDER
FUDGE CUPCAKE MURDER
SUGAR COOKIE MURDER
PEACH COBBLER MURDER
CHERRY CHEESECAKE MURDER
KEY LIME PIE MURDER
CANDY CANE MURDER
CARROT CAKE MURDER
CREAM PUFF MURDER
PLUM PUDDING MURDER
APPLE TURNOVER MURDER
DEVIL'S FOOD CAKE MURDER
GINGERBREAD COOKIE MURDER
CINNAMON ROLL MURDER
RED VELVET CUPCAKE MURDER
BLACKBERRY PIE MURDER
DOUBLE FUDGE BROWNIE MURDER
WEDDING CAKE MURDER
CHRISTMAS CARAMEL MURDER
BANANA CREAM PIE MURDER
RASPBERRY DANISH MURDER
CHRISTMAS CAKE MURDER
CHOCOLATE CREAM PIE MURDER
JOANNE FLUKE'S LAKE EDEN COOKBOOK

Suspense Novels

VIDEO KILL
WINTER CHILL
DEAD GIVEAWAY
THE OTHER CHILD
COLD JUDGMENT
FATAL IDENTITY
FINAL APPEAL
VENGEANCE IS MINE
EYES
WICKED
DEADLY MEMORIES
THE STEPCHILD

Books by Laura Levine

THIS PEN FOR HIRE
LAST WRITES
KILLER BLONDE
SHOES TO DIE FOR
THE PMS MURDER
DEATH BY PANTYHOSE
CANDY CANE MURDER
KILLING BRIDEZILLA
KILLER CRUISE
DEATH OF A TROPHY WIFE
GINGERBREAD COOKIE MURDER
PAMPERED TO DEATH
DEATH OF A NEIGHBORHOOD WITCH
KILLING CUPID
DEATH BY TIARA

CHRISTMAS SWEETS

JOANNE FLUKE
LAURA LEVINE
LESLIE MEIER

KENSINGTON BOOKS
www.kensingtonbooks.com

KENSINGTON BOOKS are published by

Kensington Publishing Corp.
119 West 40th Street
New York, NY 10018

Compilation copyright © 2019 by Kensington Publishing Corp.
"Twelve Desserts of Christmas" copyright © 2006 by Joanne Fluke
"Nightmare on Elf Street" copyright © 2013 by Laura Levine
"The Christmas Thief" copyright © 2012 by Leslie Meier

All Kensington Titles, Imprints, and Distributed Lines are available at special quantity discounts for bulk purchases for sales promotions, premiums, fund-raising, and educational or institutional use. Special book excerpts or customized printings can also be created to fit specific needs. For details, write or phone the office of the Kensington special sales manager: Kensington Publishing Corp., 119 West 40th Street, New York, NY 10018, attn: Special Sales Department, Phone: 1-800-221-2647.

Kensington and the K logo Reg. U.S. Pat. & TM Off.

ISBN-13: 978-1-4967-2693-3
ISBN-10: 1-4967-2693-6
First Kensington Trade Paperback Edition: November 2019
First Kensington Mass Market Edition: November 2020

ISBN-13: 978-1-4967-2694-0 (ebook)
ISBN-10: 1-4967-2694-4 (ebook)

10 9 8 7 6 5 4 3 2 1

Printed in the United States of America

Contents

THE TWELVE DESSERTS OF CHRISTMAS

JOANNE FLUKE

Dear Hannah Fans,

I'm really excited about seeing my Hannah Swensen story "Twelve Desserts of Christmas" in print again! I wrote it in 2006, and Hannah has experienced a lot of life since then. She's received three proposals, accepted one, danced at her mother's wedding reception, become an aunt twice-over, and solved more than twenty-five murder cases. Life speeds past at warp speed in Lake Eden, Minnesota, the little murder capital of the world!

In "Twelve Desserts of Christmas" you'll find twelve of my favorite dessert recipes. Hannah has been asked to bake desserts for a boarding school a few miles from town. It's the holiday season, but six children are still at the boarding school, unable to go home for various reasons. Hannah brings joy and plenty of sweet treats to the kids and the two teachers who have volunteered to stay with them.

Of course there's a mystery. There's always a mystery. And, just as you expect if you've read the Hannah series, Hannah plays a major part in solving it. There's plenty of fun, some wonderfully yummy recipes, a generous helping of humor, and a little romance to sweeten the story.

I do hope you like "Twelve Desserts of Christmas" and I hope you'll read Hannah's other books. Her newest adventure is in bookstores and it's called *Coconut Layer Cake Murder.* And now I have to sign off because my stove timer is ringing and I have a Coconut Layer Cake about to come out of the oven! It smells simply mouthwatering, and I wish you were here to share it with me.

Life is short, so eat dessert first!

Joanne Fluke

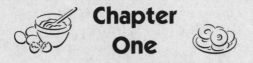

Chapter One

It was a mild day by Minnesota standards. The temperature was in the low teens, and there was no wind to kick up the foot and a half of snow on the ground. The skies were leaden gray and more snow was predicted before the day was over, but Julie Jansen didn't have time to think about the weather.

She fairly flew across the quad, sprinting for the oldest and most impressive brick building on the campus. Only the corrugated rubber soles on her snow boots kept her from wiping out as she hit the patch of ice that always formed near the flagpole. Julie was breathing hard as she pulled open the heavy door to the main building and stopped at the cloakroom to make a lightning-fast switch from boots to shoes. Then the race was on again and she dashed down the hallway, breaking the school rule about running in the halls, her dark blond ponytail whipping from side to side the way it had when she'd been a cheerleader at Jordan High. There'd been no time to braid her hair and put it up in the elaborate style she wore in the classroom to make her look older. She'd slept through her alarm, and there had been barely enough time to dress. It was departure day at Lakes Academy and Julie was late for the final faculty meeting before Christmas vacation.

Julie skidded around the corner, the ends of her silk scarf flapping, and headed into the home stretch. Perhaps they hadn't started yet. Maybe Dr. Caulder had gotten a last-minute call and she could slide into her chair before he came in. But her hopes died a quick death as she neared her destination. The door to the conference room was standing open and she could hear the headmaster's stentorian voice. His head was turned away from the door and Julie did her best to slink in unnoticed, but just as she thought she was going to succeed, he turned to look her way. Julie sank into her chair, her cheeks hot and her breath coming in little puffs from the exertion. Could her students possibly be correct when they claimed that Dr. Caulder had eyes in the back of his head?

"We're so glad you decided to join us, Miss Jansen," Dr. Caulder intoned, and thirteen pairs of eyes turned to stare at her disapprovingly. The fourteenth pair, a warm brown color that reminded Julie of melted chocolate, held only compassion for her embarrassment and what Julie hoped was the beginnings of romance. Matt Sherwood, the second-newest teacher at Lakes Academy, knew exactly why she was late. They'd attended the Christmas program in the auditorium and after their students had left, they'd taken a stroll under the tall pines that stood like sentinels outside the main gate of the academy and he'd held her close to his side. Shivering a bit after the cold excursion, Julie had suggested sharing the thermos of hot chocolate the cook always left out for teachers who worked late, and they'd stayed up until almost three in the morning.

Julie tore her eyes away from Matt's and turned to the headmaster to apologize. But instead of scowling, Dr. Caulder was smiling at her! That was ominous, and Julie clamped her lips shut and let her gaze skitter away. When she'd first arrived at the academy in September, one of the older teachers had told her that the only time Dr. Caulder ever smiled at a teacher was when he was getting ready to put one over on her.

"Ah, the enthusiasm of youth!" Dr. Caulder's smile grew a bit wider. "I happen to know that Miss Jansen was up very late last night, but here she is, only five minute late, ready to share her love of learning and her zest for life with us."

Uh-oh, Julie groaned under her breath. Dr. Caulder must have had his spies out last night. It was recommended that teachers retire before midnight and most of the older staff did just that. But someone had spotted her with Matt and squealed on them. If Julie ever found out who the rat with the big mouth was, she'd . . .

"This is one of the reasons I'm sure Miss Jansen won't mind filling in for us this year. If my wife and I weren't expected at her sister's, we'd be glad to shoulder the responsibility. Unfortunately, it's a bit late to change our plans. We'll be back here the day after Christmas to assume charge."

What's he talking about? Julie shot a silent question to her co-conspirator in late-night conversation, but Matt gave a little shrug of the broad shoulders she found so attractive. It seemed her partner in after-curfew crime didn't know either.

"As always, we're the last to know," Dr. Caulder said with a sigh. "The reasons are varied, some legitimate and others . . . shall we say, impossibly lame?"

There were several titters from the older members of the staff. Julie shot another glance at Matt and was pleased to see that he looked almost as puzzled as she felt.

"Six unfortunate children will be staying here over the semester break," Dr. Caulder went on to explain, "three girls and three boys. That means two teachers, one male and one female, must be in residence to supervise them. This is where you enter the picture, Miss Jansen. Because you're unmarried and have no pressing family obligation, I would appreciate it if you'd stay with the girls. Of course you certainly have the option to decline. And if you do, we'll simply have to make other arrangements."

Julie thought about it for a moment. She didn't have anywhere she *had* to go for Christmas. Her parents were taking the Christmas cruise they'd always dreamed of, and she'd planned to spend the holidays with her older brother. They'd never been close, and David and his wife would probably be relieved if she canceled. Then her nieces wouldn't have to double up to give her a bedroom.

"Miss Jansen?"

Julie drew a deep breath and jumped in with both feet. "I'll be glad to stay, Dr. Caulder."

"Excellent! All of us appreciate your sacrifice."

Julie noticed with surprise that there were smiles and nods around the table. It seemed all she had to do to be accepted by the rest of the staff was to take a job nobody else wanted. She smiled back and waited for the other shoe to drop. Dr. Caulder needed a male teacher for the boys and there were only two unmarried male teachers on the staff. One was Mr. Leavenger, the math teacher. He was only a year or two away from retirement and a bit of a curmudgeon. Spending Christmas vacation with Mr. Leavenger as her sole adult companion would seem endless, but she could handle it if she had to. The only other unmarried teacher was . . . dared she hope?

"Mr. Sherwood," Dr. Caulder voiced the name that was dancing across the screen of Julie's mind. "I notice that you have no family commitments. Would you mind staying here with Miss Jansen and supervising the boys?"

"Not at all."

"I thought not," Dr. Caulder said dryly.

Matt had answered so quickly, Julie's cheeks felt hot and she hoped she wasn't blushing. The kiss they'd shared at her door had been a lot more romantic than casual. And as far as Julie was concerned, it certainly beat their former colleague-to-colleague friendship. A little tingle of anticipation swept from the top of her head right down to her toes. If the speed of Matt's answer was any indication, perhaps he was starting to feel about her the way she already felt about him.

There was the usual bustle as the parents arrived. Suitcases were dropped and spilled open, apologies filled the crisp air as parents collided in a headlong rush to hug their children, and students hollered out their good-byes to their friends. The first car left, followed by the second, and less than an hour later the last car drove away through the freshly fallen snow, leaving six dejected children and two concerned teachers in their wake.

Julie glanced down at the three girls she was shepherding. Six-year-old Hope looked more dejected than hopeful, her older sister Joy wasn't at all joyful, and Serena, the oldest of the girls at almost thirteen, was about as far from serene as a girl could get. One look at Matt's boys and Julie knew they were in big trouble. Spenser, who'd just turned fourteen, and Gary and Larry, ten-year-old twins whose parents were getting a divorce, didn't look any more cheerful than the girls. She had to do something to take their minds off the fact that they wouldn't be with their families this Christmas.

"Let's plan something special for this afternoon," Matt said, beating Julie to the punch. "We've got the whole place to ourselves and we can do anything we want."

"Anything?" Julie asked him, winking at the girls.

"Well . . . almost anything. What did you have in mind, Miss Jansen?"

Julie gave him a mischievous smile. "I want to borrow a pair of roller skates and skate down the main hallway."

"But that's against the rules, Miss Jansen," Serena pointed out. "It's double demerits."

"Then it should be double the fun. What do you have to do to get a single demerit?"

"Well . . . you get one if you eat in your room, and one if you run in the hall."

"Okay. Let's do those too! We'll eat ice cream in our rooms straight out of the carton." Julie noticed that this drew smiles from all the kids, so she went on. "I ran in the halls this morning when I was late to the teacher's meeting, and it was great. We can line up and have a race from the front door all the way to Dr. Caulder's office and back again. And when we're done with that, we'll let Hope decide what's next. How about it, Hope? What would you like to do?"

"I want to talk real loud in the library." Hope's eyes began to sparkle. "That's against the rules."

"And I want to dance on top of my teacher's desk," Joy chimed in. "What do you want to do, Serena?"

"I want to draw a mustache on Dr. Caulder's picture."

Larry gasped loudly. "You can't do that! He'll find out . . ."

". . . you did it," Gary took over his twin's thought, "and he'll give you a million demerits!"

"No, he won't, not if I wash it off before he gets back. What do you want to do, Spense?"

"I want to climb up to the bell tower and throw snow-balls."

"Us too!" Gary seconded it. "Larry and I . . ."

". . . always wanted to do that," Larry finished the sentence for him.

"No way," Matt said, and everyone turned to look at him. Was he going to be a stickler and enforce the rules? But then Matt started to grin, and everyone knew he'd been teasing. "I won't let you climb up to the bell tower unless I get to throw the first snowball."

"Deal!" the boys shouted, and Julie noticed that everyone was wearing a smile . . . everyone except Hope, who looked worried again.

"What is it, Hope?" Julie asked her.

"I saw Mrs. Dryer leave. Are we going to starve to death before she comes back?"

"Of course we won't!" Julie reached out to give her a hug. "Mrs. Dryer made lots of dinners before she left, and she put them in the freezer for us. Dr. Caulder told me she even baked a ham for our Christmas dinner."

"How about Christmas cookies?" Larry wanted to know. "The ones with colored . . ."

". . . frosting that look like Santas, and Christmas trees, and stars and stuff," Gary finished the description.

"Yes," Hope chimed in. "It won't be Christmas without cookies."

"I'm sure she made those too," Matt said, stepping up to take Julie's arm. "Come on men. Let's escort the ladies to the kitchen so we can find out what goodies Mrs. Dryer left for us."

"Uh-oh." Julie gave a little groan as she read the note the school cook had taped to the refrigerator.

"What's the matter?" Matt left the children exclaiming over the menus Mrs. Dryer had written out for them and walked over to join Julie. "Mrs. Dryer didn't bake your favorite?"

"Mrs. Dryer didn't bake *anyone's* favorite."

"What do you mean?"

"She left a note apologizing, but she barely had time to make the entrees. She ordered Christmas ice cream rolls, with little green Christmas trees in the middle, but they didn't come."

"You mean . . . no desserts?"

Julie nodded, holding up the note. "She says there's a whole case of Jell-O in assorted flavors and some canned fruit cocktail in the pantry, but that's it."

"No Christmas cookies?" Hope asked, tears threatening again.

"Of course there'll be Christmas cookies," Matt assured her. "Since Mrs. Dryer didn't have time to do it, we'll bake them ourselves. You bake, don't you, Miss Jansen?"

"Actually . . . no," Julie admitted, feeling a bit like crying herself. "I'm the world's worst baker. I took home economics in high school. All the girls did. But the only one who could burn things faster than I could was Andrea Swensen. We were cheerleaders together at Jordan High, and they called us the Twinkie Twins."

"Why?"

"Because every time they held a bake sale to raise money for the pep squad, every girl was supposed to bring something to school to sell. Andrea and I used to bring Twinkies, until her sister found out about it and then Hannah . . ." Julie stopped speaking and started to smile.

"Why are you smiling like that?" Matt wanted to know.

"Hannah baked like a dream, and all we had to do was tell her when the bake sales were and she'd bake for us. I can still taste her lemon meringue pie. It was just fantastic. But here's the good part. The last time I talked to Andrea, she said Hannah was back home and she'd opened a bakery and coffee shop in Lake Eden."

"Lake Eden?" Matt began to smile too. "That's only twenty miles away."

"Exactly. Why don't I call and see if Hannah would bake us some desserts?"

"Great idea!" Matt said, and the kids all nodded.

"Okay. Then the only question is, how many desserts do we need?" Julie flipped over Mrs. Dryer's sad little note about the absence of desserts and pulled out a pen.

"One for every night," Matt said.

"Got it," Julie said, her pen moving quickly across the paper. "Do you think we should order extra desserts, like cookies and muffins and cupcakes, for snacks? Or is that too much?"

Matt glanced at the kids and saw the six hopeful expressions. "It's not too much. Let's order an even dozen."

If extra-wide smiles and grateful expressions could

have been translated into dollars, Matt would have been a rich man. As it was, he and Julie were heroes of the day, and that pleased him much more than anything else he could think of.

"Counting Mr. Sherwood and me, there are eight of us," Julie went on, "and that means everyone can choose a favorite dessert. Then we'll decide on four others together, and that'll make twelve. We'll have the Twelve Desserts of Christmas, almost like the song."

"That's right." Matt flashed Julie a smile that included their whole group. "We could even change the lyrics and sing it for our friends when they get back."

"Willie's gonna wish he stayed here," Spenser said, grinning widely.

Serena nodded. "Liz too. She kept telling me about all the presents she was getting, but I bet she won't have twelve desserts."

"That means we're special," Joy added.

"We certainly are," Julie confirmed it, smiling at each child in turn. "Let's get busy so I can call Hannah. Now who wants to choose tonight's dessert?"

It seemed to be the morning for running late. Twenty miles away in the little Minnesota town of Lake Eden, Hannah Swensen was almost an hour behind schedule. "I'm really sorry, Lisa," she apologized to her partner for the fourth time since she'd dashed into the kitchen at The Cookie Jar, their bakery and coffee shop. "I really didn't mean to saddle you with all the baking this morning."

"That's okay," Lisa said, passing a tray of Chocolate Chip Crunch Cookies to Hannah. "Herb gave me a ride to town this morning in his squad car, so I got here early.

Mayor Bascomb asked him to figure out how many tickets he gave for speeding in the school zone in front of Jordan High."

"Why does Mayor Bascomb need to know that?" Hannah asked, placing the pan of baked cookies on the baker's rack.

"The city council's voting on speed bumps this morning and the mayor wants to prove that we need them."

"Do you know what they call speed bumps in the Bahamas?" Hannah asked, turning to face her partner.

"No, what?"

"Sleeping policemen." Hannah delivered the information and then stared hard at her partner. Either Lisa had developed a facial tick or she was doing her utmost to stifle a laugh. "You think sleeping policemen is funny?"

Lisa shook her head. "It's more cute than funny."

"Then why are you trying so hard not to laugh?"

"It's your hair. It's poking up out of your cap again."

"Just call me Medusa." Hannah gave an exasperated sigh and tucked her unruly red curls back under her health board mandated cap. "The phone started ringing while I was washing it and I didn't get a chance to put on the conditioner. What do we have left to bake?"

"Just the Cherry Winks and we're through."

"Right. I'll get the cherries." Hannah headed off to the pantry to fetch the essential ingredient for the cookies her customers loved at the holidays. "Do you think it's too early to do half red and half green?"

"I don't think so. Almost everyone is already decorated for Christmas. Gil Surma put his lights up over three weeks ago."

"Gil and Bonnie are always early. They want everything to look nice for their Christmas parties."

Lisa glanced at the calendar that hung on the wall by the phone and saw the three new entries that Hannah had made. "Bonnie called you to set dates for the parties?"

"That's right. We're catering everything, just like last year."

"She gave you the order for her Brownies?"

"Yes. And yes."

Lisa looked a bit confused. "Why did you say two yeses?"

"She wants brownies for her Brownies."

"Oh. I guess that makes sense. Let's make them in bon-bon papers the way my mother used to do. Then I can frost them and put half a pecan on each one."

"The girls would love that, but are you sure you want to go to so much work?"

"I'm sure." Lisa glanced at the calendar again. "What does she want for the Cub Scout party?"

"Old-Fashioned Sugar Cookies. But the party's not just for the Cub Scouts. It's one huge party for the Boy Scouts and the Cub Scouts together, and it's going to last all afternoon."

"That's nice. I'll do the scout logo in frosting on the sugar cookies. The boys really like that. How about the Girl Scouts?"

"Bonnie's driving them to the mall so they can shop for their parents. Then they're going back to her house for hot chocolate and Cinnamon Crisps."

Lisa glanced at the calendar again. "I can help you cater the Girl Scout party. Herb's got bowling league that night."

"Great." Hannah smiled at her young partner. Lisa had more energy than anyone she'd ever met. Of course age might have something to do with it. She had just turned twenty, and Hannah was a decade and a bit past that. Not that she wanted to think about age, especially when her biological clock was ticking and her mother delighted in reminding her that she didn't have many childbearing years left. And now it was almost Christmas, and everyone was talking about families and kids.

Hannah's smile took a wistful turn. Soon her newest niece, Bethany, would be old enough to give her that wonderful wide baby grin and reach up to pat her face. Babies were delightful with their chubby little hands, their squeals of utter delight when you tickled them, and their warm, sweet scent.

"What?" Lisa asked, noticing that Hannah had stopped at the pantry door and was staring at the wall.

"Oh! Uh . . . nothing. I was just thinking, that's all."

"Don't forget to save the red cherry juice for the dough," Lisa reminded her as Hannah got out the cherries. "Green juice makes them look really yucky."

"Yucky's not good in a bakery," Hannah said, heading back to the workstation. "People want things to taste good, but they also like . . ." She stopped abruptly and turned to eye the phone on the wall as it began to ring. "Mother!" she said with the same inflection she would have voiced if she'd slid off the road into a ditch. It wasn't that she disliked her mother. It was just that Delores had already called her three times this morning.

"You're sure it's your mother?"

"I'm sure. Nobody places orders this early and we don't open for another forty-five minutes. Who else could it be?"

"But I thought your mother called you at home and that's why you were late."

"She did."

"I see. But she has to call again because she's got something she forgot to tell you?"

"You got it." Hannah turned to eye her partner suspiciously. "Has my mother been calling you too?"

"No, Marge has."

Hannah was amazed. She'd always thought calling back several times was a trait unique to her mother. "Marge does that too?"

"Yes, but I don't mind. Marge is the best mother-in-law in the world."

Warning lights flashed in Hannah's logical mind. "Hold on. You can't make that kind of a value judgment without a standard of comparison."

"Sure I can." Lisa waved away her breech of logic. "I'm perfectly happy married to Herb, and there's no way I'm ever going to get another standard of comparison. That means this is it and Marge is the best mother-in-law in the world." Lisa stopped speaking and turned toward the ringing phone. "Are you going to get that, or do you want me to?"

"Will you?" Hannah asked, heading for the workstation. She'd have to talk to her mother eventually, but at least she could get in another sip of coffee before she had to do it.

"The Cookie Jar. Lisa speaking." Hannah watched as her partner grabbed a piece of paper and a pen. "Of course we can. We just baked a big batch of Chocolate Chip Crunch Cookies and we'll put them away for you. But . . . if you don't mind me asking . . . why do you need twelve dozen chocolate chip cookies?" There was a silence and then Lisa shrugged "Okay. We'll package them up for you right now."

"Who was that?" Hannah asked when her partner had hung up the phone.

"Your sister."

"Andrea?" Hannah guessed, and she wasn't surprised when Lisa nodded. Hannah's youngest sister, Michelle, was knee deep in final exams at Macalister College in Minneapolis. "What did Andrea say when you asked her why she needed twelve dozen cookies?"

"She told me it was a crisis and the whole thing was just awful."

"*What* whole thing?"

"I don't know. She said she was driving right over and she'd tell us all about it when she got here."

CHOCOLATE CHIP CRUNCH COOKIES

Preheat oven to
350 degrees F.,
rack in the middle position.

1 cup butter *(2 sticks, ½ pound)*
1 cup white *(granulated)* sugar
1 cup brown sugar *(pack it down in the cup)*
2 teaspoons baking soda
1 teaspoon salt
2 tcaspoons vanilla
2 beaten eggs *(you can just beat them up in a cup with a fork)*
2½ cups flour *(not sifted—pack it down in the measuring cup)*
2 cups cornflakes
1 to 2 cups chocolate chips

Melt the butter, add the sugars, and stir them all together in a large mixing bowl. Add the soda, salt, vanilla, and beaten eggs. Mix well. Then add the

flour and stir it in. Measure out the cornflakes and crush them with your hands. Then add them to your bowl and mix everything thoroughly.

Let the dough set on the counter for a minute or two to rest. *(It doesn't really need to rest, but you probably do.)*

Form the dough into walnut-sized balls with your fingers and place them on a greased cookie sheet, 12 to a standard sheet. *(I used Pam to grease my cookie sheets.)* Press the dough balls down just a bit with your impeccably clean hand so they won't roll off on the way to the oven.

Bake at 350 degrees F. for 10 to 12 minutes. Cool on the cookie sheet for 2 minutes, then remove the cookies to a wire rack until they're completely cool. *(The rack is important—it makes them crisp.)*

Yield: approximately 6 to 8 dozen, depending on cookie size.

Hannah's Note: If your cookies spread out too much in the oven, either chill it in the refrigerator before baking, or turn out the dough on a floured board and knead in approximately ⅓ cup more flour.

BON-BON BROWNIES

Preheat oven to 350 degrees F.,
rack in the middle position.

1 cup butter *(2 sticks, ½ pound)*
4 squares unsweetened baking chocolate *(for a total of 4 ounces)*
4 beaten eggs *(you can just beat them up in a glass with a fork)*
2 cups white *(granulated)* sugar
½ teaspoon salt
¼ teaspoon baking soda
2 teaspoons vanilla
1 cup flour *(don't sift—pack it down in the cup)*
1 cup chopped pecans *(walnuts will work also)*
Paper mini-muffin cupliners *(mine were marked 1⅝ inches on the package)*

Put the butter and the baking chocolate in a medium-sized microwave-safe bowl and heat it on HIGH for 2 minutes. Stir to see if it's melted. If it

isn't, microwave it in 20-second intervals until it is. Set the bowl on the counter to cool to room temperature.

Beat the eggs. Add them to the cooled chocolate mixture and stir until they're thoroughly incorporated. Then add the sugar, salt, baking soda, and vanilla and mix well. Add the flour in two half-cup increments, mixing after each addition. Stir in the chopped pecans.

Set out paper cups *(I use double papers)* on a cookie sheet, 12 to a standard-size sheet, and spoon in the brownie dough until they're ⅔ full. *(Don't use mini-muffin pans—you need the papers to spread out a little as they bake.)* Bake them at 350 degrees F. for 15 minutes, or until a toothpick inserted in the center comes out clean. Cool them by placing the cookie sheet on a wire rack.

When the brownies are completely cool, count out one pecan half to top every brownie and make the Milk Chocolate Fudge Frosting.

Milk Chocolate Fudge Frosting:

2 cups milk chocolate chips *(a 12-ounce package)*
One 14-ounce can sweetened condensed milk

If you use a double boiler for this frosting, it's foolproof. You can also make it in a heavy saucepan over low to medium heat on the stovetop, but you'll have to stir it constantly with a spatula to keep it from scorching.

Fill the bottom part of the double boiler with water. Make sure the water doesn't touch the underside of the top.

Put the chocolate chips in the top of the double boiler and set it over the bottom. Place the double boiler on the stovetop at medium heat. Stir occasionally until the chocolate chips are melted.

Stir in the can of sweetened condensed milk and cook approximately 2 minutes, stirring constantly, until the frosting is shiny and of spreading consistency.

Spread the frosting on the Bon-Bon Brownies, mounding it up nicely in the middle.

Place a half-pecan on top of each brownie before the frosting is set.

Give the frosting pan to your favorite person to scrape.

Leave the Bon-Bon Brownies on a cookie sheet, uncovered, until the frosting is dry to the touch. This should take about 25 minutes or so. *(If you're in a real hurry, put the brownies in the refrigerator to speed up the hardening process.)*

Yield: Makes approximately 6 dozen attractive little brownies.

Hannah's Note: If you have any frosting left over, place it in a small container, cover it tightly, and refrigerate it. The next time you have ice cream, just heat the frosting in the microwave and spoon it over the top for a terrific milk chocolate fudge sauce.

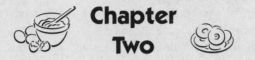

Chapter Two

"**O**h my!" Lisa gasped, staring at Andrea in shock. "That's just too sad for words."

"I know. I practically cried when Julie told me." Andrea settled herself on a stool at the workstation. She was wearing a soft rose-colored suit under a white fur jacket. Her shining blond hair was swept up in an elaborate twist, and the white fur hat that was perched on her head was far too small and dainty to protect her from the cold. Hannah glanced down at her own jeans and logo sweatshirt and quelled a small stab of jealousy. Her younger sister always dressed like a fashion model, and looked like one too.

Hannah pushed the plate of cookies closer to her sister. A few more calories wouldn't hurt Andrea's perfect figure, and it might make her feel better. "It does sound like a real tragedy."

"Absolutely," Andrea agreed, reaching for a cookie.

"Christmas is for families. No child should have to spend the holidays at boarding school."

"Oh, that's not the tragedy. Spending Christmas vacation at school is bad, but kids can survive something like that. Spending Christmas vacation without dessert is the *real* tragedy!"

"You're right." Andrea took a bite of her cookie and smiled her approval. "So you're going to bake desserts for Julie and the kids?"

"Of course. Was there ever any doubt?"

"Not really. Thank you, Hannah. I knew you'd come through for me. You remember Julie, don't you? We were on the cheerleading squad together."

"Of course I remember her. She was the only girl who could do five cartwheels in a row without getting dizzy."

"That's right. I really hate to ask, but could you run the cookies out to the academy this morning? Julie said the kids were really depressed when their friends left this morning and they need something to cheer them up. I'd do it myself, but I'm showing the old Goetz place at noon today."

Hannah was surprised. Andrea was a great real estate agent, but the Goetz place had been vacant for a year and it was practically falling down. "But the Goetz place is a real dump."

"Never say *dump*. Real estate professionals call a house like that *unloved*."

"*Unlovable* is more like it."

"Maybe to you, but these people are interested. So can you go out to the school with the cookies? Or should I take them later?"

"Hannah can take them," Lisa said. "The baking's done and the coffee's on in the shop. I don't have to open for another twenty minutes, and that gives me plenty of time to fill the serving jars and set up the tables."

Hannah wavered. She really wanted to see Julie again. "Well . . . if you're sure . . ."

"I'm sure. And while you're there, see if you can talk them into ordering apple crisp."

Julie must have been watching for her to arrive. When Hannah pulled up in the circular driveway of the school in her cookie truck, the front door opened and Julie stepped out. Hannah rushed to meet her and gave her a hug. "Hi, Julie. You haven't changed a bit."

"Yes, I have." Julie ginned widely. "See? No braces."

"That's true. So where are these poor little tykes who've been left without dessert?"

"Next door at Aames House. We thought separate dorms would be too lonely, so we're all staying there together. The kids are in the lounge, watching a movie with Matt."

Hannah went on alert as Julie said her fellow teacher's name. There was a slight breathless quality to her voice that turned the name into something approaching a vocal caress. Hannah was willing to bet the farm that whoever Matt was, he was more than just a fellow teacher.

"Who's Matt?" Hannah asked, preparing to listen for more vocal clues. Her cat, Moishe, could swivel both ears independently to pick up every nuance of sound, and for the first time in her life, Hannah wished she had that ability.

"Matt's the teacher who's staying with the boys. I'm taking care of the girls."

"And Matt is . . ." Hannah paused, trying to figure out

how to phrase it. Everyone always accused her of having no tact. "Young? Handsome? Unmarried?"

Julie gave a little chuckle and her cheeks turned pink. "He's three out of three."

"And you didn't really mind giving up your Christmas vacation as long as Matt was staying here too?"

Julie gave the type of smile that Hannah associated with Moishe, right after she'd presented him with a bowl of vanilla ice cream. "I don't mind at all," she said.

"And Matt doesn't mind either?" Hannah guessed.

"I don't think so. He's marvelous, Hannah. Tall, handsome, bright, caring, and absolutely great with children."

Hannah just grinned. It was clear that Julie had fallen harder than a novice ice-skater for Matt. She just hoped that Matt felt the same way about Julie.

"Andrea called and said you were bringing cookies. Do you want me to help you carry them?"

"Good idea." Hannah opened the back door of the cookie truck and loaded Julie up with three bakery boxes. She took the other two boxes, closed the truck door, and followed Julie to Aames House.

"Let's take them straight to the lounge," Julie said, leading the way down the long hallway with a spring in her step that reminded Hannah of a colt frolicking in a green pasture.

"We have to stop at the kitchen first. I brought dessert for tonight and it needs to go into the refrigerator."

"What is it?" Julie gave a little skip that made Hannah laugh.

"Lemon meringue pie. You used to always ask me to bake it when you were in high school."

"You remembered!" Julie looked delighted. "It's still

my favorite, Hannah. And it's on the list, because I chose it for my dessert. Nobody makes it like you do."

When they reached the large kitchen, Hannah headed straight for the refrigerator to stash the pies on a shelf. Then she glanced around at the gleaming appliances and nodded. "Nice kitchen. It's arranged just right to be really efficient."

"Is it?" Julie frowned slightly. "I really wouldn't know. Kitchens are still unexplored territory to me."

"What do you do when you're home alone? Go out to dinner every night?"

"No, that's too expensive. Teachers aren't exactly rolling in money, you know. I fix meals for myself, but if it doesn't come in a package with microwave directions, I don't buy it."

"I figured as much," Hannah said, remembering that Andrea and Julie had tied for the bottom of the class in home economics.

"Come on, Hannah." Julie started for the door. "I really want you to meet Matt. I'm hoping . . . well . . . I guess I might as well tell you."

Hannah was silent, even though she thought she knew what Julie was about to say. Her sister's cheerleading buddy was blushing again.

"I think Matt might be Mr. Right. I'm pretty sure he feels the same way, but teaching full-time is a demanding job and there's not much time for dating. This is the first time we've ever had the chance to be alone together."

"You're not alone here," Hannah couldn't help pointing out.

"I know that. We've got six chaperones, but the kids go to bed early. And then Matt and I have the whole rest of the night together."

"Really?"

Julie gulped and her already pink cheeks turned scarlet. "I didn't mean it *that* way!"

"Of course not," Hannah said, holding back a chuckle with real effort.

"Anyway, I really want to know what you think of Matt. I spent so much time with Andrea while I was growing up that you've always been like a big sister to me. Mom and Dad aren't here, so . . . you'll tell me what you think of him, won't you?"

"Absolutely," Hannah said, hoping that Matt would be everything Julie thought he was and she wouldn't have to deflate the only Jordan High cheerleader who'd ever been able to do a flip from the top of a five-person pyramid and land on her feet smiling.

LEMON MERINGUE PIE

Preheat oven to 350 degrees F.,
rack in the middle position.

One 9-inch baked pic shell

The filling:
  3 whole eggs
  4 egg yolks *(save the whites in a mixing
      bowl and let them come up to room tem-
      perature—you'll need them for the
      meringue)*
  ½ cup water
  ⅛ cup lime juice
  ⅓ cup lemon juice
  1 cup white *(granulated)* sugar
  ¼ cup cornstarch
  1 to 2 teaspoons grated lemon zest
  1 tablespoon butter

*(Using a double boiler makes this recipe fool-
proof, but if you're very careful and stir constantly
so it doesn't scorch, you can make the lemon fill-*

ing in a heavy saucepan directly on the stove over medium heat.)

Put some tap water in the bottom of a double boiler and heat it until it simmers. *(Make sure you don't use too much water—it shouldn't touch the bottom of the pan on top.)* Off the heat, beat the egg yolks with the whole eggs in the top of the double boiler. Add the ½ cup water, lemon juice, and lime juice. Combine sugar and cornstarch in a small bowl and stir until completely blended. Add this to the egg mixture in the top of the double boiler and blend thoroughly.

Place the top of the double boiler over the simmering water and cook, stirring frequently, until the lemon pie filling thickens *(5 minutes or so).* Lift the top of the double boiler and place it on a cold burner. Add the lemon zest and the butter, and stir thoroughly. Let the filling cool while you make the meringue.

The meringue *(This is a whole lot easier with an electric mixer!)*
 4 egg whites
 ½ teaspoon cream of tartar
 ⅛ teaspoon salt
 ¼ cup white *(granulated)* sugar

Add the cream of tartar and salt to the egg whites and mix them in. Beat the egg whites on high until they form soft peaks. Continue beating as you sprinkle in the sugar. When the egg whites form firm peaks, stop mixing and tip the bowl to test the meringue. If the egg whites don't slide down the side, they're ready.

Put the filling into the baked pie shell, smoothing it with a rubber spatula. Clean and dry your spatula. Spread the meringue over the filling with the clean spatula, sealing it to the edges of the crust. When the pie is completely covered with meringue, "dot" the pie with the flat side of the spatula to make points in the meringue. *(The meringue will shrink back when it bakes if you don't seal it to the edges of the crust.)*

Bake the pie at 350 degrees F. for no more than 10 minutes.

Remove the pie from the oven, let it cool to room temperature on a wire rack, and then refrigerate it if you wish. This pie can be served at room temperature, but it will slice more easily if it's chilled.

(To keep your knife from sticking to the meringue when you cut the pie, dip it in cold water.)

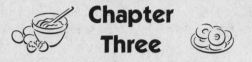

Chapter Three

"That went well," Julie said, giving a huge sigh of relief. "The kids didn't even seem to notice that I used sour cream instead of mayonnaise in their tuna salad sandwiches."

Matt squelched the urge to pull her into his arms and kiss her on the tip of her nose. There were times when Julie reminded him of a wayward elf. Of course she didn't *look* like an elf. Far from it!

He'd noticed Julie the moment she stepped out of her car on the first September morning of classes. She'd been wearing a brown tweed suit that was meant to be subdued, but it had done nothing to detract from her figure. She'd been perfectly sedate as she'd walked around her sensible black compact car and opened the trunk to take out her suitcase. But when she'd set it down on its wheels on the sidewalk and closed the trunk, she'd done something that had struck a chord in his bachelor heart. She'd glanced around, decided that no one was watching, and put her hand on the handle of the rolling travel case. Then she'd danced the first few steps of the number Gene Kelly had done when he'd partnered the lamppost in *Singing in the Rain*.

That was the beginning of their relationship, Matt decided. He adored her spontaneous sense of fun. One day, after her class had left for the afternoon, he'd found her spinning merrily away in her desk chair, humming the theme from *Carousel*. And that was another thing that he found so pleasing. Julie liked the same classic movies that he liked. She could quote whole sections from *Desk Set,* and they'd found themselves reciting Tracy–Hepburn dialogue from three different movies last night under the pine trees.

Once Julie had captured his attention, he'd watched her whenever they were in a meeting together. And although she'd been perfectly circumspect around every male member of the staff, including him, Matt suspected that Julie Jansen had hidden passions. That suspicion was based on personal observation. One telling factor was the way she licked her lips right before she tasted chocolate ice cream. Another was the way she dug into a piece of pepperoni pizza on the rare occasions Mrs. Dryer served it at a late-night staff meeting. The third factor, the one that had proven his theory beyond a shadow of a doubt, was the way she'd responded to his kiss last night.

Matt smiled just thinking about it. And then he did his best to put the memory completely out of his mind and concentrate instead on straightening the pile of napkins that were stacked on the counter. He was supposed to be supervising the kids while Julie put the cookies in a basket. If he continued to think about kissing Julie, they could have a food fight right in front of his nose and he wouldn't even notice.

Something was going on. Matt saw Serena move a little closer and accept a package wrapped in napkins from the two younger girls. They contained sandwiches, no doubt. He'd warned the kids about Julie's mistake, and they'd promised to clean their plates anyway. Matt suspected that this was the way they intended to do it, because Serena passed her package to Spenser and he stacked it on top of the one he'd taken from the younger boys. Then he stood up and headed toward the restrooms in the hall. Matt hoped he'd tear the sandwiches into small enough pieces before he flushed them. It would be embarrassing for Julie if they had to call the plumber to fix a commode plugged with tuna sandwiches.

"Earth to Matt," Julie said, reaching out to touch his shoulder. "I asked you three times if you wanted to pass around the cookies."

"Sorry," Matt said, picking up the basket Julie had lined with paper napkins.

"Don't be sorry. Just tell me what you were thinking about. You looked like you just heard the best joke in the world."

"Close," Matt said and left it at that. There was no way he was going to tell Julie that her sandwiches might even now be surfing in the sewer. "What time do you think we can get the kids to bed tonight?"

"Uh . . . well . . . regular bedtime is nine, but the older kids get to stay up to read or watch television until ten."

"Meet you in the living room at ten-thirty," Matt said, feeling as if he'd just arranged a forbidden tryst. Of course that was ridiculous. Once the kids were in bed, all they had to do was be available in case of an emergency.

"I'll be there right after I get the girls settled for the night. Are we going to discuss activities?"

"Oh yes," Matt said, putting on his best guileless smile and hoping she couldn't guess the activity that was foremost in his mind.

"Oh good! Matt wants apple crisp," Lisa said, glancing down at the list of desserts that Julie had given Hannah. They'd just closed for the night and were sharing a last cup of coffee before Herb came to pick her up.

"Why are you so happy he wants apple crisp?"

"Because I just found Grandmother Herman's recipe. I'll make two double batches of it tonight, and you can take it out there for tomorrow night's dessert. They can warm it up in the oven and serve it with ice cream."

"Perfect. I'll pick up some vanilla to go on top."

Lisa shook her head. "Get cinnamon instead. It's even better that way."

"Does the Red Owl have cinnamon ice cream?"

"Sure. Florence always stocks it over Christmas."

"Why does she stock it for Christmas?" Hannah asked, trying to figure out what cinnamon ice cream had to do with Santa and Christmas.

"They use it in Hot Candy Canes," Lisa explained.

"What are those?"

"They're drinks that Hank serves down at the Lake Eden Municipal Liquor Store."

"You've had one?"

"No, but Herb told me about it. Hank mixes hot coffee with peppermint schnapps in a big mug, and then he tops it with a scoop of cinnamon ice cream. He sticks in a candy cane for a stirrer, and it's really popular over the holidays. Herb said it brings in more revenue for the town than his parking tickets do in a whole year."

"Got it," Hannah said, jotting a note to stop by the Red Owl before Florence closed and pick up some cinnamon ice cream. Then she made a second note to fight like a Tasmanian devil if anyone ever tried to talk her into tasting anything called a Hot Candy Cane.

Lisa glanced back down at the list. "Somebody wants blueberry muffins? They're not exactly a dessert."

"I know, but one of the twins is crazy about them. I think it was Larry, but it could have been Gary. They're identical. How about the strawberry shortcake for Serena? Do you have any strawberries in your greenhouse?"

"Not right now. But you can use frozen, can't you?"

"Sure. We'll need two days to make it. My Pound Plus Cake needs to age that long."

Lisa glanced down at the next item on the list. "Fudge cupcakes should be easy. You can use the recipe you made up for Beatrice Koester."

"Right. And the peach cobbler's no problem. We'll bake our special Minnesota Peach Cobbler."

"Christmas sugar cookies are easy, and we certainly know how to make cherry cheesecake. What recipes do we have to punt on?"

"Punt?"

"You know what I mean. The ones where we're out of options and all we can do is hope everything turns out all right."

Hannah laughed. Lisa had obviously been watching football with her new husband. "I'll tell you if you'll read the rest of the list to me."

"Brownies," Lisa obliged her. "We've got that one covered. I'll make Bon-Bon Brownies the way I'm going to do for the Brownie Scouts."

"Great. What else?"

"Somebody named Spenser wants Christmas Cake. What are we going to do for that?"

"I'll make Grandma Ingrid's Date Cake, the one with the chocolate chips and nuts on top. All I have to do is figure out a way to make it really special. Is there anything else?"

"Julie's surprise. You put a little star in front of that."

"Pretend that star is a football, because that's where we have to punt. Julie wants me to teach her how to make a dessert so she can surprise Matt and the kids. And Julie's culinary skills are on a par with Andrea's."

"That'll be a punt all right! You may have to resort to ice cream sundaes with lots of store-bought toppings."

"Maybe, but I hope it doesn't come to that." Hannah glanced out the window as a car pulled up in front of the shop. Even through the lightly blowing snow, she could see who it was. "There's Herb."

"Oh *good!*"

Hannah felt a slight stab of envy as Lisa gave a delighted smile and ran to get her coat. It wasn't that she was jealous. Far from it. Herb had been a classmate of hers at Jordan High and they'd never been more than friends. But the expression on Lisa's face spoke volumes about how happy she was with her husband. Hannah wondered if she'd ever be so happily married. Despite her mother's belief that the goal was marriage and any man who was single would do in a pinch, Hannah wasn't about to go marching with Mendelssohn until she'd decided on her perfect groom.

"What?" Lisa said, coming back into the coffee shop and catching Hannah's pensive expression.

"I think I should mix up my Pound Plus Cake," Hannah said, letting Lisa think that was what had been on her mind. "If I bake it tonight, I can take it out to the academy and stick it in Julie's freezer. Then she can serve it if the weather gets bad and we can't get out there to deliver a dessert."

"Good idea. You'd better take the frozen strawberries along too. And the whipping cream and sour cream for the crème fraîche . . . unless you don't think she can whip the cream."

Hannah thought about that for a minute and then she shrugged. "That's a possibility. I'll take along a couple of cans of whipped cream, just in case. And I'll give her the instructions for thawing the berries and making the topping."

"Sounds good to me. Bye, Hannah. Don't work too late."

"I won't. Tell Herb hi for me." Hannah saw her partner out and locked the door behind her. Then she headed for the kitchen with thoughts of marriage still on her mind.

After a quick trip to the pantry and the walk-in cooler, Hannah assembled the necessary ingredients in the order her recipe listed and got out one of her largest stainless steel mixing bowls. As she mixed the softened butter with the sugar, she decided that Julie was absolutely right. Matt did appear to be perfect for her.

Hannah added eggs to her bowl and beat them in thoroughly before she mixed in the sour cream. The baking powder and vanilla were next, and as she measured out the cake flour, she wondered what would happen between Julie and Matt when all of the kids had been put to bed for the night.

DOUBLE APPLE CRISP

Preheat oven to 375 degrees F.,
rack in the middle position.

For the bottom:
    8 large apples, cored, peeled, and sliced***
    ¾ cup white *(granulated)* sugar
    1 tablespoon lemon juice
    ½ cup honey

For the topping:
    1 cup flour
    ½ cup brown sugar, firmly packed
    ½ teaspoon salt
    ½ cup *(1 stick, ¼ pound)* softened butter

   ***I used 4 Granny Smith and 4 Fuji, but any
combination will do. Half of the apples should be
tart and the other half sweeter.*

Spray a 9-inch by 13-inch cake pan with Pam or other nonstick spray. The pan can be metal, glass, or disposable foil.

Spread the sliced apples over the bottom of the pan. Sprinkle them with the white sugar and then the lemon juice.

Measure out the honey. *(I always spray my measuring cup with Pam first, so the honey won't stick to the sides as much.)* Drizzle the honey over the apples.

Mix the flour, brown sugar, and salt together in a small bowl. Use a fork to work in the softened butter, stirring until you have a crumbly mixture. *(You can also do this in a food processor using the steel blade and a stick of chilled butter cut into 8 pieces.)*

Sprinkle the topping evenly over the apples in the pan.

Bake at 375 degrees F. for 30 to 40 minutes, or until the apples are tender when pierced with a fork and the topping is golden brown.

Serve warm with whipped cream, regular cream, vanilla ice cream, or cinnamon ice cream.

Hannah's Note: If you take this out of the oven twenty minutes or so before the meal begins, it'll be a perfect temperature to serve for dessert. If you're not that organized (and who is?), dish up the apple crisp and heat it in individual bowls in the microwave. It holds up very well when reheated.

It's also good at room temperature or even cold, right out of the refrigerator. There is no wrong way to serve this Double Apple Crisp.

STRAWBERRY SHORTCAKE SWENSEN
Pound Plus Cake
The Strawberries
Hannah's Whipped Crème Fraîche

Pound Plus Cake

   WARNING: This cake must chill for at least 48 hours. Bake it 2 days before you plan to serve it. You can also bake it ahead of time, cool it, wrap it in plastic wrap and then in foil, and freeze it until the day before you need it. At that time, remove it from the freezer and let it thaw in the refrigerator for at least 24 hours.

   Pound Plus Cake will keep in the freezer for up to 4 months. This recipe makes two cakes. Each cake serves six people.

Preheat oven to 325 degrees F.,
rack in the middle position.

1½ cups softened butter *(3 sticks)*
2 cups white sugar

4 eggs
1 cup sour cream *(you can substitute unfla-
vored yogurt for a lighter cake)*
½ teaspoon baking powder
1 teaspoon vanilla
2 cups cake flour *(DO NOT SIFT—use it
right out of the box.)*

Generously butter and flour two 9-inch round cake pans. *(Don't use Pam or spray shortening—it won't work.)*

Cream softened butter and sugar in the bowl of an electric mixer. *(You can mix this cake by hand, but it takes some muscle.)* Add the eggs, one at a time, and beat until they're nice and fluffy. Then add the sour cream, baking powder, and vanilla. Mix it all up and then add the flour, one cup at a time, and beat until the batter is smooth and has no lumps.

Pour the batter into the pans and bake at 325 degrees F. for 45 to 50 minutes. *(The cakes should be golden brown on top.)*

Cool in the pans on a rack for 20 minutes. Run a knife around the inside edges of the pans to loosen the cakes and turn them out on the rack.

After the cakes are completely cool, wrap each one in plastic wrap, sealing tightly. Wrap these packages in foil and store them in the refrigerator for 48 hours. Take them out an hour before you serve, but don't unwrap them until you're ready to assemble the dessert.

The Strawberries
(Prepare these several hours before you serve.)

Wash 3 boxes of berries and remove stems. *(The easiest way to do this is to use a paring knife to cut off the top part of the berry.)* Slice all but a dozen or so, reserving the biggest and best berries to top each portion. Taste the berries and add sugar if they're too tart. Stir and refrigerate, covered tightly.

If you use frozen berries, thaw them in the refrigerator overnight by placing the whole package in a bowl. Test them for sweetness several hours be-

fore dessert and add sugar if they're too tart. Stir and refrigerate the berries in a covered container.

Hannah's Whipped Crème Fraîche
(This will hold for several hours. Make it ahead of time and refrigerate it.)

2 cups heavy whipping cream
½ cup white sugar
½ cup sour cream *(you can substitute unfla-vored yogurt, but it won't hold as well and you'll have to do it at the last minute)*

½ cup brown sugar *(to sprinkle on top after you assemble the dessert)*

Whip the cream with the white sugar. When it holds a firm peak *(test it by dipping in your spat-ula),* fold in the sour cream. You can do this by hand or by using the slowest speed on the mixer.

If you use canned whipped cream, just squirt it out until you have 2 cups and then fold in the half-

cup of sour cream. Cover and refrigerate until it's time to serve.

Assembling Strawberry Shortcake Swensen

Cut each *Pound Plus Cake* into 6 pie-shaped wedges and place the cake on dessert plates. Top with the sliced strawberries. Put several generous dollops of *Hannah's Whipped Crème Fraîche* on top and sprinkle with the brown sugar. Garnish with the whole berries you reserved *(unless you used frozen and don't have any perfect berries).* Serve and receive rave reviews.

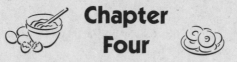

Chapter Four

"This is just heaven." Julie stretched luxuriously and snuggled a little closer to Matt. They were sitting on the overstuffed couch in the living room of Aames House, a relatively new structure that had been built for parents who were staying overnight at the school. "I wonder if parents feel like this when their kids are in bed."

Matt hugged her a little tighter. Her comment about parents and children was making him feel very fatherly. Not to Julie, of course. As far as Julie was concerned, his feelings were about as far from fatherly as . . .

"Do you think I should check to make sure they're sleeping?" Julie asked, interrupting the fantasy that was just starting to form in his mind.

"I don't think it's necessary. You told them we'd be watching a movie down here. If something's wrong, they'll come down the stairs to get us."

"You're right. Maybe it's a good thing I don't have children. I'd probably be an overprotective mother."

"That's okay. I tend to give kids their independence early. We'd balance each other out." Matt kissed the top of her head. Her hair smelled sweet, like flowers. As he tipped her face up to kiss her, he wondered idly whether she used some kind of special shampoo or if the woodsy sweetness was her own individual scent. It reminded him of morning dew, and freshly mown grasses, and precious little violets hiding deep in the forest. Then Julie gave a little sigh and molded her body to his, and Matt stopped thinking altogether.

It had been an innocent comment on her part. She'd realized she'd been worrying about the kids and she'd told him she'd probably be an overprotective mother. And then he'd said it was all right, that they'd balance each other out. Did that mean Matt wanted to have children with her? And even more important, did he even *know* what he'd said? Was it merely a slip of the tongue? Or could it be a slip of the heart?

Julie's mind spun as their kiss deepened. It was impossible to think when she was this blissful. Matt's arms were warm and protective around her, and she took delight in hearing the beat of his heart. All of her senses were alive. Every nerve and sinew was thrumming in anticipation. There would be time to think later. Right now all she wanted to do was enjoy this wonderful moment and hope it never stopped.

*   *   *

"They're kissing," Spenser reported, sticking his head in the girls' room where they all waited for the latest news.

Serena snorted. "That's what you said the last time."

"Well, they're still doing it. That's all they've done for the last five minutes. The movie's going, but they're not watching. They're just kissing."

Joy looked puzzled. "Don't they have to stop sometime so they can come up for air?"

"You can breathe while you're kissing," Serena told her. "You kiss with your lips and breathe through your nose."

"Is it like snorkeling?" Larry wanted to know.

"No, it's the other way around," Spenser explained. "You have to breathe through your mouth when you snorkel. If you breathe through your nose, you'll drown."

Serena looked dubious. "How do you know so much about snorkeling? People in Minnesota don't do it."

"I know, but they do it down in Florida. My dad used to live there, and we went snorkeling in the Keys before he died. But how do *you* know so much about kissing?"

"Uh . . . well . . ." Serena sputtered slightly. It was clear she didn't know what to say.

"I think it's because she reads those books all the time," Joy explained.

"What books?"

"Love books. You know . . . the ones that are all romantic. Serena's got one under her pillow right now."

For a moment, Serena looked as if she might deny it, but then she just nodded. "I like them. They're a lot more fun than doing homework. But this isn't about me. It's about Mr. Sherwood and Miss Jansen. You watched them for a long time, Spense. Do you think he's going to ask her to marry him?"

Spenser shrugged. "How would I know?"

"There are ways to tell. I'd better go with you to see for myself." Serena led the way to the door. "The rest of you stay here and be quiet. We'll be back in five minutes and I'll tell you what's *really* going on."

"What was *that*?" Matt asked, sitting back, startled.

Julie laughed breathlessly. "My cell phone. I put it on vibrate so it wouldn't disturb us."

"Well . . . it did." Matt started to chuckle, too. "For a second there, I thought we were having an earthquake."

Julie clamped her lips shut to keep from making a quip about how the earth had moved, or anything similar. But Matt seemed to be waiting for her response, so she said, "I don't think we have earthquakes in Minnesota."

"Sure we do. I was just reading about it on the Internet with the kids. They're not as noticeable as the temblors they have in California, but that's because the magnitude is much lower. Are you going to get that, Julie?"

"Get what?"

"Your cell phone. It's still vibrating."

"Oh. I guess I'd better. I gave Dr. Caulder my number before he left in case he wanted to check in with us."

"Don't you mean *check up on us*?"

"That too." Julie retrieved her phone. "Hello?" There was a pause while she listened, and then she laughed. "Nothing's wrong. As a matter of fact, things are going very well. It just took me a minute to answer the phone, that's all."

Matt cocked his head slightly, and Julie knew he was wondering if she was talking to Dr. Caulder. Her eyes began to sparkle as her mischievous side came out. It wouldn't hurt to tease Matt a bit. "They're all in bed, so this is our personal time alone together. We were just sitting here on the couch, watching a movie that we weren't really watching."

Matt's jaw dropped like a character in a Saturday morning cartoon, and Julie gave a little chuckle under her breath as she turned back to the phone. "Sure thing. I'll go look tomorrow. Tonight Matt and I are . . . busy."

There was a strangled sound from her fellow teacher and Julie had all she could do not to laugh out loud. "What's the matter?" she asked, as she ended the call.

"You weren't talking to . . ."

"Of course not," Julie cut him off before he could get too worried. "That was Hannah. She wanted to find out if Mrs. Dryer had any cookie cutters in the kitchen, and I'm supposed to call her back tomorrow. I was just teasing you, Matt. I'd never say anything to Dr. Caulder that would embarrass you."

Matt gave a relieved sigh, and then he looked a little sheepish. "I guess I should have known."

"Don't be so hard on yourself. There's really no way you *could* have known. We're not familiar enough with each other yet."

"That's fixable," Matt said, pulling her back into his arms and picking up right where they'd left off before Julie's phone had interrupted them.

Hannah hung up the phone with a grin. Julie was every bit as much a tease as she'd been in high school, and it was clear she'd been playing some sort of joke on Matt. She just hoped that Matt had a good sense of humor.

She'd just dumped the contents of two nearly empty containers of take-out Chinese food on top of the rice in the third container to make a sort of Oriental hotdish from the leftovers of her dinner when there was an irate yowl from her resident feline. Moishe, the orange and white tomcat she'd found shivering on her doorstep over two years ago, had cornered the duck's foot she'd bought for him between the refrigerator and the stove. He'd tried to hook it, but it was back, out of paw's reach.

"Okay, hold on a second." Hannah retrieved the yardstick that hung on a nail next to the broom closet and attempted to extricate the oriental treat. Moishe didn't eat duck's feet. He simply played with them until he got bored and then he buried them in his litter box.

Moishe gave her his best kitty smile as she fished around with the yardstick, attempting to snag it without dislodging the dust mice that were surely lurking in the small narrow space that never saw the light of day. The smile consisted of a crinkling of his eyes and a slight opening of his mouth, but that was good enough for Hannah. She got the aquatic appendage on the fourth try, grabbed it before Moishe could get it, and gave it a quick rinse under the kitchen faucet.

There was another yowl before Hannah was through drying it with a paper towel. "Here you go," she said, holding it out to him. "You can take it into the living room, but it's curtains for quackers if you lose it in back of the television. There must be a hundred wires back there, and there's no way I'm going to even try to get it out until daylight."

Moishe took the duck's foot with another kitty smile

that Hannah interpreted as a thank-you. Then he turned and headed for the living room with his head held high and his tail gently switching back and forth.

There were three high-pitched electronic dings in rhythmic succession and Hannah reached up to turn off her stove timer. She'd mixed up one of her famous cherry cheesecakes to save time tomorrow at The Cookie Jar. The cheesecake was best if it was chilled for at least a day, and two days was even better. She'd store it in her own refrigerator overnight and put it in the walk-in cooler at the shop tomorrow.

The cheesecake looked good, and Hannah set it on a wire rack to cool. Then she went off to join her furry roommate who'd managed to flip the duck's foot into the commode and was standing there staring at it balefully.

CHERRY CHEESECAKE

Preheat oven to 350 degrees F.,
rack in the middle position.

For the Crust:
   2 cups vanilla wafer cookie crumbs *(measure AFTER crushing)*
   ¾ stick melted butter *(6 tablespoons)*
   1 teaspoon almond extract

Pour melted butter and almond extract over cookie crumbs. Mix with a fork until they're evenly moistened.

Cut a circle of parchment paper *(or wax paper)* to fit inside the bottom of a 9-inch Springform pan. Spray the pan with Pam or other nonstick cooking spray, set the paper circle in place, and spray with Pam again.

Dump the moistened cookie crumbs in the pan and press them down over the paper circle and one

inch up the sides. Put the pan in the freezer for 15 to 30 minutes while you prepare the rest of the cheese-cake.

For the Topping:
    2 cups sour cream
    ½ cup sugar
    1 teaspoon vanilla

One 21-ounce can cherry pie filling*** *(I used Comstock Dark Sweet Cherry.)*

*** **If you don't like canned pie filling, make your own with canned or frozen cherries, sugar, and cornstarch.**

Mix the sour cream, sugar, and vanilla together in a small bowl. Cover and refrigerate. Set the un-opened can of cherry pie filling in the refrigerator for later.

For the Cheesecake Batter:
    1 cup white *(granulated)* sugar
    3 eight-ounce packages cream cheese at
        room temperature *(total 24 ounces)*

1 cup mayonnaise
4 eggs
2 cups white chocolate chips *(I used
    Ghirardelli's 11-ounce bag.)*
2 teaspoons vanilla

Place the sugar in the bowl of an electric mixer. Add the blocks of cream cheese and the mayonnaise, and whip it up at medium speed until it's smooth. Add the eggs, one at a time, beating after each addition.

Melt the white chocolate chips in a microwave-safe bowl for 2 minutes. *(Chips may retain their shape, so stir to see if they're melted—if not, microwave in 15-second increments until you can stir them smooth.)* Cool the melted white chocolate for a minute or two and then mix it in gradually at slow speed. Scrape down the bowl and add the vanilla, mixing it in thoroughly.

Pour the batter on top of the chilled crust, set the pan on a cookie sheet to catch any drips, and bake it at 350 degrees F. for 55 to 60 minutes. Remove the pan from the oven, but DON'T SHUT OFF THE OVEN.

Starting in the center, spoon the sour cream topping over the top of the cheesecake, spreading it out to within a half-inch of the rim. Return the pan to the oven and bake for an additional 5 minutes.

Cool the cheesecake in the pan on a wire rack. When the pan is cool enough to pick up with your bare hands, place it in the refrigerator and chill it, uncovered, for at least 8 hours.

To serve, run a knife around the inside rim of the pan, release the Springform catch, and lift off the rim. Place a piece of waxed paper on a flat plate and tip it upside down over the top of your cheesecake. Invert the cheesecake so that it rests on the paper.

Carefully pry off the bottom of the Springform pan and remove the paper from the bottom crust.

Invert a serving platter over the bottom crust of your cheesecake. Flip the cheesecake right side up, take off the top plate, and remove the waxed paper.

Spread the cherry pie filling over the sour cream topping on your cheesecake. You can drizzle a little down the sides if you wish.

Chapter Five

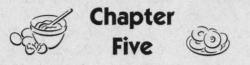

"They're in love," Serena said, sounding very sure of herself. "You don't kiss like that unless you're in love."

"Kiss like *what?*" Gary wanted to know.

"Like a raging fire that sears the emotions and scorches every inhibition to a cinder. That's the way they described it in the book I'm reading."

There was silence for a moment while everyone digested Serena's response. Then Spenser gave a little laugh. "Can you tell us in plain English?"

"Of course. They kissed like they were trying to swallow each other's tonsils."

"Yuck!" both twins exclaimed in unison.

"I feel sick," Hope added, folding her arms over her stomach.

"I know it sounds gross, but just wait until you're older," Serena advised. "Then it'll seem like fun."

Gary and Larry locked eyes. They stared at each other for a moment, and then both of them shook their heads in tandem.

"There's no way I could . . ." Gary started the thought.

". . . be *that* old." Larry finished the sentence for him.

"You'll see," Serena said, still supremely confident. "It'll happen to you too. But let's get back to Miss Jansen and Mr. Sherwood. They're in love and they're going to get married. You just watch and see if I'm right."

Joy began to frown. "But you can be in love without getting married."

"You're only seven. How do *you* know?" Spenser asked her.

"Our mother told us," Hope spoke up. "She's been in love lots of times, but she's only been married twice."

"Three times," Joy corrected her.

"Not yet!" Hope insisted, her lower lip beginning to quiver. "It won't be three times until tomorrow. And that's why we couldn't go home for Christmas. She's going on her honeymoon."

The twins glanced at each other, and then Larry said, "It's the same for us, except . . ."

". . . opposite," Gary finished his sentence. "Mom and Dad are getting divorced and they fought so much over . . ."

". . . which one got to take us, the judge said we'd be better off staying here." Larry ended the story.

"I'm here because I've got nowhere else to go," Spenser declared. "My dad's dead and Mom's on assignment in Africa."

"What's she doing *there?*" Serena asked the question that was plain on all their faces.

"She's a photographer, a good one too. She didn't want to work over Christmas, but she just switched jobs and they might have fired her, or something like that. I wanted to go over there to be with her, but she said it was too dangerous." Spenser stopped speaking and gave a deep sigh. "I should've talked her into it so I could protect her."

There was another silence, broken only when Serena cleared her throat. "You did the right thing by staying here, Spense. She would've worried about you the whole time you were there, and neither one of you would've had a good time."

"I guess . . ." Spenser shrugged, but it was clear he felt better. "What about you, Serena? Nowhere to go?"

"I've got somewhere to go. I just didn't want to, that's all. I spent enough Christmases in the Home. Believe me, this is a lot better!"

"Maybe, but it's not very exciting," Gary complained. "I wish something really . . ."

". . . exciting would happen," Larry finished the thought for his twin.

"Something exciting *is* going to happen," Serena declared. "Mr. Sherwood is going to ask Miss Jansen to marry him. And we're going to know about it before anyone else in the whole school!"

Hope started to smile. "We'll know first and we can tell everybody else when they come back."

"That's right," Joy said, sounding delighted. "All our friends will wish they'd stayed here."

Spenser looked doubtful as he turned to Serena. "How do you know Mr. Sherwood's really going to ask her?"

"I just know, that's all."

"Then it's like my dad used to say . . . put your money where you mouth is."

"You mean you want to bet?"

"Why not? If you're so sure you're going to win, you should go for it, right?"

"Right. But . . . I don't have any money."

"Then bet something else."

"Like what?"

"Like how about doing my chores for a month if you lose?"

Serena glanced around at the rest of the kids who were intent on their conversation. It was clear she didn't want to back down. "It all depends on what you have to do."

"I have to pick up after Queenie every day."

"Mrs. Caulder's toy poodle?"

"Right," Spenser answered what he knew would be her next question. "I know she's small, but she can . . . well . . . let's just say it takes me at least a half hour to do it."

Serena shrugged. "That doesn't sound so bad. I wouldn't mind walking Queenie around."

"Oh, you don't get to walk her. Mrs. Caulder does that. What you have to do is pick up all the . . . uh . . . *stuff* in Dr. Caulder's backyard. And if you miss any, he's not exactly delighted, if you get what I mean. So is it a bet?"

Serena thought about that for a minute. "Not unless you have to pay if you're wrong."

"What do you mean?"

"This goes both ways. If you lose and I win, you have to do my chores for a month."

"Deal," Spenser declared, holding out his hand.

"But don't you want to know what my chores are?"

"Doesn't matter, since I'm not going to lose. But just for the purposes of discussion, what are they?"

"I have to help Mrs. Dryer clean up the kitchen after supper."

Spenser's hand quivered with the effort not to pull it back. He'd heard that Mrs. Dryer made her helpers scour every surface of the kitchen after every meal.

"So do you want to back out?" Serena asked smugly.

"No way. It's a deal by me. Let's shake on it."

The other four watched as Serena and Spenser shook hands. Then Joy hopped off the bed.

"I want to bet too," she said. "I'll do Gary's chores if we lose, and he can do mine if we win."

"Deal," Gary said quickly, holding out his hand so that Joy could shake it.

"Me too," Hope declared, holding out her hand to Larry.

"That's it then," Spenser said. "It's the boys against the girls. If Mr. Sherwood asks Miss Jansen to marry him before Christmas is over, we have to do the girls' chores. Is that right, men?"

"Right!" the twins chorused.

"And if they don't get engaged before Christmas is over, the girls have to do *our* chores. Right, girls?"

"Right," Hope said.

"Yes," Joy added, turning to Serena.

"It's a bet," Serena confirmed. "We'll write it down so there won't be any misunderstandings, and we'll all sign it. And then you boys have to go to your own room. It's late and we need to get some sleep."

Hope waited until the boys had left and then she turned to Serena. "You're not sleepy, are you?"

"No. I think I'll read another chapter in my book. But first I want to get a glass of water."

Joy gave a little giggle as she caught on. "From the front bathroom at the top of the stairs?"

"So you can see how our bet is going?" Hope added.

"You girls are pretty smart for your age," Serena said as she got up and headed for the door.

"Don't they ever get tired of kissing?" Gary asked, as Spenser returned to their room.

"I guess not. They're still at it."

"You'd think their lips would start . . ." Gary stopped and waited for his twin to finish the sentence, but Larry was sitting in front of his laptop computer, surfing the net.

"Forget him. He's in another world. You'd think their lips would start to what?" Spenser asked.

"Swell up, or get chapped, or something," Gary completed the thought by himself, but he started to look a bit worried. "They're doing an awful lot of kissing down there. Do you think Serena might be right and we could lose?"

"The only way we'll lose is if we sit back and don't do anything to break things up."

"What things?"

"Them. We have to figure out a way to break up Miss Jansen and Mr. Sherwood."

"But that's not fair!"

"I know, but if we don't do it, we'll lose. Do you and Larry really want to spend a month doing chores for the girls?"

Gary wavered. "I don't know. What do they have to do?"

"Hope and Joy have to go to Mrs. Caulder's house and pass around trays at her Wednesday night musicales."

"That's not horrible."

"You wouldn't say that if you'd ever heard Mrs. Caulder sing. And she sings at every musicale."

"We could always wear earplugs."

"Wait. There's more. On Saturday afternoons, they have to go shopping with her and carry her packages."

"No way Larry and I want to do that!" Gary made a face that perfectly expressed his feelings. "But I still hate to break up Mr. Sherwood and Miss Jansen."

"So do I, but it won't be permanent. They're doomed to get together eventually. But not until we've won our bet."

Julie was snuggled warm in Matt's arms, half-watching the movie. Normally, she would have been engrossed in the silver screen classic, but the beating of Matt's heart was so comforting, she just wanted to close her eyes, relish the moment, and dream of the future. If Matt asked her to marry him, she'd say yes. There was no doubt about that. They were perfectly compatible, and she was perfectly in love. All she had to do was hope that Matt was beginning to feel the same way.

Her sleepy mind drifted off to thoughts of a perfect wedding. Matt stood in the front, unbelievably handsome in a black tux, waiting for his bride. And there she was, a lovely vision in a white lace tablecloth and tiara. One hand rested on her father's arm, and the other was holding a beautiful bridal bouquet of dandelions.

Dr. Caulder was officiating. She hadn't known he had the authority, but it wasn't surprising with the long string of initials after his name. And there was her mother in the front row, smiling and happy in a lovely dress, sitting next to Joy.

Julie turned slightly so that she could see her brides-maids. There was Serena, looking quite lovely in her school uniform. Her partner was Spenser, one of Matt's groomsmen, and he cut a dashing figure in his hockey gear. Hope was the flower girl, holding a white basket of pine needles to strew in her wake, and one of the twins was the ring bearer. Julie wasn't sure which twin it was, but that didn't really matter because he was much too old for the honor anyway. The other twin, Gary or Larry, whichever this one wasn't, would be really upset. Julie didn't see him and suspected he'd stayed in his room to pout. She should have invited him, because he might just come here to disrupt the whole thing and . . .

"Miss Jansen?"

Julie's eyes flickered, and she did her best to banish him from her dream. This was her wedding. He shouldn't be here if he couldn't behave.

"Miss Jansen?"

There was no help for it. She had to take time to ex-plain that there could be only one ring bearer per wedding and he'd just have to wait until the next faculty member got married.

"Something's wrong, Miss Jansen!"

Julie sat up with a start. Gary or Larry was leaning over the back of the couch and he looked worried. "What's wrong?"

"Gary's not in his bed. He isn't in the bathroom either. Spenser and I checked."

Julie glanced at Matt. He was sleeping peacefully, his chest rising slowly up and down. His hair was tousled like a little boy, and he looked years younger than he did when he was awake. "Matt?" she said, reaching out to shake his arm. "Wake up, Matt. We need you."

"What?"

Julie could barely believe her eyes when Matt straightened up, blinked twice, and was fully alert. "What is it, Larry?"

"I just told Miss Jansen. I woke up and Gary wasn't in his bed. Spense and I looked, but he's not in the bathroom. We wanted to search the house, but Spense thought we should come and get you first."

"Spenser thought right. Has Gary ever done any sleepwalking?"

"I don't think so."

"That's good. It's cold out there." Matt turned to Julie. "Would you check the front door, Miss Jansen? I threw the deadbolt when we were all in for the night. If it's still locked, that means Gary's somewhere inside. I'll go check the back door with Larry."

The door was securely locked, and Julie gave a huge sigh of relief. She was very glad Gary hadn't gone out in the dead of winter. The wind had kicked up, and it was howling so loud, she could hear it inside the snug walls of Aames House. While she was there, she pulled back the curtains and checked the thermometer mounted on the outside frame of the window next to the door. It was eleven below zero, and she hoped Gary hadn't gone out the back way.

"The bolt was still thrown." Matt came back looking relieved.

Julie nodded. "Same with the front door."

"Good. That means he's got to be here somewhere. Will you check the downstairs, Miss Jansen? And when you're through, come up and find us. We'll be checking all the vacant rooms on the second floor."

"While you're at it, you'd better check the girls' room. Gary could be there."

"Why would he be in the girls' room?" Larry wanted to know.

"He could have gotten up for some reason and taken a wrong turn when he tried to get back to your room. This is the first night we've spent at Aames House, and he's used to being in the dorm."

Matt gave her an approving smile. "I wouldn't have thought of that, but you're right. We'll check the girls' room last. No sense in waking them up if we find him somewhere else."

When Matt and Larry had gone up the stairs, Julie headed for the kitchen. Aames House was designed like a very large private residence with more upstairs bedrooms than the normal-size family would require, but with a single kitchen, a giant living room, a dining room that would easily seat twenty, and several fully equipped offices for the convenience of working parents who had come to visit their children.

Julie switched on the kitchen lights and blinked in the sudden flood that illuminated the marble-topped counters and gleaming appliances. She'd expected to find Gary here. It was a natural place to look. She hadn't forgotten her nights as a child and the times she'd stolen downstairs in the middle of the night for a snack.

But Gary wasn't in the kitchen. That was apparent at a glance. Julie checked the pantry and even opened the broom closet, but no one was hiding there.

The laundry room was next, and then the dining room. Julie went through the offices and even double-checked the living room, but Gary was nowhere to be found. She was halfway up the stairs when she heard Matt start to laugh. They must have found him!

"Gary!" Julie arrived at the boys' room in a rush and hurried to put her arms around him. "Thank goodness you're safe. We were worried about you."

Gary squirmed slightly and Julie let him go, suddenly remembering that ten-year-old boys didn't like to be held for long. She turned to Matt. "Where was he?"

"Under his bed. He must have tumbled out, rolled under it, and fallen asleep again."

Once the boys were back in bed, Julie and Matt went back downstairs. Matt checked the doors again, to make sure they were secure, and Julie folded the afghan and placed it on the back of the couch.

"Now that the crisis is over, I think I'd better call it a night," Julie said. "The girls slept right through everything and they'll probably be up early tomorrow."

"You're probably right. I'll just stay here for a while and see if I can find some late news. I'd really like to hear the weather report."

"Mostly overcast, temperatures below zero, and variable winds," Julie recited.

"And that means it'll be sunny, unusually warm, and perfectly calm?"

"You got it," Julie said, blowing him a kiss before she headed up the stairs to the guest room she'd staked out as her own.

Chapter Six

It was the kind of perfectly beautiful winter day that painters loved and weathermen hated. The temperature had climbed to slightly above thirty degrees and the sunlight gleamed on the icy banks of snow, making them shimmer as if they were studded with diamonds. The icicles that hung from the stark black branches of the trees glistened like silver Christmas ornaments, and brightly colored winter birds flitted from branch to branch turning black and white to Technicolor.

Hannah turned into the driveway that led to Lakes Academy. It was the fourth round-trip she'd made in as many days, but she really didn't mind. She opened her window to enjoy the fresh pine scent that Christmas trees in warmer climates could never begin to replicate when she noticed another more subtle scent on the breeze. It was that indefinable something that some people claimed they could smell when snow was on the way. Hannah could smell it, her grandmother had taught her, and she hoped that the winter storm wouldn't hit too hard. It would be a pity if Julie, Matt, and the kids were snowed in and she couldn't carry out the Christmas plans she'd made for them.

Hannah had just pulled up and was preparing to unload when she heard the sound of childish laughter on the wind. Curious, she got out of her truck and followed the sound through the tall pine trees to Aames House. It seemed to be coming from the rear and Hannah walked around the red brick structure. What she saw when she came around the corner made her blink several times in surprise.

Julie and Matt were helping the kids make snowmen, but they were unlike any other snowmen Hannah had ever seen. They had the traditional stacked snowballs—a large one for the body, a medium one for the chest, and a smaller one for the head. But instead of white snowmen, these icy creations were in rollicking colors. One snowman had a red body with a yellow chest and an orange head. Another had a green body with a peach middle and a blue head. The one that they were working on now had a blue body and a yellow chest. Hope was rolling the head, and it was still white.

"Is this the right size?" Hope called out, sitting back on her heels to look at her work.

"Perfect," Matt replied, and he helped Hope move the head to a small gardener's tarp that had been spread out on the snow at the foot of the uncompleted snowman.

"What color do you want for his head, Hope?" Julie asked.

"I want purple."

"I need the grape, please," Julie called out to Spenser, who was holding a tray containing several thermoses.

Spenser hurried over with a thermos, and Hannah watched as Julie shook it. Then she uncorked it and poured a thin stream of liquid all over the top of the snowman's head until it was streaked with purple. A few moments later the color began to spread, and within a minute or two the snowman's head resembled the top of a huge grape snow cone.

"Okay?" Matt asked Julie.

"Go ahead. It should be cold enough by now."

Matt lifted the slightly irregular ball of snow and carefully placed it on top of the larger yellow ball. "That does it, except for dressing them. I found some old hats and scarves."

"And I found some little pinecones we can use for the eyes," Serena said.

"Let's wait until after lunch to do that. I want to make sure they're frozen hard." Julie turned to Spenser. "Will you bring in the thermoses, Spenser?"

"Sure, right after I take a picture to send to my mom. I sent her an instant message about the snowmen, and she wants me to e-mail some photos."

"Okay. Come in when you're through then."

Julie headed for the back door with Matt and the kids, and that was when she spotted Hannah. "Hi, Hannah. Did you see our snowmen?"

"I did. They're pretty colorful characters. How did you do that?"

"Jell-O. The kids got tired of eating Jell-O with fruit cocktail for lunch, so we thought we'd use it up another way."

"Very clever. I had no idea it would color the snow that evenly."

"Neither did I, but I hoped it would. And believe me, it took some doing! The temperature of the Jell-O liquid has to be just right, and the snow needs to be really icy. I don't think I would have figured it out if I hadn't spent one whole summer at Eden Lake Bait and Tackle making snow cones."

"I'll do the sandwiches, Miss Jansen," Serena offered, catching up with them. "I know you want to talk to Miss Swensen."

"Thanks, Serena. I was going to make peanut butter and jelly on toast."

"Okay. I'll make the toast, Joy can spread the peanut butter, and Hope will put on the jam. Gary and Larry can set the table and pour the milk."

"There's a big box of cookies in the back of my truck if someone wants to go out and get them," Hannah told Matt. "It's the box with the cutout handles. The bakery boxes are filled with Blue Blueberry Muffins for tonight's dessert and they can come in too."

Matt turned around and motioned to Spense, who'd just finished taking his pictures. "We'll rinse out the thermoses, and then Spense and I'll carry them in."

Hannah waited until the back door had closed behind the kids and Matt, and then she turned to Julie. "So?"

"So what?" Julie started to grin.

"So how's the romance going?"

Julie's grin faded abruptly. "It's not," she said.

"You had a fight with Matt?"

"Oh, no. It's nothing like that. It's just that we can't seem to get any time alone. Every time we think we've got them all settled down and tucked in for the night, one of them wants something or other."

"I think that's pretty common with kids. They want to be the center of attention twenty-four hours a day. I remember Andrea saying that it was really hard to get any time alone with Bill after Tracey was born. And you and Matt have that problem times six!"

"That's true. I really didn't think the kids would be that needy, but I guess it's understandable. I'd feel pretty lonely too if I had to stay at boarding school over Christmas."

"You *do* have to stay at boarding school over Christmas."

Julie laughed and Hannah was glad. Andrea's high school friend had looked just a bit depressed.

"I wonder if it bothers Matt as much as it bothers me," Julie mused. "I'd come right out and ask, but I think that's a little blatant, don't you?"

"Maybe," Hannah conceded, although that was probably what she would have done in the same circumstance.

"Why don't *you* ask him for me? You can kind of approach the subject obliquely, so he won't know I asked you to."

"You mean I should be tactful?"

"Exactly."

Hannah sighed. If Julie expected her to be tactful, she was in deep trouble. She'd been told often enough by many people that there wasn't a tactful bone in her body.

"Will you at least try to find out?"

How could she resist a plea like that? Hannah caved in without a whimper. "Okay. I'm not very good at things like that, but I guess I can try."

* * *

There was no chance for Hannah to talk to Matt during lunch. The kids were in high spirits and the noon meal was filled with laughter and wisecracks. But after they'd finished eating, Julie organized the cleanup, and Hannah found herself straightening the chairs and putting on a clean tablecloth with Matt.

"Do you have a second?" she asked, moving as far away from the kitchen door as the confines of the room would allow.

"Sure. I figured you'd want to ask about the peach cobbler when Julie wasn't around."

Hannah started to say that wasn't what had been on her mind, but she quickly changed tactics. A discussion of Julie's culinary limitations might give her a clue to their relationship. "Did she manage to heat it in the oven?"

"Yes. She did a good job too. Only one corner got a little brown, and I ate it before she could notice."

Love, Hannah thought to herself. She'd thought it was love before, but now she had the proof. Any man who would eat the corner of a burned dessert rather than embarrass the woman who'd heated it was definitely in love. "Then it doesn't really bother you that Julie can't cook?"

"Not at all. I like to cook, and I don't think Julie would mind being my helper. She's better than I am with a knife, and she's great at plating. All I can do is follow a recipe."

"But you're not doing the cooking here."

"I would have offered, but I thought it might make Julie feel bad. She's very proud of being able to make lunches and snacks for the kids."

Definitely love, Hannah decided, giving Matt an approving smile. "Do you bake?"

"I never really learned, but I'd like to get into it. Maybe later, when I have more time."

Time. Hannah heard her cue word and picked up on it. "Julie said the kids are needy right now, and they demand almost constant attention."

"She's right. Not the girls so much, but the boys seem to really need us. We've been trying to watch *Roman Holiday* for three nights now, and Gregory Peck's still got his arm in the gargoyle."

Hannah laughed and so did Matt, but she quickly sobered. "About the kids . . . Julie thinks they're probably lonely, missing their parents and all that."

"Well . . ." Matt sounded as if he'd been about to agree when he'd had second thoughts. "That *does* make perfect sense, but I don't think it's the only reason."

"Why not?"

"It's a whole bunch of things. Let me give you some examples. Last night, an hour after he was supposed to be asleep, Spenser came down to tell us the window in their room was stuck and Larry wanted it open a crack."

"It wasn't stuck?" Hannah guessed.

"It slid right up when I tried it. Spense said he must have loosened it up and he should have tried it one more time before he came to get me, but I noticed that he couldn't look me in the eye when he said it."

"You found that a little suspicious?"

"Yes, in light of everything else. The night before that, Gary came down to tell us that the faucet in their connecting bathroom was dripping and he couldn't get to sleep. I went up to fix it, and all I had to do was tighten it with my hand."

"And Gary could have done that?"

"Of course. It's almost as if the boys are jealous of the time I spend alone with Julie."

"That's interesting. And it must be frustrating for you and Julie, never getting any time alone together."

"You have *no* idea!" Matt said, sighing deeply. "The only time we can talk without one of the boys standing there listening is when they're eating dessert."

"Good thing I brought extra Blue Blueberry Muffins," Hannah said, proud of the way she'd managed to gather the information Julie wanted. "The next time I drive out, I'll bring triple dessert and you might actually have time to finish that movie."

BLUE BLUEBERRY MUFFINS

Preheat oven to 375 degrees F.,
rack in the middle position.

The Batter:

¾ cup melted butter *(1½ sticks)*
1 cup sugar
2 beaten eggs *(just whip them up with a fork)*
2 teaspoons baking powder
½ teaspoon salt
1 cup fresh or frozen blueberries *(no need to thaw if they're frozen)*
2 cups plus one tablespoon flour *(no need to sift)*
½ cup milk
½ cup blueberry pie filling

Crumb Topping:

½ cup sugar
⅓ cup flour
¼ cup softened butter *(½ stick)*

Grease the <u>bottoms only</u> of a 12-cup muffin pan *(or line the cups with double cupcake papers— that's what I do at The Cookie Jar).* Melt the butter. Mix in the sugar. Then add the beaten eggs, baking powder, and salt. Mix it all up thoroughly.

Put one tablespoon of flour in a baggie with your cup of fresh or frozen blueberries. Shake it gently to coat the blueberries and leave them in the bag for now.

Add half of the remaining two cups of flour to your bowl and mix it in with half of the milk. Then add the rest of the flour and the milk and mix thoroughly.

Here comes the fun part: Add ½ cup of blueberry pie filling to your bowl and mix it in. *(Your dough will turn a shade of blue, but don't let that stop you—once the muffins are baked, they'll look just fine.)* When your dough is thoroughly mixed, fold in the flour-coated fresh or frozen blueberries.

Fill the muffin tins three-quarters full and set them aside. If you have dough left over, grease the

bottom of a small tea-bread loaf pan and fill it with your remaining dough.

The crumb topping: Mix the sugar and the flour in a small bowl. Add the softened butter and cut it in until it's crumbly. *(You can also do this in a food processor with chilled butter and the steel blade.)*

Fill the remaining space in the muffin cups with the crumb topping. Then bake the muffins in a 375 degree F. oven for 25 to 30 minutes. *(The tea-bread should bake about 10 minutes longer than the muffins.)*

While your muffins are baking, divide the rest of your blueberry pie filling into half-cup portions and pop it in the freezer. I use paper cups to hold it and freeze them inside a freezer bag. All you have to do is thaw a cup the next time you want to make a batch of Blue Blueberry Muffins.

When your muffins are baked, set the muffin pan on a wire rack to cool for at least 30 minutes. *(The muffins need to cool in the pan for easy removal.)* Then just tip them out of the cups and enjoy.

These are wonderful when they're slightly warm, but the blueberry flavor will intensify if you store them in a covered container overnight.

Hannah's Note: Grandma Ingrid's muffin pans were large enough to hold all the dough from this recipe. My muffin tins are smaller and I always make a loaf of Blue Blueberry tea-bread with the leftover dough. If I make it for Mother, I leave off the crumb topping. She loves to eat it sliced, toasted, and buttered for breakfast.

MINNESOTA PEACH COBBLER

Preheat oven to 350 degrees F.,
rack in the middle position.

**Hannah's Note: Don't thaw your peaches be-
fore you make this—leave them frozen.**

Spray a 13-inch by 9-inch cake pan with Pam or
other nonstick cooking spray.

10 cups frozen sliced peaches
  (approximately
  2½ pounds)
⅛ cup lemon juice *(2 tablespoons)*
1½ cups white *(granulated)* sugar
¼ teaspoon salt
¾ cup flour *(no need to sift)*
½ teaspoon cinnamon
½ cup melted butter *(1 stick, ¼ pound)*

Measure the peaches and put them in a large
mixing bowl. Let them sit on the counter and thaw

for 10 minutes. Then sprinkle them with lemon juice and toss.

In another smaller bowl combine white sugar, salt, flour, and cinnamon. Mix them together with a fork until they're evenly combined.

Pour the dry mixture over the peaches and toss them. *(This works best if you use your impeccably clean hands.)* Once most of the dry mixture is clinging to the peaches, dump them into the cake pan you've prepared. Sprinkle any dry mixture left in the bowl on top of the peaches in the pan.

Melt the butter. Drizzle it over the peaches. Then cover the cake pan tightly with foil.

Bake the peach mixture at 350 degrees F., for 40 minutes. Take it out of the oven and set it on a heat-proof surface, but DON'T TURN OFF THE OVEN!

Top Crust:
    1 cup flour *(no need to sift)*
    1 cup white *(granulated)* sugar
    1½ teaspoons baking powder

¼ teaspoon cinnamon
½ teaspoon salt
½ stick softened butter *(¼ cup, ⅛ pound)*
2 beaten eggs *(just stir them up in a glass
  with a fork)*

Combine the flour, sugar, baking powder, cinnamon, and salt in the smaller bowl you used earlier. Cut in the softened butter with a couple of forks until the mixture looks like coarse cornmeal. Add the beaten eggs and mix them in with a fork. For those of you who remember your school library with fondness, the result will resemble library paste but it'll smell a whole lot better! *(If you have a food processor, you can also make the crust using the steel blade and chilled butter cut into 4 chunks.)*

Remove the foil cover from the peaches and drop on spoonfuls of the topping. Because the topping is thick, you'll have to do this in little dibs and dabs scraped from the spoon with another spoon, a rubber spatula, or with your freshly washed finger. Dab on the topping until the whole pan is polka-dotted. *(Don't worry if some spots aren't covered very well—the batter will spread out and fill in as it bakes and result in a crunchy crust.)*

Bake at 350 degrees F., uncovered, for an additional 50 minutes.

Minnesota Peach Cobbler can be eaten hot, warm, room temperature, or chilled. It can be served by itself in a bowl, or topped with cream or ice cream.

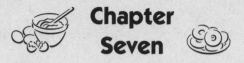 # Chapter Seven

"Maybe tonight is our lucky night," Matt said, sitting down on the couch next to Julie and reaching for the remote control. "Hannah brought us a quadruple batch of fudge cupcakes, and the boys ate four apiece. With stomachs that full, they should sleep for hours."

"Don't count on anything when it comes to the kids. Even after we put them to bed, there's always something they need."

"There's always something *the boys* need," Matt corrected her. "It's never the girls."

"That's true. The girls are no trouble at all." Julie glanced at the screen where *The Quiet Man* was playing without sound. "Where were we anyway?"

"I think I was kissing you and you were making those little purring noises in your throat, the ones that make me feel like I'm the most important guy in the world."

Julie laughed, but her cheeks turned pink "Well, you

are the most important guy in the world, but I was talking about the movie. What scene were we watching the last time the boys interrupted us?"

"The one where Maureen O'Hara bolts the door and John Wayne breaks it open. But I don't really care about that. I'd rather research those little purring noises."

"Research is very important for a teacher," Julie replied, snuggling into his arms and leaving John and Maureen to their own devices.

"Mr. Sherwood?"

Matt groaned. This couldn't be real. No one was that unlucky. He must be imagining the night's worst scenario, because he was afraid it might happen again.

"Mr. Sherwood?"

Yup. It was happening. That was Larry's voice, and the boys were interrupting his night with Julie again.

Resolutely, Matt pulled away from Julie's willing arms and turned to face his ten-year-old tormentor. "What is it, Larry?"

"Gary had a nightmare."

There was a beat of silence while Matt considered the logic of that statement. "I'm sorry to hear that. But if Gary had a nightmare, why didn't *he* come down here to get us?"

"Because he's hiding in the closet and he won't come out. He thinks Spense and I are aliens. We think he's still dreaming."

It was the lamest excuse Matt had ever heard, and he was about to say so when Julie interrupted.

"I'll go," she offered, standing up and moving past him. "You find the scene where John Wayne fights with

Victor McLaglen while I'm gone. When I come back, we can start watching everything all over again."

"Of course I'm sure," Larry said, once Julie had gone back downstairs. "We broke them up, but not for long. They're just going to start kissing again."

Spenser nodded. "I think you're right. And if they keep this up, we're going to lose to the girls for sure. It's time to pull out the big guns."

"What big guns?" Gary and Larry asked together.

"I'm not sure yet, but I'll come up with something. Just give me a little time to think about it."

Larry looked worried. "Better think fast, before . . ."

". . . Mr. Sherwood asks her to marry him and we have to wear aprons and listen to Mrs. Caulder sing," Gary finished.

FUDGE CUPCAKES

Preheat oven to 350 degrees F.,
rack in the middle position.

4 squares unsweetened baking chocolate
   (1 ounce each)
¼ cup white *(granulated)* sugar
½ cup raspberry syrup *(for pancakes—I
   used Knott's red raspberry)****
1⅔ cups flour *(unsifted)*
1½ teaspoons baking powder
½ teaspoon salt
½ cup butter, room temperature *(one stick,
   ¼ pound)*
1½ cups white sugar *(not a misprint—you'll
   use one and three-quarters cups sugar in
   all)*
3 eggs
⅓ cup milk

*** *If you can't find raspberry syrup, mix
¼ cup seedless raspberry jam with ¼ cup light
Karo syrup and use that.*

Line a 12-cup muffin pan with double cupcake papers. Since this recipe makes 18 cupcakes, you can use an additional 6-cup muffin pan lined with double papers, or you can butter and flour an 8-inch square cake pan or the equivalent.

Microwave the chocolate, raspberry syrup, and ¼ cup sugar in a microwave-safe bowl on high for 1 minute. Stir. Microwave again, for another minute. At this point, the chocolate will be almost melted, but it will maintain its shape. Stir the mixture until smooth and let cool to lukewarm. *(You can also do this in a double boiler on the stove.)*

Measure the flour, mix in the baking powder and salt, and set it aside. With an electric mixer *(or with a VERY strong arm)* beat the butter and 1½ cups sugar until light and fluffy. *(About 3 minutes with a mixer—an additional 2 minutes if you're doing it by hand.)* Add the eggs, one at a time, beating after each addition to make sure they're thoroughly incorporated. Add approximately a third of the flour mixture and a third of the milk. *(You don't have to be exact—adding the flour and milk in increments makes the batter smoother.)* When that's all mixed

in, add another third of the flour and another third of the milk. And when that's incorporated, add the remainder of the flour and the remainder of the milk. Mix thoroughly.

Test your chocolate mixture to make sure it's cool enough to add. *(You don't want to cook the eggs!)* If it's fairly warm to the touch but not so hot you have to pull your hand away, you can add it at this point. Stir thoroughly and you're done.

Let the batter rest for five minutes. Then stir it again by hand and fill each cupcake paper three-quarters full. If you decided to use the 8-inch cake pan instead of the 6-cup muffin tin, fill it with the remaining batter.

Bake the cupcakes in a 350 degree F. oven for 20 to 25 minutes. The 8-inch cake should bake an additional 5 minutes.

Fudge Frosting:
    2 cups semi-sweet *(regular)* chocolate chips
      (a 12-ounce package)
    One 14-ounce can sweetened condensed milk

18 cupcakes, or 12 cupcakes and 1 small
    cake, cooled to room temperature and
    ready to frost.

If you use a double boiler for this frosting, it's
foolproof. You can also make it in a heavy saucepan
over low to medium heat on the stovetop, but you'll
have to stir it constantly with a spatula to keep it
from scorching.

Fill the bottom part of the double boiler with
water. Make sure it doesn't touch the underside of
the top.

Put the chocolate chips in the top of the double
boiler, set it over the bottom, and place the double
boiler on the stovetop at medium heat. Stir occasionally until the chocolate chips are melted.

Stir in the can of sweetened condensed milk and
cook approximately 2 minutes, stirring constantly,
until the frosting is shiny and of spreading consistency.

Spread it on the cupcakes, making sure to fill in the "frosting pocket."

Give the frosting pan to your favorite person to scrape.

These cupcakes are even better if you cool them, cover them, and let them sit for several hours (or even overnight) before frosting them.

Hannah's Note: If you want to make them in mini-cupcake tins, fill those ⅔ full and bake them at 350 degrees F. for 15 minutes.

Chapter Eight

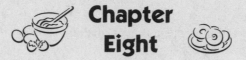

"**D**o you know how to preheat the oven to three hundred and fifty degrees?" Hannah asked, taking nothing for granted as far as Julie's domestic skills were concerned.

Julie nodded. "I can handle that part of it. It's the job they used to give me when we baked in a group in high school. Do I have to do something with the rack?"

"It should be in the middle position," Serena told her after glancing down at the recipe Hannah had brought. "Do you want us to unpack the box with the ingredients, Miss Swensen?"

"Not until Miss Jansen's had time to read through the recipe," Hannah said, handing the recipe to Julie as she came back to the workstation in the middle of the kitchen.

Julie scanned the recipe and started to smile. "What

fun! I've never heard of Multiple-Choice Bar Cookies before."

"You mean it's like a test?" Serena asked.

"No, it's like a buffet," Julie said, placing the recipe on the surface of the workstation and motioning for the girls to come closer. "Just look. There are four columns, and you get to choose one ingredient from each column. You could make a lot of different bar cookies from this recipe."

"One thousand five hundred and eighty-two," Hannah said.

"You figured it out that fast?" Serena looked impressed.

"No, I made it up. Whenever I do math problems like that, I forget to subtract for the number of factors to avoid the duplicates."

"Right," Julie said, looking every bit as confused as the kids. "Whenever I see a math problem like that, I'm glad I majored in English."

Serena cracked up, and so did the two younger girls. Hannah could tell that Julie had a good relationship with them. It would be an unusual child indeed who didn't like Julie. She was funny and caring at the same time.

"Since there are four columns, let's split this up," Julie continued. "You can choose one from each column. Take the first column, Serena. Hope? You've got the second column. And you've got the third column, Joy. I'll take the fourth, and we'll have our own creation."

Leaving the girls to discuss their choices and argue the merits of graham cracker crumbs over chocolate wafer crumbs, Hannah pulled Julie aside to teach her how to melt butter in the microwave and pour it in the pan. Once that was done, they had time for a brief, private conversation.

"How are things developing with Matt?" Hannah discarded any fleeting notion she might have had at subtlety and waded in with both feet.

"We'd be fine if the kids would just leave us alone," Julie said, and then she shook her head. "Matt and I talked about it, and he pointed out that it's just the boys. The girls have been perfect angels. They never interrupt us when we're together. I think they're really sensitive to the way we feel about each other. It's almost as if they're encouraging us to get together."

"Miss Jansen?" Hope called out. "Can I use M&Ms *and* raisins? It says two cups, and Serena thought it might be okay if I used one cup of each."

"Hannah?" Julie turned to her.

"Absolutely. And that makes one thousand five hundred and eighty-*three* ways to make them. You're a natural-born baker, Hope."

"Thanks, Miss Swensen."

While Julie was sprinkling the chosen ingredient from column A in the pan, Hannah thought about how the boys didn't want Julie and Matt to get together and the girls did. It was a little strange, considering that both the boys and the girls seemed to like Matt and Julie a lot. Something didn't make sense, but Hannah couldn't quite put her finger on what it was. Then Julie asked about the best way to cover the pan evenly with sweetened condensed milk, and Hannah shoved the romantic puzzle aside to consider later.

Spenser was worried. He'd thought it was suspicious when Mr. Sherwood said he was going out for supplies.

The storeroom was fully stocked and there really wasn't anything they needed. It was the reason he'd offered to help Mr. Sherwood unload when he came back, and just as he'd expected, Mr. Sherwood had insisted that he could handle it himself.

His curiosity aroused, Spenser had watched from an upstairs window as his teacher carried things in. Most of the packages Mr. Sherwood had bought were for them. Spenser recognized the toy store logo on the bags. But then Mr. Sherwood had gone back out to his car to retrieve a red bag with a logo on the side. It was a silver heart with an arrow, the trademark symbol of Cupid's Jewelry. Since there was no way Mr. Sherwood had purchased jewelry for one of them, it had to be for Miss Jansen. And Spenser was pretty sure the bag contained a diamond engagement ring.

Spenser ducked around a corner as Mr. Sherwood came up the stairs to stash the bag in his room. Things were coming to a head much too fast. It was time for them to act, or all was lost.

"Something's wrong in the office, Mr. Sherwood." Gary arrived at his teacher's side panting slightly, with Larry following a second or two behind him.

"What office?"

"The one down the hall," Larry answered. "Gary and I were walking down . . ."

". . . the hall when we heard this loud noise," Gary finished.

"It was sort of like a ringing sound," Larry tried to describe, "except it buzzed too. We thought it was . . ."

". . . a phone off the hook, or something like that."

"Thanks for telling me," Matt said. "It sounds like a fax machine, or something electronic. I've got the master keys in my pocket. Show me which office it is, and we'll go take a look."

This time it seemed that the twins had a legitimate reason for needing him. As they neared the office that Julie used to check her e-mail and generate daily reports to Dr. Caulder, he could hear the beeping noise Larry and Gary had told him about.

"It's definitely electronic," Matt said, making short work of unlocking the door and flicking on the lights.

Gary headed straight for the computer desk. "It's coming from here."

"What is it?" Matt asked.

Larry gave a little laugh. "It's an alarm clock. One of the guests must have left it in here . . ."

". . . and it got turned on accidentally," Gary finished. "But it's a good thing we came in. This is the computer Miss Jansen used, and she . . ."

". . . must have forgotten to turn it off," Larry completed the thought. "Do you want me to do it, Mr. Sherwood?"

Matt nodded. Both Gary and Larry were computer gurus. Even though they were only ten, they'd already written several small programs, and they knew more about the computers in the offices than Matt did. "Go ahead. Just make sure you save any files Miss Jansen might have open."

"Don't worry about that. We always check everything to . . ." Gary stopped and stared at the screen. "What do you think . . . ?"

"I don't know. Maybe it's some kind of security . . ."

"No way! It looks more like an illegal operation that led into an internal conflict with . . ."

"No, it doesn't. Just let me . . ."

"Better not. Look at that . . ."

"Uh-oh," Larry groaned.

Matt began to frown. "Uh-oh what?"

"Miss Jansen's computer just went to the blue screen of death."

"*What* blue screen of death?" Matt interjected before they could revert to twin talk again.

"You know, Mr. Sherwood," Larry started to explain. "You only get the bright blue screen when , , ,"

". . . your operating system's compromised," Gary ended the explanation.

"That sounds bad," Matt said, remembering his old college roommate talking about getting a blue screen and not being able to access the term paper he'd just finished.

Gary gave a short laugh. "It's always bad, and sometimes it's a disaster. But we know a couple of fixes that might . . ."

". . . get it back online again," Larry took over. "Just give us a minute, and we'll get into the CMOS and run some internal checks."

"Take your time," Matt said, sitting down on the couch by the window.

The twins worked in silence for a moment, and then Gary gave a little cheer. "Okay. It's up."

"That's just the operating system," Larry pointed out. "How about her files and her Internet provider?"

"The files are here. Let me just sign on and see if . . ." Gary stopped speaking as the computer rang like a bell several times in succession. "It's an instant message."

Larry frowned. "Better retrieve it and save it. If you don't, she might lose it."

"Okay. I'll just pull it up and . . . Wow!"

"Wow, what?" Matt asked, leaning forward slightly.

"I didn't know Miss Jansen was engaged!"

"Engaged?" both Matt and Larry asked at once.

"Well, she must be. He's asking her questions about their wedding."

Matt felt sick, and he was glad he was sitting down. "You shouldn't read somebody else's e-mail," he said weakly.

"But he's talking about *you*," Gary insisted. "You want to know what he says, don't you?"

"Yes, but we really ought to respect her privacy." Matt's voice trailed off. Of course he wanted to know what the message said. He'd been about to propose to Julie and that meant he *needed* to know.

"How can it be private if it's about you?" Larry challenged, and then he turned to his twin. "Go ahead and tell Mr. Sherwood what it says. Don't read it out loud 'cause that would be snooping, but tell him the important parts."

"Okay. His name is Dan and he's talking about something called a bachelor party. Do you know what that is?"

"Oh, yes," Matt said, the sick feeling rising in his stomach.

"The wedding's going to be in June, and Dan's telling Miss Jansen that he just sent an e-mail to her colleague to invite him to the bachelor party."

"Me?" Matt managed to ask.

"That's right. He says, *your colleague, Mr. Sherwood.* And then he says something about how he's looking forward to meeting you, and how glad he is that you're keeping her amused over Christmas."

Amused? Julie had told her fiancé that he'd *amused* her? Matt felt like swearing a blue streak, or throwing something through the picture window that overlooked the quad, or tracking down Julie's fiancé and taking him out with his bare hands. Any one of the three might have made him feel better, but he did none of them. Instead, Matt took a deep breath and let it out again slowly, hoping that his equilibrium would return and the twins wouldn't notice how his hands were shaking.

"That's very interesting," he said, pleased that his voice sounded calm, "but it's really none of our business. Save the message and then go find Spenser. Tell him I'm going to drive you boys out to the mall for hamburgers, and after that we'll take in a movie, or go bowling, or something."

"How about the girls?" Larry asked.

"They can stay here with Miss Jansen. It'll be boys night out, no girls allowed."

"Like a bachelor party?" Gary wanted to know.

"'Course not," Larry corrected him. "Spense told me about bachelor parties. All the guys drink a lot, and a lady in a bikini pops out of a cake."

"Do they eat the cake after she pops out?"

"Spense didn't say. Come on, Gary. Let's go find him."

Gary started to join his twin, but then he turned back to the computer. "Do you want me to shut this off, Mr. Sherwood?"

"I'll do it. I've got an e-mail I have to send, and I need to check something in that last report Miss Jansen wrote for Dr. Caulder. Just meet me by the car at five o'clock sharp and we'll leave."

"Thanks, Mr. Sherwood," Gary said.

"It'll be fun," Larry added.

The twins headed for the door, but just as they got there, Matt thought of something else. "Better not say anything to anybody about that e-mail from Miss Jansen's fiancé."

"Right," Larry agreed.

"We won't," Gary promised. "She might not understand how we had to open it to save it."

Once the boys had left and closed the door behind them, Matt sat down at the computer desk and opened Julie's e-mail. He was going to do something he knew he shouldn't do, but in the interests of his own sanity, he had to know exactly what was going on with the woman he'd intended to make his wife.

MULTIPLE-CHOICE BAR COOKIES

Preheat oven to 350 degrees F.,
rack in the middle position.

½ cup butter *(one stick, ¼ pound)*
1 can *(14 ounces)* sweetened condensed milk

Column A
(1½ cups of)
Graham Cracker Crumbs
Vanilla Wafer Crumbs
Chocolate Wafer Crumbs
Animal Cracker Crumbs
Sugar Cookie Crumbs

Column B
(2 cups of)
Chocolate Chips
Butterscotch Chips
Peanut Butter Chips
Raisins *(regular or golden)*
M & M's *(without nuts)*

Column C
(1½ cups of)
Flaked Coconut *(5 oz.)*
Rice Krispies
Miniature Marshmallows
   (2½ cups)
Frosted Cornflakes
   (crumbled)

Column D
(1 cup of)
Chopped Walnuts
Chopped Pecans
Chopped Peanuts
Chopped Cashews

Melt the butter and pour it into in a 9-inch by 13-inch cake pan. Tip the pan to coat the bottom.

1. Evenly sprinkle one from Column A over the melted butter.
2. Drizzle sweetened condensed milk over the crumbs.
3. Evenly sprinkle one from Column B on top.
4. Evenly sprinkle one from Column C on top of that.
5. Evenly sprinkle something from Column D over the very top.

Press everything down with the palms of your impeccably clean hands. Bake at 350 degrees F. for 30 minutes. Cool thoroughly on a wire rack and cut into brownie-sized bars.

Make sure you cut these before you refrigerate them or they'll be very difficult to cut.

Hannah's Note: Kids love to help make these bars when they get to choose the ingredients.

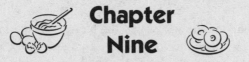

Chapter Nine

The moment that Hannah pulled open the heavy front door of Aames House, she knew that something was wrong. Instead of the childish laughter that had greeted her on every other visit, there was only the sound of quiet voices from the kitchen where Julie and the girls were waiting for her. The group baking yesterday afternoon had been so much fun, the girls had asked if they could do it again today. Of course Hannah had agreed. Tonight was Christmas Eve, and The Cookie Jar was closed. Hannah and Lisa had plenty of time to start the holiday fun by baking Christmas sugar cookies with Julie and the girls.

"What's the matter?" Lisa asked, as Hannah stopped and listened.

"It's quiet . . . too quiet."

"Like in an old western when the Indians are about to ride up over the top of the hill and attack?"

"Not exactly, but the general concept's the same. Something's wrong, and I've got the feeling it's something big. Let's go find out if I'm right or if I've seen too many movies."

Hannah led the way down the hallway to the kitchen and pushed open the door. Julie was standing at the central workstation with the girls, who were talking quietly among themselves.

"Uh-oh," Hannah said under her breath as she caught sight of Julie. Even though she'd tried to cover the traces of tears with makeup and there was a brave little smile on her face, Julie's eyelids were puffy, and Hannah suspected she'd been crying most of the night.

Lisa nudged Hannah and moved closer so she wouldn't be overheard. "You're right. It's something big. I'll take over with the cookies and the girls if you want to have coffee with Julie in the dining room and find out what's wrong."

"Good idea." Hannah took a deep breath and waded into deep waters. Julie might resist her probing, but she looked so miserable, they couldn't just stand by and pretend nothing was wrong.

"Hi, Hannah," Julie said as Hannah approached her. "The girls are all ready to bake Christmas cookies."

"And Lisa's all ready to teach them how to do it. Let's get a cup of coffee and go into the dining room."

It was proof of Julie's misery that she didn't even voice an objection or say something about how she should help to supervise her students. She just poured coffee for both of them and carried the cups into the adjoining room.

"I guess the makeup didn't work," Julie said, setting the cups down on place mats.

"It might fool someone who was visually challenged

on a night with no moon." Hannah opened one of the bakery boxes she'd carried in with her. "We brought along all the leftover cookies for the kids. These are Twin Chocolate Delights. Eat one."

"Thanks, Hannah, but I'm not really hungry."

"You don't have to be hungry. Just eat one. The endorphins in the chocolate will help."

"Help what?"

"Whatever it is that's making you cry. You want to feel better, don't you?"

"Of course I do, but . . ."

"Then take a bite. It'll work, I almost guarantee it. Chocolate creates a feeling of well-being, calms frazzled nerves, relieves stress, and puts daily problems into perspective."

Julie gave a brief little smile, and Hannah was very glad to see it. "You sound like a commercial for a new drug. The only thing you're missing is the part about the side effects."

"You may experience a slight weight gain if you overdose," Hannah said in her best announcer's voice. "Ask your local baker if chocolate is right for you."

This time Julie's smile was a bit wider. She reached into the box, chose a cookie, and took a bite. "These are good," she said, after she'd swallowed.

"Of course they are. If I calculated right, they're over seventy percent good stuff."

"What's *good stuff*?"

"Chocolate, butter, and sugar. But let's not talk about nutrition."

"Or the lack of it," Julie countered, finishing her first cookie and reaching for a second.

"Right." Hannah was pleased as Julie's second cookie

began to go the way of the first. "Now tell me what's got you so upset. I'm assuming you had a fight with Matt?"

"Yes."

"Over what?"

"Over e-mail."

Hannah thought fast. Asking Julie questions was a little like cracking almonds. If she applied too much pressure, Julie might be crushed by the weight of her problem and start crying again. Still, she had to know the facts. "You mean Matt's been sending you e-mail?"

"No, he's been getting e-mail . . ." Julie stopped to take a deep breath, ". . . from my fiancé. And I don't even *have* a fiancé!"

"Then how did . . . What . . . Did he . . ." Hannah sputtered while she went through the possibilities in her mind. "Let me get this straight. Matt got an e-mail from a guy who said he was your fiancé, and now he thinks you're engaged?"

"Exactly. And Matt also thinks I was just amusing myself with him because I was bored and this Dan who claims to be my fiancé is all the way out in Montana."

"Uh-oh."

"Uh-oh is right. I tried to tell Matt that it must be a case of mistaken identity, that there must be another Julie Jansen and that I don't even *know* a guy named Dan. But he wouldn't listen." Julie's eyes filled with tears.

Hannah thought about that for a moment, and then she stood up. "Okay. I'm going to go talk to Matt."

"It won't do any good," Julie warned.

"Maybe not, but I have to try. You stay here and eat a couple more cookies. I'll be back just as soon as I can."

* * *

"I really don't want to talk about it. Not only that, it's really none of your business."

"Yes, it is," Hannah countered. Matt was being rude, but she didn't take offense. It was clear by his expression that believing Julie was engaged had wounded him deeply. "I talked to Julie and she told me about the man who claims to be her fiancé."

"The man who *is* her fiancé."

"Whatever. Let's leave that open for now. I'd like to see the e-mail he sent, if you still have it."

"Why?"

"Because I just can't believe that Julie would lie to both of us about being engaged. I admit I haven't seen her since she was in high school, but it seems so out of character for her."

Matt hesitated, but then he nodded. "Okay. I understand how you feel, Hannah. I was taken in by her too. Come with me. It's in the room I'm using as an office."

It was only a few steps to Matt's office, and Hannah waited while he unlocked the door. Once she was seated on the couch next to the windows, Matt brought her a sheaf of papers. "What's all this?" she asked.

"The top one's the e-mail I got from Dan. The others are copies of the messages he sent to Julie. I know it was wrong to do it, but I read them and printed them out."

"I don't understand how you got her e-mail."

"The twins must have known her password or gotten around it somehow. They're both computer whizzes."

"You asked the boys to break into Julie's computer?" Hannah asked, clearly shocked.

"No. The whole thing was accidental. The boys came to me because they heard something buzzing in Julie's office and the door was locked. It turned out to be an alarm clock, but her computer was on. While we were there, the computer started acting up and the twins tried to fix it. They got it back online, but then an e-mail message came in and they were afraid that if they didn't open it and save it, Julie would lose it."

"I see," Hannah said, and both meanings of the word applied. While they'd been talking, she'd paged through the messages, and one thing had popped out loud and clear. "So the twins are computer experts?"

"That's right. They even dabble in programming. Both of their parents are in the technology field."

"So if anyone could make a computer act up, it would be the twins."

"True." Matt's eyes narrowed slightly. "But they don't have a key to Julie's office. How could they get the alarm clock to go off?"

"I'm not sure, but I bet if you check you'll find out that they went into Julie's office while she was there. If one twin did or said something to distract her, it would be easy for the other one to set that alarm clock."

"You could be right, but how about all these messages from Julie's fiancé? I've got them right here in black and white."

"Let me read you something," Hannah said, paging through the stack to find the one she wanted. "According to the date, this one came in yesterday. *I yearn for you more each day and fervently anticipate the instance when we can be united continually.* Does that sound like something a guy would write to his fiancée?"

"Not really. I guess I was too upset to notice it before, but the wording's very awkward."

"How about this one?" Hannah located a second sheet

of paper. "*The moments we're estranged are anguish, but the future will soon arrive. I adore you more with each second that elapses.*"

Matt began to frown. "That's even worse. It reminds me of something, but I can't quite put my finger on it."

"It's writing for Roget," Hannah told him. "Somebody looked up some perfectly good words in the thesaurus and substituted bigger ones."

"You're right! But who'd go to all that trouble for an e-mail?"

Matt and Hannah exchanged glances. And then he answered his own question. "There's only one person who'd do it. It was a kid who was trying to sound like an adult."

Hannah headed for the kitchen at a trot. She'd check in with Lisa and the girls, tell Julie what was going on, and then she'd confront the boys. Matt said they were watching television in the lounge and that was a perfect place to elicit a confession from the three pranksters who'd almost been Julie and Matt's undoing.

A lovely scent wafted down the hallway as Hannah neared the kitchen. The girls were already baking. She'd mixed up the dough at The Cookie Jar before she'd left last night. Today the only thing to do was roll it out, cut it in Christmas shapes, bake it, and then frost it. From the mouthwatering aroma that hit her nostrils as she pushed the kitchen door open, Hannah could tell that the girls were well on their way to finishing the sugary Christmas treats.

"Will you come look at my cookies, Miss Swensen?"

Hope asked, running up to grab Hannah's hand and pull her to the far end of the workstation. "I'm decorating the bells."

"And you're doing a wonderful job, Hope. I especially like that one." Hannah pointed to a red and green bell with markedly irregular stripes.

"Serena likes that one too. She wants it for her Christmas present."

To the girls' delight, Hannah inspected all the cookies and pronounced them good enough to eat. Then Lisa shooed her out of the kitchen and into the dining room to talk to Julie.

"What did Matt say?" Julie sounded calm, but the way her hands twisted in her lap was testament to her anxiety.

"He believes you now."

"It's about time! He should have believed me when I first said that . . ."

"Stop!" Hannah held up her hand and Julie fell silent. "Let's not compound the problem. Matt didn't want to believe it, but he was tricked."

"Who tricked him?"

"We don't know for sure, but we think it was the boys."

"But . . . I thought the boys liked me," Julie said, looking very confused.

"Oh, they do. And they like Matt too."

"Then why did they try to break us up?"

"That's what I'm about to find out. You wait here. Matt's coming to ask you to forgive him, and I want you to do it. It's true that he should have trusted you, but everyone makes mistakes."

Julie thought about that for a minute. "You're right,

Hannah. I just hate to think the boys did this deliberately, though. Maybe they were just playing a prank and it got out of control."

"Maybe," Hannah said. Julie was kind, giving the boys the benefit of the doubt, but Hannah didn't believe it for a second. The boys had planned all this very carefully and she was determined to find out why.

CHRISTMAS SUGAR COOKIES

Do not preheat oven—this dough
must chill before baking.

*I came up with the cookie recipe and Lisa did
the frosting.*

  1½ cups melted butter *(3 sticks, ¾ pound)*
  2 cups white *(granulated)* sugar
  4 beaten eggs
  2 teaspoons baking powder
  1½ teaspoons salt
  1 teaspoon flavor extract *(lemon, almond,
       vanilla, orange, rum, whatever)*
  5 cups flour *(no need to sift)*

Mix the melted butter with the sugar. Let cool.
Add the beaten eggs, baking powder, salt, and fla-
voring.

Add the flour in one-cup increments, stirring after
each addition.

Refrigerate dough for at least two hours. Overnight is fine, too.

When you're ready to bake, preheat the oven to 375 degrees F., rack in the center position.

Divide the dough into four parts for ease in rolling. Roll out the first part of the dough on a floured board. It should be approximately ⅛ inch thick.

Dip the cookie cutters in flour and cut out cookies, getting as many as you can from the sheet of dough. *(If you don't have cookie cutters, you can cut free-form cookies with a sharp knife.)* Use a metal spatula to remove the cookies from the rest of the sheet of dough and place them on an UN-GREASED cookie sheet. Leave at least an inch and a half between cookies.

If you want to use colored sugar or sprinkles to decorate, put it on now, before baking. If you'd rather frost the cookies, wait until they're baked and cooled.

Bake at 375 degrees F. for 8 to 10 minutes, or just until delicately golden in color. Leave them on the sheet for a minute or two and then transfer them to a wire rack to complete cooling.

Icing:
>   2 cups sifted confectioner's sugar *(powdered sugar)*
>   Pinch of salt
>   ½ teaspoon vanilla *(or other flavoring)*
>   ¼ cup cream

Mix up icing, adding a little more cream if it's too thick and a little more powdered sugar if it's too thin.

If you'd like to frost the cookies in different colors, divide the icing and put it in several small bowls. Add drops of the desired food coloring to each bowl.

Use a frosting knife or a brush to "paint" the cookies you've baked.

Chapter Ten

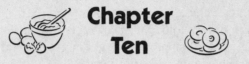

"Hello, boys," Hannah said.

"Hi, Miss Swensen," the boys chorused, and three faces with identical innocent expressions turned to greet her.

"So why did you do it?"

"Do what?" one of the twins asked, but a dull red stain crept up his neck and spread to his cheeks.

"Yes, what?" the other twin chimed in, pulling his collar up a bit to hide his telltale color.

"You know what you did. What I want to know is why."

"It was my fault," Spenser said manfully, squaring his shoulders a bit. "I talked them into making the bet, and these guys had no choice but to go along with me."

"Yes we did," one of the twins said. "We could have . . ."

". . . said we didn't want to bet," the other twin finished the explanation.

"Tell me about the bet," Hannah said, sitting down in the chair next to the couch and switching off the television with the remote control.

Spenser drew a folded piece of paper from his pocket. "You can read all about it. I've got our copy right here. All of us signed it to make it official."

Hannah took the paper and read it. "The girls win if Mr. Sherwood asks Miss Jansen to marry him. And you win if they don't get engaged. Is that right?"

"That's right," Spenser said, and the twins nodded.

"I don't get it. You must not like Mr. Sherwood and Miss Jansen."

Spenser shook his head. "We like them a lot," he said.

"It's just that the girls were being so . . ." one twin started the thought, but he got stuck for a word.

". . . confident," the other twin provided it. "And stuck up. They thought they knew better than we did."

"They *did* know better than we did," Spenser pointed out. "Mr. Sherwood was going to propose to Miss Jansen. I saw him carry in the jeweler's bag with the ring that he bought at the mall. The girls were right and we were wrong, and that meant we had to do their chores for a month. We couldn't let that happen. It was just too awful."

"What do the girls have to do for chores?" Hannah asked, thinking that it must be pretty bad for the boys to go to such lengths to win.

"Hope and Joy have to go shopping with Mrs. Caulder every Saturday and carry her packages," one twin said, shuddering slightly.

"And they have to pass trays of sandwiches with their crusts cut off on Wednesday at her musical sorry," the other twin added.

"Soirée," Spenser corrected. "Serena's chores are pretty bad too. She has to help Mrs. Dryer clean up the kitchen after dinner."

"When does this bet end?" Hannah said, an idea beginning to form in her mind.

"The day after Christmas," Spenser told her. "We didn't know that Mr. Sherwood and Miss Jansen would feel this bad. Now we wish we hadn't done it."

"Okay," Hannah said, handing the remote control to Spenser and standing up. "I've got to go. I need to bake a dessert for tonight's dinner."

"Are we busted?" one of the twins wanted to know.

"I'm not going to punish you, if that's what you mean. Your own consciences will do that."

"Do you think Mr. Sherwood will propose before Christmas is over?" Spenser wanted to know.

"I have no idea. All we can do is wait and see," Hannah said, heading for the hallway and leaving the three guilty boys to think about the havoc they'd caused.

"Hannah's right," Julie confirmed it when Matt told her Hannah's theory. "The twins came into my office yesterday morning while I was getting my e-mail. Larry said he wanted to see if I had the latest virus protection and he offered to teach me how to check. I was busy with him, and I didn't pay much attention to Gary."

"That must be when Larry got your password and Gary set the alarm clock."

Julie thought about it for a moment. "I remember Larry asking me to type in my password so he could download an update to my security program. It all makes sense."

"I think Spenser must have planned it. He's quite the strategist. That boy is going to go far."

"Let's just hope he doesn't turn to a life of crime. He might just get away with it. He almost did this time."

"That was my fault." Matt slipped his arm around Julie's shoulders. "I should have trusted you when you said you didn't have a fiancé."

"And I should have been more insistent that you listen to me. I just gave up without a fight."

"We'll learn," Matt promised, bending down to kiss her. "With every day that passes, we'll trust each other more."

"Yes, we will," Julie agreed. And as he pulled her tightly into his arms, it was as if the whole misunderstanding had been a bad dream and they'd never been apart for an instant.

Hannah pulled aside the curtains and peered out at the driveway. Her family and friends should arrive any minute. When Jordan High's cook, Edna Ferguson, had heard that Julie and her young charges were going to eat frozen dinners for the holiday, she'd volunteered to come out and cook a "proper" Christmas Eve dinner.

The two men Hannah was dating, Mike Kingston and Norman Rhodes, had volunteered next. Along with Lisa's husband, Herb, and Andrea's husband, Bill, they were bringing out snowmobiles to entertain the boys. Not to be outdone, Andrea had offered to take charge of the girls and decorate Aames House for Christmas. There would be presents, of course. Hannah's mother had organized that. And Hannah would bake her special Christmas Date

Cake complete with the surprises her mother had suggested.

The big grandfather clock in the lobby had just struck noon when the first car drove up with Edna Ferguson and her sister, Hattie. Hannah rushed to the door to greet them, and then she called for Matt and the boys to help them carry in their load of goodies for the holiday feast.

The next to arrive was Andrea, and she brought Tracey, baby Bethany, and her live-in nanny, "Grandma" McCann. Once Julie and the girls had exclaimed over the baby and made Tracey feel welcome, Hannah got baby and nanny settled in the lounge while Andrea took the girls off to unpack the decorations she'd brought.

Just about the time good smells were beginning to waft in from the kitchen, Bill and Mike drove in, towing a large three-passenger snowmobile behind Mike's Hummer. Hannah's other boyfriend, Norman, was next, and he was also towing a snowmobile. Lisa's husband, Herb, was right behind him with the third, and when the boys raced out to look at the snowmobiles, Matt turned to Hannah.

"Is all this for us?" he asked.

Hannah shrugged, but she was smiling. "I just mentioned that I was coming out to spend Christmas Eve with you, and the word spread. The guys decided to take the boys out for a ride and give you a little break this afternoon."

"That's really nice of them."

"They're all nice guys. Mike's got a Christmas tree in the back of his Hummer. Why don't you go out and help him carry it in before he takes off on his snowmobile with the kids?"

Once the tree was inside and securely fixed in the stand, Andrea and the girls began to decorate it. Matt watched the boys leave with the four men, and Hannah thought he looked a bit lost.

"Is there anything you need me to do while they're gone?" Matt asked her.

"Yes," Hannah said, her mind racing to think of something he could do with Julie. "Andrea could use some mistletoe for her decorations. I spotted some hanging from the old oak tree near the end of the driveway when I drove in. Would you and Julie go out to cut some?"

With everyone busy and happy, Hannah was about to head for the kitchen to bake her cake when her mother arrived. Delores was dressed for the occasion in a red satin pantsuit that would have looked ridiculous on any other Lake Eden woman even approaching her age. She wore gold high-heeled shoes and carried a gold-beaded purse. Anyone who saw her for the first time immediately knew how Andrea had acquired her perfect petite figure and her sense of fashion.

"Nice outfit, Mother," Hannah said, taking her mother's coat.

"Thank you, dear. I wanted to be festive." Delores reached in her purse and drew out a tissue-wrapped packet. "I brought the silver charms for the cake, dear."

"Thanks. And speaking of the cake, I'd better go make it." Hannah headed for the kitchen at a trot. Once there, she worked fast, getting out the ingredients she'd brought with her and mixing up her batter. She was just slipping the cake into the oven when Julie came into the kitchen.

"You look happy," Hannah remarked, noticing that her younger friend was practically glowing.

"That's because I *am* happy. I think Matt's going to

ask me to marry him, Hannah. And I wouldn't be surprised if it's tonight."

"Uh-oh," Hannah said, thinking of the boys and their bet. Then she noticed the frown on Julie's face and hurried to reassure her. "I'm delighted, Julie. I think you and Matt are perfect for each other. There's just one small problem. Come over to the sink with me while I wash these things, and I'll tell you all about it."

Hannah finished explaining the terms of the bet about the same time Julie dried the last bowl. "I know they deserve to lose for what they've done. And doing the girls' chores won't be that bad."

"Oh yes it will. You have no idea how the other boys will tease Spenser when he has to work for Mrs. Dryer in the kitchen. And the twins will just die if they have to follow Mrs. Caulder around the mall. I want Matt to ask me to marry him, but I don't want the boys to suffer. Isn't there a way that the boys and the girls could both win?"

Hannah thought about that for a minute, and then she started to smile. "No, but there's a way they could both lose. It'll take some doing and you'll have to clue in Matt, but I think it should work."

When the last succulent bite of roast turkey had been eaten, and the final morsel of sweet potato with marshmallow and brown sugar topping had found a willing mouth, it was time to serve the dessert.

"Will you explain dessert, Mother?" Hannah asked, turning to Delores.

"Yes, dear," Delores stood up and smiled at everyone seated around the oval table. "We're having a Regency Love Cake for dessert."

"What's that, Mrs. Swensen?" Serena asked, clearly enthralled by the concept.

"It's a little something they served at parties in England in the early nineteenth century. Hannah has baked the modern-day version, a Christmas Date Cake. Each piece has a little prize inside, a small keepsake to remind you of this marvelous Christmas Eve. It's wrapped in a foil packet so you won't inadvertently eat it."

"That's good," Norman said, and everyone laughed.

"All the prizes are the same," Delores went on, "except for one. And that special prize is what makes it a Regency Love Cake."

"What's the special prize, Mrs. Swensen?" Joy asked.

"A gold ring. Is everybody here willing to abide by the old Regency rules and reveal the name of the person they love if they get the piece with the gold ring?"

The adults at the table laughed and nodded. In sharp contrast, the kids looked very uncomfortable.

"But Mrs. Swensen," Spenser gulped slightly. "What if we don't have someone we love?"

Delores smiled to reassure him. "Don't worry, Spenser. The gold ring is only for adults. If you or one of your friends gets it, just give it to me and I'll pass it on to Hannah."

Hannah gave her mother a dirty look. Delores was matchmaking again.

"And now it's time for the Regency Love Cake." Delores walked over to dim the lights, and Hannah ducked in the kitchen to light the candles on the platter of cake. Each piece had a dollop of whipped cream on top to camouflage the spot where she'd inserted the prize. She quickly located the piece with the double swirl of whipped cream and carried the platter out to the applause of the kids and the assembled guests.

Once the candles were blown out and the lights were back on, Hannah plated the cake the way they'd planned, making certain that Julie got the piece with the double swirl. She gave Julie a conspiratorial wink, and then she put on her best guileless smile.

Everyone tasted the cake and pronounced it excellent, and one by one, they found their prizes, a little silver whistle for everyone except . . .

Julie unwrapped her prize and let out a little shriek. "Oh my!" she exclaimed, acting very surprised. "I've got the gold ring!"

"How marvelous, dear!" Delores reached over to pat her on the shoulder. "You're our lucky winner. Will you tell us the name of the person you love?"

Julie nodded, blushing slightly as she smiled at Matt. "It's Matt and I'll give him this ring if he'll marry me."

Matt did a good job of feigning surprise, but he quickly recovered. "Yes, I will. Remember the day I went out to the mall to pick up a few gifts for the kids? Well, I stopped at the jewelry store and bought an engagement ring for you. I was planning on asking you to marry me later tonight, but you beat me to the punch."

"Oh no!" Spenser groaned as Matt reached over and placed the ring on Julie's finger. "Mr. Sherwood asked her to marry him!"

"No, he didn't," Larry pointed out. "Miss Jansen asked . . ."

". . . Mr. Sherwood to marry *her*," Gary finished the thought.

"Then we win the bet?" It was clear that Spenser could scarcely believe his good fortune.

"What bet?" Delores asked.

"I'll explain later," Hannah told her, and then she turned to Spenser. "You lose the bet, Spenser. You bet the girls that Mr. Sherwood and Miss Jansen wouldn't get engaged until after Christmas was over. Take a look at that ring on her finger. They're engaged."

"So you have to do *our* chores!" Serena crowed, giving Joy and Hope a high five. "We win!"

"No, you don't," Hannah said, taking great relish in pointing it out. "You bet that Mr. Sherwood would ask Miss Jansen to marry him, and that didn't happen. Miss Jansen asked Mr. Sherwood instead."

"So we both lost?" Spenser asked, looking very confused.

"That depends on your point of view. I think you both won. The important thing is that no one has to do anyone else's chores."

"Right!" Spenser said, smiling again. "I don't think I want to bet on anything again for a really long time."

"Good idea," Hannah said, glad that he'd learned something from the experience.

"There's one more thing we have to do before this Christmas Eve dinner is over," Andrea said, nudging Bill.

Bill stood up and lifted Tracey onto his shoulders. He walked over to the beam where the ball of mistletoe was hanging, and Tracey reached up to remove it. Then Bill took her over to Matt and Julie, and she leaned forward to hold the mistletoe over Julie's head.

"You know what mistletoe means, don't you?" she asked.

"I certainly do," Matt said, taking his cue and leaning over to kiss his bride-to-be to the accompaniment of cheers from everyone there.

CHRISTMAS DATE CAKE

Preheat oven to 325 degrees F.,
rack in the middle position.

Hannah's Note: This recipe is from my Grandma Ingrid. She used to make this cake every Christmas.

2 cups chopped pitted dates *(You can buy chopped dates, or sprinkle whole pitted dates with flour and then chop them in a food processor.)*
3 cups boiling water
2 teaspoons baking soda

Pour the boiling water over the dates, add the soda *(it foams up a bit),* and set them aside to cool. While they're cooling, cream the following ingredients together in a large mixing bowl:

1 cup soft or melted butter *(2 sticks, ½ pound)*

2 cups white *(granulated)* sugar
4 eggs
½ teaspoon salt
3 cups flour *(don't sift—pack it down in the cup when you measure it)*

Once the above are thoroughly mixed, add the cooled date mixture to your bowl and stir thoroughly.

Butter and flour a 9-inch by 13-inch rectangular cake pan. *(This cake rises about an inch and a half, so make sure the sides are tall enough.)* Pour the batter into the pan. Then sprinkle the following on the top, in this order, BEFORE baking:

12 ounces chocolate chips *(2 cups)*
1 cup white *(granulated)* sugar
1 cup chopped nuts *(use any nuts you like— I prefer walnuts or pecans)*

Bake at 325 degrees F. for 80 minutes. A cake tester or a long toothpick should come out clean one inch from the center when the cake is done. *(If you happen to stick the toothpick in and hit a*

chocolate chip, it'll come out covered with melted chocolate—just wipe it off and stick it in again to test the actual cake batter.)

Let the cake cool in the pan on a wire rack. It can be served slightly warm, at room temperature, or chilled.

If you want to be truly decadent, serve it the way Hannah did in the story, with a generous dollop of sweetened whipped cream on each slice.

Index of Recipes

Baking Conversion Chart

These conversions are approximate, but they'll work just fine for Hannah Swensen's recipes.

VOLUME:

U.S.	Metric
½ teaspoon	2 milliliters
1 teaspoon	5 milliliters
1 tablespoon	15 milliliters
¼ cup	50 milliliters
⅓ cup	75 milliliters
½ cup	125 milliliters
¾ cup	175 milliliters
1 cup	¼ liter

WEIGHT:

U.S.	Metric
1 ounce	28 grams
1 pound	454 grams

OVEN TEMPERATURE:

Degrees Fahrenheit	Degrees Centigrade	British (Regulo) Gas Mark
325 degrees F.	165 degrees C.	3
350 degrees F.	175 degrees C.	4
375 degrees F.	190 degrees C.	5

Note: Hannah's rectangular sheet cake pan, 9 inches by 13 inches, is approximately 23 centimeters by 32.5 centimeters.

NIGHTMARE ON
ELF STREET

LAURA LEVINE

Chapter One

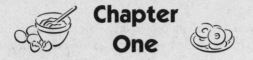

You'd think after all I've done for my cat—the belly rubs, the back scratches, the endless cans of Fancy Feast—you'd think she could at least wear a pair of reindeer antlers for three minutes while I took her picture for my annual Christmas card. But, no, Prozac, the little drama queen, had decided that the fuzzy felt antlers I'd ordered online were emissaries from the devil and was determined to avoid them at all costs.

"Pumpkin face," I pleaded. "Just think how adorable you'll look."

But she just glared at me balefully.

I'm already adorable. And don't call me pumpkin face.

I was on my knees that late November morning, begging her for the umpteenth time to let me put the antlers on her stubborn little head, when the phone rang.

Wearily I picked it up to hear:

"Fabulous news, Jaine! I've just spent the past forty-five minutes fondling the feet of a fabulously wealthy Malibu blonde."

No, you haven't stumbled on a foot fetish novella. The voice on the other end of the line was my neighbor Lance Venable, who happens to fondle feet for a living as a shoe salesman at Neiman Marcus.

"She wound up buying five pair of Jimmy Choos," Lance was saying. "And guess what? It turns out her husband owns that new mall out in Santa Monica—Conspicuous Consumption Plaza."

Of course that wasn't what it was really called. I've changed the mall's name to protect the innocent—namely *moi*—from a lawsuit.

"It seems they're looking for someone to write their ads, and I told her all about you and your award-winning campaign for Apple computers."

"But Lance, I've never worked for Apple. My biggest client is Toiletmasters Plumbers. And the only award I've ever won is the Golden Plunger from the L.A. Plumbers Association."

"A mere technicality, honey. The bottom line is you've got an interview with their HR gal tomorrow morning at ten o'clock."

I have to admit I was excited. How nice it would be to have something glamorous to write in between toilet bowl ads.

"Oh, Lance. You're an angel!"

"Try to remember that when shopping for my Christmas present—Oops. Gotta run. Trophy Wife over by the Ferragamos. Damn. Looks like she's got bunions."

I hung up the phone in a much better frame of mind than when I'd picked it up, my head spinning with visions of all that a new job could buy: A high-def TV. New slipcovers for my sofa. Maybe even a lifetime membership in the Fudge-of-the-Month Club.

"Fabulous news, Pro!" I said, whirling around in a happy glow. "I've got a job interview!"

To which she merely rolled over on her back, her paws poised daintily in the air.

And I've got a belly that needs scratching. So hop to it.

"No belly rubs for you, young lady," I said, marching straight past her to my bedroom. "Not after your churlish behavior with those felt antlers."

Okay, so I didn't march straight past her.

I may have stopped to give her belly a teeny scratch. But I swear it wasn't for more than two minutes. Five, tops.

Okay, twenty, if you must know.

Conspicuous Consumption Plaza was an upscale mall with valet parking, froufrou boutiques and stocking stuffers that cost more than my Corolla.

To fool the Human Resources gal into thinking I actually belonged there, I showed up in my one and only Prada suit and one and only pair of Manolo Blahniks. I'd blown my mop of unruly curls reasonably smooth, and was now clacking along on the mall's travertine marble floors on my way to the executive offices. Shiny baubles glistened in shop windows, lush garlands hung overhead, and the air was redolent with the scent of cinnamon spice and new money.

All the glitz came to a screeching halt, however, when I walked through the door to the staff offices. Suddenly everything was linoleum and fluorescent lights.

I found Molly Grover, the head of Human Resources, in a no frills cubicle down at the end of a corridor.

I'd been expecting a kamikaze fashionista straight from the pages of *Vogue*, but instead I found a somewhat frazzled thirtysomething woman in a wrinkled pantsuit.

She gazed up from a pile of papers, her face pale and pasty, her mousy brown hair hanging in limp clumps on her shoulders.

"Have a seat." She gestured vaguely to a cracked plastic visitor's chair. Then, with a hopeful smile, she said, "I hear you've written for Apple."

Oh, gulp.

"I'm afraid there's been a bit of a mix up. I haven't actually handled any computer accounts. Although some of the septic tanks sold by one of my top clients, Toiletmasters Plumbers, do come with a computerized control panel."

"Is that so?" she said, her smile rapidly fading. "Well, let me take a look at your samples anyway."

I handed her my book of writing samples, and she began leafing through them. Every once in a while she paused to gaze at me intently, then back to the book.

Finally she slammed the book shut, shooting me one last penetrating look.

"You're perfect!" she exclaimed.

Wow. Talk about your dream interviews.

I'd been there less than five minutes, and already I'd landed the job.

"Here." She reached down under her desk and pulled out a shopping bag. "Try it on."

"What is it?"

"Your elf suit."

"My elf suit?"

"Yes, one of my Santa's elves just quit and I'm in desperate need of a replacement."

"But what about the writing job?"

"Oh, that. I like your samples, very impressive. You're definitely on the short list. But let's just say you'd be a lot higher up on that list if you helped me out and worked as Santa's elf for a few weeks."

"In other words, you're bribing me."

"Not in other words. In those words. Put on the elf suit," she commanded, suddenly tough as a marine drill sergeant, "or you don't have a snowball's chance in hell of getting the writing gig."

Well! If she thought I was the kind of person who would sacrifice my dignity and self-respect just to better my chances at landing a job—she was absolutely right. It had been a long time between toilet bowl ads, and I needed the bucks.

"So how about it?" she asked. "Are you game?"

If I'd known what was in store for me, I would have grabbed my sample book and skedaddled straight to the food court. But I knew nothing of the disastrous events waiting in the wings. So with hope in my heart, and a pair of curly-toed shoes in my hands, I said yes.

A mistake, I would soon learn, of monumental proportions.

Chapter Two

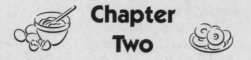

I got my first hint of how truly ghastly my days as an elf would be when I hustled off to the employees' ladies' room to try on my elf suit. I still shudder to think of that hideous costume. The green velvet tunic, piped in gold, wasn't too horrible, if you didn't mind looking like Peter Pan on estrogen. Nor was the stocking cap with the fuzzy pompom at the tip. Or the green curly-toed shoes.

But those godawful red and green striped tights! That was truly the fashion accessory from hell. Those damn stripes added at least five extra pounds to my thighs—which had all the poundage they needed, thank you very much.

But on the bright side, I reminded myself, I'd actually managed to squeeze into an elf costume. For those of you who don't know me, I am not ordinarily considered the elfin type. Far from it, as my scale will be the first to assure you.

To tell the truth, when Molly said I'd be perfect for the part, I'd actually been a tiny bit flattered. But my bubble was quickly burst when, back in Molly's office, she looked at me and beamed, "Oh, marvelous! The costume fits you so much better than it fit Kenny."

"Kenny?"

I was wearing a *guy's* elf suit?

"Yes, the elf you're replacing. He quit to concentrate on his Weight Watchers classes."

I was wearing a *fat guy's* elf suit?

Ouch.

At which point, there was a knock on Molly's cubicle door and a truly elfin elf waltzed in. A tiny pixie of a thing with a pert little nose, enormous brown eyes, and waist the size of my red and green striped thigh.

"Hi, Molly," she said, looking adorable in her elf costume. "You wanted to see me?"

"Yes, Gigi. Say hi to Jaine Austen, our new elf. Jaine, this is Gigi Harris."

The pixie and I exchanged hellos.

"Would you mind taking Jaine around and showing her the ropes?"

"Not at all."

Gigi shot me a friendly grin. And, grabbing my sample book, I followed her tiny tush out into the hallway.

My first shift did not officially start until the next day. So thank heavens I was allowed to change out of my elf suit before returning to the mall. As Gigi explained while I struggled out of my hideous tights in the employees' ladies' room, she and I were the two weekday elves, working Mondays through Fridays, taking turns with the day and night shifts. Working alongside us were two weekday Santas, while a whole other crew took over on the weekends.

"We get minimum wage," she said, popping a wad of gum in her mouth and sending a blast of Juicy Fruit my way. "Plus a twenty percent employee discount. Of course, the discount doesn't help much with the ridiculous prices they charge around here. The real reason I'm working at Conspicuous Consumption is the exposure."

"Exposure?"

"Sure. A lot of show business insiders shop here. A gal never knows when she's going to get discovered."

"So you're an actress?"

"Couldn't you tell?" she asked, batting her saucer eyes. "Practically everybody who works in Santa Land is in the biz. Or trying to break in, anyway. Scotty, one of the Santas, has done a Taco Bell commercial, and Barnaby, the other Santa, used to play Shakespeare on Broadway."

By now I'd changed back into my civvies, and Gigi led me to a fluorescent-lit employees' locker room.

"The lockers are co-ed," she explained, "which is why we have to change into our costumes in the ladies' room. Here's yours." She pointed to a rusty cubbyhole against the wall. "It's right next to Barnaby's. He's a real sweetie. Scotty, on the other hand, can be a bit of a handful."

That, as I was about to discover, was putting it mildly.

"Well, c'mon," she said, popping her gum. "Time for you to see Santa Land."

Conspicuous Consumption's Santa Land was an extravaganza of the highest order—the highlight of which was a ginormous Christmas tree sitting on a bed of fake snow, its boughs bedecked with glimmering baubles. Nearby a life-sized Rudolph with a blinking red nose stood watch over a sleigh piled high with ornately wrapped presents. Off to the side was a miniature cottage with a sign on the door that said "Santa's Work-shop." And meandering through it all was a candy cane lane leading up to Santa's chair, a rococo gold affair straight out of Versailles.

The only thing missing from Santa Land was, in fact, Santa.

Several kids were lined up in their Tommy Hilfiger/ Ralph Lauren finest, asking the bewildered Hispanic maids who had been delegated to schlep them to the mall, "*Donde está* Santa?"

"Damn!" Gigi muttered as she surveyed the scene.

Then she plastered on a bright smile and turned to the children waiting on line.

"Santa must be busy wrapping presents in his work-shop. I'll go get him."

"Darn that Scotty," she muttered as she stomped over to the workshop. "He's on another bender."

She opened the door to Santa's workshop, and poked her head inside.

"Wake up, Scotty!" she hissed. "You've got kids wait-ing."

Peering over her shoulder, I saw a guy in a Santa suit sprawled out, clutching a bottle of tequila.

"Tell 'em Santa's got a hangover," he mumbled.

"Are you crazy?" Gigi snapped.

"Okay, okay." Reluctantly he got up and started to crawl out the door, his Santa's beard dangling from his neck. Just before he pulled it up, I took a look at his face, and realized that he was one heck of a handsome Santa.

Small but deep blue eyes, fabulous cheekbones, and pouty Brad Pitt lips. He had Out Of Work Actor written all over him.

Blearily he glanced over at me.

"Who the hell are you?"

"The new elf," Gigi said. "Kenny's replacement."

"She's supposed to be an *elf*?" he said, with a none too flattering glance at my thighs.

Taking a deep breath, he walked over to his throne and muttered to Gigi, "Bring on the brats."

The heart melts, *n'est-ce pas*?

I watched as Gigi led a skinny little girl over to his lap.

"Ho-ho-ho!" he boomed, practically melting the tot's eyebrows with his tequila breath. The kid started to whimper, and Gigi quickly whisked her off Scotty's lap and into the safety of her nanny's arms.

As another, much braver, kid took her place and whipped out a spreadsheet printout of the gifts he expected Santa to bring him, Gigi sprinted over to my side.

"I better stick around," she said, "otherwise Lord knows what hell will break loose."

"Is he always this bad?" I asked.

"Pretty much. Just remember. When you work with him, never loan him money. Don't let him flirt with the pretty moms. And whatever you do, try to keep him away from his 'hot chocolate' thermos. It's filled with tequila."

"Yikes. How come he hasn't been fired?"

"Because he's dating Molly, that's why."

My mind boggled at the thought of mousy little Molly with the soused Santa.

"Well, thanks for showing me around," I said.

And with the sound of some poor tyke wailing on

Scotty's lap, I scooted off, about to begin My Life as a Santa's helper.

Or, as I'd soon come to know it, Nightmare on Elf Street.

I headed for the Conspicuous Consumption parking lot, my elf costume in a garment bag, dreading the thought of wearing the damn thing in public. As I tossed it in the backseat of my Corolla, I prayed that somehow it would morph into a tasteful Eileen Fisher pantsuit by the time I got back to my duplex in the slums of Beverly Hills.

(Contrary to popular belief, not every street in Beverly Hills is studded with mansions and Mercedes. There are quite a few humble pockets in town—none quite so humble as the duplex-and-Toyota lined street that I call home.)

Driving along, I shuddered at the memory of how I'd looked in my elf suit, my thighs glowing like giant neon barber poles.

But then a ray of hope dawned on my horizon. Maybe the mirror at the mall was a "fattening" mirror—one of those distorted mirrors I so often find in department stores when I'm trying on bathing suits.

That was it. I bet I'd look much thinner in my mirror at home!

And so, filled with a desperate burst of optimism, the minute I got back to my apartment, I raced to my bedroom and tried on my elf costume again, hoping the Conspicuous Consumption mirror was all wrong.

And indeed, it was.

As it turned out, my striped tights did not add another five pounds to my thighs. No, siree. In my mirror at home, they added another *ten* pounds.

I was standing there groaning in dismay when there was a knock on my front door.

"Open up, Jaine. It's me. Lance. I want to hear all about your job interview."

I trudged to the door to find Lance on my doorstep, spiffed up in his Neiman-Marcus work togs, his blond curls moussed to perfection.

He took one look at me and gasped.

"My God, Jaine. What happened? You look like you were mugged by a leprechaun."

Wearily I told him how Molly had offered me a chance at the Conspicuous Consumption writing gig, but only if I agreed to be a Santa's elf.

"The pay stinks, the hours are awful, I get a twenty percent discount on things I can't begin to afford, and worst of all, I have to work with a Santa from hell."

"You poor thing," Lance tsked soothingly. "You can't possibly be seen in public in that outfit. You're going to have to quit."

"You think so?"

"Absolutely! But not before you use your twenty percent discount to get me a Hugo Boss tie for Greg."

"Greg?"

"The most adorable guy at work. I pulled a few thousand strings and I'm his Secret Santa! I saw the perfect tie for him at your mall the other day."

A tiny alarm bell went off in my head.

"How much does this tie happen to cost?"

"About two hundred bucks. But don't worry. I'll pay you back as soon as I get my Christmas bonus in December. No, wait. I might need that money for last minute gifts. How about early January? Possibly February. April at the latest."

"Forget it, Lance. I'm not laying out two hundred bucks so you can impress a guy you barely know. Besides, Secret Santa gifts are supposed to be inexpensive. This Greg guy will think you're coming on way too strong if you hit him with Hugo Boss."

"You're probably right," he said, with a pensive scratch at his curls. "But I've got to get him the perfect gift. I'll start making a list tonight. Don't quit your job, hon, until I know for sure what I'm getting him. I may need your discount."

How gratifying to know he had my best interests at heart.

While Lance trotted off to his apartment to work on his Secret Santa list, I headed back to my bedroom and began struggling out of my tights. I was in the midst of yanking them off my hips, flushed from the effort, my elf hat askew on my head, when Prozac wandered in and stopped in her tracks.

She looked up at me with what I can only describe as a smirk on her face.

And I thought I looked silly in my antlers.

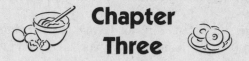

Chapter Three

As much as I was tempted, I was not about to throw away my chance at a lucrative copywriting gig.

I'd be an elf if it killed me.

And my first day on the job damn near did.

I can't tell you how mortifying it was standing there in that moronic elf suit. The bright green tunic top barely covered my striped tush, leaving my neon thighs on display for all the world to see. There was no getting around it. I was a hot elfin mess—from the top of my pointy green hat to the tips of my curly toes.

Somewhere in time, I was convinced, some medieval court was missing its jester.

Not five minutes into my shift a towheaded tyke in a tiny blue blazer and red bow tie looked me over with the soulless eyes of a future hedge fund manager.

"I thought elves were supposed to be *skinny*," he

sneered, much to the delight of the other kids on line, all of whom broke into a most humiliating round of giggles.

Where's a lump of coal when you need one?

But the truly hellish part of the day was working with Scotty.

The guy was lazy, rude, egotistical, and mean spirited.

And those were his good points.

It was clear from the moment he came swaggering down Santa Lane that he hated working there.

"I can't believe I'm wasting my talents like this," he muttered, taking a swig from his "hot chocolate" bottle.

Good heavens. Was he actually drinking tequila at nine o'clock in the morning?

"I'm up for a starring part in a TV pilot," he told me, "and the minute I get it, I'm outta here."

That day could not come a moment too soon, as far as I was concerned.

Mr. Showbiz couldn't be bothered to remember my name, so he called me Elf #2. (Gigi, apparently, got top billing as Elf #1.)

And I was lucky that's all Scotty called me. He was capable of worse. Much worse—as I would find out when a large, ruddy-faced woman in a mall security uniform walked by Santa Land speaking into her walkie-talkie.

Scotty looked up from the kid who was on his lap and called out, "How's it going, Porky?"

The woman flushed and, gritting her teeth, walked on, ignoring him.

"Her real name's Corky," he said. "What a tub of lard, huh? I love to get a rise out of her."

By now, I was ready to strangle the guy, and I hadn't even been there an hour.

As for his duties as Santa, Scotty was one sly son of a gun. When kids showed up with a nanny or a low-income parent, he barely gave them the time of day, whipping them off his lap with lightning speed.

But if a little tyke was holding the hand of a well-heeled parent, Scotty was all smiles and ho-ho-ho's.

And if that parent happened to be a pretty blonde, he was in full-tilt flirtation mode.

"What can Santa get *you* for Christmas, pretty lady?" he'd leer.

The really aggravating thing was that most of the women fell for it. He was a good looking dude, and those deep blue eyes of his made the designer moms giggle with adolescent glee.

Elf #2, I can assure you, was ready to puke.

He refused to wear any padding, and when kids asked him why he wasn't fat, his standard reply was, "Santa's been working out."

Then, with a snarky glance in my direction, he'd add, "His elf, not so much."

In slow periods when there were no kids on line, he was off like a shot to Santa's Workshop to guzzle tequila or take a nap.

Frankly, those were the highlights of my day.

It was during one such lull, just as Scotty was about to scoot off for a nap, that Molly from Human Resources showed up.

He quickly sat back down in his chair, all smiles.

"Molly, babe." He grinned. "How's my favorite boss?"

I looked down and saw his hand on her fanny.

Like the designer moms, she burst out in giggles.

"Really, Scotty," she said, reluctantly removing his hand from her tush. "People are looking."

And indeed, over by a roasted chestnut cart, Corky the security guard was glaring in Scotty's direction.

"Let 'em look," Scotty said. "You're my main squeeze, and I don't care who knows it."

With that, he shot her his idea of a sultry look.

Somehow Molly restrained herself from jumping on his lap and turned to me.

"So how's your day going, Jaine?"

"Great," I lied. "Just great."

"Isn't Scotty a terrific Santa? He's so wonderful with the children."

This time I could barely manage to nod my head.

Talk about love being blind.

Eventually Molly tore herself away from Scotty and headed back to her office. The minute she was gone, he zipped over to his workshop for a nap.

The rest of the day dragged by, with Scotty barking orders at me in between naps and nips of tequila. At one point, he actually snapped his fingers and said, "I'm hungry, Elf #2! Go get me some donuts at the food court."

Like I was his own personal servant or something.

"Get your own damn donuts!"

Okay, I didn't actually say that. Mainly because I was sort of hungry myself, and a donut sounded like a pretty good idea at the time.

Needless to say, I counted the milliseconds till the end of my shift, and practically kissed the toes of her curly shoes when Gigi showed up to relieve me.

Thank heavens I'd made it through Day One.

Only twenty-eight to go.

But who's counting?

*   *   *

Thoroughly exhausted, I changed into my civvies and headed for the food court for an espresso latte. (Okay, and another donut.)

I'd just paid for a chocolate-glazed beauty when I turned and saw Corky, the security guard Scotty had been taunting all day. She sat at a table by herself, a bag of fries and a can of Coke in front of her.

At that very moment, she glanced up and caught me looking at her.

I smiled feebly and waved. To which she just nodded curtly and shoved a fry in her mouth.

Somehow I got the feeling she didn't like me. Maybe she thought I was laughing at her when Scotty called her "Porky."

The last thing I wanted to do was hurt her feelings, so I walked over to her table to make amends.

"Hi," I said, with my brightest smile. "I'm Jaine, the new elf."

"I know," she said, dunking a fry in some ketchup. "I saw you in Santa Land."

For such a hefty gal, she had a surprisingly childlike face: big baby blues, button nose, and pale blonde hair scraped back into a sparse ponytail.

"I'm so sorry about what happened today," I said. "I hope you don't think I had anything to do with Scotty's stupid comments."

"Nah," she said with a shake of her ponytail. "He's been calling me Porky ever since he started working here. What a prince, huh?"

"The worst!"

At last she broke out in a tentative smile.

"Mind if I join you?" I asked.

"Help yourself," she said, gesturing to an empty chair.

I plopped down, and without any further ado, chomped into my donut.

"Yum!" I exclaimed after my first heavenly bite.

"You should try the cheesecake donut," Corky advised. "And the chocolate with sprinkles. They're fantab."

Clearly I'd met my junk food soul mate.

We soon launched into a discussion of the best places to go for soft ice cream; Corky extolling the joys of Carvel, me mounting an impressive campaign for Dairy Queen. I was in the middle of a paean to Dairy Queen's Blizzard when I was interrupted by a loud, braying laugh.

I looked up to see Scotty walking by with Molly, looking annoyingly handsome in his street clothes, laughing his silly head off. How irritating that he was in such a good mood after all the hell he'd put me through.

"There goes Satan's Santa," I muttered. "I don't know how you've put up with him all these weeks."

"Oh, he doesn't bother me," Corky said with a shrug. "Not one bit. I'm used to fools like him."

Her angel face was calm as could be, but when I looked down at her fist, I saw she'd smashed her Coke can tighter than a trash compactor.

He bothered her, all right. More than a bit.

I'd bet my bottom Blizzard on it.

Chapter Four

All I can say is thank heavens for Barnaby.

I'll never forget the morning I met him. I'd just changed into my elf suit and was walking into the employees' locker room to lock up my purse, when I heard a deep plummy voice intone:

> *She walks in beauty like the night*
> *Of cloudless climes and starry skies*
> *And all that's best of dark and bright*
> *Meet in her aspect and her eyes.*

I looked over by the locker next to mine and saw a skinny guy in a Santa suit several sizes too big for him.

At first I thought he was making fun of me with his "she walks in beauty" crack; after all, I was a woman in striped tights and curly-toed shoes.

But no, there was a warm smile on his face as he said, "You must be the new elf Gigi told me about, the lovely Jaine. A pleasure to meet you, my dear."

With that, he took my hand and actually kissed it.

"Allow me to introduce myself. I'm Barnaby King."

"Nice to meet you," I said, wondering how this skinny little guy with a face like Mr. Magoo had actually landed a job as a Santa.

"It seems as if we're working together today," he said. "I so look forward to it. Wait for me while I finish getting ready and then we can walk out together."

I sat down on the locker bench and watched as he took a giant hunk of padding from his locker and strapped it around his waist.

"Oh, that this too too solid flesh would melt!" he said, fluffing it up with a wink.

First Lord Byron. Now Shakespeare. Obviously a former English major.

Once his tummy was in place under his Santa jacket, he reached into his locker and took out a makeup brush and began dotting his cheeks with blush. After which he donned a white bushy beard, wire-rimmed glasses, and finished off his ensemble with a Santa hat perched rakishly over his wisps of curly gray hair.

Before my very eyes, Mr. Magoo had become St. Nick.

"Well, how do I look?" he asked, turning around for my approval.

"Like you've just come down a chimney."

"Oh, my dear. I can tell we're going to have such fun together."

And we did.

Compared to Scotty, Barnaby was heaven to work with. Of course, compared to Scotty, the Marquis de Sade would have been heaven to work with.

And the kids adored him.

His favorite shtick was to surprise them by knowing their names before they even sat on his lap.

"Well, well!" he'd cry out. "If it isn't Courtney!"

Courtney's eyes would grow wide with wonder, and Barnaby would tell her how just last night he'd seen her name on his list of Good Little Girls.

I, of course, was his accomplice in this magical feat, asking the kids their names as I led them up Candy Cane Lane, and whispering their answers in Santa's ear.

And what a fuss he made over them.

"Why, I bet you're the prettiest little girl I've seen all day!" he'd whisper confidentially, so the other girls on line wouldn't hear. "I bet you're a movie star, aren't you, sweetheart?"

Inevitably, the little girl would blush with pleasure. The plainer they were, the more they soaked up his praise.

Occasionally, this being Conspicuous Consumption Plaza, the kid actually *was* in show biz and would tell Santa about her most recent parts. Sometimes, she'd even show Barnaby her head shots.

With the tiny tots, the ones who tended to cry on Santa's lap, Barnaby was gentle, whispering a soothing, "There, there," before handing the child back to his parent.

With the older kids, Barnaby zeroed in on what they wanted—or needed—to hear.

The plain girls were all beautiful princesses.

The shy boys were all action heroes.

And the bratty ones, the ones with their Excel spreadsheet gift lists, those were the ones he always asked, "And what are you *giving* for Christmas?"

The kids would inevitably sit there, blinking, for the first time considering that the world did not revolve around them.

Every once in a while, he'd break out in a Shakespearean fit of fancy. Especially if I brought him a girl whose name sounded anything like "Juliet."

"But soft!" he'd cry. "What light through yonder window breaks? It is the east, and Juliet (or Julie or Julianne) is the sun!"

"Do you know who Juliet (Julie or Julianne) was?" he'd ask the little girl on his lap, re-writing Shakespeare a bit if need be. "A beautiful maiden who lived a long time ago, so beautiful she shone brighter than the sun! And you know what?" he'd say. "You look just like her younger sister!"

Usually little Juliet/Julie/Julianne would squirm in delight.

And the kids weren't the only ones whose egos he bolstered. He insisted I looked "cute as a button" in my elf suit, that he was sick of all the "skinny minnies" he saw on TV and the movies. "Some of these mothers," he would say, shaking his head at the designer moms in their size zero jeans, "look like they could use some intravenous Quarter Pounders."

In those moments, my neon stripe thighs didn't seem so bad, after all.

When it was slow, we chewed the fat and snacked on roasted chestnuts from a kiosk next to the Christmas tree. I told him about my life as a freelance advertising writer, and he told me about his career as an actor—starting out playing Lady Macbeth in his all-boys prep school, going on to do Shakespeare in the park in New York City, and starring as Tevye in the national touring company of *Fiddler on the Roof.*

"My acting days are pretty much over," he told me during one such gabfest. "Except for some community theater and my Santa gig. And there's the Tiny Tim Project, of course."

"The Tiny Tim Project?"

He pointed to a large plastic bin right outside Santa Land.

"We collect toys for underprivileged kids. I started it a couple of years ago when I realized how many children never even get a gift on Christmas."

What a welcome change from the insufferable Scotty, whose favorite charity was, no doubt, himself.

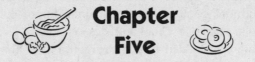

Chapter Five

And so the days passed as I dragged myself through my shifts with Scotty, the hours flying by with Barnaby.

It was on one of those days from hell with Scotty when I was listening to a twelve-year-old explain why she needed a pair of diamond studs from Tiffany that I heard my name called out.

"Jaine Austen! Is that you?"

I turned to see a mucho attractive guy with jet black hair and a crooked smile, carrying a Godiva shopping bag.

Omigod. I'd know that smile anywhere. It was Jason Nicoletti. I'd had quite a crush on him back in high school in Hermosa Beach, when we worked together on our school newspaper, the *Hermosa Herald*.

From the first day I saw him in our editorial offices (which we shared with the janitorial supplies), my heart melted just a tad.

Much to my delight, Jason had taken a liking to me, too. Working at adjacent desks, we shared our teenage angst and took great pleasure in making fun of the "A" listers who ruled our school with despotic glee.

The more we kidded around, the more I liked him, and the more I was convinced he liked me, too.

Then one day, he turned to me. For once looking quite serious, he said, "Jaine, there's something I need to ask you."

Omigosh! This was it. He was going to ask me out on a date.

"Go ahead!" I said, grinning like a maniac. "Ask."

He cleared his throat nervously and then quickly blurted out: "Do you think I stand a chance with Becca Washton?"

My maniacal grin froze.

Becca was a cheerleader, an insanely popular redhead, a prominent member of the Reign of Terror we always made fun of. My heart sank. Surely Jason couldn't possibly be interested in her? All along I'd assumed he was the kind of guy who looked past the superficial and saw the true beauty inside a person with slightly generous hips.

But clearly I'd been wrong.

"So?" he asked eagerly. "What do you think? Do I have a shot with Becca?"

"Sure," I managed to say. I had no idea if Jason stood a chance with Becca, and I didn't care.

Somehow our friendship was never the same after that, and I'm ashamed to confess that I took great pleasure when Jason asked Becca to the prom and she turned him down.

And now here he was all these years later, looking

more attractive than ever. The soft lines of adolescence were gone, replaced by craggy cheekbones and sharply etched laugh lines.

In spite of myself, I felt a jolt of excitement.

"Jason!" I said. "How've you been?"

"Great. Just great. I'm a creative director over at Saatchi."

Yikes. Saatchi & Saatchi was one of the world's biggest ad agencies.

"And what about you?" he asked. "What have you been up to?"

Oh, Lord. It suddenly dawned on me that I was standing there in my elf suit, my striped thighs glowing like spandex flares.

How mortifying. I couldn't possibly let him know that I'd been reduced to going on donut runs for an out of work actor.

"I'm a freelance writer," I said.

At which point, Scotty barked out, "Oh, Elf #2! Santa needs an espresso latte. Now!"

I shot him an angry glare and turned back to Jason who was no doubt wondering why a freelance writer was hanging around Santa Land in a cheesy elf suit.

And then I thought of the most marvelous explanation. True, it was a bit of a whopper, but it was all I could think of at the time, so I went with it.

"Actually," I said, "I'm writing a piece for *L.A. Magazine* on what it's like to work as a Santa's elf."

His eyes lit up.

"You write for *L.A. Magazine*? Very impressive."

Yes! He bought it!

"Gosh, Jaine," he said. "We used to have so much fun together at the *Hermosa Herald*, didn't we?"

He shot me that crooked smile, the same smile that first melted my heart next to the janitor's mops.

"You know," he said, staring deeply into my eyes. "I've never forgotten our time together."

Was it my imagination or was he interested in me? Had he finally grown up and realized what he passed up all those years ago?

"I'm throwing a little Christmas party," he said, "and I'd love for you to stop by."

"Sounds wonderful."

Indeed it did.

"What's your number?" he asked. "I'll text you an official invite."

"My phone number?"

Oh, darn. His smile had me so rattled, it had totally slipped my mind.

"My phone number. Of course. It's right on the tip of my tongue."

When at last I finally remembered my own phone number, Jason typed it into his phone.

"Can't wait to catch up," he said, blasting me with another killer smile.

"Me, too," was my witty rejoinder.

Then he headed off to do some Christmas shopping while I proceeded to zoom straight up to Cloud Nine.

Looked like Santa had just brought me an early Christmas present.

Later that night, I was stretched out in my bathtub, up to my neck in strawberry-scented bubbles. Perched across from me on the toilet tank, Prozac was deep in sleep, her pink mouth slightly open as she snored.

We'd just spent a rather vigorous half hour running around my apartment, me chasing Prozac with my camera, trying desperately to get her to stay still for one millisecond while I got a shot of her for my holiday greeting card. I had long since given up any notion of sticking felt antlers on her head. All I wanted at this point was a plain old photo, and even that was proving impossible.

I'd taken at least twenty-five shots of her, one blurrier than the next.

"How can one cat be so aggravating?" I'd finally wailed, tossing my camera on the sofa in defeat.

She looked up at me with huge green eyes.

It's not easy, but I try.

Soon the hot bubbly water began to work its wonders and ease away my stress. (The glass of chardonnay perched on the edge of the tub didn't hurt either.)

And my thoughts drifted back to Jason Nicoletti. I told myself not to get my hopes up, but I couldn't help it. I saw the way he'd been looking at me. He was interested. Most definitely.

Clearly he'd outgrown his shallow Becca Washton days and realized that flaming red hair and skinny hips did not a soul mate make.

I couldn't help thinking that our chance encounter at the mall might be the start of something big.

Before long I was lost in a fantasy, walking down the aisle with Jason on a beach in the Bahamas, then settling down in a Santa Monica cottage and raising a passel of adorable moppets while writing my Great American Novel. I was in the middle of telling our future grandkids how Jason and I made our love connection at Santa Land when I heard a disembodied voice float through the air.

"Hey, you've been in that tub long enough!"

No it was not the voice of my conscience, but Lance, whose X-ray hearing allows him to hear toilets flushing in Pomona.

"I need to talk to you!" he called out, banging on our paper thin walls. "On an extremely urgent matter!"

Lance's idea of an urgent matter is a BOGO sale at Old Navy, so I took this with a grain of salt. Nevertheless I dredged myself out of the tub and fifteen minutes later I was perched across from him on my living-room sofa, a bowl of pretzels between us.

"So what's this urgent matter?" I asked, helping myself to a pretzel or three.

"Russian River Pinot Noir or Singing Chihuahua?" he asked.

"What on earth are you talking about?"

"I've narrowed Greg's Secret Santa gift down to two choices. A bottle of Russian River Pinot Noir, or a mechanical Chihuahua that sings 'Feliz Navidad.'"

"A Chihuahua that sings 'Feliz Navidad'?"

"It was either that, or a moose that pooped M&M's."

Remind me never to go gift shopping with Lance.

"The Pinot Noir says I'm an urban sophisticate, suave and debonair. While the singing Chihuahua shows him my fun side, the zany, madcap me. So which one should I choose?"

He bit into a pretzel, eagerly awaiting my answer.

"I'd go with the Pinot Noir."

"But the Chihuahua is pretty darn funny. I mean, a sense of humor is very important in a relationship."

"Okay, then go with the Chihuahua."

Lance's brow furrowed in doubt.

"But then Greg might think it's silly. I'm probably better off playing it safe and going with the Pinot."

"That's what I think."

"Really?"

"Really. That's what I think."

"Then I'll stick with the Chihuahua."

"What???"

"C'mon, Jaine. Let's face it. You don't exactly have the greatest track record winning over the opposite sex."

"For your info," I said, whipping the bowl of pretzels from his hands, "my track record with the opposite sex is about to take a gigantic leap forward."

"Why?" he asked, perking up at the scent of some hot news. "What's up?"

I told him all about my chance encounter with Jason, how cute he looked in his jeans and blazer, carrying his Godiva shopping bag. I told him how we'd met all those years ago at the *Hermosa Herald* and how he was now a big cheese advertising man and how we locked eyeballs over Candy Cane Lane and the next thing I knew he was asking me to his Christmas party.

"Omigod!" he cried, jumping up. "That's fantastic! Just fantastic!"

How nice that he was so excited for me.

"That's what I'll get Greg! Godiva chocolates!"

"What??"

"They're sweet and sensuous at the same time. Just like me. So what do you think? Should I get him milk chocolate or dark?"

Like a fool, I said, "Dark."

"Then milk chocolate, it is."

One of these days, I've got to stop answering my door.

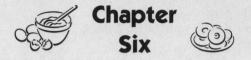

Chapter Six

I knew I was in for trouble when I showed up at Santa Land the next day and saw Scotty sprawled out in his Santa chair, his beard in his lap, grousing to Molly.

"Those fools wouldn't know acting talent if it bit them on the fanny," he whined.

I remembered him telling me he was up for a role in a TV pilot. From the pout on his pretty boy lips, it looked like he hadn't gotten it.

"They were idiots to turn you down, honey," Molly said with a placating smile. "But I'm sure a much better part will come along soon."

"Like what?" he sneered. "The Easter bunny?" He waved his beard in disgust. "God, I hate this crummy job."

What an ingrate. He was damned lucky to have this gig. If I were Molly, I would've sent him packing on the spot.

But I was not Molly. She was actually in love with the creep.

"I'd better get to work," she said, checking her watch. "Love you," she added, clearly waiting for him to echo her sentiment.

But all she got in reply was an abrupt, "Yeah, right."

She walked away with a worried look in her eyes, and Scotty took out his "hot chocolate" thermos for his morning slug of tequila.

Then for the first time he noticed me standing there.

"Not you again," he moaned. "Why the hell do I always get stuck working with you?"

The feeling, I can assure you, was mutual.

But not wishing to set off the powder keg I sensed was brewing under his Santa cap, I merely replied, "And a good morning to you, too."

By now the mall was open and a few kids were heading over to Santa Land.

"Better put on your beard," I told him. "And pop an Altoid. You don't want the kids passing out from the tequila fumes."

"Fooey on you."

(Technically he didn't use the word "fooey." But this is a family novel, so I'll spare you the real F-word involved.)

After another slug from his thermos, he muttered, "Bring on the brats."

Fasten your seat belts, kids, I felt like saying. *It's gonna be a bumpy sleigh ride.*

* * *

And indeed it was. The kids were on and off Scotty's lap so fast their little heads were spinning. He was in such a foul mood, he didn't even bother flirting with the cute moms.

He refused to pose for any photos, snarling, "Santa's having a bad beard day."

One of his favorite gags, when the kids would tell him what they wanted, was to say, "Sorry, we're out of that this year. Elf #2 was supposed to make them, but she's too lazy, so it ain't gonna happen."

"Santa's only kidding," I'd hasten to assure them, glaring at Scotty. "He's going to try his very best to get you your gift, aren't you, Santa?"

"Oh, all right," he'd pout.

A couple of hours of this nonsense had passed when, with a redheaded tyke perched on his knee, Scotty looked up and saw Corky walking by.

She'd already walked by several times that morning, and each time he saw her, he'd called out, "How's it going, Porky?"

Each time she'd gritted her teeth and ignored him.

This time, however, Corky was not alone. She was walking with a fellow security officer, a young hunk with muscles the size of ham hocks. They were laughing about something, and from the way Corky was looking at her co-worker, I sensed she had a bit of a crush on him.

She was punching him on the shoulder playfully when, in a booming voice, Scotty called out his familiar refrain:

"How's it going, Porky?"

Corky stopped in her tracks, her face flushed.

Then she left Mr. Ham Hocks and marched up Candy Cane Lane, fire burning in her eyes.

She gently lifted the little redhead off Scotty's lap and,

with bulging biceps, grabbed Scotty by the collar of his Santa suit.

Up close I could see a knotted vein throbbing in her forehead.

"You call me Porky one more time," she hissed, "and you're a dead man."

By now, her grip was so tight, Scotty was gasping for air.

"Corky!" I cried. "Cut it out! You're strangling him."

"Am I?" she sneered. "What a shame. Next time," she practically spat in Scotty's face, "I'll finish the job."

Then reluctantly, she let go and marched off.

Scotty sat there hacking for a few seconds. Then, hands trembling, he screwed open his thermos to take a slug of tequila.

"Fat cow," he muttered when his breathing had returned to normal. "She doesn't scare me."

Like hell she hadn't.

From that point on, Scotty was a train wreck, guzzling tequila and barely talking to the tots. It got so bad that, after a while, *I* was the one the kids were telling what they wanted for Christmas.

The hours dragged by and at long last we reached the end of our shift. Outside Santa Land I saw Barnaby and Gigi waving to us in their street clothes, having come to relieve us.

"Thank goodness you guys are here!" I said, racing over to them.

"Bad day?" Barnaby asked.

"The worst. Scotty got turned down for his TV pilot and has been on a rampage ever since."

We looked over to where a gawky little girl was sitting on Scotty's lap, whispering in his ear.

"A Barbie doll?" we heard him sneer. "Better ask Santa for a nose job, sweetie. That's what you really need."

A long-limbed moppet with wide doe eyes, the little girl would probably grow up to be an Audrey Hepburn lookalike, but at this stage in her life, her nose was large for her face. With cruel accuracy, Scotty had zeroed in on her weak spot.

Her hands flew up to her face, covering her nose. Tears welled in her eyes.

Next to me, Barnaby gasped in disbelief and scooted over to the little girl, who had left Scotty's lap, sobbing.

"Honestly," I muttered to Gigi, "sometimes I feel like strangling Scotty with his own sleigh bells."

Barnaby now kneeled down to talk to the little girl.

"You're beautiful, sweetheart," he said. "And your nose is just fine. Santa didn't mean what he said. In fact, he's not really Santa. He's just an out of work actor." He turned to glare at Scotty. "And a bad one at that."

At which point, Scotty bolted out of his chair and marched over to Barnaby.

"You're calling *me* a bad actor?" he fumed. "Why, you two bit fraud. You may have everybody else fooled, but I know all about you. You never did Shakespeare in the Park. Or toured with *Fiddler on the Roof.* The closest you ever got to Broadway was the TKTs booth in Times Square. You're a joke, that's what you are. A joke!"

With a colorful expletive, not at all suitable for little ears, he kicked Rudolph in the shins and stormed off.

I turned to the crowd of astonished kids and their parents.

"Well, kids," I said. "Santa's imposter has gone to his

anger management class. But if you wait just a few minutes, the real Santa will be here to talk to you."

And as I walked off with Barnaby and Gigi to the employees' locker room, I prayed that Scotty had at last gone too far, and that Molly would be forced to fire him.

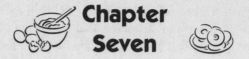

Chapter Seven

Days passed, and much to my disgust, Scotty did not get fired. I don't know how many strings Molly had to pull, but somehow he kept his job.

What's worse, Molly clearly hadn't read him the riot act, because he was as obnoxious as ever. Although I couldn't help noticing that now, whenever Corky walked by, he was dead silent.

As for Barnaby, he was the same jolly Santa he'd always been. If he'd been upset by Scotty's tirade, he showed no signs of it.

It wasn't until one day after our shift when Barnaby and I were sitting on one of the mall benches, munching on roasted chestnuts, that he brought up the subject.

"Remember what Scotty said the other day?" he said, cracking open a shell. "About me being a phony?"

"I didn't believe him for a minute," I assured him.

"He was right, Jaine."

I blinked in surprise.

"He was?"

"I never did play Shakespeare in Central Park. Or Tevye in *Fiddler on the Roof*. But I've done some community theater. And I *was* Lady Macbeth in prep school," he added with a wry smile.

"Actually, I was a high school English teacher for thirty-two years before I retired. I don't know why I lied about my past. I guess I just wanted to live the dream I never had the courage to pursue. After a while, I got to believe it myself. It was fun being a professional actor. Even if it wasn't true."

He looked up at me sheepishly.

"I hope you don't think any the less of me."

"Oh, no! I totally understand."

I looked over at him and for the first time I saw sadness behind those twinkling blue eyes.

Popping a chestnut in my mouth, I hoped I'd lead the kind of life that wouldn't require a re-write.

If you happened to have walked by Casa Austen later that night, you would not have seen me sipping eggnog. Or writing out my gift list. Or belting out jolly Christmas carols. No, you would have found me hiding in my hall closet, crouched among my boots, my vacuum cleaner jammed into my ribs.

My latest ploy in the Battle of the Christmas Photo.

Up until then, I'd tried everything to get Prozac to sit for a picture. I'd tried kitty treats. I'd tried squeaky toys.

I'd even tried attaching feathers to my camera, hoping she'd think it was a bird.

All to no avail.

But this, my latest plan, the Candy Cane Caper, felt destined for success.

I'd cleverly placed a candy cane smeared with Minced Mackerel Guts on my living-room coffee table. Surely Prozac would not be able to resist this holiday treat.

It was just a matter of time before she came wandering in from the kitchen where I'd left her meowing for her dinner.

Her little nose would twitch at the scent of the fetid fish, and before I knew it I'd be snapping hilarious photos of Prozac licking a candy cane. Perhaps I'd even send them in to one of those photo contest web sites.

Honestly, sometimes I surprise myself with my creativity.

I sat in the closet, thinking of how cute my Christmas cards would be, and not incidentally about the moo shoo pork I'd picked up for dinner, waiting for Prozac to take the bait.

Five minutes passed. Then ten. Then fifteen. Then twenty. Where the heck was she? And why the heck wasn't she howling for her chow?

Hunched over with that damn vacuum cleaner still jammed in my ribs, every one of my muscles were now aching at full throttle.

Finally, when me and my muscles could stand it no longer, I conceded defeat. Hobbling out of the closet, I headed for the kitchen, eager to pour myself a glass of chardonnay and dig into my moo shoo pork.

You know where this is going, right?

You know what I saw the minute I stepped into the kitchen:

Prozac sprawled out on the kitchen counter, belching up the remains of my Chinese dinner.

Somehow she'd clawed open the carton, and now just a few shards of pork lay scattered around her on the counter.

She was kind enough to leave me the fortune cookie, though.

Covered with cat spit.

What a disaster that had been, I thought, rinsing mackerel guts off the candy cane before I ate it.

The next day I shared my woes with Barnaby. We were at the end of our shift, waiting for Scotty and Gigi to show up, and at the moment there were no kids on line.

"I've had it with that cat," I said. "I guess I'll just take the easy way out and send e-cards."

"Have you tried the Cat Whisperer?" Barnaby asked.

"The Cat Whisperer?"

"Yes. A fellow named Ernie DeVito. He owns a shop right here in the mall called Picture Perfect. He specializes in photos of children and animals, and I hear he works wonders with cats."

"Really?"

Suddenly I was filled with hope. Maybe this Cat Whisperer could somehow wrangle Prozac into submission. Maybe he could even get her to wear those reindeer antlers!

A designer-clad kidlet now showed up with her Conspicuous Consumption mom in tow.

As I trotted over to greet them, I heard Mom say, "Now, remember, sweetie. No biting Santa like you did last year!"

I led The Biter over to Barnaby and plopped her on his knee, hoping no rabies shots would be required. She then proceeded to give him detailed instructions about exactly what kind of pony she wanted for Christmas.

"All white. No spots. Pure bred. And not smelly."

Barnaby reminded her about the needy kids who couldn't afford ponies and got her off his lap with admirable finesse.

"Poor kid," he sighed when she'd gone. "With expectations that high, life's not going to be easy for her."

I, however, was not thinking about The Biter's future.

My mind was still on the Cat Whisperer. I was dying to hustle over and make an appointment. But Scotty and Gigi had still not shown up to relieve us.

"Where the heck are those two?" I sighed.

"You go ahead, Jaine," Barnaby said. "I can handle the kids."

"Are you sure?"

"Of course."

"Thanks, Barn. You're a doll."

Happily I trotted over to the employees' locker room to change, visions of Reindeer Prozac floating in my head.

My visions came to a screeching halt, however, when I turned the corner to my locker and saw Scotty locked in a steamy embrace.

At first I could not make out his embrace. But then I caught a whiff of Juicy Fruit gum and recognized that pert little figure.

Omigosh. It was Gigi! It looked like she really was Scotty's #1 Elf!

And all along I assumed she hated him just as much as the rest of us.

I stood there, boggled, as she clamped her lips on his.

And I was not the only one to witness this touching scene. After a second or two I realized I was not alone. I turned to see Molly standing behind me, fury oozing from every pore.

"Scotty!" she hissed, her fists clamped in tight balls at her sides.

The lovebirds flew apart, Scotty's eyes darting like a trapped rat.

"Molly, babe," he cried. "This isn't what it looks like."

"Oh? Then what is it? Mouth to mouth root canal?"

I could practically see the wheels spinning in Scotty's brain trying to tap dance his way out of this mess. But then Gigi spoke up.

"It's no use, Scotty," she said. "You've got to tell her the truth."

The truth was clearly a novel approach for a guy like Scotty, but apparently he decided to go with it.

"I didn't mean for this to happen, Molly," he said with his idea of a penitent look. "I fought it, really I did." Then, placing his arm around Gigi, he dealt the *coup de grace*. "But Gigi and I are in love."

"Well, goody for you," Molly said, dripping sarcasm.

"I suppose this means we're fired," Gigi said, her voice practically a whisper.

"No, I'll never be able to replace you this close to Christmas. You can keep your jobs. Just don't ever talk to me again. Either of you."

Gigi had the good grace to look ashamed as Molly turned on her heel and started for the door.

"Molly, babe," Scotty called after her lamely. "I'll make it up to you somehow. I promise."

She whirled around, fire burning in her eyes.

"You want to make it up to me, Scotty? Drop dead."

Whaddaya know? It looked like the mouse had claws, after all.

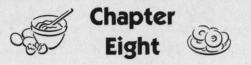

Chapter Eight

By the next day I'd forgotten all about the drama in the employees' locker room.

That's because I'd managed to set up an appointment with Ernie DeVito, aka The Cat Whisperer. He was squeezing me in that very morning to take Prozac's photo. Which would give me plenty of time to bring her in before reporting for work on the night shift.

"My gosh, Pro," I said as I brushed her fur to a glossy shine. "Isn't this exciting? We're going to the photographer who took the original head shots for the Taco Bell Chihuahua!"

(I'd looked up Ernie on the Internet, and his credits were quite impressive.)

Prozac, I regret to say, was not nearly as stoked as I was.

She spent the entire drive over to the mall yowling at the top of her lungs.

The humane society is going to hear about this!

"Oh, please. Do you know how many cats would kill to be photographed by the Cat Whisperer?"

But Prozac just hissed.

The only thing I'd kill for right now is a new owner.

At last we arrived at the mall and I made my way over to the Cat Whisperer's studio, Prozac yowling every inch of the way.

Help! Police! Someone report this woman to the ASPCA!—Whoa! Is that a corn dog you're eating, mister?

What can I say? She's easily distracted.

I headed into Ernie's studio and announced myself to the receptionist—a middle-aged woman with a blunt cut brown bob and an *I* ♥ *My Cat* pin on the lapel of her polyester suit jacket.

"Mr. DeVito!" she called out. "Ms. Austen is here."

And then the great Cat Whisperer himself came out from behind a curtain that separated the reception area from his photo studio.

I must admit I was shocked.

You'd expect a guy named Ernie DeVito to be short and stocky with more hair in his ears than on his head. You would not expect him to look like he'd just stepped out of a *GQ* fashion spread. Tall and sinewy, with patent leather slicked-back hair and smoldering bedroom eyes, Ernie was one suave signor indeed.

"Ah, Signorina Austen," he said, "what beautiful eyes you have. So big and round, like the Taco Bell Chihuahua. I took his head shots, you know."

"Yes, I know," I said, wondering if he expected a round of applause. "I read all about it."

"And who do we have here?" he said to Prozac, who had mercifully stopped wailing and had confined herself to merely shooting me dagger looks.

He took her carrier from me and set it down on the reception counter.

"Be careful," I warned him, as he started to open the latch. "She's in a terrible snit. She'll probably scratch."

"Oh, no. Not this bella principessa."

When he reached in to get her, I fully expected the fur to fly, but much to my amazement, she took one look at Ernie and began purring like a buzzsaw.

Hubba hubba, hot stuff!

"Ciao, bella!" he said, scratching the sweet spot behind her ears.

She lay nestled in his arms, much like Scarlett O'Hara on her honeymoon with Rhett, as Ernie carried her past the curtain into his studio, where a bank of cameras were set up across from a raised platform.

"Aren't you the most beautiful kitty in the world?" Ernie cooed, still scratching her sweet spot.

She gazed up at him dreamily.

That's what I've always thought.

"I can't wait to take your picture, *cara mia*!"

Ernie kept on scratching. Prozac kept on purring. It was quite a love fest. In fact, I was almost tempted to tell them to get a room, when he finally carried her over to the raised platform, on top of which was a pedestal draped with black velvet.

"Cats like to be high up," he explained, perching Prozac on the pedestal. "It makes them so much easier to work with."

Oh, yeah? Just wait till he took out his camera. Let's see how easy to work with she was then.

"Once she sees your camera," I warned him, "she's going to be impossible."

Prozac looked up at him with innocent green eyes.

Don't listen to her. I'm very easygoing. She's the impossible one.

"I don't suppose you could get her to wear these?" I whispered, showing Ernie the fuzzy reindeer antlers I'd shoved into a shopping bag.

"Of course!" he beamed. "You are looking at the man who once got Vin Diesel's pit bull to wear a tutu."

He took the antlers from the bag and headed over to Prozac.

At this point, I expected her to leap up and fly off the pedestal, but she barely moved a muscle as he put the antlers on her head and tied the straps under her chin.

Then she cocked her head at a coquettish angle.

Ready for my close up, Mr. DeVito.

I blinked in amazement. Suddenly she was Heidi Klum with retractable claws.

"Why the heck couldn't you do this for me," I muttered, "the woman who's fed you and scratched your belly for the past umpteen years?"

She shot me an impatient glare.

Move it, willya? You're blocking my view of his tush.

By now, Ernie had his camera in his hand. I feared that once Prozac saw it, all would be lost. But no. She kept on purring and posing like a pro.

It looked like Ernie really was a miracle worker! I'd be getting the holiday photo of my dreams, after all.

And then, just as he raised the camera to take his first shot, disaster struck.

At that moment a toddler, whose name I would later find out from the news reports was Wesley Thorndal III, was being wheeled in his stroller past Ernie's studio. His nanny had just bought him a corn dog from the food court.

Now you must remember Prozac is a cat who can smell food cooking in Beirut.

At the first whiff of that corn dog, Ernie's charms were totally forgotten and Prozac was off her pedestal like a rocket, bounding out the studio at the speed of light.

Where she then proceeded, as Wesley's nanny told the Eyewitness News reporter, to nab the corn dog straight out of little Wesley's hand and sprint off down the mall.

I, of course, was in hot pursuit, chasing Prozac past startled shoppers as she sped by, reindeer antlers on her head, a corn dog in her mouth.

Before I knew it, I'd chased her all the way over to Santa Land, where Scotty and Gigi were on duty.

Prozac, the fickle hussy, took one look at the ginormous Christmas tree on display, and forgot all about Operation Corn Dog.

Because there, standing before her, were at least a hundred shiny ornaments, all of which she could destroy.

It was her fondest Christmas dream come true!

I raced over to get her before she could do any damage, but, alas, I was too late.

Just as I was about to reach out and grab her, she leaped up into the tree, flying past screaming kids and a terrified old lady in a holly berry scarf.

"Omigod!" the old woman cried out. "It's a bat. Somebody call animal control!"

"It's not a bat!" I said. "It's just a cat in reindeer antlers."

"A cat in reindeer antlers?" huffed an indignant mom. "What sort of person puts a cat in reindeer antlers? Everybody knows cats hate costumes."

Well, excuse me for trying to get into the holiday spirit with a simple little photo.

"Some people shouldn't be allowed to have pets!" sniffed PETA mom, whose own tyke at that very moment was busy kicking another kid in the shins.

I was hoping that Santa would say something to calm down the crowd, but Scotty, in his usual helpful way, just took a big snort from his thermos.

At which point, Corky came huffing on the scene.

"What's going on here?" she asked.

"There's a bat in the Christmas tree!" the old lady screamed.

"It's not a bat!" I snapped. "It's a cat in some perfectly pet-friendly reindeer antlers."

Catching sight of my antlered darling on one of the Christmas tree branches, Corky sprang into action, lunging for Prozac, who nimbly sprinted to a higher branch. Corky lunged again, hurling her rather hefty bod against the tree.

A major mistake.

Because this time she rammed into the tree with just a little too much force.

The massive tree teetered for an agonizing second and then began to fall. We all watched in horror as, on its way down, the tree toppled the umbrella from the nearby roasted chestnut stand. Which in turn landed smack dab in the chestnut cooker. Seconds later, the umbrella was up in flames. Which, naturally, triggered the sprinkler system.

Bedlam ensued as water gushed from the ceiling.

I rushed over to the felled Christmas tree, my heart pounding, afraid Prozac might have been injured in the fall.

But no, there she was, keeping dry under the shelter of some branches, happily batting around a glass ornament like a hockey puck.

The minute I realized she wasn't hurt, a wave of anger came washing over me.

"Bad kitty!" I tsked, sweeping her up in my arms. "Look what you've done."

I gestured to the chaos around us.

She preened with pride.

I know. Isn't it great?

By now the sprinklers had shut off and when I looked over at the crowd, I saw that Molly had shown up.

Which meant it was time for me to make tracks.

Lest you forget, I desperately wanted that copywriting gig, and the last thing I needed was for Molly to find out my cat was at the epicenter of this little fiasco.

No, I'd quickly slink away and avoid any possible collateral damage.

And so I was tiptoeing out of Santa Land when I happened to pass Scotty's chair.

How odd. He was just sitting there like a lump, his thermos in his lap.

Was he so drunk that he slept through this whole disaster?

"Wake up, Scotty!" I hissed.

But he didn't move a muscle.

I went over to shake him awake, and that's when I saw it—the sharp metal snowflake ornament plunged in his heart.

For once, Scotty wasn't dead drunk on the job.

This time, he was just dead.

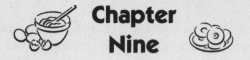

Chapter Nine

So much for keeping a low profile.

Before I knew it, the cops had shown up on the scene, and I soon found myself sitting in the mall's security office, shivering in my wet clothes, Prozac snoozing peacefully on my lap. Across from me sat a freckle-faced young cop who looked less like an officer of the law than a boy scout on steroids.

"So you're the one who first discovered the body," he said.

"Right," I replied, staring at a rebel cowlick popping up from his copper colored hair. First the freckles. Now the cowlick. Good heavens. I was being questioned by Huck Finn.

"Notice anyone else near the deceased before you walked over?" Huck asked.

"No, nobody."

"Can you think of anyone who wanted to kill him?"

Could I think of anyone who *didn't* want to kill him, would be more like it.

But I wasn't about to get an innocent person in trouble. Surely, the Conspicuous Consumption security department would have the whole crime captured on their security cameras.

"Nobody liked Scotty," I said, "but I wouldn't go so far as to accuse someone of murder."

"What about you?" asked my freckle-faced inquisitor. "How would you describe your relationship with the deceased? Were you on friendly terms?"

"Not exactly," I confessed.

Now Huck started rifling through a small pad, brows knit in concentration.

"According to your co-worker, a Ms. Gigi Harris," he said, reading from his notes, "you were quoted as saying, in reference to the deceased, *I'd like to strangle him with his own sleigh bells*."

Oh, for crying out loud.

That's what I'd told Gigi the day of Scotty's meltdown.

I couldn't believe she actually felt the need to share that little tidbit with the authorities.

I was sorely tempted to rat on her in return, but unfortunately, she was the only one I could think of at the moment who actually seemed to like Scotty. Loved him, in fact.

"It's true I said I wanted to strangle Scotty, but I didn't really mean it. It was a figure of speech. And besides, Scotty was killed with a Christmas ornament. Not sleigh bells."

"Uh huh." Huck nodded dubiously, making a note on his pad.

"On another matter," he said, "is it true that your cat is responsible for the mess over in Santa Land?"

At the sound of her name, Prozac's eyes fluttered open.

"Well, yes," I confessed. "I should have never taken her in to get her photo taken. It's just that I thought she'd look so cute in those reindeer antlers—"

"You put antlers on your cat? Don't you know cats hate wearing costumes?"

Prozac shot him her patented Little Orphan Annie look.

You can't imagine how I suffer.

"What a little sweetheart," he said, reaching over to scratch her under the chin.

My God, was there no one on this planet who could see her for the demon feline she was?

"You can go now," Huck said. "But from now on, take care of your cat."

Prozac wiggled happily in my arms.

That's telling her, officer!

"And one more thing," he added as I got up to go. "Don't leave town."

Don't leave town??

Oh, hell. Isn't that what they tell murder suspects?

Prozac was an absolute angel that night—rubbing herself against my ankles and gazing at me goo-goo eyed. Stuff she normally saves for strangers.

She knew she'd been a bad cat and was desperately trying to ease her way back into my good graces.

Usually all it takes is the touch of her soft fur against my shins for my heart to melt. But not that night.

I was steamed. I mean, here I was—a murder suspect. All because of Prozac.

Whoever killed Scotty clearly had taken advantage of the fiasco in Santa Land to plunge that snowflake in Scotty's heart. A fiasco that never would have happened in the first place had it not been for the antics of my mischievous feline.

"Honestly, Pro," I muttered as I climbed into bed. "Sometimes I wonder why I ever adopted you."

She hopped in bed right after me, eyes wide as saucers.

Hey, I know what'll make you feel better. Rubbing my belly for the next half-hour or so.

She rolled spread-eagled on her back, waiting for the rubbing to begin. But she waited in vain. Ignoring her belly, I reached for the remote and turned on *House Hunters*.

Finally she got the hint and shot me a dirty look.

Well, if that's the way you're going to be—

With that, she leaped down from the bed and stalked off to the living room.

Usually in these little tiffs of ours, I'm the first to crack, jumping out of bed and running after her, begging her forgiveness with ear scratches and kitty treats.

But not that night. That night I was just too darn mad.

I watched TV for a while, then after the 3,768th couple in the history of *House Hunters* had chosen a three-bedroom, two-bath house with an open floor plan, granite countertops and stainless steel appliances, I turned out the light.

Without Prozac cuddled next to me, it was hard to fall asleep, but I'd be damned if I went running after her.

I'd finally managed to drift off when out of nowhere I felt someone shaking my arm.

My heart began beating like a bongo.

Someone had broken into my apartment!

"Lance?" I called out, hoping it was him and that he'd used the key he knows I keep under my flower pot.

"No, it's not Lance," a woman's voice replied.

Suddenly the light snapped on and I saw the old lady in the holly berry scarf from the mall. The one who thought Prozac was a bat. There she was, standing at the foot of my bed. Wearing the same velour jog suit she'd worn that afternoon.

"Who are you?" I asked. "And how did you get into my apartment?"

"I," she said with a toss of her scarf, "am your fairy godmother."

"What?" I blinked in disbelief.

"But you can call me Hazel."

"My fairy godmother??"

"Hey, some of us wear jog suits and bunion pads. Live with it."

Yikes. Somehow this nutcase had followed me home and broken into my apartment. I tried to reach over to call 9-1-1, but my hand felt like lead. I simply couldn't get it to move.

"You said you wondered why you ever adopted your darling kitty," Hazel was saying. "Well, now you're about to find out what your life would be like without her." She snapped her fingers. "Voilà! You are now a cat-free woman."

Honestly, the old gal was certifiable.

"Let's go see what life is like without Prozac, shall we?"

With that, she took me by the hand, and led me to my living room.

I looked around and, indeed, Prozac was nowhere to be found. Not snoring on the sofa. Not curled up next to P.G. Wodehouse on the bookshelf. Not trolling for left-overs in the kitchen.

"Where is she?" I whirled around to Hazel. "What have you done with her?"

"I haven't done anything with her. You never adopted her, remember? And I'm sad to say, it hasn't seemed to work out very well. See for yourself."

She pointed over to the sofa.

Holy cow. I almost fainted when I saw myself, sitting on my couch, staring dully into space.

"Life's pretty lonely for you now," Hazel said, "with only your philodendron for company."

She pointed to a wilted philodendron on my book-shelf.

"You call it 'Phil' and pet its leaves, but it's not the same. It's not Prozac. You're so lonely, you've even started naming your socks."

I looked over at Lonely Me on the couch. And damned if she wasn't right. I was talking to my own socks!

"Hi, Jack! Hi, Jill!" I heard myself saying. "How's it going?"

Oh, Lord. This was beyond pathetic.

"Let's get out of here!" I wailed. "I need to see Lance."

I ran out of the apartment, Hazel puffing to keep up with me, and banged on Lance's door.

Seconds later, he opened it, a puzzled look on his face.

"Yes? Can I help you?"

"Lance. It's me. Jaine!"

But he just stared at me blankly.

"Don't you see?" Hazel crooned in my ear. "You never

made friends with Lance, because Prozac wasn't here to dig up his geraniums. So he never came knocking on your front door to complain. And you never invited him in to make amends over margaritas."

"Lance and me—not friends?"

At which point he slammed the door in my face.

"Apparently not," Hazel said. "C'mon, I've got some other things to show you."

Suddenly I found myself on the sidewalk outside my local dry cleaners.

"What're we doing in front of Jiffy Clean?" I asked.

"Look closely," Hazel said.

"Omigosh. The windows are all boarded up."

"A shame, isn't it?" Hazel tsked. "They went out of business because you weren't there to bring all the clothes Prozac threw up on."

"But Mr. Jiffy was such a nice man!"

"Oh, well," Hazel said with a bright smile. "What does it matter? At least you're saving on dry cleaning bills. Now c'mon. Let's go shopping."

And with a snap of her fingers, we were in my local supermarket.

"What are we doing here?"

"Just follow me," Hazel said, leading me to the cat food aisle.

"Look," she said, pointing to the rows and rows of cat food. "Notice anything missing?"

"Omigosh! There's no Fancy Feast."

"They went belly up years ago, what with Prozac not around to eat their inventory."

"Poor Fancy Feast!" I moaned. "Poor Mr. Jiffy! Poor Prozac!" I burst into tears. "To think, she was never even born!"

"I didn't say that," Hazel said, wagging a finger in my face. "I just said you never adopted her."

"You mean, Prozac's alive somewhere?"

"Indeed she is."

"Can I see her?"

"Are you sure you want to? You might not like what you see."

Oh, God, what if my poor little angel was being mistreated somewhere? I'd find some way to bring her back to safety!

"No, no! I must see her. Take me to her right now."

"Okay, if you say so."

Another snap of her fingers, and we were walking up the path to an enormous Spanish hacienda styled estate.

"Where are we?"

"Bel Air, California. Birthplace of the one percent."

Suddenly we were in what I can only describe as a designer showcase bedroom, replete with pink satin linens, priceless antique side tables, and Persian rugs on gleaming hardwood floors.

And there, perched on a pink silk chaise longue, was Prozac, noshing on a Limoges plate of bacon bits and caviar.

"Prozac!" I cried out.

But she didn't even look up.

"She can't hear you," Hazel reminded me.

"Her new owner must be awfully rich," I said, "to have such a fabulous bedroom."

"Actually, this is Prozac's room."

"She has this room all to herself?"

"And a personal maid, too." Hazel nodded.

Just then, an impossibly tall blonde with a flawless

complexion and figure to match, came drifting into the room on a cloud of designer perfume.

"Tinkerbelle, sweetie!" she cooed. "How's mommy's little angel?"

"Tinkerbelle?" I cried. "She doesn't have a silly name like Tinkerbelle! She has a perfectly sensible name—Prozac!"

But once again, I was not heard, as the blonde joined Prozac on the chaise longue and scooped her up in her arms.

"Was the caviar fresh enough for you, sweetums?"

Prozac let out a satisfied belch in reply.

"Are you happy, darling?"

Prozac looked up at her with loving eyes.

Am I ever! Thank God I'm living here with you and not in some crummy duplex with a part time Santa's elf!

"Prozac," I cried, "you can't mean that! Think of all the fun times we had together! Think of the furniture you clawed, the pantyhose you ruined. Think of the back scratches, the belly rubs, the hairballs in my slippers!"

But Prozac just went on purring in her new owner's arms.

"Oh, Prozac!" I wailed. "Prozac! Prozac!"

Suddenly I was choked with tears, so choked I could hardly breathe.

And that's when I woke up from what had to be my worst dream ever and realized Prozac's tail was draped across my nose.

Gently I removed it, and swept my precious kitty in my arms.

"Oh, Pro, honey. I didn't mean what I said. Adopting you was the happiest day of my life!"

Prozac looked up at me with enormous green eyes that could mean only one thing:

Yeah, right. Whatever. So when do we eat?

Then she tucked her furry little head under my chin and began to purr. And I knew then that all was right with the world.

Except for that pesky little murder, of course.

Chapter Ten

It took them two days to restore Santa Land to its former glory, and when it was up and running again, Barnaby had taken over Scotty's shift, working from nine in the morning till nine at night. Which he didn't seem to mind at all.

"What can I say?" Barnaby confided to me between ho-ho-hos. "I love performing, even if half my audience is still teething."

Needless to say, Scotty's absence wasn't missed a bit, and Barnaby reigned happily over a tension-free, tequila-free Santa Land.

In the bad news department, however, it turned out that, due to faulty wiring in Conspicuous Consumption's electrical system, the security cameras were short-circuited by the sprinklers when Scotty was killed.

Which meant there were no surveillance tapes of the murder. Or the murderer.

Zippo. Nada. Nothing.

Which meant I was still a suspect, still unable to leave town.

As much as my parents drive me crazy at times, I was not about to pass up my annual visit to see them in Florida for a week of coddling, cuddling, and fudge on tap 24/7.

And who knew how long it would take the cops to wrap up the case? So I made up my mind to stick around and give them a hand. They didn't know it (and you might not, either), but I happened to have solved quite a few murders in my day, action packed tales of adventure and Chunky Monkey binges listed at the front of this book.

And so the morning after the murder, I was ensconced on my living-room sofa, chomping on a cinnamon raisin bagel, going over my list of suspects.

There was Molly, Scotty's scorned lover. And Corky, who'd threatened to kill Scotty if he called her "Porky" one more time. There was also Gigi, Scotty's secret squeeze, but for the life of me, I couldn't see why she'd want to knock him off. (Unless she'd caught him cheating on her with some other elfin cutie.)

Finally, as much as I hated to consider it, there was Barnaby. After all, Scotty had exposed him as a fraud in front of a whole crowd of Christmas shoppers. Barnaby had laughed it off, but maybe he was more upset than he'd let on.

You can imagine how distressed I was my first day back at work when I saw him talking with Detective Huck Finn.

My heart sunk. What if Barnaby was about to be arrested?

Sidling up to where they were chatting in the employees' locker room, I heard Huck tell Barnaby, "You'll be happy to hear we checked out the movie theater, and several witnesses confirmed seeing you there the morning of the murder."

Yay! Barnaby had been at the movies at the time of the murder!

"Looks like you're in the clear," Huck said.

"But you're not," he said to me as he walked by. "So don't leave town."

It was all I could do not to yank on his cowlick.

With Barnaby safely off my Suspect List, I turned to my two top contenders:

Corky and Molly.

I decided to start my investigation with Scotty's spurned lover. I remembered how Molly told Scotty to drop dead in the employees' locker room.

Now I wondered if she'd turned her suggestion into a reality.

Before I could think of an excuse to stop by her office, I was summoned to see her on my lunch break.

"It has come to my attention," she said, looking up from a stack of papers on her desk, "that it was your cat who was responsible for the disaster at Santa Land the other day."

"Yes, I'm so sorry. I should have never brought her to the mall to have her picture taken."

"It wasn't easy," she said, "but I talked Mr. Halavi out of suing you."

"Mr. Halavi?"

"The man who owns the roasted chestnut concession. Thank heavens his insurance paid for a new umbrella. But I'd steer clear of roasted chestnuts for a while if I were you."

"Absolutely!" I assured her. "And I just want you to know that this little incident does not at all reflect my work ethic. If you hire me as a copywriter, I can guarantee you it will never happen again."

"I should hope not. Just be sure to leave your cat home on Bring Your Pet to Work Day," she added with a wink.

It suddenly occurred to me that she was awfully chipper for someone who'd just had an employee stabbed on her watch.

In fact, never had I seen her hair quite so shiny or her skin so radiant.

Death (Scotty's, that is) certainly seemed to have agreed with her.

At which point, I remembered my mission and switched to part-time semi-professional P.I. mode.

"I still can't believe what happened to Scotty," I said, shaking my head.

"I can believe it," she replied, steely-eyed. "The way he lived his life, he was just asking for trouble."

Then she sat back in her chair with a sigh.

"I won't pretend I'm heartbroken that he's gone. You saw for yourself how he was cheating on me. I suppose deep down I knew all along he was using me, but I was too much of a wuss to face the truth.

"I wasted way too much of my life on that bum," she said, shaking her head ruefully. "I should've stuck with my old boyfriend. I didn't know a good thing when I had it."

Then she sat up straight again, back in bizgal mode.

"Well, if you'll excuse me, I've got work to do. Insurance reports to file for the damage in Santa Land."

I cringed at the thought of all the havoc Prozac had caused.

"Thanks again for everything," I said.

She nodded and reached for her phone. As she did, I noticed something very interesting. There on her arm were a bunch of scabbed-over scratches.

She must have seen me staring because she quickly piped up:

"You're not the only one with a cat. I've got a mighty frisky feline of my own. Got these the other night," she said, pointing to the scratches, "giving her a bath."

Maybe, I thought, as I headed out the door.

Or maybe she got them from Scotty, trying to defend himself as she stabbed him to death.

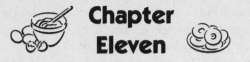

Chapter Eleven

After my tête-à-tête with Molly, I made a beeline for the food court for a quick corn dog. And, if you must know, a side of fries. (Okay, two sides. A gal can build up quite an appetite working as an undercover detective elf.)

I was just chowing down on my last fry, when I glanced up and saw Corky, strolling side by side with the muscle-bound co-worker I'd seen her with the day she blew up at Scotty.

Now her ruddy face was flushed with pleasure, her sparse ponytail bobbing merrily behind her. I watched as she gazed into Mr. Muscle's eyes with the kind of gooey-eyed adoration normally found in puppy dogs and Viagra commercials.

She was in love, all right.

I couldn't help thinking that with Scotty and his nasty comments out of the way, her romance could proceed unimpeded.

Indeed, she and Mr. Muscle looked quite chummy strolling along, Mr. Muscle's hand just millimeters from Corky's ample tush. Finally, he gave her a pat on said tush and stepped on the escalator, bidding her a fond adieu.

Which was my cue to leap into action.

"Hey, Corky," I cried, scurrying to her side. "I wanted to thank you for trying to rescue my cat the other day."

"No problem," she replied. "That's some little monster you got there."

Hey! I'm the only one who's allowed to call my little monster a monster. But somehow I managed to rein in my annoyance.

"So how's it going?" I asked.

"Pretty good," she replied. "Except for the damn shoplifters. They're out in droves at Christmas. Figure they can get away with it, with the stores so crowded. Gotta watch for the ones with the big totes," she said, eyeing a tiny brunette with an enormous purse.

"Just yesterday I caught some gal with a KitchenAid mixer in her bag. Said it must've fallen in when she wasn't looking. She actually expected me to believe her. And here's the crazy thing. Turns out she was married to some gazillionaire movie director out in Malibu. Can you beat that? She could've bought seventeen of those mixers without batting an eye.

"The worst offenders," she said with a knowing wink, "are always the rich ones."

"Speaking of crime," I said, in an effort to wrench the conversation away from mall theft, "I still can't get over Scotty getting killed the way he did."

At the mention of Scotty's name, Corky's spine stiffened.

"Couldn't have happened to a more deserving guy."

Spoken like a woman who might have done the job herself.

Once again I remembered her threat to Scotty:

Call me "Porky" one more time, and you're a dead man!

Had Scotty called her "Porky" one more time? And had Corky made good on her threat?

"Don't get me wrong," she said, as if reading my thoughts. "I didn't kill him. I sure as heck wanted to. But I'm no murderer."

"I don't suppose you have any idea who did it?" I asked.

"Not a clue."

"Did you notice anyone near him after the sprinklers went off?"

"Just you."

Gee, thanks for the vote of confidence.

"Sure you didn't see anybody else?"

"Say, what's with all these questions, anyway? You some sort of reporter?"

"Actually, I'm a private eye."

"You? A private eye?"

She blinked in amazement. Can't say I blamed her. Standing there in my pointy elf shoes and striped tights, I was not exactly the image of a hard-boiled dick.

"I work part-time, semi-professional," I explained.

"Wow." She gazed at me with new-found respect. "I've always wanted to be a detective. I tried to join the L.A.P.D. But they turned me down because of the time I spent in juvie."

"You were in juvie?"

Now it was my turn to be shocked. Corky, our genial security guard, had once done time in a kiddie correctional institution!

"Yeah, I had some anger issues when I was growing up. I've always been on the chubby side. Got bullied a lot in school. One day some kid went too far, and I beat the stuffing out of him. Just my rotten luck I busted a couple of his ribs. Spent six months in juvie. They sent me to a shrink to help me get a handle on things.

"But that's all behind me now," she added with a toss of her ponytail.

I wasn't so sure about that. For all I knew, history had just repeated itself in Santa Land.

By now, we'd reached the employees' locker room, and I followed Corky as she headed for her locker.

"I'm just grateful Molly gave me a break," she was saying, "and hired me here at Conspicuous Consumption. It's not easy getting a job when you've got a record."

She opened her locker, revealing a monumental stash of M&M's on her top shelf, as well as a locker door plastered with photos.

There was a picture of Arnold Schwarzenegger in his Pumping Iron days. Another of Bruce Lee. And another of Corky, decked out in a kimono, assuming a karate pose.

Clearly the woman had a thing for brute force.

"So you know karate?" I said.

"You bet." She nodded.

No doubt about it. Corky certainly had the strength to have rammed that snowflake in Scotty's heart.

"I graduated second in my class at the Kung Pow Academy of Martial Arts," she said, pointing to another picture, a group shot of about a dozen men and women, all in karate garb. Sure enough, Corky was in the back row, grinning with pride.

And then I noticed someone standing in the row in front of her. A thin wiry woman with mousy brown hair.

"Wait a minute," I said, squinting at the photo. "Is that Molly?"

"Sure is. She's the one who graduated first in the class. You should see that woman chop her way through a cinder block."

Holy Moses. First those scratches on Molly's arms. Now this.

Just a few seconds ago, I was convinced Corky was my Number One Suspect.

But now, thanks to the Kung Pow Academy of Martial Arts, it looked like Molly was back in the running.

Later that night I was at my dining room table, writing out my Prozac-free Christmas cards. Alongside me on the table was a mug of hot chocolate and a plate of Oreos. Well, technically there was no plate. I was munching on them straight from the bag. Things tend to be a tad informal here at Casa Austen.

Somehow I'd managed to nibble my way through a frightening number of the chocolate beauties, and I now decided to save the last one as a reward for when I finished my cards.

I spent the next twenty minutes diligently sending XOXO's to friends and relatives and was just putting the stamp on my last card, when I heard Lance's familiar knock on my front door.

"I've been meaning to stop by for days," he said, breezing in, "but it's been crazy busy at work—Mmm, an Oreo!"

Without so much as a "Do you mind?" he scooped up my Reward Oreo and shoved it in his mouth.

"Hey! I was going to eat that!"

"You'll thank me in the morning, hon. I've just saved you scads of unsightly calories which would've gone straight to your thighs. Whereas I, on the other hand, will zap them away at the gym before they even know what hit them."

He did not lie. The man spends so much time at his gym, they've practically named a StairMaster in his honor.

"So," he said, plopping down next to Prozac on the sofa. "I heard some nutty cat set fire to your mall—"

Prozac sat up and preened.

That would be moi.

"—and that one of the Santas got killed."

"I know," I sighed. "I was there when it happened."

"Omigosh!" His eyes lit up with excitement. "Tell all! Don't leave out a single detail!"

I told him. How Prozac stole the corn dog and jumped on the Christmas tree. How Corky knocked the tree over onto the roasted chestnut stand. How the umbrella caught fire and set off the sprinklers. And how someone had taken advantage of the pandemonium to kill Scotty with a Christmas tree ornament.

"Wow," Lance said when I was through. "A Christmas tree ornament, huh? I thought about getting one of those for Greg for his Secret Santa gift."

"Forget about the damn Secret Santa gift, Lance! The point is, a murder has been committed, and the cops won't let me leave town till the case is solved. Technically I'm one of the suspects."

"Oh, sweetie," he said, "I'm sure they'll find the killer. If worse comes to worst you can always spend Christmas with me and my family and watch my uncle Delmar fall head first into the candied yams after his fifth martini. That's always good for a chuckle."

"Sounds delightful," I replied with a wan smile.

"Try not to worry, hon," he said, taking my hand. "Everything's going to be okay. Just promise me you won't go chasing after the killer yourself. Really. That stuff is dangerous."

"Yes, but—"

"But nothing! I know how you get the minute you sniff a corpse. You're like a bloodhound in elastic-waist pants. For once, promise me you'll leave everything to the police."

"I promise," I lied.

"That's my girl," he said, wrapping me in a hug. "And remember. You've always got my dysfunctional family to come home to at Christmas."

Lance may be a royal pain at times, but when I'm in a fix, he's always there for me with a hug.

"By the way, honey," he said, "I've got a weeny favor to ask."

I should've known there was a catch to that hug.

"Neiman's having a crisis down at their Newport Beach store. A couple of their top shoe salesmen got food poisoning at a Christmas party. I need to go down there to pitch in for the next few days. So would you mind taking in my mail while I'm gone?"

"Is that all? No problem."

"One more thing. I need you to watch over Greg's Secret Santa gift."

"You need me to watch over a box of Godiva chocolates?"

If you remember, class, when last we left Lance, that's what he'd decided to buy.

"Oh, no," he said, with a dismissive wave of his hand. "I didn't get chocolates. That's so passé. I thought of a much better idea. Wait! I'll go get it."

He zipped out the door and minutes later returned with a canvas-covered dome.

"What on earth is that?" I asked.

"The perfect Christmas gift!"

He whipped off the cover and revealed an ornate wrought iron bird cage. In the center of which was a bright green and orange parrot.

Prozac looked up eagerly from the sofa.

Oh, goody! Dinner!

I blinked in amazement. "You're giving a parrot as your Secret Santa gift?"

"Not just any parrot. A Christmas parrot! Look. His wings are red and green!"

"They're orange and green."

"Close enough. Anyhow, his name is Bogie. I bought him on Craigslist for only thirty bucks! His owner says he talks, but so far he hasn't said a thing."

"I can't keep a bird here, Lance. Not with Prozac."

"Don't be silly. The bird's in a cage. What harm can Prozac possibly do?"

Prozac's nose twitched with anticipatory glee.

Don't worry. I'll think of something!

"Just cover the cage at night so Bogie can sleep."

Then he dashed outside, only to come back seconds later with a bag of bird seed and a stand for the cage.

"Thanks, Jaine, sweetie! You're an angel."

"But, Lance—"

Before I could get in another word, he was off and running.

Gritting my teeth at the prospect of guarding Bogie the Parrot for the next few days, I put the birdcage the one place I knew Prozac was least likely to go—inside the bathtub. She has not ventured inside that tub since the one and only time I tried to give her a bath—a harrowing experience featuring much hissing, scratching, and decibel shattering wails.

(And Prozac wasn't too crazy about it, either.)

Bogie fluttered his wings a bit, then gazed at me with bright beady eyes.

"If you want anything," I said, striking a pose against the doorjamb, "just whistle. You know how to whistle, don't you, Bogie? Just put your upper and lower mandibles together, and blow."

Then, after that very poor Lauren Bacall impersonation, I returned to the living room where Prozac was staring dreamily off into space.

I knew just what she was dreaming about.

"You leave that bird alone," I warned her. "For your information, parrots happen to be one of nature's most treasured creatures."

She looked up at me with sly green eyes.

Especially with ketchup.

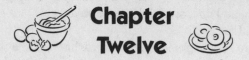

Chapter Twelve

Gigi was subdued in the days following Scotty's death. Gone was the spring in her step and the sparkle in her eye. She led her charges up to Santa's chair with all the *joie de vivre* of a condemned man tootling off to the electric chair.

Rumor had it she was seeing a shrink.

I tried to question her about Scotty's murder, hoping she could provide me with a valuable clue. After all, she was on duty with him when he was killed. But every time I tried to talk to her, she seemed to be in a hurry somewhere—to her acting class, to her gym, to her aromatherapist . . .

If I didn't know better I'd say she was avoiding me.

Well, she wasn't going to lose me that easily.

With a quick trip to Molly's office, and a fib about wanting to send Gigi a Christmas card, I was able to obtain her address.

I planned to pay her a visit in person. Nothing like a face-to-face chat to wring the truth out of a witness.

I waited till the following Saturday when the weekend Santa Land crew had taken over and neither of us was working. Then I called her to make sure she was home, using a pay phone at the public library so she wouldn't see my name on her caller ID.

She answered the phone with a weary "hello," and I immediately hung up and dashed to my car—eager to zip over to her apartment for our long-delayed chat.

Gigi Harris lived in Westwood, in one of the many courtyard buildings that dot the neighborhood around UCLA. I walked up the front path to a security gate, and peering inside, saw a tiny pool, surrounded by rusty lounge chairs. An abandoned volleyball bobbed forlornly in the turquoise water.

Unwilling to ring Gigi's buzzer and risk having her blow me off, I waited at the gate, examining the names on the intercom, until at last one of the tenants came out, a lanky guy toting a backpack and wheeling his bike. After he pushed the gate open, I held it out for him, and then scooted inside.

Safe in the courtyard, I trotted over to Gigi's apartment and knocked on her door.

"Who is it?" she called out.

"It's me. Jaine Austen, from work."

I heard footsteps shuffling and then the door opened a crack.

Gigi peered out at me with glazed eyes, her uncombed hair sticking out in messy spikes. Yet somehow she still managed to look cute.

Life's sure not fair, is it? When my hair sticks out in messy spikes, I look like Medusa on uppers.

"How did you get past the security gate?" she asked.

"It was open," I fibbed.

"Well?" she said, making no move to let me in. "How can I help you?"

"Look, I know you're unhappy about what happened to Scotty, but I really need to talk to you. Can I come in for just a minute?"

"Oh, all right," she sighed.

She opened the door, and I almost gasped when I saw that she was standing there in a long, white wedding dress, nipped in at the waist, with acres of tulle cascading from her slim hips.

"Scotty bought this for me," she said, doing a half-hearted pirouette. "Today was supposed to be our wedding day."

I followed as she led me to her tiny living room, furnished in Early Starving Actor—rump-sprung sofa flanked by worn director's chairs, steamer trunk coffee table, and cinderblock book cases. Up on the wall above her sofa, Gigi had sandwiched a framed glamor shot of herself in between posters of James Dean and Marilyn Monroe.

At least she was aiming high.

She picked up a bottle of opened champagne from the coffee table.

"Want some?" she asked, holding it out to me.

Not at 10:30 in the morning, I didn't.

"No, thanks. I'll pass."

"All the more for me," she said, slumping down onto her sofa and taking a big slug.

"Sit." She gestured for me to take a seat in one of the director's chairs.

"Round about now," she said, checking her watch, "I

was supposed to be picking up Scotty. We were going to drive to Vegas and get married in one of those corny Elvis chapels. The best laid plans, huh?"

Another slug of champagne.

I looked over and saw that about half of the bottle was gone. Gigi was well on her way to being snockered. I needed to hurry and get in some questions while she was still lucid.

"I'm so sorry about what happened to Scotty," I tsked. "Such a tragedy."

Of course what I really wanted to tell her was that she was better off without him, that he was a sleazebag of the highest order, and that he'd only have made her life miserable in the end.

But of course I said none of this.

Instead I just murmured, "I know how unhappy you must be. And I'm sure, more than anyone, you'd like to see the killer brought to justice."

She nodded in agreement, picking at the foil on the neck of the champagne bottle.

"So I was wondering if I could ask you a few questions about the murder."

"Go ahead. Shoot. Corky tells me you're some kind of detective."

"Part-time, semi-professional."

"Who woulda thunk it?" she said, shaking her head in disbelief.

I get that a lot. For some strange reason, most people tend to underestimate the investigative skills of a woman in elastic-waist pants and a *Cuckoo for Cocoa Puffs* T-shirt.

"Like I told the police," Gigi said, "I didn't see a thing that day. I was too busy trying to calm down the kids, what with the Christmas tree falling and the sprinklers going off."

"Are you sure you didn't see anybody approach Scotty at the time he was killed?"

"I'm pretty sure," she said, a note of doubt creeping into her voice.

"Think back to the scene. Try to remember anyone, anyone at all, going near Scotty's chair."

"Okay."

She leaned back against the sofa, closing her eyes to concentrate. I waited for her to speak, but she said nothing. At first, I thought she was lost in thought. Until I heard her start to snore.

Oh, hell! She'd passed out.

A fat lot of good this interview was getting me. I got to question her for a whole thirty-two seconds.

I was just about to get up and leave when I glanced down and saw the spine of a book peeking out from under one of Gigi's sofa cushions—as if it had been shoved there hastily before she'd answered the door.

I reached over and began to slowly ease it out.

At one point my heart lurched as I saw her eyelids flutter. But thankfully she kept on snoring.

At last I'd pulled the book free, and I now saw that it was a high school yearbook.

I flipped the pages until I came to the H's, looking for Gigi's picture.

I blinked in disbelief when I found it. There she was, listed as Virginia Harris, a chubby girl with clunky dark-rimmed glasses. A far cry from the elfin Gigi of Santa Land. But there was no doubt about it. Underneath all those extra pounds, that chubby girl scowling out at the camera was indeed Gigi.

Talk about your amazing transformations.

I continued to flip the pages until I saw something that made me stop dead in my tracks. There under the class officers, voted "Most Handsome," was a picture of Scotty. A younger version of the same handsome, cocksure Scotty who had driven everybody crazy in Santa Land.

So he and Gigi had gone to high school together.

Had they known each other? Had they been friends?

I sincerely doubted it. First, because Scotty didn't strike me as the kind of guy who would have been friends with a chubby, unattractive girl in high school.

And mainly because Gigi had slashed a big X across his photo.

What's more, she'd crossed out the word "Handsome" from his "Most Handsome" caption, and written "Loathsome" in its place.

Clearly Gigi had hated Scotty's guts back then.

Had she held on to that hate all these years and taken it out on him with a Christmas tree ornament?

But that was impossible.

After all, she was going to marry the guy. Wasn't she?

Suddenly from the depths of my reverie I heard a snort. I looked up and saw that Gigi was awake and staring at her yearbook clenched in my hands.

"I see you found my yearbook," she said. "A treasured memento of my golden high school years."

Her voice fairly dripped with sarcasm.

"I suppose you're wondering why I defaced Scotty's photo."

"Sort of."

"Would you believe I hated him back in high school but fell madly in love with him when we met again in Santa Land?"

"No, frankly, I wouldn't."

"Good for you. Go straight to the head of the class." She stopped to take another swig of champagne. "You want the truth, Jaine? I hated Scotty then. I hate Scotty now. I'll always hate Scotty."

"Then why on earth were you going to marry him?"

"Oh, but I wasn't. I was going to do to him what he did to me back in high school. Back then, I was a fat pimply senior and he was a golden boy on the track team. I didn't think he even knew I was alive. But then one day when I was sitting in the cafeteria—alone, of course—he came and sat next to me. He told me that he'd seen me in a couple of classes and thought I had really pretty eyes. Then he said he'd just broken up with his girlfriend and was wondering if I'd like to go to the senior prom with him. I was foolish enough to think he actually meant it. I didn't know it was just a joke, a crazy prank he'd thought up with his stupid buddies.

"I ran out and spent every penny in my savings account on a prom dress. My parents were so excited for me; at last their unpopular daughter had a boyfriend! They couldn't wait to meet him. He said he'd pick me up at seven. Seven came and went. So did eight. And nine. By ten o'clock I got into my pajamas and cried myself to sleep.

"I later found out he'd gone to the prom with his girlfriend, that he'd never broken up with her. Every time he saw me after that, he'd snicker, 'Wanna go to the prom?'

"God, I wanted to kill him. Then, all these years later, we wound up working together at Santa Land. He didn't recognize me, of course. I'd lost all that weight. My face had cleared up. And I'd started calling myself Gigi. So he had no idea who I was.

"But I remembered him, all right. A guy that awful, you never forget. I wanted to puke when he started coming on to me. I wanted to kick him in the groin and tell him exactly what I thought of him. But then I had a better idea. I'd do to him what he did to me. I made him fall in love with me. Lots of guys do, you know."

I believed her. The new improved Gigi was one hot cookie.

"True," she said, "I had to let him touch me." She gave a tiny shiver of disgust. "It made me sick, but it was worth it. Before long he asked me to marry him. He even went and bought me this silly dress. All this lace and tulle. So romantic. If he only knew how much I detested him.

"Like I said, I was supposed to pick him up this morning and drive him to Vegas for our wedding. But I was never going to show. I was going to keep him waiting hour after hour, just like he kept me waiting all those years ago. I wanted him to feel what it was like to have his heart broken. Oh, that was going to be so much fun.

"But then somebody killed him and spoiled everything. Scotty died thinking I actually loved him."

She shook her head ruefully and slugged down the last of her champagne.

"I should've kicked him in the groin when I had the chance," she sighed. "Oh, well. Gotta look on the bright side. At least he won't be around to insult any more fat women.

"Now if you'll excuse me," she said, getting up on shaky feet, "I'm going to pass out in my bed where it's nice and comfy. Let yourself out, will you?"

* * *

I walked past the volleyball bobbing in Gigi's tiny pool, my mind buzzing with the story she had just told me. Not for one second did I doubt that Scotty had played that awful trick on her in high school. And not for one second did I doubt that Gigi had been out for revenge. Maybe all she planned at first was to stand him up at the altar.

But who's to say she didn't change her mind and stab him in the heart with a Christmas tree ornament instead?

Just something to think about between Christmas cookies.

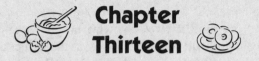

Chapter Thirteen

Back home, I found my answering machine blinking. My heart did a flip flop when I pressed the Play button and heard Jason Nicoletti's voice.

Hi, Jaine. Jason here. Just calling to remind you about my holiday party on Tuesday. Really looking forward to re-connecting. See you then!

In the sturm und drang of Scotty's murder I'd forgotten all about the party. But now Jason and his crooked smile came roaring back into my consciousness.

He was interested in reconnecting. With *moi*! All too exciting for words.

I hurried to my bedroom where I spent the next hour or so trying on potential outfits. After piling my bed high with clothes, I came to the perfectly logical conclusion that I had nothing to wear and raced over to Nordstrom where I found a divine Eileen Fisher outfit—hip-slimming black velvet elastic waist pants and matching black beaded sweater.

Even on sale, it was way too rich for my anemic budget, but I bought it anyway—vowing not to buy another thing for myself till after Labor Day at the earliest. Not one thing. Except maybe a fabulous Very Berry lipstick in Cosmetics. And a darling pair of chandelier earrings on sale in Costume Jewelry.

I headed home, exhilarated from the hunt. Nothing gets a gal's endorphins flowing like black velvet and dangly earrings.

My good mood came to a screeching halt, however, when I picked up my mail from where my mailman had tossed it on my front step, just in case there were any burglars in the area who needed to know I was out shopping.

There among the bills and flyers was a particularly galling invoice from Ernie, the Cat Whisperer. Would you believe he was charging me $100 for our photo session? A hundred buckeroos—and he hadn't snapped a single picture of Prozac!

I was on the phone in a flash.

"Picture Perfect Photo Studio. Edna speaking," Ernie's receptionist answered.

"This is Jaine Austen calling."

"Oh, yes. The lady with the crazy cat."

I opted to take the high road, and let that slip by.

"I believe your billing department has made a mistake, Edna. I just got a bill for $100."

"That was no mistake," Edna informed me.

"But Ernie didn't take a single picture."

"I'm sorry, but we booked an hour of studio time for you. And that's one hundred dollars."

"That's outrageous!" I fumed. "Simply outrageous. I demand to speak with Ernie."

"I'm afraid he's busy right now."

"Have him call me back as soon as possible," I said in my most authoritative voice.

Needless to say, I didn't hear a peep from Ernie that day. Or the next. So on Monday when I got back to work, I decided to pay him a visit in person.

I strode into the Cat Whisperer's studio in full tilt Tough Gal mode. Which wasn't all that easy considering I was wearing my elf suit at the time. Let's just say that a gal in a pointy green hat and curly-toed slippers does not exactly scream "I am woman; hear me roar."

"May I help you, Ms. Austen?" asked Edna, gazing up at me from behind the reception counter.

"I need to speak with Ernie about this," I said, waving my invoice in her face. "Now!"

"I'm sorry," she said icily, "but he can't be disturbed."

That's what *she* thought. I wasn't about to be put on hold for one moment longer.

Seething with righteous indignation, I started for the curtain that separated the reception area from the photography studio. As I did, Edna sprang out from behind the counter.

Whoa. When I met Edna the day of Prozac's photo shoot, she seemed like an ordinary middle-aged woman, the kind you see squeezing cantaloupes in the produce section. But now, as she came out from behind her reception counter, I realized she was a rather intimidating gal. In fact, if I'd met her in a dark alley, I would've sworn she was a linebacker for the Green Bay Packers.

Yes, along with her *I* ❤ *My Cat* pin and Easy Spirit Walkers, she had quite an impressive set of muscles on display.

But if you think for one minute that I was going to be the least bit intimidated by a mere show of brute force— you're absolutely right.

"Guess I'll come back later," I said, me and my curly-toed slippers skedaddling out the door with lightning speed.

Okay, so I've got to work on my Tough Gal act.

After several hours hoisting kids on Santa's lap, I took a break from my elf duties and headed back to Ernie's studio.

It was after six and I was hoping maybe Edna had left for the day, but no, there she was, still on guard, just waiting to tackle interlopers.

How on earth was I going to get past her into Ernie's inner sanctum?

Then I had an idea. A rather clever one if I do say so myself.

I put in a call to Lance in Newport.

Luckily he deigned to pick up his cell phone.

"Lance, you've got to do me a favor. Call the Picture Perfect Photo Studio in L.A. and keep the receptionist on the line as long as possible."

"Can't it wait, Jaine?" he whined. "I'm in the middle of a very important Happy Hour. Martinis are only three bucks."

"Lance!"

"Okay, okay. I'll call."

I waited impatiently outside Ernie's studio as Lance tore himself away from his martinis to make the call. Finally I saw Edna pick up the phone. Which was my cue to march on over.

"Yes, of course," I heard her say as I approached the entrance. "Mr. DeVito photographs events. What sort of event are you planning?"

I scooted over the threshold.

"Your cat is getting married? To the poodle next door?"

Oh, for crying out loud. Couldn't he have thought up something more believable than that?

But for some reason, the gargoyle was buying it.

"Yes, I'll be happy to take your credit card to reserve the date."

Once I saw her writing what I was certain was Lance's bogus credit card number, I strode inside and sailed past her with a jolly wave.

I could see she was tempted to leave the phone, but the lure of a big booking was simply too great to resist. Gritting her teeth in frustration, she allowed me to slip past the curtain into Ernie's studio. Which was empty at the time.

Then I looked around and saw the door to what I assumed was an office in the back where Ernie was probably hard at work overcharging other innocent customers.

I stormed across the room and was just about to barge in when I heard voices coming from inside.

"Oh, Ernie. I'm so sorry I ever broke up with you."

Wait. I knew that voice. It was Molly.

"I must've been crazy to fall for a bum like Scotty," she was saying. "Can you ever forgive me?"

"Of course, *cara mia*," Ernie crooned in reply. "It wasn't your fault. Scotty had you under his spell. But I knew somehow, some way I'd win you back."

Yikes. Molly had mentioned something about an old boyfriend. But I never dreamed it was Ernie, the Cat Whisperer! Was it possible Ernie had decided to win back his old love by getting rid of his competition—permanently?

My head was spinning with the idea of the Cat Whisperer as the killer—not to mention Molly as a femme fatale—when I looked around and for the first time I noticed a Christmas tree Ernie had set up in the corner of his studio—a plump, artificial affair, studded with tinsel and gold balls.

I almost gasped when I saw it.

Not because of the tinsels. Or the gold balls.

But because of the dozen or so snowflake ornaments hanging from its branches.

Good heavens. It was the exact same kind of ornament that had killed Scotty!

Had Ernie looked out his shop the day of the murder and, seeing the pandemonium in Santa Land, pocketed a snowflake from his own tree to plunge into Scotty's heart?

Maybe the murder weapon didn't come from the tree in Santa Land, but from right here in the Cat Whisperer's studio!

My musings were interrupted just then by Edna, charging in and yelling, "Exactly what do you think you're doing, missy?"

Before I got a chance to answer, the lovebirds came out of Ernie's office to see what the ruckus was about.

"She slipped right by me," Edna sputtered, "just as I was booking another cat-poodle wedding."

They'd actually done this cat-poodle wedding thing before??

Only in L.A.

"That's all right, Edna," Ernie assured her. Then he turned to me with a suave smile. "How may I help you, Ms. Austen?"

"For starters, you can tell me if you knocked off Scotty with one of your snowflake ornaments."

Of course I didn't really ask him that. But oh, how I wanted to.

Instead I launched into an indignant complaint about my bill, how a hundred dollars was a bit much for what had amounted to only about ten minutes of his time.

All the while I was yakking, I couldn't help staring at his hands. For such a slim guy, he had the hands of a dockworker. How easy it would have been for those hands to have plunged a sharp metal snowflake into Scotty's chest.

Undoubtedly trying to show Molly what a good sport he was, Ernie agreed to charge me only twenty-five bucks, and I headed back to Santa Land with a seventy-five dollar savings—and a hot new murder suspect.

Chapter Fourteen

I was lying in bed that night, Prozac sprawled across my chest, watching *Diners, Drive-Ins and Dives*. Well, Prozac was watching (she has a thing for Guy Fieri). I was busy thinking about my murder suspects, wondering which one of them could have plunged that snowflake into Scotty's heart.

Was it Molly, his scorned lover? She certainly had the strength, what with her black belt in karate. And there were those scratches on her arm, possible evidence that Scotty had put up a fight as she stabbed him to death.

What about Corky? She had, after all, threatened to kill Scotty if he called her Porky one more time. Had she carried out her threat in a moment of insane rage? There was also Gigi, who'd been nursing a grudge against Scotty ever since high school. Was it true that all she planned to do was ditch him at the altar? Or had she upped the ante and decided to kill him instead?

Finally, there was Ernie, the Cat Whisperer. I couldn't stop thinking about what I overheard him saying to Molly that afternoon:

I knew somehow, some way, I'd win you back.

Had he found the way—with a snowflake ornament from his own Christmas tree?

I laid there, pondering these questions, and whether or not I had the energy to get out of bed for a couple of Oreos.

I opted to forgo the Oreos. (Alert the media.) As much as I wanted them, I simply didn't have the strength to move. My days as a part-time, semi-professional P.I./Santa's Elf had been draining, to say the least. Juggling murder suspects and kiddies on candy cane highs was exhausting work.

So I turned off the TV and drifted off into an uneasy sleep. Before long I was deep into nightmare territory, dreaming about a toddler stabbing Santa in the heart with a snowflake ornament while I stood by helpless, eating a Double Stuf Oreo.

Suddenly I was jolted awake from this hellish vision by the sound of a deep male voice saying:

"Stick 'em up, or I'll shoot."

Omigod. It was Ernie! He was the killer! I should have known all along. There was something about his oily charm that screamed homicidal maniac. Besides, anyone who could get Prozac to sit still for the camera had clearly made a pact with the devil.

I remembered those dockworker hands of his. Oh, Lord. Any minute now, they'd be pulling the trigger and blowing me to kingdom come! I peered into the darkness, but I saw no one. He had to be hiding somewhere.

"I swear, Ernie," I said, bolting up in bed, my hands

high in the air. "Just because I saw the murder weapon in your studio doesn't mean I think you killed Scotty to get him out of the way so you could get Molly back.

"Honest," I lied, "that's the last thing on my mind!"

But all I heard in reply was:

"Stick 'em up, or I'll shoot."

Whoa. It suddenly occurred to me that the guy didn't have an Italian accent. So it couldn't be Ernie. Then who the heck was it? Yikes! It was probably a burglar!

"Look, I don't have much," I called out. "Just a gold locket from my parents, and a supposed diamond engagement ring from my ex-husband, the Blob, but knowing my ex-husband, I'm sure it's just cubic zirconia. Oh, yes, and a darling pair of dangly earrings I bought on sale at Nordstrom for a Christmas party I'm going to on Tuesday. Old friend from high school, says he wants to reconnect."

I tend to babble when I'm nervous.

"You can have everything," I said, "including the twenty dollars in the Pringles can on top of the refrigerator. Just don't hurt my cat."

I waited for what seemed like an eternity, my arms aching. It felt like I'd been holding them in the air for hours.

Then I heard the voice again:

"Stick 'em up, or I'll shoot."

But this time it was accompanied by an extremely screechy: *Awwwwwwk!*

Oh, for crying out loud, it was Bogie, Lance's silly parrot!

I'd been taking care of him for the past few days, running myself ragged moving him from room to room, keeping him out of Prozac's striking zone.

Lance said he knew how to talk. Apparently "Stick 'em up, or I'll shoot" was what he knew how to say. Picked up, no doubt, from one of the real Bogie's early gangster movies.

I turned on the light, and sure enough there were no intruders in my bedroom. Just me and Prozac.

I clambered out of bed and hurried to the bathroom, where Bogie was happily awwking away.

No wonder he'd been making such a racket; I'd forgotten to cover his cage.

"Stick 'em up, or I'll shoot," he said by way of greeting.

"Oh, Bogie," I sighed. "Of all the duplexes in all the towns in all the world, why did you have to wind up in mine?"

To which he just blinked his beady eyes and let loose with a fairly hefty poop.

Guess he wasn't much of a *Casablanca* fan.

# Chapter Fifteen

Lance came home from Newport early the next afternoon, and wasting no time, I hustled over to his apartment to return Bogie, lock, stock, and birdseed.

"Was he much trouble?" Lance asked.

"A lot, actually."

"Aw, thanks, hon. You're a true friend. Greg and I will name our first parakeet after you."

Leaving Lance to his fantasy relationship, I headed off to Conspicuous Consumption.

I was working the three to nine o'clock shift that day, which was a shame, since Jason's party was that night. I'd tried to get Gigi to switch shifts with me, but she had an audition she had to go to, so I was stuck.

I just hoped the party wouldn't be over by the time I got there.

Somehow the day crawled by. I led the kids up to see Santa, my head in the clouds, mentally mapping the shortest route to Jason's house in the Hollywood Hills and deciding whether to wear my hair loose and flowing or swept back in an elegant updo.

Finally eight o'clock rolled around. Just one more hour to go.

Usually after eight o'clock, the line at Santa Land died down; most kids were home getting ready for bed. But wouldn't you know, at eight thirty that night there was a line of kids snaking halfway down the mall.

After about the 367th time Barnaby saw me checking my watch, he asked me what was up, and I told him about Jason's party.

"A Christmas party? With your old high school crush? Don't just stand there, girl. Go!"

"But I can't leave you alone."

"Of course you can."

"Are you sure you'll be okay?"

"I'll be fine. Just have fun."

What a doll. I really had to remember to buy a toy for his Tiny Tim Project.

"Santa's elf," he announced to the crowd, "has to go help Mrs. Claus wrap presents, so she's going to say good night to you now."

I waved good-bye to the kids and, blowing Barnaby a kiss, raced off to grab my stuff from my locker. Then I hurried out to my car and roared out of the parking lot—only to be caught in the kind of hellish traffic that descends upon Los Angeles every year during Christmas party season.

I inched home gritting my teeth and cursing, my knuckles white on the steering wheel.

By the time I got back to my apartment, it was after nine.

Having silenced Prozac's indignant howls with a bowl of Hearty Halibut Guts, I dashed into my bedroom where I threw on my new Eileen Fisher black velvet elastic-waist pants set. I was in such a hurry, I didn't even bother taking off my striped elf tights, rolling them up at the ankles so they wouldn't show under my pants.

After slapping on some makeup, I took a quick pass at my bangs with the blow dryer. (So much for that glam updo.) Then I slipped on my dangly earrings, spritzed on some perf, and I was out the door.

"Wish me luck," I called out to Prozac.

She gazed up from where she was sprawled on the sofa, belching hearty halibut fumes.

Yeah, right. Whatever. Bring back leftovers.

Wending my way over to the Hollywood Hills, "Feliz Navidad" blaring from my radio, I fairly buzzed with anticipation, wondering if that spark I'd felt with Jason way back in high school was about to be ignited.

I found Jason's house—an ultra-modern concrete and glass affair—on a winding road deep in the hills. When I got there, the narrow street was jammed with cars. In a clearing I saw a valet in a red vest. Normally, I'd rather die than fork over money to a valet, but I couldn't afford to waste another minute, so I pulled up alongside him.

He peered in at me through my passenger window.

"You here with the cleaning crew?"

I get that a lot in my ancient Corolla.

"No, I'm a guest," I said, stepping out of the car and brushing an Almond Joy wrapper from where it was clinging to my thigh.

(Okay, so I had a teeny snack on the way over.)

Then I tossed him my keys and, with as much dignity as I could muster, I headed up the steps to Jason's party.

From the open front door, I could hear the sounds of laughter and tinkling glasses, a jazz rendition of "Jingle Bells" playing in the background.

I stepped inside, and suddenly my svelte new Eileen Fisher outfit seemed a lot less svelte than it had just two seconds ago. Everywhere I looked, I saw people far hipper than *moi*. Way too many willowy blondes in size zero cocktail dresses.

Oh, dear. Maybe this reconnection thing hadn't been such a good idea.

Then I spotted Jason across the room, chatting with a tall, aristocratic looking fellow in a tweedy blazer.

Jason caught sight of me and flashed me his crooked smile.

And just like that, my insecurities vanished.

My heart skipped a beat or three as he made his way through the crowd to my side, looking tres adorable in jeans and a bright red sweater.

"So glad you could make it, Jaine!" he said, wrapping me in the most divine hug.

Where's the mistletoe when you need some?

I was standing there, fantasizing about the two of us celebrating future holidays together, bingeing on Christmas fudge, when suddenly I was brought back down to earth with a resounding thud.

"Guess who's here?" Jason said, releasing me from his hug. "Jim Nelson." He pointed to the tall guy in the tweedy blazer. "The features editor at *L.A. Magazine*."

"That's nice," I said with a vague smile, wondering why he thought I'd be so excited to see a magazine editor. And then it all came flooding back to me—that whopper of a lie I told about writing an article for *L.A. Magazine*.

"I figured you two would have plenty to talk about

since you're writing that story for him. Let me go get him."

Oh, hell. I couldn't possibly talk to this Nelson guy and have him unmask me as the fake that I was.

My first thought was to jump back in my Corolla and race home. But I'd already given it to the valet. And Lord knows where he'd parked it. Probably somewhere in West Covina. It could take ages for him to bring it back. What if Jason spotted me out front and came trotting after me, with his editor friend in tow?

No, there was only one sensible thing to do:

Hide until the party was over and then sneak out in the dead of night.

Quickly, I nipped up a nearby stairway to the second floor and ducked into the first room I saw, closing the door behind me. It was dark inside and, unable to see where I was going, I stumbled over something in my path. Something big and hairy with sharp pointy teeth. A Doberman to be precise, as I discovered when I flipped on the light. And he was not alone. A fellow Doberman stood beside him.

(For the purposes of this narration and to avoid confusion, I shall call the first Doberman "Abbott" and the second Doberman "Costello.")

"Nice doggies!" I said, with a sickly smile.

Sadly, Abbott and Costello were not in the mood to be chummy.

On the contrary, they bared their pointy teeth and growled most menacingly.

"Well, nice meeting you," I said, starting for the door.

But Abbott and Costello were not about to let me go.

Like a flash they were at the doorway blocking my exit, fangs bared, massive jaws dripping with drool.

How I yearned for the good old days of Edna the receptionist.

Now they started advancing on me, backing me into the room, which seemed to be some sort of guest bedroom. Any minute, they'd be pinning me to the bed, lunging at my neck, going for the jugular.

Frantically I looked around for an escape route.

And then—hallelujah!—I saw two French doors leading out onto a balcony.

If I could make it outside, I'd be safe.

My heart in my throat (better there than in Abbott and Costello's jaws), I started sprinting across the room. But I hadn't taken two steps when one of the Dobermans, I believe it was Abbott, clamped down on the leg of my expensive new Eileen Fisher pants.

Oh, hell. He had the velvet in his iron jaws and refused to let go.

Desperate to break free, I slipped out of the pants (thank heavens for elastic waists!) and let him have them.

I hated to lose them, but it was clearly all for the best, since Abbott, now busy chomping on Eileen Fisher, had forgotten all about Yours Truly.

Which left me free to dash over to the French doors.

Unfortunately at that juncture, Costello, heretofore busy sniffing at Abbott's tush, sprang into action and came lunging at me.

Or, I should say, at my Eileen Fisher beaded top.

I quickly pulled it off and tossed it at him.

Apparently Costello was an Eileen Fisher fan, too, because seconds later he was next to Abbott on the floor, both of them happily noshing on my new outfit.

Grateful it was not me under their grinding teeth, I

raced out onto the balcony, shutting the door firmly behind me.

I stood there, breathing an enormous sigh of relief,
when suddenly flood lights snapped on from the garden
below.

"Jaine?"

I looked down and saw Jason standing with the guy
from *L.A. Magazine*. They were both staring up at me,
mouths gaping. And I suddenly realized I was standing
there wearing nothing but a wonderbra and striped elf
tights.

"This is Jim Nelson from *L.A. Magazine*," Jason called
up. "He says he's never heard of you."

Oh, gulp.

"And this," he said, putting his arm around one of the
size zero blondes I'd seen earlier that evening, "is my fiancée, Dawn."

Uh-oh. Time to cancel that mistletoe.

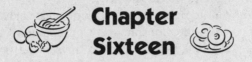

Chapter Sixteen

"Oh, Lord. What a disaster!"

It was the next day during one of our lulls in Santa Land, and I was baring my soul to Barnaby.

"There I was practically naked out on that balcony, everybody staring at me."

It's true. Soon after I was discovered in my elf tights and wonderbra, the whole party had trotted outside to see what the commotion was about.

Eventually Jason came upstairs and called off the dogs. And I slunk off in disgrace, my Eileen Fisher outfit shredded to bits and soaked with Doberman drool.

"How could I have been so wrong about Jason?" I sighed. "It was like high school all over again. I'd convinced myself he liked me when all he wanted was to be friends. When will I ever learn?"

"You're being too hard on yourself, kiddo," Barnaby said. "This Jason character talked about reconnecting and

didn't mention Word One about a girlfriend. It's no wonder you thought he was available."

"I guess you're right," I said, sucking on a candy cane
I'd nabbed from the Conspicuous Consumption Christmas tree. "But still, when I think of myself out on that
balcony in nothing but a wonderbra and elf tights, I want
to die."

"I've got an idea," Barnaby said, a Santa-like twinkle
in his eye. "After work tonight, why don't we go over to
Ben & Jerry's and drown your sorrows in a hot fudge
sundae? My treat."

If he were twenty years younger, I would've asked
him to marry me.

"Sounds wonderful," I said.

"Uh-oh," he said, fluffing his beard. "Here come some
kiddies. Better put on a happy face."

We resumed our roles as Santa and loyal elf until closing time at nine when we headed off to the locker room
together.

"I think I'll order the Brownie Special," Barnaby said,
opening his locker door. "A warm brownie topped with
ice cream, hot fudge sauce, and a mini-mountain of whipped
cream."

"I'm feeling better already." I grinned.

"See? By tomorrow you'll have forgotten all about
Jason."

He reached into his locker to get his street clothes, and
as he did something fell to the floor.

"I'll get it," I said, bending down to pick it up.

And suddenly all thoughts of Brownie Specials evapo-
rated into the ether.

There lying on the floor was a bright red scarf. With a
holly berry pattern. I'd seen that scarf somewhere before.

On the day of Scotty's murder. I remembered the old lady who screamed in terror when Prozac leaped onto the Christmas tree—the crazy dame who'd insisted Prozac was a bat. That old lady had been wearing a scarf just like this.

Omigosh. Was it possible that the old lady in the mall hadn't been an old lady—but Barnaby in disguise?

Barnaby was a diminutive guy. With the right makeup, he could easily pass for a woman. Hadn't he said he'd played Lady Macbeth in prep school?

According to witnesses, Barnaby was supposed to have been at the movies when Scotty was killed. Had he somehow slipped out of the theater and nipped across town to plunge a lethal snowflake in Scotty's heart?

I so did not want to believe that my cherubic co-worker was the killer, but something was telling me he was. Namely, that holly berry scarf, still lying on the floor between us.

But I couldn't let Barnaby see that I suspected anything. I had to be bright and cheery and act like nothing was wrong.

Alas, it was too late. When I got up to hand him the scarf, I found myself looking smack dab into the nuzzle of a snub-nosed revolver.

"Oh, dear," he tsked, grabbing the scarf from me. "I should have burned it. But I hated to give it up. The Crazy Mall Lady was one of my favorite roles."

"So it was you at the mall that day," I said, my heart plummeting.

"I was quite magnificent, wasn't I?" he asked, the revolver now aimed at my gut.

I nodded woodenly, determined to keep him talking. Surely the Conspicuous Consumption security cameras would pick up this little scene, and before long someone would come racing to my rescue.

"But I don't understand," I said. "Why did you kill Scotty? Just because he told everyone you'd never been a big time actor?"

"Heavens, no. That was most annoying. But it's not why I killed him. You see, when Scotty said I was a fraud, he wasn't just talking about my acting. He was talking about the Tiny Tim Project."

"The Tiny Tim Project?"

"It's a complete scam, sweetie. I keep every dime I collect from my corporate sponsors. And I sell the toys on eBay." He actually seemed proud of himself. "Somehow Scotty found out about it and was threatening to turn me over to the cops."

His bushy brows furrowed in consternation.

"I couldn't let that happen, could I? After all, nobody wants to see Santa go to jail. Think of how disappointed all the kiddies would be."

"Absolutely." I nodded, hoping to get on his good side with a little faked sympathy. "I understand totally."

"So I went to the movies and made a point of talking to the ticket taker and the other people on line. I purposely chose a movie I knew wouldn't be crowded. Once in the theater, I sat in the back row by myself and slipped on a wig and a jacket I'd brought along in a shopping bag. Then I sailed back out again, a completely different person, and hurried home to disguise myself as the Crazy Old Lady. So many costume changes that day. My, it was fun!"

"I'll bet," I said, doing my best to fake a smile.

For crying out loud, the guy was practically telling me his life story, and still no one had come to my rescue.

Where the hell was the Conspicuous Consumption security team?

"C'mon," he said. "Time to take a little trip to Santa Land."

With his gun lodged firmly in my back, he shoved me out into the mall. So bright and festive during the day, at night, with the people gone and the lights dimmed, it now had the antiseptic look of a hospital corridor.

"My original plan," Barnaby said as he prodded me over to Santa Land, "was to slip a little poison into Scotty's 'hot chocolate' thermos, but when your cat went ballistic, I decided to take advantage of the chaos and stab Scotty in the heart instead.

"Much more satisfying," he added with a happy nod.

By now we'd reached Santa's Workshop.

"Get in," Barnaby said, nudging me with his gun.

Oh, dear. I didn't like the looks of this. Not one bit.

"Whatever you're planning, Barnaby, you'll never get away with it. There are security cameras all over the place," I said, waving at the cameras, hoping that whichever idiot was asleep at the wheel would finally wake up and notice me.

"Forget it, hon. The security cameras got fried by the sprinklers the day of the murder and they've never been fixed."

"They've never been fixed?" I blinked in disbelief.

"Unfortunately the gentleman who owns Conspicuous Consumption has made some rather unwise investments and is in dire financial straights. He can barely pay the light bills, let alone fix his high tech security system.

"That's what Corky told me, anyway, on one of her many snack breaks. Everyone always seems to confide in me. I'm so darn likeable, aren't I?"

He smiled at me, the twinkle in his eye no longer a twinkle, but a manic gleam.

"Now get in the damn workshop!" he growled, waving the gun in my face.

I crawled into the small hideaway where Scotty had enjoyed so many tequila breaks, sick with fear. I was about to die at the hands of a nutcase Santa, all because I'd been trying to land a job at a mall that couldn't afford to hire me in the first place.

Then Barnaby crouched in the doorway and, much to my surprise, dropped his gun.

Frantically, I grabbed it.

"Won't do you any good, Jaine. It's just a prop."

"Just a prop?"

I pulled the trigger, and sure enough, all I heard was a harmless click.

"Stole it from a community theater production of *Sleuth*. I played the Larry Olivier part. Got fantastic reviews. Personally, I thought I gave old Larry a run for his money."

Dammit. I'd let myself be conned by a silly prop!

"But *this* murder weapon is very real, my dear," he said, whipping out a switchblade knife from his Santa boot. "Souvenir of an impromptu performance I did in a back alley in Koreatown. An ugly story. I won't bore you with the details."

Oh, God. The maniac was going to eviscerate me. Here—in Santa's Workshop! And no one was coming to help.

How the hell was I going to get out of this mess?

And then I saw it. My salvation:

An empty tequila bottle, left over from one of Scotty's binges.

As Barnaby ducked his head to crawl into the workshop, I was ready for him. The minute he came through the door, I whacked him over the head with Jose Cuervo's finest. A satisfying crack rang out as the glass made contact with his skull. He crumpled to the ground, groaning.

Kicking him aside, I began scrambling out of Santa's Workshop, screaming bloody murder. I'd just gotten to my feet when I felt a hand clamp down on my calf.

Oh, crud. I hadn't knocked Barnaby out; I'd just stunned him. Now I peered down into the workshop and saw he was reaching for his knife with his other hand. Why the hell had I left it in there?

I tried to shake myself free of his grasp but it was like a manacle. Any minute now he'd be slashing my legs to ribbons.

Then suddenly I remembered The Biter—the little girl who'd come marching in to see Santa to demand a pony. I remembered how her mother had pleaded with her not to chomp down on Santa.

Pulling a page from The Biter's book, I bent over and sunk my teeth into Barnaby's bony arm. Chunky Monkey, it wasn't. But it did the trick. With a piercing wail, he released his hold on me.

Taking no chances, I then stomped on his hand, and seconds later when he came crawling out from the workshop, I was waiting for him with the *Giant Book of Mother Goose Nursery Rhymes*, a hefty tome I'd snatched from the Tiny Tim toy bin.

As Barnaby crawled into view, brandishing his knife, I whacked him on the bean with every ounce of strength I had. Jose Cuervo may have let me down, but Mother Goose did the trick. This time Barnaby was out for good.

How fitting, I thought, that he was felled by a gift from his own scuzzy charity scam.

At which point, Corky finally came rushing over.

"Jaine! What's going on?"

"Quick!" I cried. "Call the police. Barnaby's the one who killed Scotty!"

"Sweet little Barnaby?" she asked, peering down at his crumpled body. "Really?"

"Yes, and he just tried to kill me, too."

"Wow," she said, shaking her head in disbelief. "This sure hasn't been our year for Santas."

Corky got on her cell phone and minutes later the place was swarming with cops. After I told them my story and showed them Barnaby's switchblade, they hauled the psychotic Santa off to the medical wing of USC county jail.

Somehow I managed to drive myself back to my apartment, vowing that from that day forward I would do all my Christmas shopping online.

Home at last, I collapsed onto my sofa, Prozac nestled on my chest.

"Prozac, honey. You won't believe what happened. I was almost stabbed to death in Santa's Workshop by a deranged Santa Claus, but thank heavens I managed to bop him over the head with a tequila bottle and a book of nursery rhymes before he could eviscerate me."

Yeah, right. Whatever. Is that brownie I smell on your breath?

Okay, so I stopped off for that Brownie Special.

(With extra whipped cream, if you must know.)

* * *

I woke up the next morning to find a message on my answering machine.

What with my near death experience, I hadn't noticed it blinking the night before.

I pressed the play button, and almost choked on my morning coffee when I heard:

Hello, Jaine. This is Jim Nelson calling from Los Angeles Magazine. We . . . um . . . sort of met the other night at Jason's party. Anyhow, Jason told me about your Christmas Elf idea, and I think it would be a great story for the magazine. Why don't we get together for lunch to talk over the details? Or dinner, if you're free. Give me a buzz.

Holy Moly. It looked like it was going to be a Merry Christmas, after all.

One More Thing

It turns out that Greg, Lance's Secret Santa crush, is allergic to birds. So if anyone wants a parrot who can say, *Here's looking at you, kid,* just let me know.

Hi, there!

I hope you enjoyed reading "Nightmare on Elf Street" as much as I enjoyed writing it. I had so much fun squeezing Jaine into those ghastly striped tights.

Those of you familiar with my books already know what crazy scrapes I put Jaine through. Not only is she constantly stumbling over dead bodies, she's kissed more frogs than me and Miss Piggy combined.

One of these days, after we've shared a margarita or three, you must remind me to tell you about the time my date tried to toss me off the Santa Monica pier. Happy to report I survived, only to see the guy show up on TV a few days later as a staid stock market analyst!

But that's a whole other story, one I'm saving for my memoirs, and my therapist.

Until then, I'm focusing all my attention on Jaine.

Since her nightmare on Elf Street, Jaine has solved murders at a health spa, a teen beauty pageant, and a far-away Pacific island (where, amid swaying palms and Godzilla-sized water bugs, a native island king is determined to make Jaine his twelfth bride).

My intrepid heroine has tracked down killers on cruise ships and weddings; and dealt with murder weapons as diverse as designer shoes, a chocolate yule log, and—in her very first adventure, *This Pen for Hire*—a Thigh-master. She's crossed paths with so many dead bodies, she's practically got an honorary crypt at the L.A. County morgue.

In Jaine's latest outing, *Death of a Gigolo,* she gets a job ghost-writing a romance novel for a wealthy society matron. When the woman's boy toy—a sleazy nogoodnik loathed by one and all—is murdered, Jaine sets out to find the killer—all the while trying to impress the new love in her own life.

Yes! For once, Jaine is dating someone she actually likes! Unfortunately, Prozac doesn't share Jaine's enthusiasm and mounts an aggressive campaign to sabotage their budding romance.

Will Jaine find the killer? Will she master the art of romance writing? And, most important, will she foil Prozac's dastardly attempts to come between her and her hot new honey?

The answers to these and other burning questions are waiting to be revealed in *Death of a Gigolo*.

Until we meet again (I hope!)—

Laura Levine

P.S. Whatever you do, stay away from guys who want to take you for an after-dinner stroll on the Santa Monica Pier!

THE CHRISTMAS THIEF

LESLIE MEIER

Chapter One

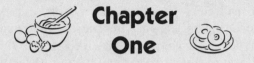

"That bag is to die for."

As a graduate of the Cavendish Hotel chain's Guests Come First program, Toni Leone was too well trained to point, but Elizabeth Stone followed her colleague's gaze, which was fixed on a Chanel-style handbag made of silver quilted leather with a long, woven leather and chain strap. The woman carrying the bag was dressed in tight black jeans, stiletto heels, and a fluttering silk tunic. Her hair was bleached blond and she was hanging onto the arm of an extremely muscular man.

"It's probably not real," Elizabeth replied, speaking in a whisper. The two young women were wearing matching forest green blazers and standing behind the reception desk at the very posh, very expensive Cavendish Palm Beach Hotel. It was strictly against hotel policy to comment on the guests, but the staff members all did it, especially during the quiet times. The hotel was a historic landmark and attracted the rich and famous from around the world. Located right on the beach, the pink stucco building had eight restaurants, four pools, a spa, and recreational options ranging from tennis courts and an eighteen-hole golf course to paddleboats and shuffleboard. It was also steps away from Worth Avenue, which was lined with designer boutiques such as Gucci, Armani, Ralph Lauren, and Cartier.

"Of course it's real," Toni replied, giving her wavy blond hair a toss. "I saw it in the window at the Chanel store. I can tell the difference between a genuine Chanel bag and a knockoff and I'm surprised you can't."

Elizabeth shrugged and tucked her short, dark hair behind her ears. "If it's real, it's the only genuine thing about her. Her hair's bleached, and I bet she's had quite a bit of work done." She gazed across the vast, luxuriously appointed lobby—where a round gilt and marble table with an enormous display of pink poinsettias was centered beneath a fabulous crystal chandelier—and through the glass doors, where the sun was shining brightly on a flower bed filled with colorful tropical plants. She shook her head. "I've been in Florida for almost six months and I'm still not used to this weather. Eighty-two degrees and sunny—can you believe it's almost Christmas?"

"Uh, yeah," Toni said, winding a lock of hair around her finger. "They put the poinsettias and amaryllis plants in the lobby weeks ago." She'd lived in Florida her entire life and didn't find the climate the least bit odd, unlike Elizabeth, who had grown up in Tinker's Cove, a small town located on the coast of Maine. "Don't tell me you miss the snow—most people come to Florida to get away from the cold winters up north."

Elizabeth hit a few keys on her computer and went to a

favorite site. "It's twenty-five and snowing in Tinker's Cove," she said. "Looks like we're going to have a white Christmas."

Toni looked over her shoulder at the live-cam image showing a lighthouse with snow swirling all around it and rough surf crashing on the rugged gray rocks below. "I don't get it," she said. "Why do you want to go *there* for Christmas?"

Elizabeth smiled. "It's home. There'll be tree trimming and carol singing. . . ."

"You can do that here."

"It's not the same," Elizabeth said. "You have to go caroling in the snow and have hot chocolate afterward, in front of a roaring fire."

"I'd rather have a chilled martini on a deck overlooking the ocean, watching the sunset."

Elizabeth laughed. "That's nice, too, but Christmas is about family. I miss my mom and dad and my sisters and my brother and especially my little nephew, Patrick. He's almost three now and he's very excited about Santa Claus."

"Well, you've only got to wait a little more than two weeks and you'll be on your way, flying north." She shivered. "Personally, I think you're crazy to take your vacation in December. The hotel's really busy at Christmas and I'm going to be keeping an eye out for Mr. Right."

"Tell me, again, what makes him Mr. Right?" Elizabeth urged.

"Well, he has to be tall, and good-looking, and sweet, really considerate," said Toni, just as a very ugly, very short man came through the revolving door, dressed head to toe in Ralph Lauren resort wear and sporting an enormous gold watch on a very hairy wrist. "But I'll be willing to overlook all that if he's rich," she added, under her breath as she pasted on a smile. "Welcome to the Cavendish, Mr. Moore. It's so nice to see you again."

"It's nice to be back," he replied. "This place feels like home. I don't know how you do it but I know I'm going to find my bags waiting for me in my room, there'll be an extra-firm pillow on my bed with a sugar-free chocolate, and my favorite low-cal beer is going to be in the mini-bar."

"That's our little secret," Toni said. "Is it the same Visa account?"

"No, no." Mr. Moore produced an American Express platinum card. "I've got a new one."

"Very well." Toni was clicking away at her keyboard, adding the new information to the extensive database the Cavendish chain maintained about all its customers. That database, envied throughout the entire hospitality industry, allowed Cavendish employees to provide top notch service personally tailored to every guest, and was the reason why Mr. Moore found that extra-firm pillow, sugar-free chocolate, and light beer waiting for him in his room. "Have a pleasant stay," Toni said, handing him the key card. "Room three-oh-five, overlooking the pool."

"See?" he asked Elizabeth, holding up the key card. "My favorite room. You guys take better care of me than my wife does."

"It's our pleasure," she said. "Just give us a call if there's anything we can do for you."

"Right-o," he said, giving them a little salute with his key card and making his way to the elevator, pausing here and there to admire the blooming orchids and other holiday decorations.

"You know why he likes room three-oh-five, don't you?" Toni asked.

"The view of the pool?" Elizabeth suggested.

"Think again. It's not the pool, it's the women in skimpy swimsuits."

"So Mr. Moore is a bit of a voyeur," said Elizabeth, giggling, just as the hotel manager, Sergei Dimitri, came out of his office, which was located behind the reception desk.

Mr. Dimitri was a neat, middle-aged man with slicked back hair, a small mustache, and a pronounced French accent. Guests adored him, frequently commenting on his warm smile and accommodating nature, but staff members had a somewhat less favorable opinion of him. "Ladies, ladies, how many times must I warn you not to talk about the guests? They pay your salaries, remember that."

"Of course, Mr. Dimitri," Toni said with an innocent expression.

His gaze rested on Elizabeth. "I'm surprised at you, Elizabeth. I don't want to have to place you on probation."

Elizabeth didn't like the sound of that—employees who were on probation could not take vacation time. "Oh, please no, Mr. Dimitri," she said. "I'm terribly sorry."

Mr. Dimitri's eyes were hard, like round black buttons, and his mustache bristled. "You've been warned. Don't let it happen again."

"Oh, it won't," she said. "I promise."

"And don't forget," he told them, "there's a staff meeting this afternoon, when your shift ends."

Elizabeth felt like groaning, but restrained the impulse.

Staff meetings were held off the clock, on employees' own time, and she had been planning to spend the evening digging her cold-weather clothes out of storage, in anticipation of her vacation.

"We'll be there," Toni said. "Never fear."

"Good," Mr. Dimitri said, spying an elderly guest exiting the elevator, looking a bit lost. "Mrs. Fahnstock," he cooed, hurrying toward her. "What can I do for you?"

Mrs. Fahnstock's wrinkled face immediately brightened. "Oh, Mr. Dimitri, how lovely to see you."

"Is something the matter, dear lady?"

"Well, this is so silly of me, but I'm supposed to meet my friend, Doris, and I can't seem to find the Victorian Tea Room. Has it been moved?" she asked, furrowing her brow.

"Never fear, these corridors can be confusing." Mr. Dimitri snapped his fingers. "Elizabeth, please escort Mrs. Fahnstock to the Victorian Tea Room."

Elizabeth hurried across the thickly carpeted space and Mrs. Fahnstock's look of befuddlement was replaced with a serene smile. "You're such a darling to help me," she said.

"It's my pleasure, Mrs. Fahnstock," Elizabeth said, taking her arm. "Now if you'll just come this way I'm sure we'll find your friend waiting for you."

Mr. Dimitri stood watching, a thoughtful expression on his face, as Elizabeth escorted the elderly guest through the spacious lobby, which was dotted with numerous luxuriously appointed seating areas. He noticed with approval the way she matched her pace to the old woman's, and kept up a lively conversation as they proceeded along the paneled and carpeted corridor leading to the tea room.

* * *

The hotel's largest function room, the Bougainvillea Room, was packed with employees when Elizabeth and Toni arrived, and everybody was talking, expressing different expectations about the staff meeting.

"Bonuses . . . holiday bonuses. I'm sure they're going to announce bonuses," Toni said, taking a seat next to Kieran, one of the doormen.

"Don't be daft," Kieran said gloomily. "Layoffs. It's this recession, don't you see? They're going to cut staff. The hotel's got something like five hundred rooms and more than fifteen hundred employees. Do the math."

"Nonsense," said Ada, one of the housekeepers. She was wearing the lavender shirtwaist dress with a white lace collar that all the housekeepers wore. "The rich are doing just fine, there's no recession for them, and that's who comes to this hotel. The one percent."

"If you ask me, occupancy's been down," Kieran insisted. "I know my tips are."

"Maybe it's something about the health insurance plan," Elizabeth said, following her mother Lucy's oft-expressed advice not to panic until you had to.

"There aren't any charts or books," Toni observed, indicating the single podium in the front of the room. "Wouldn't there be stuff like that if it's only a new health plan?"

Elizabeth suspected her friend was right and her heart gave a little jump when Mr. Dimitri appeared and took his place, tapping the microphone. "Attention, attention," he said. "I promise to be brief."

The room quieted as everyone waited to hear what he had to say; a few fingers were crossed, and a few people were holding their breath.

"I see some anxious faces," he began with a laugh. "Well, you can relax. I have good news."

The employees who were holding their breath exhaled, some even chuckled.

"I have the pleasure of announcing that our hotel has been chosen for a great honor—the entire hotel has been booked by Wall Street financier Jonah Gruber for a Christmas extravaganza for six hundred of his closest friends."

Mr. Dimitri nodded, waiting for the employees to absorb this information. While not exactly ecstatic, everyone seemed interested, wondering what the extravaganza meant for them personally. Elizabeth found herself feeling a bit let down since the event would most likely take place during her vacation and she'd miss it. She almost wished she could stay to see all the famous people who would be attending.

"The highlight of this four-day celebration will be a fantastic black-tie dinner dance, the Blingle Bells Ball, at which Mr. Gruber's wife, the lovely cinema star Noelle Jones, will wear the amazing ruby and emerald Imperial Parure. You may remember that Mr. Gruber bought the parure, which was originally created for Empress Marie Louise, at auction for forty-seven million dollars."

Finally, Mr. Dimitri got the reaction he wanted: there was a collective gasp from the assembled employees.

"That's correct, forty-seven million dollars. Needless to say, security will be a top concern. And that is why I would like to turn this meeting over to our security director, Dan Wrayburn."

Wrayburn, who had been standing to the side of the room, came forward. He was a stocky, muscular man in early middle age with a gray brush cut, and he had the easy, bouncing movement of a former boxer but rumor had it he was actually ex-FBI.

"My top concern—and yours, too—is the safety of our guests," Wrayburn began, his eyes moving restlessly over the group. "This event will bring extra challenges, not only because of the presence of the valuable jewels, but also because the guest list will include European royalty, celebrities, politicians, even the First Lady. All of these high-profile people are potential targets for crimes ranging from simple theft to kidnapping. I am asking you all to remain vigilant—you are the first line against criminal activity. You must keep your eyes and ears open and report anything, anything at all, that appears suspicious to you. If you see something, say something."

Everyone nodded in agreement and Wrayburn cracked a grin. "I'll be issuing more specific instructions in the future, so for now I'll turn things back to Mr. Dimitri. But first let me say I have every confidence that together we can make this a safe and secure celebration for our guests."

Elizabeth nudged Toni. "Sounds like you'll have some prime husband-hunting opportunities."

To her surprise, Toni didn't look pleased. "Don't count on it. We're all going to be under a microscope. And believe me, if anything goes wrong—and something will, count on it—we're the ones who will be blamed."

Mr. Dimitri was again tapping the microphone, demanding silence. "Thank you, Mr. Wrayburn. I know I can count on you all to cooperate with Mr. Wrayburn's plans for security. And now, just one more thing before you go. . . ."

There was suddenly an air of tension in the room; they

all knew Mr. Dimitri's habit of delivering bad news just before he ended a meeting.

"All vacations scheduled for the rest of the month are canceled—we need all hands on deck to prepare for this special event."

It hit Elizabeth like a hammer. No vacation! No white Christmas! No little Patrick, squealing with delight at the presents under the tree.

"Too bad," Toni said, sympathizing.

"Yeah," Elizabeth said, remembering another favorite expression of her mother's: be careful what you wish for. For a moment, only a moment, she'd wished she wouldn't be missing seeing all the famous people—and now she'd gotten that wish.

"Cheer up," Toni urged. "We'll have fun. You'll see."

"I guess it could be worse," Elizabeth grumbled, joining the crowd of employees flowing through the doors. Absorbed in disappointment, she didn't notice Mr. Dimitri until he tapped her on the arm.

"A word, please, Elizabeth."

Her eyes met Toni's in a shared look of dismay, then she followed Mr. Dimitri to his office, certain she was about to be fired, or at the very least, placed on probation. Things weren't going her way today, that was for sure. She never should have made that remark about Mr. Moore.

"Sit down, Elizabeth," he urged, shutting the door after they stepped into the room and seating himself behind his desk.

Elizabeth obeyed, bracing herself for the bad news. No matter what happened, she vowed, she wasn't going to cry. And if she got fired, well, she'd be able to go home for Christmas.

"You've been noticed," he said, smiling.

What a sadist, Elizabeth thought. He was actually enjoying this.

"Your excellent work has been noticed."

Elizabeth sat up straighter. What the heck was going on?

"You may have noticed that our assistant concierge, Annemarie, has been on sick leave. She called today and told me she has Epstein-Barr and won't be able to return for at least four weeks."

"My sister had that once," Elizabeth said. "That's too bad."

"Indeed," Mr. Dimitri said. "And Annemarie's absence at this busy time of year poses a problem for us. I've discussed the matter with the head concierge, Mr. Kronenberg, and he agrees with me that you should take her place."

This wasn't what she'd been expecting and Elizabeth struggled to process this new information. For a moment she pictured herself sitting at Annemarie's curvy little French desk in an alcove off the lobby, impressing guests with her knowledge and expertise. Or not, she thought, assailed by doubt. Did she really have the skills and experience the job required? She was still learning to find her way around Palm Beach. But, she realized, brightening, this might be a genuine opportunity. And Mr. Dimitri wouldn't have suggested it if he didn't have confidence in her abilities.

Finally, she spoke. "I'm very flattered," she said. "I'll do my best."

"Good," he said. "You can start tomorrow."

* * *

Elizabeth was seated at Annemarie's desk the next morning, waiting impatiently for Toni's arrival. She couldn't wait to see her friend's reaction, and Toni didn't disappoint when she took her place at the reception desk. Her eyes rounded in astonishment when she spotted Elizabeth and she hurried right over.

"What's this?" she asked. "Did you get a promotion?"

Elizabeth shrugged. "It's temporary. Annemarie's got Epstein-Barr."

"Lucky you."

"We'll see. I feel like a fake. I don't really know what I'm doing."

Toni grinned. "Just pretend," she said in parting, dashing back to her post when she spotted the head concierge, Walter Kronenberg, stepping out of the elevator and heading in Elizabeth's direction. He was a tall man with gray hair brushed straight back; from his stiff, formal manner Elizabeth suspected he might be a retired military officer.

She stood up to greet him, and said, "I'm very honored to take Annemarie's place. I know it's a challenging job but I'm a fast learner and a hard worker."

"Very well, Elizabeth," he said. "Now we must get to work. You have a lot to learn, and we're under pressure with the Gruber event in just two weeks." He sat down in her chair, indicating she should take one of the chairs provided for guests and sit beside him. "First of all, you need the computer password."

Elizabeth knew that concierges had a higher level of access to the Cavendish data bank and was interested to see what information was now available to her.

"I must warn you, all of this information is highly confidential. We don't want to be reading in the *National En-*

quirer that one of our guests has a passion for cashew nuts."

Elizabeth was tempted to giggle but stifled the impulse; she didn't think Mr. Kronenberg was joking. "Of course not," she said with a serious nod, watching as he wrote the password on a slip of paper.

"Got it?" he asked, and when she nodded, he tore the paper into tiny bits, which he pocketed.

Elizabeth had a strange sense of dislocation. Was she being trained as an assistant concierge in a posh hotel or was she being briefed for a mission to defend national security?

"Now, Elizabeth," Mr. Kronenberg continued, "on occasion one of our guests will require access to the hotel safe when neither I nor Mr. Dimitri will be available. In that case, you will need the combination."

Elizabeth swallowed hard. This was quite a bit more responsibility than she expected and she remembered Toni's warning that if something went wrong, the staff would be blamed. "Right," she said.

"The combination is in this box," he continued, producing a small gray metal cash box from a side drawer. "The key to this box is kept with the paper clips."

Elizabeth opened the shallow central drawer and found the compartment filled with paper clips and dug through them, producing a small, silver key.

"Remember," he said, "it is most unlikely that both Mr. Dimitri and I would be unavailable but it does occasionally happen and we don't want our guests to be inconvenienced."

"I understand," Elizabeth said.

"You must tell no one about the combination," he warned in a most serious tone.

"Of course not."

"But I think you will enjoy this job," he said, standing up. "You'll find our guests are most delightful and you'll see that it's a pleasure to help them. Sometimes their requests are challenging, but there's great satisfaction in coming up with the perfect solution." A quick smile flickered across his lips, then he wished her good luck and left Elizabeth on her own.

She had a busy morning, arranging horseback riding for one guest, making dinner reservations for several others, and changing an airplane flight for Mrs. Fahnstock, who had decided to stay a few more days. Around eleven she caught a breather, but when she glanced across the lobby at the reception desk and gave Toni a little wave, she only got an odd little smirk in response. She was about to go over and ask what the problem was when another guest approached her desk.

"I'm sorry to bother you," said a tall, good-looking guy in his early thirties, removing his Ray-Bans to reveal bright blue eyes. He was dressed casually in a polo shirt and khaki shorts with Teva sandals on his bare feet.

"Not a problem," Elizabeth said, taking in his tousled, sun-bleached hair, broad shoulders, and lean torso and finding him terribly attractive. "I'm here to help."

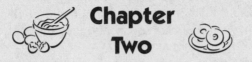

Chapter Two

"Who was the good-looking guy?" Toni asked, seating herself beside Elizabeth at the scuffed Formica-topped table in the employees' break room. The two always had lunch together, usually eating bag lunches they brought from home.

"I don't know," Elizabeth said, prying the lid off a plastic container of salad. "He wanted to know where he could get a flat bike tire fixed and I sent him to the sports center."

Toni's eyebrows shot up. "You should have got his name so you could Google him."

Elizabeth speared a cherry tomato. "He just had a simple question and I was on the phone with Delta, trying to get them to drop the change fee for Mrs. Fahnstock."

"I would have dropped Delta and called back later. He wasn't wearing a wedding ring, you know."

"How do you know that?" Elizabeth asked. "What have you got, X-ray vision or something?"

"I make a point of checking," Toni replied, licking the last of the yogurt off her spoon. "It saves a lot of trouble later."

"Rings can be removed, you know," Elizabeth said. "They're not permanently attached."

"I know," Toni admitted in a rueful tone, taking a sip of Diet Coke. "Maybe men should be required to get tattoos on their ring fingers when they get married. So tell me, did Dimitri give you access to the supersecret database?"

As all Cavendish employees knew, there were various levels of access to the company's famous database. Desk clerks were among those with the lowest access, mainly to credit card account numbers and personal preferences; concierges inevitably accumulated more data as they maintained records of guest requests; and executives like Mr. Dimitri had the highest level of information, which according to rumor was more complete than data collected by the FBI and CIA. All employees, whatever their level, were required to sign strict confidentiality agreements and anyone caught sharing information was subject to immediate dismissal.

Elizabeth remembered Mr. Kronenberg's warning and shrugged. "So far I haven't seen anything that would interest the *National Enquirer*, if that's what you want to know."

Toni ran her finger around the top of the Coke can. "I was thinking that maybe you could tip me off about rich male guests, say whether they're married or not."

"And their credit limits?" Elizabeth teased.

"Well, yeah, that would be good, too."

Elizabeth wasn't exactly surprised at Toni's request, but she was a little hurt that Toni would ask her to put her job in jeopardy. "No way. I'm not taking any chances. This temporary job could be a big break for me." She paused. "I've already been scolded by Mr. Dimitri for failing to address a guest by name. Apparently the concierge gets an IM alert when a guest checks in, but if I miss it for some reason I'm supposed to politely ask them to introduce themselves. It's a bit awkward—I'm not comfortable doing it."

Toni shrugged. "The guests love hearing their names. It makes them feel like they're the lords of the manor and we're their servants or something."

Elizabeth stood up. "Yeah, well, back in Tinker's Cove, where I come from, people treat everybody the same. It doesn't matter if they're millionaires or garbage collectors."

"Maybe that's fine for you," Toni said, "but personally I'd much rather marry a millionaire than a garbage man."

"I guess I would, too," Elizabeth admitted, laughing.

Elizabeth was ordering a same-day flower delivery for a guest who had forgotten his mother's birthday when the good-looking biker reappeared.

"Hi," he said, grinning and revealing a prominent set of very large, very white teeth.

Elizabeth held up a finger, indicating she was on the phone, and he seated himself in one of the chairs provided for guests. She took the opportunity of looking him over while she completed negotiating the flower order, noting his tanned face and arms, his long, muscular legs, the chunky gold watch on his wrist. Toni was right—there was no wedding ring. Finally ending the call, she smiled and asked, "What can I do for you?"

"I just wanted to thank you for helping me out earlier. They fixed the bike for me at the sports center, no questions asked."

Elizabeth, who had gone to college in Boston, thought she detected a hint of a Boston accent, which she liked. "Guests come first at Cavendish," she said, repeating the company motto in a teasing voice.

"I guess I better fess up," he said. "I'm not actually a guest. I was just biking by when the tire went flat." He bit his lip. "My name's Chris Kennedy, by the way."

"Elizabeth Stone."

"I know," he said, indicating her name tag.

Elizabeth blushed. "Well, maybe you'll be a guest in the future."

"I'd like that. But in the meantime, I was hoping you'd go out to dinner with me. How about tonight?"

The request caught Elizabeth off guard. "Oh!" she exclaimed. "I guess that would be okay."

"Don't sound so enthusiastic," he said sarcastically.

Again, Elizabeth blushed. "It's just . . ."

"I know," he said. "I had you at a disadvantage. So, shall I pick you up here?"

Elizabeth thought of the ratty old shorts and T-shirt she'd worn to work that morning before changing into her uniform in the hotel locker room. It was hardly the outfit she wanted to wear on a first date. "No, I'd like to go home and change out of this uniform," she said.

He tilted his head. "I think it's kind of cute."

Rolling her eyes, she wrote her address and phone number on a slip of paper. "What time?" she asked, giving it to him.

"Seven?"

"See you then."

Chris had no sooner left than Toni dashed across the lobby. "So what was that all about?" she asked.

"He asked me out to dinner."

"That was fast," Toni said. "Who is he?"

"His name's Chris Kennedy."

"Kennedy! He's probably one of *those* Kennedys. They have a place here in Palm Beach, you know."

"He does have a Boston accent," Elizabeth said.

"And those teeth. Those are definitely Kennedy teeth."

Elizabeth was doubtful. "You think?"

"Absolutely. And no wedding ring. That makes him husband material—with money. That's the best kind."

"We'll see," Elizabeth said, not nearly as convinced as her friend. Chris Kennedy was good-looking and she certainly found him attractive, but she didn't really know anything about him. She'd been raised to be cautious in matters of the heart and she wanted to know what kind of person he was before she got too involved.

When her doorbell rang precisely at seven, Elizabeth was ready, dressed in a pastel tunic, a pair of skinny white jeans, and her prized Jack Rogers sandals. She'd figured Chris was a casual sort of guy and didn't want to be too dressed up. She'd used a light hand with her makeup, too, applying only mascara and a slick of lip gloss. When she hurried out of her apartment and down the stairs, meeting him at the door to the apartment block, she was glad she'd worn pants because he had arrived on a motorcycle.

"I hope the bike's okay," he said. "I have a spare helmet."

"Fine with me," Elizabeth said, eager for a bit of an adventure.

"Great," he said, giving her the helmet. "I'll take good care of you."

"You better, 'cause my dad will come roaring into town from Maine and track you down and wring your neck if anything bad happens to me." Setting the helmet on her head, she discovered the straps were too long.

"I can fix that," he said, bending down to adjust them. Feeling his warm hands at her neck and scenting his minty fresh breath, she wondered what it would be like to kiss him. "There," he said, straightening up. "Even your dad would approve."

"I'm not sure of that," she said, climbing on the seat and wrapping her arms around his waist. He was every bit as lean as he looked, she discovered, feeling the firm muscles beneath his polo shirt.

He laughed. "I wouldn't blame him, but I'm really the kind of guy even an overprotective dad can't object to," he said as they rolled off down the driveway.

It was a warm evening and dusk was lingering as they rode over the bridge and along Ocean Boulevard, where moored boats bobbed in the peaceful navy blue water. Some had strings of twinkling lights, a few even had Christmas trees fixed to their masts, and Elizabeth thought of the annual arrival of Santa by boat back home in Tinker's Cove. She had a brief moment of homesickness but Chris took a curve a little bit fast and she tightened her grip around his waist and discovered she was definitely enjoying the present moment, and this ride with this exciting guy.

He pulled up at a tiki bar by the beach, where tables with shaggy grass umbrellas were set up on the sand, and they ordered captain's plates and cold beer. The night air was warm and silky when they seated themselves at one of the tables, waiting for their number to be called. Flaming tiki torches illuminated their faces and Elizabeth thought she was a very long way from home.

"So your family is in Maine?" he asked, taking that first sip of beer.

"Yup," Elizabeth said, meeting his blue eyes. "I grew up in Tinker's Cove, a little town on the coast. My mom's a reporter for a local newspaper and my dad's a restoration carpenter. I went to Chamberlain College in Boston, and this is my first real job, though I worked summers back home." She licked a bit of foam off her lip. "What about you? You sound like you come from Boston."

"Guilty," he said, grinning. "I was supposed to go to Harvard—that's what the family wanted—but I love sailing and biking and I chose the University of Florida instead. I went on to law school and now I'm working with a, uh, conservation trust."

"That must be interesting," Elizabeth said, impressed. "And it's a meaningful job that makes a difference, that makes the world a better place."

He raised his shoulders. "I don't know about that, but it does pay the rent. What about you? Do you like your job at the Cavendish?"

"I guess it's okay," she replied, "but I don't think I want to do it for the rest of my life. I sort of fell into it because I had a little experience. I worked summers at an inn back home." The sun was long gone and they were enclosed in a flickering circle of light from the tiki torches. Elizabeth slipped off her sandals and curled her toes, feeling the cool sand beneath her feet. "Don't you miss winter?" she asked. "I just can't get used to the idea of Christmas without snow. Instead of balsam wreaths they've got pink and white poinsettias in the hotel—it seems so wrong. I don't mind poinsettias but they ought to be red."

Chris shrugged. "I guess you get used to it. It's Christmas everywhere, after all. When I was a kid I had this book: *Christmas Around the World*. Eskimos sitting around Christmas trees in their igloos and African kids opening presents in grass huts and Japanese kids hanging up stockings in their pagodas."

"I'm not sure that book was culturally correct," Elizabeth said skeptically.

"Now that you mention it," he said, laughing, "I don't think it was." Hearing their number called, Chris got up and returned with a tray loaded with fried fish, French fries, and coleslaw.

"That's enough food for an army," Elizabeth said, taking her plate.

"Eat up," he said. "You'll need some insulation when you go back north for Christmas. You are going, aren't you?"

"No," Elizabeth said, biting into a fry. "All December vacations are canceled for this big party Jonah Gruber is giving. He's some rich Wall Street guy who's booked the entire hotel for four days. Lots of VIPs are coming and everybody's going to have to work extra hours." She popped the rest of the fry into her mouth. "I was really looking forward to seeing my little nephew, Patrick."

"That's too bad," Chris said. "Christmas is all about family. We have this tradition—we all go skiing in New Hampshire. My dad, Joe, he's a great skier, and my cousin, Robbie, he's a fiend on the slopes."

Elizabeth noticed little stars in the sky; the water was a smooth black surface reflecting the lights on the moored boats. Joe and Robbie, she thought, those were names she'd heard in connection with *the* Kennedy family. Joe Kennedy ran a program that provided heating oil to low income people in Massachusetts and Robbie was a nickname for Robert, JFK's brother who was also assassinated. Cousin Robbie might be his son or grandson. Should she come right out and ask him? Would that be pushy? Rude? Too personal for a first date?

"Penny for your thoughts," Chris said.

"Oh, sorry." Elizabeth decided that she certainly didn't want to seem like a celebrity hound or, worse, a gold digger. "I was just looking at the stars. Isn't the sky beautiful tonight?"

"Sure is," he answered, but he wasn't looking at the sky. He was gazing at Elizabeth.

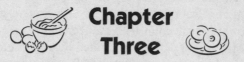

Chapter
Three

The next morning Elizabeth was still basking in the afterglow of her date with Chris. She'd never been one of those girls like Toni who made up a checklist for the perfect mate, but if she had, Chris would have a check in every box. He was tall and good-looking. He had a good job as a lawyer working in the public interest. Family was important to him. And he'd been a terrific date, fun to be with and considerate. When they'd finally ended the evening, standing in front of her door, he'd given her a long, lingering kiss that made her wish for more. But he didn't press her. He said he wanted to see her again and then he was gone.

Toni, of course, couldn't wait to dissect the date. "So how was it?" she demanded, encountering Elizabeth in the locker room, where she was putting on her Cavendish blazer. "Did you go all the way?"

Elizabeth was shocked. "Not on a first date! Besides, he was a perfect gentleman."

Toni narrowed her eyes. "Maybe he wasn't that into you."

"He sure seemed interested. We had a great time and he said he wanted to see me again."

"They always say that," Toni warned. "I bet you'll never hear from him again."

That idea bothered Elizabeth more than she cared to let on. "Well, my mother always says never run after a man because they're like streetcars—another one always comes along."

"Well, if that's the way you feel, I guess it's okay then. Too bad you didn't have that spark, that chemistry."

"Yeah," Elizabeth said, thinking their chemistry had been just fine. Every time she thought about Chris, which was pretty much all the time, she felt the stirrings of desire. And once seated at her concierge desk, she found her heart jumped every time the phone rang, in hope that he was calling. He didn't call, however, and she was kept busy by the guests and their endless demands. Busy as she was, she couldn't forget Toni's prophecy that he wasn't that into her, which squatted like some evil toad in the back of her mind.

Then, when he finally did call, she didn't have time to talk. She'd been conscripted to assist Layla Fine, the professional party planner Jonah Gruber had hired to organize the festive gala. Mr. Kronenberg had minced no words when he gave her the assignment. "You'll find she has a rather forceful personality," he said with a sigh. "Just do whatever she wants and we'll add it to Mr. Gruber's account."

Elizabeth nodded, thinking the bill for the four-day gala was going to be astronomical. Gruber probably wasn't paying the rack rate, which began at over five hundred dollars for a room in season and went up to over five thousand for the top-floor suites; she was sure he'd negotiated a sizable discount. Even so, this was a big deal for the hotel and now, suddenly, she was responsible for making it all go smoothly.

"I just know we're going to get along like a house afire," Layla told her, plunking her tiny little bottom in one of the gilt chairs next to Elizabeth's desk. Up close, Elizabeth could see that Layla wasn't quite as young as she first appeared; long lines ran from her nose to either side of her mouth, and the skin around her eyes was crepey. Nevertheless, she was a bundle of energy and gave a youthful impression, tossing her long blond hair extensions this way and that and dashing about on impossibly high, needle-thin stiletto heels. "So, first let's see what the hotel can offer in the way of activities. These folks are going to be here for four days and we need to provide lots of fun things for them to do."

"We offer lots of options for our guests," Elizabeth said, trying to put Chris out of her mind so she could concentrate on the task at hand. "There's a fitness center, of course, and we're right on the beach. There's boating, golf, tennis, all right here. And I can arrange for horseback riding, helicopter rides, pretty much anything anyone wants."

Layla was shaking her head. "That's all well and good, but these are very special people, the crème de la crème, and they will want unique entertainments, things that ordinary people can't do."

Elizabeth was stumped, painfully aware that she was

an ordinary person and didn't have a clue what the extra-ordinary people did. "What do you have in mind?"

"Well, say a special performance at a theater, or perhaps a private showing in an art museum, things like that. Danny Simpson, the tennis star, is one of the guests. Maybe we could have an exhibition match with Sharapova. That would be fun, wouldn't it? Boy versus girl?"

Elizabeth had a sinking feeling; she knew she was out of her depth here. "I'll do my best," she began.

"Oh, don't worry—I'll help. I'll give you names and numbers. We'll plan four days that they'll never forget." Layla turned her head, giving her wavy extensions yet another toss, and studied the holiday decorations in the lobby, which Elizabeth considered a tasteful assortment of seasonal flowering plants and wreaths, with a few twinkly lights here and there. "You know, these decorations are rather restrained, wouldn't you say?"

"That's intentional," Elizabeth said. "We cater to a wide variety of guests here—Jewish people and Muslims and quite a few Asians and Indians—and they don't celebrate Christmas. It's supposed to be seasonal, not particularly Christmas."

"Well, we'll have to change that," Layla declared. "We need a lot more sparkle, a lot more bling. It's the Blingle Bells Ball!"

When Layla finally left, leaving Elizabeth with several single-spaced pages listing all the things she wanted her to do, Elizabeth tried to return Chris's call. She dialed his cell but only got voice mail, so she left a quick message saying she was sorry they hadn't had time to talk but she'd been busy at work. She half expected him to return her call immediately; she'd called his cell phone, after all, and knew he always carried it. When he didn't call back, she reluctantly concluded it was because he'd decided to ignore her call and blow her off, just like Toni had predicted. She found that thought terribly depressing and threw herself into her work.

It wasn't until she was headed home in her used Corolla, three hours later than usual due to the extra work for the Gruber party, that her cell phone finally rang.

"Hi!" he said, "I missed you. Want to go for a beer or something?"

Elizabeth's heart leaped—he missed her! But she was dead tired. Layla had run her off her feet, trimming dozens of fake white Christmas trees, making calls, packing elaborate gift baskets for Gruber's guests, and fending off reporters who'd gotten wind of the exclusive gala and wanted information. And then there'd been a stressful one-on-one session with Dan Wrayburn, the security director, who had warned her about data breaches and computer viruses and worms. "A beer would be great," she finally said, deciding she didn't want to put him off and risk the chance of letting his ardor cool.

"Great," he said. "Do you want to meet me somewhere? Say Charley's Crab?"

Elizabeth agreed, thinking she was glad she'd worn her Lilly dress to work that morning, instead of her usual workout clothes, just in case Chris called.

He was waiting for her in front of the casually elegant restaurant, dressed in khakis and a pale blue polo shirt, with boat shoes and no socks. She smiled, aware that she was a sucker for the preppy look.

"What are you smiling about?" he asked, when they were seated at a table in a cozy corner of the bar.

"I'm just giddy with relief," she said. "I've been dealing with this awful woman all day. She's the party planner Gruber hired to organize this shindig and she's a piece of work."

"Well, now you can relax," he said. "What will you have?"

"A glass of chardonnay," she said.

He nodded at the waitress and ordered the wine for her and a Sam Adams for himself. "You can take the boy out of Boston but you can't take the Boston out of the boy," he quipped.

"My dad loves their Winter Lager," Elizabeth said. "But you hardly need that down here."

"Sometimes the nights get chilly," he said, with a mischievous grin.

Elizabeth didn't quite know how to take this, so she decided to make a joke. "I know—that's why I wear flannel to bed, even here in Florida."

"I hope you're teasing me," he said, when their drinks arrived. He raised his beer and tapped her glass. "Here's to Yankee girls, or one very special Yankee girl."

Elizabeth laughed. "I don't comb my hair with codfish bones," she said, referring to the silly rhyme she'd learned as a child.

"I like short hair on girls," he said, reaching across the table and smoothing a lock of her hair. "You don't get all tangled up in it."

She took a swallow of wine. "I've got to get an early start tomorrow. I've got a seven o'clock meeting with the security director."

"What does he want with you?" Chris asked, in a casual tone.

"I don't know." Elizabeth shook her head. "Something about the jewels, I think. You know, the whole point of this party is for Gruber to show off these jewels he

bought for his wife for millions of dollars. The hotel
doesn't want responsibility for them until the last minute,
but Layla, the party planner, told me that they've got to
come sooner because of some photo shoot for *Town &
Country* magazine." She paused, thinking perhaps she
was saying too much, and changed the subject from the
jewels. "The photographer is only available on one day.
His name is Sammie Wong. I never heard of him but
Layla says he's famous."

"I've heard of Sammie Wong. He had a show here at
Four Arts," said Chris. "It will be interesting to see what
he does with the jewels. When are they supposed to arrive?"

Elizabeth was tired and the wine wasn't helping. "I
don't know, I guess I'll find out tomorrow," she said, sti-
fling a yawn.

"You're beat," he said, laughing. "What do you say we
call it a night? I've got to catch an early flight to Seattle for
a conference tomorrow. But save Saturday night for me?"

"Okay." Elizabeth kept her voice cool so as not to reveal her fluttering heart. "It's a date."

But when Saturday finally rolled around, Layla insisted she needed Elizabeth to finalize the seating plan for
the Blingle Bells Ball and she had to cancel her date.
"I'm so sorry," she told Chris, breaking the bad news on
the phone, "but I have to work tonight."

"You're working an awful lot," Chris grumbled.

"Tell me about it. It's temporary, just until this Gruber
event is over."

"So what all do you have to do? Fluff the pillows in
the Presidential Suite?"

"No, housekeeping does that. It's mostly helping the party planner. She had me trimming awful fake white Christmas trees for days, and wrapping gift baskets and making plans for special events including a celebrity tennis match and a golf tournament and studio visits with artists. You know, I thought I knew how the other half lives, but this isn't the other half, it's the one percent!"

"You must be getting some time off," Chris said. "What about tomorrow? It's Sunday."

"Actually, I am off tomorrow, but I've got to clean house and do laundry and buy some groceries. I've been working ten and eleven hours a day."

"Okay, we'll grocery shop," Chris said. "It'll be fun. Let's say I'll pick you up at one, we'll get a late brunch, and afterward we'll go to Publix, and then I'll cook dinner for you."

Elizabeth couldn't stop smiling; this guy was too good to be true. "See you tomorrow," she said.

Later that afternoon Elizabeth was surprised when Chris paid her a visit at work. She was at her desk, arranging for limousines to pick up guests at the airport, when she looked up and saw Chris standing there.

"I couldn't wait until tomorrow," he said. "How's it going?"

"Crazy, crazy. I know it's hard to believe, but there's a terrible shortage of limousines in Palm Beach."

"I could offer my services," he said with a grin.

"I don't think a motorcycle will cut it, not with these folks."

He seated himself, propping one ankle on the other knee. "So when is this party starting?"

"The guests are arriving on the sixteenth—that's next

Friday—but Jonah and Noelle are coming earlier, to get ready." She sighed. "And then there's those darn jewels."

"Oh, yeah?" Chris's voice was studiedly casual. "What's that got to do with you?" he asked, gazing into her eyes.

"Well, I've got to schedule the delivery and make sure hotel security has the details," Elizabeth said, thinking perhaps she was saying too much. "This thing is turning into a nightmare."

Chris looked concerned. "What do you mean? Problems with Brinks?"

Elizabeth decided she wasn't going to say anything more about the jewels. "It's just all so over the top. Layla—she's the party planner—well, the way she acts you'd think this was life and death and it's really just a rich guy showing off. There are people who are really in terrible situations—dreadful flooding in Indonesia and in Africa they're starving and getting raped and killed by rogue militias. But Layla seems to think the world will end if the vichyssoise isn't chilled correctly or the roses are the wrong color."

Chris looked amused. "So you're a closet revolutionary?"

Elizabeth gave him a crooked grin. "This thing is turning me into one, that's for sure."

"A revolutionary with access to all that supersecret, confidential information about the masters of the universe. You could be dangerous."

Remembering Wrayburn's warnings, Elizabeth grew wary. What did Chris know about the database? And why was he even mentioning it? "Oh, I'm far too insignificant to see much of anything except whether the guests prefer plain or sparkling mineral water."

Chris laughed. "Well, I guess I better let you get back to work." He stood up, then leaned down and whispered in her ear, "See you tomorrow."

His warm lips brushed her ear and she wished for a moment that she could lean against him, like she had on the motorcycle, feeling his body against hers. Then she remembered where she was and gave him a businesslike smile. "See you then," she said.

The moment he was gone, Toni dashed across the lobby. "What was that all about?" she demanded.

"He just stopped by to say hi," Elizabeth said. She knew she was blushing and it was making her furious; she didn't want Toni to know how much she liked Chris.

"He's awfully cute," Toni said, "but I don't think he's really a member of the Kennedy clan. Did you hear about that guy in Boston who was pretending to be a Rockefeller?"

"I did," Elizabeth said. It was all over the news, you really couldn't miss it. But Chris wasn't like that, at least she didn't think he was. For one thing, he'd never actually said he was a member of the Kennedy clan.

"The funny thing is, that guy never claimed to be a rich Rockefeller. He just sort of let people assume it," Toni continued, as if reading her mind.

"Well, I don't care if he's JFK's great-nephew or not," Elizabeth said. "I'm just getting to know him."

"I'm only saying this 'cause I think he might be as fake as that Rolex he wears."

"It's fake? How can you tell?"

"I can tell," Toni said. "And those polo shirts he wears—they're from Target."

"So he's careful with his money. That's not a crime,"

Elizabeth insisted. But as she said the words, she remembered how uncomfortable she'd felt when Chris mentioned the database. Maybe Toni was on to something and he didn't really like her but was only trying to use her for some purpose of his own.

"I just think you'd better be careful, that's all," Toni said, hurrying back to the reception desk.

Elizabeth went back to her list of limo companies but her thoughts were miles away. Toni had upset her and she figured that was her intention. She was probably just jealous because Elizabeth had a boyfriend. Or did she? They'd only had two dates, actually one and a half, and here she was falling head over heels, struggling to keep her mind on her work when all she wanted to think about was that kiss. That one kiss.

She was being ridiculous, she told herself. It was never good to let a guy know you really liked him. If she kept this up she'd scare him off. It was better to play hard to get, that's what everybody said. She decided she was simply going to put Chris Kennedy completely out of her mind. She'd throw herself into her work and wouldn't give him a single thought until one o'clock tomorrow.

But when Sunday dawned, she was in a state of high anticipation. She quickly tidied her little apartment, showered and dried her hair, and finally confronted the problem of what to wear. Shorts and a tank top? Would that be too revealing? What about a skirt? No good on a motorcycle! Jeans again? Then the phone rang and she learned she didn't have to decide what to wear after all.

"I'm really sorry," he said. "Something's come up and I have to go out of town."

Elizabeth's heart fell to the floor and landed with a thud. "Oh," was all she could say.

"I was really looking forward to being with you," he said.

"It's too bad," she said, determined not to let him know how disappointed she was. "But I really have a lot to do anyway."

"I'll call you when I get back, okay?"

"If you want," she said, trying to sound as if it didn't matter to her whether he called or not.

"Oh, I want," he said, in a thick voice.

"Have a good trip," she said, hanging up and grabbing a handful of tissues as the tears started to flow. Finally wiping her eyes, she decided she didn't know what was worse: Chris calling off their date or having to admit it to Toni on Monday morning.

As she expected, Toni couldn't wait to ask if she'd had a good time on her date with Chris when they met in the locker room.

Elizabeth opened her locker, took out her makeup bag, and concentrated on applying a fresh coat of lip gloss. "Never happened," she said with a shrug, waving the little wand.

"Why not? What happened?"

Elizabeth pressed her lips together, then examined the effect in the mirror on her locker door. "He had a business trip."

"Or he met somebody else," Toni said.

"Or he met somebody else," Elizabeth repeated with a shrug. Honestly, she thought, she ought to get an Academy Award for acting.

Toni's eyebrows rose in astonishment. "Aren't you upset?"

"It was just a couple of dates," Elizabeth said. "And frankly, I'm too busy to worry about it. You know, the jewels are coming today. It's going to be a madhouse around here."

The arrival of the Imperial Parure was supposed to be a highly guarded secret. Jonah Gruber had outbid an Arab sheik and a Japanese industrialist for the set, which included an emerald and ruby necklace with a removable pendant featuring the twenty-three-carat Star of Bethlehem diamond that could also be worn as a brooch, plus a tiara, two bracelets, and a ring. His winning bid was many millions above the presale estimate and security was naturally a top concern. Mr. Dimitri had stressed that fact at a special staff meeting, and Dan Wrayburn had bombarded employees with memos threatening immediate dismissal to anyone who leaked information about the jewels. Nevertheless, Elizabeth noticed a handful of reporters and photographers gathering outside the hotel doors shortly before the armored truck was due to arrive.

"How did they find out?" she asked Layla, who was on hand for the delivery.

"Probably Gruber tipped them off himself," she replied.

"Why would he do that?"

"He paid a lot for those baubles and he wants to get his money's worth in publicity. He's got a deal with *Town and Country* magazine; Sammie Wong's going to photograph Noelle wearing the jewels. She's actually here and I need you to help out."

This was news to Elizabeth. "She's here? Now?" Elizabeth asked.

"Yup. We took advantage of the jewelry delivery to sneak her in through the hotel garage. She's waiting up in the Royal Suite, but that's top secret. Don't you breathe a word of it to that crowd out there."

"I wouldn't," Elizabeth said.

"Good." Layla handed her a sheaf of papers. "This is a press release. You can distribute it once the jewels are secured. Then I want you to meet me upstairs in the Royal Suite."

The moment the elevator doors closed behind Layla the armored truck rolled up and the media gang went into action, snapping photos and yelling questions to the guards as they unloaded the metal-clad case containing the jewels. Extra doormen, actually security guards dressed as doormen, blocked access to the lobby, and Dan Wrayburn escorted the armored truck guards to Mr. Dimitri's office, where the hotel safe was located. Once she was sure the recently reinforced office door was tightly closed and the jewels safe inside, Elizabeth stepped through the entrance, distributing the press releases to the crowd of reporters who were clamoring for information outside. They still peppered her with questions: "Did you see the jewels? Are they really worth forty-seven million? Is the hotel worried about jewel thieves?"

"It's all in the press release," she said, ducking back inside and leaving the doormen to handle the crowd. Then she was hurrying upstairs to the Royal Suite, her special knowledge bubbling inside her. She was one of the few who knew that Noelle Jones was actually in the hotel; she was going to see, and perhaps even handle, the incredibly valuable Imperial Parure. If only the folks back home in Tinker's Cove, Maine, could see her now!

When Layla answered her knock and opened the door, Elizabeth had to restrain herself from exclaiming "Wow!" The hotel's four best suites, the Imperial, the Royal, the

Majestic, and the Presidential, never failed to impress. Over fifteen hundred square feet apiece, they were bigger than her apartment, and included luxurious bedrooms, a living room complete with wet bar, a dining area, and numerous balconies with ocean views. The decor was elegant and restrained, so as not to compete with the fabulous views.

But even more breathtaking than the view, was the Imperial Parure, which had arrived ahead of her and was displayed in its case on a white lacquered coffee table. Elizabeth couldn't take her eyes off the rubies and emeralds. There must have been hundreds all told. And the huge diamond glittered so brightly in the sunlight that poured through the windows.

Sammie Wong was beside himself with excitement. "This is going to be great," he said, and Elizabeth could almost see the wheels turning in that shaved head, behind those bright, black eyes, imagining the photo possibilities. He was a tiny man, dressed in a black turtleneck and loose pants, bouncing around on bright aqua spring-loaded athletic shoes. "I think we should have the jewels in incongruous settings. . . ."

"Like the bathtub?" Noelle suggested. She was a stunning woman, with a curvy body, luscious red lips, and long black hair that tumbled halfway down her back. She was dressed in a white knit dress that clung to her figure and had discarded a fabulous white fur coat, which lay in a luxurious heap on the carpeted floor.

"We'll see," Sammie said, picking up the emerald and ruby tiara and holding it up to admire it. Then he set it gently on Noelle's head.

"Ohmigod!" she exclaimed. "This thing weighs a ton!"

"Bear up, dearie," Sammie said, disregarding her complaint and hanging the enormous necklace around her neck. The huge Star of Bethlehem diamond nestled just above her breasts, its facets catching the light and splashing the walls and ceiling with patches of shimmering color.

"Look! It's a rainbow!" Sammie exclaimed, pointing at the scraps of vibrant color that danced with Noelle's slightest movements. Then he slipped the ring with its huge emerald on her finger, and wrapped each wrist in a band of alternating rubies and emeralds. Noelle stood perfectly still in front of the pale green silk draperies that screened the room's French doors, and Elizabeth thought she looked like one of those bejeweled royals in an Elizabethan painting. All she was lacking was a lace ruff and a long skirt.

Sammie was already snapping photos, but this was only the beginning. Lugging bags of clothing and props, Elizabeth followed the photographer and his subject through the hotel as Noelle was photographed in the jewels and a swimsuit at the hotel pool, in the jewels and a Chanel suit at a table in the hotel restaurant, in the jewels and an evening gown in the ballroom.

Finally they returned to the Royal Suite, where Noelle started stripping off the jewels and tossing them on the bed. "Whew," she said, "those suckers are heavy, and that necklace poked into my skin. Look!" Pointing with a manicured finger, she indicated a slight, whitened dent on her tanned chest, where the Star of Bethlehem had been.

"You poor thing!" Layla commiserated. "But we're done. You did great and now you can rest."

"No, not done," Sammie said, pulling back the bedcovers and tossing the pillows into a pile, which he covered with the white fur coat.

Noelle smiled slyly. "I think I know what you have in mind."

Sammie winked. "Okay with you? You strip?"

"Sure," Noelle shrugged, slipping out of the terry cloth robe she was wearing and casually arranging her naked body on the fur-covered pillows.

"Beautiful, beautiful," Sammie cooed, lovingly placing the tiara on her head, and once again wrapping her arms in the enormous bracelets.

Elizabeth was stunned, watching the casual way in which Noelle stripped and allowed Sammie to arrange her body in various poses.

"Don't look so surprised," Layla said, amused at her reaction. "She's done this before."

"She has?" Elizabeth whispered, clutching the terry robe.

"Sure. She used to be a porn star. She did it all in front of the camera—and I mean everything."

Elizabeth's jaw dropped. "Really?"

"And she was a centerfold for *Playboy* magazine."

"Where I come from, some people never take their long johns off all winter."

Now it was Layla's turn to be horrified. "Really?"

"Just joking," said Elizabeth, who was growing more comfortable with the situation. If Noelle wasn't bothered, she decided, she shouldn't be either. And she could see why Sammie was so enthusiastic; the contrasting textures of Noelle's flawless caramel skin, the lush white fur, and the glittering jewels made for fabulous visuals.

Finally, the staccato clicking of the camera stopped,

and Sammie's assistant handed him a towel, which the exhausted photographer used to wipe his brow.

"About time," his subject declared, yanking the tiara off her head and tossing it on the floor. The necklace, bracelets, and ring soon followed as she stretched, sauntered casually up to Elizabeth and grabbed the robe, then continued on into the bathroom, still entirely nude.

Getting a nod from Layla, Elizabeth scrambled to pick up the jewels and replace them in the case. She could hardly believe she was handling them, actually touching these amazing gems worth millions of dollars. She laid one bracelet across her wrist, examining the effect, imagining what it would be like to wear them all. Then, afraid she would be seen, she tucked the bracelet into its compartment. All the jewelry fit beautifully into the hollows of the velvet-lined case designed to hold each piece. . . . All except the huge emerald ring, which seemed to be missing. It had been there a moment ago, Elizabeth thought, panicking. She'd seen Noelle pull it off. Where was it?

Horrified, Elizabeth began searching through the tumbled bedclothes. How could Noelle be so careless? she wondered anxiously. The thing was worth a fortune—all the jewels were—and she had thrown them around as if they were nothing to her.

Sammie and his assistant were packing up the photographic equipment, Layla had followed Noelle into the bathroom, so only Elizabeth was concerned about the missing ring. She picked up the pillows and stacked them on the nightstand, she pulled off the sheets and bedspread, she looked under the bed. . . .

And finally found the priceless bauble under the nightstand, where it had rolled into a tangle of wires. Her hand was shaking when she slipped the ring into its groove and snapped the case shut.

"He doesn't really love me," Noelle was telling Layla, as the two emerged from the bathroom. She was wearing the robe now, and her feet were in the floppy terry slippers the hotel provided. "I'm just another acquisition, like these jewels."

So that's why she doesn't care about them, Elizabeth thought with a flash of insight. "Do you have the key?" she asked Layla.

"The key! What did I do with the key?" Layla exclaimed, clutching her head with her hands.

Her panic was contagious and everybody started scrambling, searching for the key to the jewelry case, tossing the contents of the room this way and that. Everybody except Noelle, who drifted out of the bedroom and into the living room, where she settled into a plush upholstered chair and called room service, ordering a turkey club sandwich and a double Scotch.

Finally, when the bedroom had been thoroughly tossed and everybody had searched everywhere, Layla triumphantly proclaimed, "I've found it!" and held up the key. "It was in my pocket the whole time."

Chapter Four

Elizabeth let out a huge sigh of relief when the hotel safe clicked shut. She had been entrusted with returning the jewelry case to the safe and was a nervous wreck, hurrying through the carpeted hall to the special elevator that provided access to the exclusive penthouse level with its four luxury suites. That elevator was tucked discreetly away in a corner of the lobby, behind the regular bank of elevators, and only rose to the top floor when a special key card was inserted into a slot.

When the elevator descended and she reached the lobby, Elizabeth dashed across the richly carpeted expanse between the elevator doors and the reception counter and waited impatiently, her heart thudding in her chest, until Toni hit the buzzer and the door to the manager's office opened. She was breathing heavily when she handed the case to Mr. Dimitri.

"Everything's okay?" Mr. Dimitri asked. "All the jewels are inside? And the case is locked?"

"I put the jewels in and Layla locked it," she said. She paused, wondering whether to tell Mr. Dimitri about the frantic search for the key, but noticing a pulsating vein near his eye, decided not to add to his already high level of stress. "After she locked the case Layla gave the key to Ms. Jones."

"Good," Mr. Dimitri said, letting out a big sigh. "That's very good. Now, go and have some lunch. You look a bit pale."

In truth, Elizabeth was dead on her feet, but she was surprised that Mr. Dimitri noticed. Maybe there was more to the old tyrant than she'd realized. Though today he appeared to be more considerate than she'd believed him to be, she still thought she'd been right not to mention the search for the key.

The next few days were a whirlwind of activity as final preparations were made for the guests' expected arrival on Friday. Enola Stitch, the famous fashion designer, came earlier, on Thursday, to make final adjustments to Noelle's gown for the Blingle Bells Ball. There was much speculation about the gown, which had been shrouded in secrecy, much like Kate Middleton's dress before her marriage to Prince William. The secrecy only drove the fashion press wild with anticipation and there were various predictions as to the design, although all agreed it would feature a plunging neckline.

Other notables that reporters would have loved to question included junk bond pioneer Matt Milkweed, hedge fund investor Adrian Robinson, and Goldsmith

Shoffner CEO Floyd T. Dewey, but they all dodged the press, arriving through the garage entrance in limos with tinted glass. Aware of the general unpopularity of Wall Street bankers and financiers, they had decided discretion was the better part of valor and were maintaining extremely low profiles.

Others, including Jonah Gruber himself, weren't so shy and gave statements to the reporters gathered outside the hotel doors. Gruber, Elizabeth noted with interest, was a short, slim man with a receding hairline and an odd sense of appropriate leisure wear; he arrived wearing a turtleneck sweater, shiny bike shorts, black socks, and Birkenstock clogs. He kept his comments brief but beamed with pride, standing to the side, as Senator Clark Timson and New York City mayor Samuel Hayes both praised his philanthropic contributions. Guests who were media stars also took advantage of the gathered reporters to add to their luster. Daytime TV diva Norah gushed about her "best friend" Noelle Jones and radio shock jock Howie Storch commented that Noelle was "a real hottie."

The most highly anticipated guest, and the last to arrive, was flamboyant pop star Merton Paul, who was going to sing at the ball. Hundreds of his fans were gathered outside, waiting for a glimpse of the rocker, and their screams heralded the arrival of his white stretch Hummer.

"He's here! He's here!" Toni exclaimed, barely able to contain her excitement. "Can I ask him for an autograph, do you think?"

Spying Mr. Dimitri hurrying to greet the star, Elizabeth shook her head. "Not now, but maybe you'll get a chance later."

"Oh, I love him," Toni cooed. "Look! There he is!"

Elizabeth saw a pudgy middle-aged man wearing a

shaggy fur jacket, bell-bottom pants, and a rather obvious wig, but Toni was blinded by Merton Paul's fame. "It's really him," she said, hanging onto Elizabeth's arm. "I think I'm going to faint."

"And who are these lovelies?" Merton Paul asked Mr. Dimitri, approaching the two young women.

Elizabeth took Merton Paul's proffered hand and introduced herself. "I'm the assistant concierge. I'll be happy to help you with anything you need," she said.

When he offered his hand to Toni she apparently found herself unable to speak, hanging on to Merton Paul like a drowning woman.

"This is Toni Leone," Elizabeth said. "She's at the front desk."

"Call anytime," Toni said, finding her voice. "It's marked on the phone: D-E-S-K."

"I'll keep that in mind," Merton Paul said, withdrawing his hand. "Take care, ladies."

"I can't believe I did that," Toni moaned, watching as Mr. Dimitri escorted the rocker to the penthouse elevator. "I mean, I spelled out *desk*, like he doesn't know how to spell."

"You were charming," Elizabeth said, amused at Toni's reaction. "I'm sure he's used to adoring fans."

"I made a fool of myself. Now I'll be so embarrassed every time I see him."

"He's only a person, with a head, two arms, and two legs," Elizabeth said, hearing her phone ringing. "Try to keep that in mind," she said, hurrying to answer it.

Elizabeth spent the rest of the afternoon coping with the demands of the glitterati. Enola Stitch discovered a crease in her pillowcase and required another—freshly pressed but not starched, and linen, of course. Matt Milkweed wanted a case of Cristal (no problem) and a basket of fresh peaches (a problem, in December). Senator Timson called for a masseuse and Elizabeth got him one, but wasn't convinced that Leon was exactly what he had in mind. Norah wasn't happy with the hairdresser her personal assistant had booked in advance and required someone more in sync with her astral sign. Howie Storch wasn't fussy—any stylist would do, so long as she had a large bust. After Howie's call, Elizabeth thought she'd heard it all, but then she got an e-mail from Sammie Wong asking for a jar of Crème de la Mer, the fabulously expensive skin cream. "I can't believe I forgot to pack it," he moaned.

Elizabeth was on the phone with Neiman Marcus, arranging an emergency delivery for Sammie Wong, when she noticed the lobby was unusually crowded. Suspecting that fans, or even the press, had managed to infiltrate the building, she sent an instant message to Dan Wrayburn. She was aware, as were all the hotel employees, that Jonah Gruber had specified that access to the building was strictly limited to his guests and selected media. Gruber was apparently unable to pass up any profit-making opportunity and had sold exclusive media rights to the event to *People* magazine.

She was keeping a nervous eye on the situation and her fears were confirmed when a bearded guy in a fishing vest approached TV sitcom star Dawn Richards and produced a tiny tape recorder. On the other side of the lobby, behind one of the glittering white Christmas trees that Layla had insisted on adding, she saw a series of camera flashes.

Wrayburn, who was stepping out of the elevator, also saw them and hurried to investigate.

"This is absolutely absurd," Richards protested. She was a curvaceous brunet dressed in a very short skirt and very high heels. "Bobby here is my friend—he's just taking a snapshot."

"Good try," Wrayburn said, "but I know Bobby. In fact, I called him last week and told him the hotel was strictly off-limits."

Bobby started to leave but Dawn grabbed him by the sleeve. "Don't be silly, Bobby. You don't have to leave. This is America. We have free speech here, and I want to put these photos on my Facebook page."

"The hotel is private property," Wrayburn explained, but his message was undermined by a guy in a fake brown UPS uniform who was photographing the encounter on his cell phone, as was a woman carrying a boxed flower arrangement.

"This is a warning," said Wrayburn, raising his voice. "I'm ordering our hotel security guards to clear the lobby. Only registered guests will be allowed to stay."

"Good luck with that," Howie Storch said, stepping out of the hotel bar with a pair of statuesque, bikini-clad twins hanging on his arms. "You can find me and my friends at the pool." He continued on his way, strolling across the lobby with his companions, and suddenly cameras were everywhere as reporters and photographers trailed the trio.

Wrayburn marched off with a grim expression on his face and Elizabeth realized her phone was ringing—again.

"Concierge, how may I help you?"

"This is Merton," the caller said, unnecessarily identifying himself. It was impossible not to recognize the famous voice.

"What can I do for you, Mr. Paul?"

"It seems I forgot my bubble bath."

"Not a problem. I'm sure we can provide some bubble bath."

"It may be a problem," said Merton. "This is special bubble bath. From Tibet."

Elizabeth wasn't aware that bubble bath was manufactured in Tibet, but she was learning something new every day. "Can you tell me what it's called, and where you usually get it?"

"It's called Lama's Tears; Bono gave it to me. He said it's great and he was right. I'm addicted."

Elizabeth was beginning to suspect this might be more difficult than she thought. "I'll do my best," she said. "But if I can't find Lama's Tears, is there another brand you could use?"

"No way, babe," said Merton. "It's out of my control. I'm hooked. It's gotta be Lama's Tears."

Nordstrom had never heard of Lama's Tears, neither had Saks or Sephora or Neiman Marcus. Elizabeth tried all the drugstores and every bath and body boutique in the Palm Beach area. Batting zero, she finally tried asking Toni, thinking that since she was such a big Merton Paul fan she might have heard of the rocker's favorite bubble bath.

"You haven't heard of Lama's Tears?" Toni was amazed.

"No, and nobody else I've called has either."

"Well, you've been calling the wrong places."

"Obviously," Elizabeth admitted, growing impatient.

"Well, I'll tell you but you're going to have to do something for me."

"What?"

"If I tell you where you can get Lama's Tears, you have to let me take them up to Merton Paul, okay?"

"Okay, okay," Elizabeth promised. "Where do I get it?"

"There's this cool place where all the hip people go. It's kind of a head shop, but they've got some clothes, some vintage. It's called Metaphor."

Elizabeth was on the computer, looking it up, jotting down the phone number. "You're a lifesaver!" she exclaimed, dialing the number.

"Just remember your promise. I get to take it up to Merton's suite."

"I won't forget, I promise," Elizabeth said, placing the order.

When she finished she realized she needed to use a bathroom and decided to break the rules just this once and use the facilities off the lobby, which were a lot closer than those provided for staff. She didn't want to be away from her desk for long, especially since there were so many people milling about in the lobby. The security guards had managed to remove a few paparazzi but others had drifted in, along with dedicated fans of the celebrity guests.

She'd taken a few steps when she encountered Wrayburn, who was looking extremely harried. "I've got to use the ladies' room," she told him. "Can you have somebody keep an eye on my desk?"

"I'll do it myself," he said, seating himself in her chair.

When she returned she saw he had propped both elbows on the desk and was rubbing his forehead. "Thanks," she said.

"No problem," he replied, standing up. Then he gave an abrupt laugh. "No problem. That was wishful thinking."

Elizabeth watched as Enola Stitch was accosted by three very thin women dressed entirely in black, obviously members of the fashion press. Enola greeted them warmly, then shepherded them into the coffee shop. "There isn't much you can do when the guests are the ones breaking the rules," she said.

"You said it," Wrayburn agreed. "I wish I was back in Washington. They take security seriously there."

Elizabeth was about to reply when four very serious-looking men in suits and wearing earpieces entered the lobby and took up positions; their presence was both imposing and forbidding. Conversation stopped as people became aware of them, everyone suddenly watchful.

"Secret Service," Wrayburn said, using his phone to alert Mr. Dimitri. "The First Lady is arriving."

The atmosphere in the lobby was hushed and expectant, everyone waiting and hoping for a glimpse of the president's wife, and perhaps even a chance to greet her and shake her hand. She was far more popular than her beleaguered husband, who had to cope with the woes of the world, and thanks to her support for disabled veterans, she enjoyed record-high approval ratings from both Democrats and Republicans.

Mr. Dimitri was hurrying into the lobby, straightening his cuffs as he walked to the front entrance. He had taken his place when the door flew open and a uniformed courier barreled in. The Secret Service officers, moving in unison, all reached for their guns.

The courier's hands flew up. "I'm making a delivery," he said. "From Metaphor, attention concierge."

"That's right," Elizabeth said as the agents patted the courier down. "I'm expecting a delivery for a guest."

One of the agents was examining the package closely,

finally concluding it was harmless and giving it to Elizabeth. The courier was sent on his way and Elizabeth, rattled by the incident, forgot her promise to Toni and summoned a bellboy to take the package to Merton Paul in the Majestic penthouse suite.

Then the motorcade arrived and Mr. Dimitri rushed out and greeted the First Lady, who was smiling and gracious and insisted on greeting everyone, staff and guests and paparazzi alike. It was a full half hour later that she finally stepped into the penthouse level elevator and the crowd began to disperse.

Elizabeth, wondering why a smile and a handshake from the First Lady could possibly make her feel so good, noticed Chris Kennedy coming through the door. He wasn't out of town at all, she realized. He'd just said that as an excuse for canceling their date. Suddenly, all that warm, good feeling was gone and Elizabeth wished she could disappear, just sink through the floor. At the same time she couldn't take her eyes off him. When he looked at her, straight on, she had to do something so she gave him a little wave. Darn it, she thought, she wasn't going to let him know how upset she was.

By way of response Chris nodded and continued on his way down the hallway that led to the bar and coffee shop. Elizabeth was tempted to follow but knew it was a bad idea. Besides, Toni was at her elbow.

"What a creep," she said. "Coming here like that."

"It's a free country," said Elizabeth, feeling her knees go weak under her and sitting down.

"I wonder what he's doing here."

"I haven't the faintest idea," said Elizabeth. Her phone was ringing and her computer was informing her she had fourteen instant messages.

"Are you going to answer that?" Toni asked.

Elizabeth picked up the receiver and heard Merton Paul's voice, thanking her for the Lama's Tears. That distinctive voice of his carried, and Toni could hear him, too.

"You got the Lama's Tears?" she demanded, when Elizabeth hung up. "And you didn't tell me?"

"I meant to," Elizabeth said lamely.

"You promised!"

"I'm sorry. It was so crazy here. You know how it's been this morning."

Toni's face was tight. "If it wasn't for me, you'd never have known even where to get the bubble bath!"

"That's true," Elizabeth said, miserably. "I just forgot."

"I thought we were friends." Toni narrowed her eyes. "I'll get you for this, Elizabeth. Don't think I won't."

Chapter Five

Toni was as good as her word, giving Elizabeth the silent treatment whenever they met, which wasn't actually that often because they were both insanely busy. At the front desk, Toni's phone rang constantly with demands from the guests for everything from fresh towels to the weather report. When she wasn't answering the phone, Mr. Kronenberg gave her the task of hand-addressing the Christmas cards Cavendish sent to every guest who had stayed at the hotel in the past year. "It's these little personal touches that count," he told her, giving her a box containing one hundred envelopes and telling her there were more in his office when she finished those. "I simply can't manage to do it all myself this year, not with all that's going on."

"I'm happy to help," said Toni, giving the head concierge a big smile. "If there's anything else I can do, just let me know." She lowered her voice. "I think Elizabeth is in a bit over her head. She was complaining to me, saying some of the guests are terribly demanding."

Kronenberg glanced across the lobby, where Elizabeth had the phone tucked on her shoulder and was scribbling frantically on a notepad. Her hair was mussed and her harassed attitude was a stark contrast to the confident, professional demeanor that Annemarie had always projected. "I'm sure she's doing her best," he said. "It's unfortunate timing that Annemarie got sick just now."

"Epstein-Barr can last for weeks, too," Toni said in a sympathetic voice. Then her tone brightened. "I'll get right to work on those cards—don't give it another thought."

Kronenberg's anxious expression softened. "You're a trooper, Toni."

In truth, Elizabeth was frantically scrambling, without a moment to catch her breath, trying to fulfill guests' special requests while also assisting Layla with the schedule of activities they had planned. Luxury coaches came and went, taking guests on tours of art galleries and museums, shopping expeditions, nature hikes, and golf matches. The golf tournament, in which every foursome included a member of the PGA tour, was a big success. The boy versus girl tennis tournament pitting Simpson against Sharapova became an instant sports legend, and Gruber's guests would be able to fascinate friends and acquaintances with play-by-play accounts for years.

But the main event, the Blingle Bells Ball, was still to come. Every employee was working overtime, preparing for the gala. There were decorations to put up, tables to set, and food to prepare, and the pace grew more frantic as the time drew closer. The doors to the Grand Ballroom would open at nine Sunday evening, and at eight o'clock Layla invited interested staff members in for a sneak peek.

"You've all been working so hard," she told the hundred or so staff members who had accepted the invitation and gathered in the Grand Ballroom's service hallway. "This is what you've done!" She opened the door and they entered reverently, awestruck, almost as if they were visiting a great cathedral, and paraded single file around the perimeter of the room. Even though they had all been involved in the preparations, only a few workers had seen the room in its final glory, complete with dramatic lighting designed for the event by theatrical lighting expert Stefan Ludwig.

Elizabeth found herself awed by the banks of orchids on every table, the swags of silk suspended from the ceiling, and the hand-painted wallpaper panels that had been installed for the occasion. Every table was covered with sparkling crystal and silver, the specially monogrammed porcelain plates sat on silver chargers, and two gilt thrones would be occupied by Noelle and Jonah.

"Every guest will receive a diamond gift," Layla said. "The gentlemen will receive gold and diamond money clips and the ladies will all get one-carat pendants."

"How much are those worth, do you think?" one of the housekeepers, Marketa, whispered, speaking in her lightly accented voice. Elizabeth knew she worked extremely hard, often taking double shifts so she could send money home to her family in Serbia.

"I don't think you can get a one-carat diamond for less than a couple thousand dollars," Angela replied. A bookkeeper for the hotel, she had just gotten engaged. "And that doesn't include the setting. Gold is really high right now."

"You mean, in addition to a ball for four hundred guests, Gruber is giving each a gift worth two thousand dollars? What does that come out to?" Elizabeth asked. "I can't do the math—it's too many zeroes."

"Eight hundred thousand dollars," said Angela, who was a whiz with numbers. "Almost a million."

Elizabeth suddenly felt sick to her stomach. "A million dollars on gifts for people who already have everything they could possibly want."

"I bet some of these women won't even appreciate a single-carat diamond," Marketa sniffed. "It's nothing to them."

"You're right," Elizabeth said, remembering the way Noelle had tossed forty-seven million dollars worth of jewels on the bed, as if they were little more than a ripped pair of panty hose. "So, Angela, what do you think the total bill for this do is going to be?" she asked.

"Millions and millions," Angela said. "But Gruber's got it. I read in the paper that he's worth something like a billion dollars."

"You know," Elizabeth said, "back home in Maine, my mom and her friends have this little charity they call the Hat and Mitten Fund. They have bake sales and beg for contributions so they can give poor kids in our town warm clothes and school supplies. I think their entire budget is maybe a thousand dollars."

"Imagine what they could do with one of these trinkets," Marketa said.

"Yeah, I know what you're thinking," Angela said.

"But look at it this way. Gruber's money creates a lot of jobs for folks like us. I heard that Dimitri was considering layoffs because holiday reservations were down. If it wasn't for Gruber some of us would be having a pretty miserable Christmas."

"Ho-ho-ho," said Elizabeth, causing the others to chuckle as they completed their circuit of the glittering ballroom and exited into the dank, fluorescent-lit chill of the concrete-walled service hall.

An hour later, just before nine, Elizabeth was back at her desk. A few early arrivals were drifting about in the lobby, waiting for the doors to the Grand Ballroom to open. Elizabeth recognized several of them, people she'd dealt with in the past few days. There was Katrina Muldaur, a sweet middle-aged woman whose novel about the Spanish-American War was a surprise best seller; she was clearly thrilled to have been invited and was wearing a black lace dress Elizabeth had seen at Macy's for a hundred and forty-nine dollars. The lady author was accompanied by a middle-aged man in a badly fitting tux who tugged on his cummerbund from time to time as he paced about impatiently. Elizabeth suspected he was probably wondering why they couldn't have served dinner at six, which was exactly what her own father would be wondering, if he were here.

Matt Milkweed, the financier, also caught Elizabeth's eye. He was tapping his foot by the elevator, waiting for someone. That someone turned out to be a tiny Asian woman, whose ruffled red evening gown seemed to swallow her up. She had to hold the ruffle encircling her neck down with one hand just so Milkweed could give her a kiss, then she took his arm and they drifted off in the direction of the bar.

Elizabeth was glancing at the clock over the desk and saw it was just five minutes to nine when the office door opened and Mr. Dimitri appeared carrying the metal-clad jewel case. He gave her a nod as he traversed the distance to the penthouse elevator. Then it was nine o'clock and two hotel waiters dressed as footmen complete with white powdered wigs and knee breeches opened the doors to the ballroom and the rush was on.

The band was playing a familiar tune, light and nice for dancing, and the elevator was arriving regularly and discharging guests. Elizabeth found she was enjoying the show, despite her uneasiness with Gruber's display of conspicuous consumption. It was better than a fashion show, she decided, watching Howie Storch's twin dates hobble past in very tight, very low-cut dresses that seemed ready to pop, revealing all. Merton Paul was flamboyant as ever, in a ruby red silk tux that contrasted nicely with the emerald green wig he'd chosen for the occasion. Norah, however, was the very picture of elegance, in white satin and silver sequins. Her insistence on a hairdresser with a compatible astrological sign had resulted in a smooth updo that perfectly framed her heart-shaped face.

Elizabeth was wondering what the First Lady would be wearing when she noticed Dan Wrayburn hurrying across the lobby to the elevators with the look of a man who was very worried about something but trying not to show it. He disappeared behind the elevator doors only to return a few minutes later, deep in conversation with Mr. Dimitri and Mr. Kronenberg. After a brief conference, he left to make an announcement on the hotel's emergency PA system.

"Attention please," Wrayburn began. "This is an official announcement from the hotel management. The Imperial Parure is missing and the hotel is on lockdown, awaiting the arrival of the police. Mr. and Mrs. Gruber hope that everyone will continue to enjoy the evening, but no one will be able to leave until further notice."

That set off a shocked buzz, with everyone frantically talking, wondering how such a thing could happen. The band, which had stopped playing for the announcement, resumed, but nobody was dancing. Everyone was uneasy, almost as if they were expecting a mob armed with pitchforks to storm the building.

Then, appearing almost magically, as if she'd simply materialized in the ballroom, Noelle was standing on the bandstand. Leaving her desk and standing by the door, Elizabeth had a clear view of the gorgeous woman. Enola Stitch's design more than lived up to the anticipatory hype. She had created a long, strapless sheath of hot pink satin that clung to every curve of Noelle's amazing body, and then gilded the lily by adding a fabulous puffy bustle and train. Every eye in the room was on Noelle, but she unnecessarily tapped the microphone, as if she needed to call the guests to attention.

"I just want to say," she began, in a whispery, little girl voice, "that I hope you will all cooperate with the police and tell them anything you might have seen or consider suspicious. With your help I'm sure we will get the jewels back, and in the meantime, I hope you'll all have a wonderful time. So take your seats because dinner will be served in a few minutes and afterward Merton Paul will entertain with his biggest hits."

She then left the room, clutching Layla Fine's hand, leaving the two extravagant gilt thrones unoccupied.

"You know what this means, don't you?" Toni asked after joining Elizabeth in the doorway.

"It means the party's over," Elizabeth said. The waiters were serving grilled foie gras appetizers but few of the guests appeared to have any appetite. News of the theft had definitely cast a pall over the gala. "They're all going to be scrutinized by the police and they've probably all got something to hide."

"Not just them," said Toni. "The police will start with the staff and I bet quite a few of us have something to hide, too. Mark my words, it's going to be a lot worse for us than it is for them."

Elizabeth knew she was right. The staff members were good, hardworking people but she knew that many of the lowest-paying jobs were filled by illegal immigrants, who feared deportation if their status was discovered. There were also undoubtedly some who had drug or alcohol problems, or a gambling addiction, and they would automatically be suspected of stealing the jewels to feed their habits. Elizabeth was most worried about the handful of employees who had come to the hotel through a program that found jobs for prisoners upon their release. She expected those workers would also face close scrutiny from investigators, so it was quite a shock when she was one of the first called to Wrayburn's office

Of course, she thought, making her way down the hall, she was one of the few employees who had actually seen and handled the jewels. That must be the reason why they wanted to talk to her.

Wrayburn seemed pleasant enough when she arrived, pointing out a chair for her to sit in and introducing Detective Michael Tabak of the Palm Beach Police Department. Tabak, she noticed with some unease, was accompanied by two uniformed officers who had stationed themselves by the door, blocking any escape attempt. As if she would even think of it! She was innocent!

"You are Elizabeth Stone," Tabak began. "Is that right?"

Once she had affirmed her identity she was shocked to hear him deliver the Miranda warning, adding that the entire interview would be recorded by a hidden CCTV camera. "Do you understand?" he asked.

Simply a formality, Elizabeth thought, nodding. They were probably doing this with everyone.

"I would like to show you some video footage taken yesterday," said Tabak, flicking on a small TV.

Elizabeth studied the grainy footage that showed people coming and going in the lobby. She herself appeared as a small figure in the background, seated at her desk.

"Look here," said Tabak, pointing out a male figure carrying a large duffel bag. He seemed to be in a hurry, but there was a moment when he looked in her direction and she waved at him. It was Chris Kennedy, she realized, with a shock.

"Who is this man?" Tabak demanded.

"That's Chris Kennedy," she said reluctantly. "I had a couple of dates with him."

"Why the wave?" Tabak asked, fixing his small, dark eyes on her.

"Just a friendly wave," said Elizabeth. "That's all."

"It looks like a signal to me."

Elizabeth was almost too shocked by this accusation to reply. "That's ridiculous," she finally said. "Why would I do that? What would I be signaling?"

"Letting him know the coast was clear," Tabak said. "That he could get into the office and steal the jewels."

Elizabeth thought she saw a way out of this nightmare. "But even if he got access to the office, and even if I opened the safe for him, which I definitely did not do, the jewels were still in a locked case."

"He could easily substitute a matching case, especially since you'd seen the real case and could describe it to him. Then he could take the case with the jewels, hiding it in that bag of his, and open it later," said Tabak.

Elizabeth felt as if she were in a scene from a very bad movie, but knew it was all really happening. She shook her head. "This is crazy."

"There's no sense protecting him," Wrayburn warned. "We have reason to believe he stole the parure. This is your opportunity to tell everything you know before he has a chance to implicate you. Which he will, believe me."

Elizabeth didn't know what to think. She'd liked Chris a lot, but then he'd broken their date and lied about the reason. Maybe he'd been lying about everything, like Toni said. Maybe he was a fake, like his Rolex. Maybe he hadn't been interested in her at all but had just been using her to get information about the hotel and the jewels.

"Listen, I'm not very happy with Chris Kennedy. In fact I'm not even sure he really is named Chris Kennedy. I have no reason to protect him. If I knew he'd stolen the jewels, I'd tell you, but I don't. I simply don't have anything to tell you," Elizabeth protested.

"You're in serious trouble," Tabak said, fastening that dark stare on her. "Once we catch him—and believe me, we will—he'll do everything he can to put the blame on you."

Elizabeth's head was spinning. She felt like Alice, falling through the rabbit hole into a completely strange and nonsensical world. "I can't believe Chris Kennedy stole the jewels, but if he did, I certainly had nothing to do with it."

"So that's your story," Tabak said.

"It's not a story, it's the truth."

Wrayburn sighed. "That's all for now, Elizabeth."

"I can leave?"

"Yes, but you need to see Mr. Dimitri first."

Tabak had something to add. "And don't leave town."

Elizabeth stood up, surprised to see that her legs still worked. It was with a sinking feeling, however, that she made her way with heavy steps to the hotel manager's office. She was pretty sure she wasn't going to like what he had to say.

When she reached the lobby, she found it empty, except for a few uniformed police officers. There was a subdued hum of conversation coming from the Grand Ballroom, and the orchestra had been replaced with a pianist, who was providing dinner music. The party must go on, she thought, even if the bling was missing from the Blingle Bells Ball.

Stepping behind the reception desk, she was surprised when the door to Mr. Dimitri's office flew open and Toni popped out.

"Hi!" Elizabeth exclaimed, glad to see a friendly face.

Except the face wasn't all that friendly. "Uh, hi," Toni muttered, ducking past her and rushing off in the direction of the employee's locker room.

What on earth was happening? How could Toni even know that she was suspected of involvement in the theft? And if she did know, why wasn't Toni sticking up for her?

Elizabeth opened the door and saw Mr. Dimitri. He was seated at his desk, looking through a file.

"Elizabeth," he said, a note of disappointment in his voice. "Sit down."

Here we go again, she thought, seating herself.

"I am not one to rush to judgment," he began. "I want you to answer one question, and to tell me the truth."

"Absolutely," Elizabeth said, relieved that somebody seemed willing to believe her.

"Did you have anything to do with the theft of the jewels?"

"No, I did not," she replied.

He sighed. "Are you absolutely sure that the jewels were in the case when you returned it to me after the photo shoot?"

Elizabeth decided it was time to tell the truth. "No, I'm not sure."

"You're not?" Mr. Dimitri looked horrified.

"There was some confusion. Noelle had been throwing the jewels around and—"

"That will be enough, Elizabeth," he said, cutting her off, apparently unable, or unwilling, to hear a Cavendish employee speak ill of a guest. "I'm afraid I'm going to place you on leave pending further developments."

"Leave?" Elizabeth asked. "What does that mean?"

"It means we will hold your job for you until the investigation is complete. If you are exonerated, and I most certainly hope you will be, you will be welcome to return to the Cavendish family."

Elizabeth did a rapid calculation and figured she had eighty-two dollars in her checking account, and only a couple of thousand in her emergency savings account. "Is this a paid leave?" she asked hopefully.

"No," he said, "but you will be paid for the days you worked in this pay period."

That was the first good news she'd had since the theft was announced, she thought, slightly relieved.

"If I were you," Mr. Dimitri said, "I'd hire a good lawyer."

Elizabeth nodded and left the office. At the door she was met by one of the hotel's security guards, who escorted her to the locker room. He stood by, watching as she opened her locker and hung up her green Cavendish jacket, feeling a bit like a disgraced officer being stripped of her military insignia. She turned her back and slipped off the green skirt, then pulled on the shorts she'd worn to work that morning. When she picked up her purse he took it and looked through it carefully; she blushed when he opened the plastic tampon container. "Okay," he said, handing the bag back to her.

She took it and left the building, stepping into the dark night and following the dimly lit path to the employees' parking lot. There, she discovered, the one halogen lamp that lit the lot was out. She unlocked the Corolla and sat behind the driver's wheel, looking back at the golden, glittering hotel and wondering if she would ever be able to return.

Tears sprang to her eyes. Tabak was right. She was in trouble, the worst trouble of her young life, and there was only one thing to do. Call home.

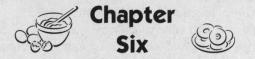

Chapter
Six

After talking to her mother, Elizabeth followed her advice and took a long bath and went to bed. "Everything will look better in the morning," Lucy Stone told her daughter, but Elizabeth found that hard to believe. Every time she closed her eyes she saw another disturbing vision: Tabak warning her not to leave town or Mr. Dimitri's curt dismissal or Wrayburn's bulldog expression. And then there was Toni, smirking and speculating that Chris wasn't genuine. Was Toni right? Had she been a complete idiot? Or, worst of all, had she actually aided and abetted the thieves without realizing it?

Exhausted at four a.m., she gave up and took the one remaining Ambien in the vial Doc Ryder had prescribed when she'd had a bout of insomnia last summer, anxious about leaving home and beginning her new job. She then fell sound asleep and didn't wake until noon.

Her first impulse upon waking was to call Chris Kennedy, but she couldn't quite make up her mind to do it. Finally, spitting a mouthful of toothpaste into the sink, she gave in, only to get a recording informing her he wasn't available but she could leave a message.

She was about to do so, then remembered the police were most certainly monitoring his calls and snapped the phone shut. Too late, she realized. Her call would be retained by the system as a missed call. In fact, she realized, it was quite probable that she was under surveillance herself. She went to the front window and looked out, wondering if she was being watched.

There was no black sedan parked out front, no unmarked white van on the other side of the street, but she was too paranoid to feel relieved. What was it they said? It wasn't paranoia if they were out to get you. And Elizabeth had the uncomfortable knowledge that she was under suspicion, the police were out to get her and wanted to implicate her in the jewel robbery.

She was making herself a cup of tea—she couldn't face coffee this morning, actually this afternoon—when Toni's face popped into her consciousness. That bitch! There was no other word, she thought, stirring a scant teaspoon of sugar into the mug. It must have been Toni who fingered her, who had told investigators about her and Chris dating. Impulsively, she grabbed the phone, determined to have it out with her.

"Why did you do it? Why did you even mention me to the cops?" she demanded, when Toni answered. "Thanks to you I'm in big trouble."

"I was only trying to help," Toni replied. "I told them you were under the influence of this Chris Kennedy guy, that it wasn't your fault. I told them how he had won you over, using a fake identity."

"How could you know that?" Elizabeth demanded.

"It was obvious. He's a big phony but you were too infatuated with him to realize it. I was only trying to help you, honest."

"Well, you've gotten me in real trouble. They think I conspired with Chris," Elizabeth wailed.

"I didn't realize . . . I was only trying to be a good friend."

Elizabeth doubted that Toni was telling the truth, but didn't want to think badly of her colleague. "I guess it won't matter in the end," she said. "The truth will out and I have nothing to fear because I'm innocent."

"I'm sure that's right," Toni said. "By the way, they gave me your concierge job. Temporarily."

Something in the way Toni said "temporarily" gave Elizabeth pause. She remembered Toni's threat, after Elizabeth had forgotten to let her deliver the bubble bath to Merton Paul, that she would get back at her. Now, it seemed, Toni had succeeded. Maybe she wasn't really a friend after all.

Suddenly, Elizabeth didn't want to have anything to do with Toni. "I've got to go," she said, tossing the phone on the table as if a spider had crawled out of it.

She picked up her mug of tea and wrapped both hands around it, as if its warmth could somehow console her. Reassure her.

She was a good person, she told herself. It was ridiculous that she should find herself suspected of a crime. She worked hard, she tried to please, and this is what it got her. How could Toni be so mean? She simply didn't understand it. And Chris? Was it possible that Toni was right? Had she been played for a fool?

She sat down on her futon, crossing her legs Indian style, and tasted the tea. It was sweet and spicy, and it seemed to help her clarify her thoughts. She sipped and tried to remember every conversation she'd had with Chris. Had she unwittingly given him valuable information? It was true that he'd mentioned the Cavendish data system, she realized with a start, but she hadn't given him any information. Or had she?

Was it really possible that he wasn't who he'd claimed to be? He looked like a Kennedy, but so did a lot of people. Toni had been suspicious of him right from the start. Was Chris Kennedy as fake as that big Rolex he always wore? And why hadn't he answered her call?

Setting the tea aside, she decided to get dressed and work off her nervous energy in the apartment complex's gym. She threw herself into her workout, starting on the treadmill, then advancing to the Stairmaster and elliptical trainer, then finishing off with a half hour's worth of lazy laps in the pool. When she headed back to her apartment her joints were loose and a bit rubbery, and she was very hungry. She was wondering what she had in the fridge when she saw a strange apparition climbing out of a taxi.

It was a very old woman with a head of curly white hair, carrying a bright red winter coat looped over her arm. There was nothing unusual about seeing an elderly woman in Florida but Elizabeth thought this particular old lady bore an uncanny resemblance to her mother's friend in Tinker's Cove, Miss Tilley. Christened Julia Ward Howe Tilley many years ago, she was known as Julia to only a few very dear contemporaries, and was Miss Tilley to everyone else.

Elizabeth blinked a few times, staring at this incongruous figure standing on the sidewalk, apparently examining a leathery anthurium blossom. They said everyone had a double—was this Miss Tilley's double?

The apparition turned and smiled at Elizabeth, giving her a wave. Then another figure climbed out of the taxi and began collecting luggage and there was no question at all about her identity. It was her mother, Lucy Stone. There was no mistaking that cap of shining hair or that hideous orange plaid jacket her mother was so fond of.

"What are you doing here?" Elizabeth asked, running up and greeting them both with hugs and smiles. For the first time since she was accused, she was beginning to feel that things might work out for her, that it was going to be all right.

"You're all wet," Miss Tilley observed.

"I was swimming," said Elizabeth, who was still in her swimsuit with a towel draped over her shoulders.

"I was afraid we'd find you in jail," Miss Tilley said. "We took the first flight."

"She insisted," said Lucy, handing Elizabeth one suitcase and taking the other herself.

"I didn't think we'd find you lolling about the pool," Miss Tilley said in a disapproving tone. She patted the snap purse she was carrying. "I brought cash to bail you out."

"If it makes you feel better, prison is still a very real possibility," said Elizabeth. She was pulling a rolling suitcase behind her, leading the way through the apartment complex's landscaped grounds to her building. It was slow going, however, as Miss Tilley and Lucy kept stopping to examine the tropical plants.

"At home, those are houseplants," said Lucy, pointing to a clump of spiky snake plants that were flourishing against a wall.

"Mother-in-law's tongues, that's what my mother used to call them. And look at those poinsettias," said Miss Tilley. "They're as big as my lilac bushes."

"It's amazing," said Lucy, finally shrugging out of her jacket. "It was snowing at home when we left."

"Well, come on in and get settled," Elizabeth invited, unlocking her door and wondering how she was going to accommodate the two women in her tiny apartment, located off the island in the more affordable town of West Palm Beach.

"This is lovely," said Miss Tilley, glancing around at Elizabeth's mix of IKEA and thrift shop furniture. Peeking into the bedroom, she nodded in approval at the queen-size bed. "We'll take the bedroom and you can have the couch. You don't mind sharing, do you, Lucy?"

"Not at all, as long as you don't get fresh," said Lucy, busy hanging up their winter coats in the hall closet. "Now, what's for dinner?"

Lucy opened the refrigerator and examined the contents, Elizabeth went into the bedroom to get dressed, and Miss Tilley settled herself in a sunny spot on the little screened deck off the living room.

"There's nothing to eat," called Lucy. "All you've got is yogurt."

"There are microwave dinners in the freezer," Elizabeth replied.

Opening the compartment, Lucy discovered she was right. "Elizabeth, this is no way to live," she scolded, choosing three of the packaged meals.

Ten minutes later, Lucy had set the table on the deck, thrown some salad in a bowl, and zapped three dinners.

"Warm weather is so nice when you're older," Miss Tilley observed, when Lucy and Elizabeth joined her on the deck and seated themselves on the mismatched chairs at Elizabeth's rickety plastic table. Miss Tilley raised her wrinkled face to the sun, reminding Elizabeth of a tough old lizard.

"With this heat it doesn't seem at all like Christmas," Lucy said, glancing about at the collection of flowering plants that Elizabeth had set on the deck railing. "And you haven't put up any decorations, not even a Christmas tree."

"I haven't had time," Elizabeth said defensively. Her mother's offhand comment had stung. "Most days I've been working from eight in the morning to nine or ten at night."

"Maybe we can find a little tree for you," said Lucy.

"Maybe we should tackle the problem at hand," Miss Tilley snapped. "Now tell me all about it, starting with the young man."

Elizabeth's chin dropped. "How did you know there's a young man?"

Miss Tilley looked at her. "When a young woman finds herself in a predicament, it's always because of a young man. Always."

"I disagree," said Lucy, who had two other daughters besides Elizabeth and often found herself refereeing squabbles and consoling them when mean girls got up to their tricks. "Girls can cause a lot of grief, too."

Elizabeth chewed a bite of chicken parmigiana and swallowed. "In this case," she said, "I think my troubles are due to a woman. Several women, in fact."

"I'm sure there's a man in there somewhere," said Miss Tilley.

"Okay," Elizabeth agreed. "I'll start at the beginning. I'd just been promoted to assistant concierge, it was my first day, and this guy came in with a flat bike tire. I sent him to the hotel's sports center and they fixed it and then he asked me out. We had a great time, and he asked me out a couple more times, but when we were supposed to go out last Sunday—the last day I had off—he canceled at the last minute."

"Does he have a name?" Miss Tilley inquired.

"Chris Kennedy."

"One of *those* Kennedys?" Lucy asked.

"I don't know. Toni, who I work with at the hotel, said she thinks he's an imposter, pretending to be a member of the Kennedy clan, but he never claimed any connection. He told me he was a lawyer and worked for some environmental organization. I thought he was a pretty nice guy. However, the investigators think he stole the jewels and that I was an accomplice."

"I suppose Toni had something to do with that," Lucy remarked.

"How did you guess? She told the investigators about her suspicions and she told them about me. She told them he was taking advantage of me. She said she did it to help me but I don't believe her. She's got my concierge job now."

"And I imagine she was jealous because you had a boyfriend," said Lucy, spearing a cherry tomato.

"I don't know about that. She was always kind of down on Chris. I think the thing that really got her mad at me was that I promised to let her deliver a package to Merton Paul—he was in the hotel—and I forgot. She was furious, and she said she'd get back at me."

"And she did," said Lucy.

"It certainly sounds that way," Miss Tilley agreed. "You mentioned several women caused you problems. Who are the others?"

"Well, Noelle Jones, Jonah Gruber's wife. I was assigned to help with a photo shoot, pictures of her with the jewels, and she was terribly careless with them. She said they were uncomfortable and threw them on the bed. A ring even rolled under a nightstand and I had to scramble around on my hands and knees to find it." Elizabeth found her frustration was getting the better of her. "She acted like a spoiled brat."

Lucy clucked her tongue. "She certainly doesn't sound very nice."

"She isn't," Elizabeth said. She was beginning to enjoy dishing about the hotel guests; she'd been working so hard for so long and hadn't been able to vent her frustration with anyone. "A lot of the guests are like that. They think the world revolves around them. If you saw the money Jonah Gruber spent on this Blingle Bells Ball, you'd be horrified. He hired this party planner, Layla Fine, and she spent two weeks ordering everybody around, but mostly me. I had to plan special events for Gruber's guests, 'extraordinary events for extraordinary people,' she said. Like they were better somehow than everybody else, and entitled to the best of everything. Orchids and foie gras and diamond gifts for every guest at the ball. . . ."

"My goodness," Miss Tilley tutted. "Such ostentation. And so unnecessary. My dear father used to say that there was nothing better than sweet water from our well and my mother's home-baked anadama bread, and he was right. That and a clear conscience."

"I don't think anyone at that party had a clear conscience," Elizabeth said. "I don't see how they could. I mean, I kept thinking about people back home who don't have jobs and their houses are in foreclosure and they have to depend on the food pantry to feed their kids."

"This Gruber's priorities certainly seem to be a little skewed," Lucy said, "but I've seen big events like weddings get way out of control in Tinker's Cove, too, especially if there's a professional planner in the picture. What's this Layla person like?"

"I had nightmares about her," Elizabeth admitted. "She was so demanding, she had me running all over the place. Everything had to be perfect, but she was the one deciding what perfect was. I mean, white roses, pink roses, who cares? And they couldn't be just any white roses, they had to be Patience white roses from some outfit in England. Everything was like that. Every day was an impossible quest to find some crazy thing, and if I couldn't find it she'd rip into me, saying I was stupid and lazy."

Lucy gave her daughter's hand a squeeze. "That's terrible," she said. "Nobody should treat you like that."

Miss Tilley, however, wasn't about to be distracted by Elizabeth's complaints. "This has all been very interesting, and therapeutic, I suppose, if you believe in that Freudian nonsense, but we need to focus on the problem, which is that Elizabeth has been falsely accused of being involved in a jewel robbery."

Reminded of the gravity of her situation, Elizabeth's spirits fell. She was in big trouble and she didn't see how these two were going to help her. Her mother was a part-time reporter for a small town newspaper, and had had some success in solving crimes, but Elizabeth suspected that was mostly luck. As for Miss Tilley, she was sharp and had been the town librarian, but she was well over ninety years old. When you got right down to it, they were well intentioned, but that was about all they had going for them.

"So tell me about this young man," Miss Tilley said. "Chris Kennedy. Do you think he stole the jewels?"

"I don't know what to think," Elizabeth said. "I really liked him."

"What do you know about him?"

"Not that much. He was fun to be with, and he was from Boston, so we had a lot in common. He had a motorcycle. . . ."

Lucy was horrified. "A motorcycle!"

"But he had a helmet for me and he made sure that I wore it. He took good care of me."

"And did you—" Lucy began, but she bit her tongue. Some things were personal and Elizabeth was entitled to her privacy.

"He was a gentleman, Mom. We kissed but that was all." Elizabeth's face softened at the memory.

"So if you put everything else aside and just trusted your reaction to him, do you think he is a thief?" Lucy asked.

"Take your time," Miss Tilley urged. "Give it some thought."

"I don't have to," Elizabeth said. "My gut reaction *was* that he's a good guy. I *thought* he was a really, truly good person—but I'm beginning to think I can't trust my instincts. I thought Toni was my friend, for example, and she ratted me out to the police. I've been way too trusting but I'm learning that people are not always who they seem to be, or what they want you to think they are."

"And where is this young man now?" Miss Tilley asked.

"That's the problem," Elizabeth answered glumly. "He hasn't returned my call. I don't know where he is."

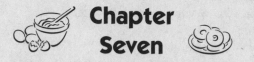

Chapter Seven

"Let's stick to the facts," Lucy said in a brisk tone. "I've been a reporter for a long time, I've interviewed all sorts of people, and I have to say it's almost impossible to tell what people are really like underneath that social veneer. You have to see what they do and how they treat other people, get to know them over a period of time so you can see how they act and not just what they say."

"I agree," Miss Tilley said. "I suppose there's no question that the jewels are really missing. That's the first fact we have to verify."

"You mean, the whole thing could have been staged?" Lucy was definitely intrigued by the possibility. "To defraud an insurance company, for example?"

"I can't imagine why Jonah Gruber, or Noelle, would do that. They're rolling in money. He's the second richest man in the world, something like that. He's got billions," Elizabeth said.

"How do we know that?" Miss Tilley asked. "He has a reputation for being rich, but maybe he isn't. Maybe he's strapped for cash."

"*Forbes* magazine thinks he's rich. They put him right at the top of their list," Elizabeth said. "And he paid forty-seven million dollars for the Imperial Parure. I'm pretty sure Christie's didn't let those jewels go until they got their money."

"That's something we could check," Miss Tilley said. "We could find out their payment policy."

"I'll make a list of questions," Lucy offered, extracting a notebook from her handbag. "First off, we want to know if Jonah Gruber is really as rich as everybody thinks he is, right? And we want to know if Chris Kennedy is really who he says he is."

"Have you actually seen the jewels, Elizabeth?" Miss Tilley asked. "And if you did, do you think they were real?"

"Oh, I saw them. I touched them." Elizabeth remembered laying the bracelet across her arm, how it had felt warm and heavy. "They sure looked real to me, but how would I know? I can't tell real pearls from fakes, or cubic zirconia from a diamond."

"Real pearls feel warm to the skin," Miss Tilley said, "and you can scratch glass with a genuine diamond."

"I didn't really have a chance to do that," Elizabeth said defensively. "I was too busy chasing after Noelle and that photographer."

Her sarcastic tone got her a sharp look from her mother, but Miss Tilley ignored it. "And you say Noelle was quite careless with the jewels?"

"She acted as if it was all a big chore, all except the last photos they set up. She seemed to enjoy that."

"Because it was the end of the session?" Lucy asked.

Elizabeth remembered Noelle's casual attitude as she arranged herself on the white fur coat, entirely naked except for the jewels. "Because she's an exhibitionist," Elizabeth said. "She stripped completely naked for the last photos. At first I didn't know where to look but Layla told me that Noelle was in porn films and loves to show off her body."

"A week or two in Tinker's Cove would fix that," Lucy said primly. "What was the temperature when we left?"

"Not bad," Miss Tilley said. "It was at least ten degrees, but that doesn't take the wind chill into account. It's the northeast wind off the water that really cools things off."

"That's true," Lucy said with a little shiver. "So after the photo session, what happened?"

"Well, Noelle tossed the jewels on the bed and she drifted off to the bathroom with Layla, carrying a terry cloth robe—one of the robes the hotel provides. There were a lot of costume changes and Layla was wearing it between photos. I gathered up the jewels and put them in the case. Layla came out of the bathroom, wearing the robe, and I told her that the jewels were in the case so she could lock it. She couldn't find the key right away. I sort of lost track of things when I joined in the search, but the key was eventually found—she had it all along—and the case was locked and I carried it down to the manager's office so he could put it in the safe."

"He didn't ask to see the jewels, to check that they were all there?" Lucy wondered.

"He couldn't. The case was locked."

"Did Layla still have the key?" Miss Tilley asked.

"No. She gave it to Noelle after she locked the case."

"And what did Noelle do with the key?"

Elizabeth furrowed her brow, trying to remember. "I'm pretty sure she put it in the pocket of her robe."

"And probably forgot it," Lucy said, thinking of all the times she'd searched high and low for her reading glasses only to find them in her bathrobe pocket. "Anyone could have taken it. One of the maids, for instance."

"But the case was locked away, in the safe."

"Ah, the safe," Miss Tilley said, sounding like Sherlock Holmes finding an important clue. "Who has the combination to the safe? Do you?"

"Only the manager and the head concierge have the combination," said Elizabeth. "The official hotel policy is quite strict. The safe is only to be opened by Mr. Dimitri or Mr. Kronenberg."

"But what if a guest needs something from the safe when they're not available?" Lucy asked, making eye contact with her daughter. "If I ever heard of a rule that was made to be broken . . ."

Miss Tilley's eyebrows rose to a startling elevation.

"You said it," Elizabeth admitted. "It was the first thing Mr. Kronenberg showed me when I was promoted to assistant concierge. He made me promise to keep it secret, then showed me where he kept the combination."

"So you could get into the safe?"

"I could," Elizabeth admitted, wondering if she'd been set up by the head concierge, or the hotel manager, or both. Wouldn't that be rich? The two most senior employees conspiring to rob a guest!

Miss Tilley broke into her thoughts. "And what if the

key to the case was missing for a short while? Would Noelle have noticed?"

"I doubt it," Lucy said. "I suspect she forgot all about the key until she needed it to open the jewel case just before the ball."

Elizabeth suddenly felt very cold, even though it was at least eighty degrees on her sunny, plant-filled deck. Looked at this way, it wasn't at all surprising that she was suspected of being involved with the theft. After all, she was one of the few employees entrusted with the combination to the hotel safe, and she knew how careless Noelle was with the key to the jewel case. "I didn't do it," she said, feeling the need to proclaim her innocence, even to herself.

"Of course not," Lucy said, giving her a hug. "That's why we're here."

Miss Tilley grasped the edge of Elizabeth's wobbly plastic table with her knobby hands and began to raise herself, prompting Lucy to jump up and assist her at the same time Elizabeth steadied the table.

"Really!" Miss Tilley exclaimed. "I'm perfectly able, you know."

"Of course you are." Lucy released her grip on the old woman's arm.

Miss Tilley turned to Elizabeth. "Where is your computer? I presume you have one?"

Lucy tidied up the lunch dishes while Elizabeth settled Miss Tilley at her little café table and showed her how to use her laptop. Then Lucy went off to her storage unit to dig out her small collection of Christmas decorations. When she returned, Miss Tilley had a plan.

"First thing tomorrow I think you should take a look at

this Chris Kennedy's apartment and see what you can find out," she said, peering at them over the laptop.

"You mean break in?" Lucy asked, opening the box and examining the contents. "I don't think that's a good idea. It's probably been sealed by the police."

"No way," Elizabeth protested. "I don't want anything to do with him."

"I think you have to," Miss Tilley said. "I fear the police may be right about him after all."

Elizabeth felt sick; she'd been a fool. "What have you found?"

"He lied to you about his job. I've done a computer search checking every environmental organization in Florida and he is not employed by any of them as a lawyer or in any other capacity. He's not registered with the Florida bar either."

"So Toni was right about him," Elizabeth said. "But what good will searching his apartment do?"

Miss Tilley scowled and glared at them through her wire-rimmed glasses. "You can find out a lot about a person when you see his home. Take Audrey Wilson, for example. She ran for selectman last spring promising to straighten out town government, but everybody knew she lived in absolute squalor. Even her yard was filled with junk. So nobody believed her and she lost the election."

"That's true," Lucy said thoughtfully, holding up a twig and berry wreath Elizabeth had hung on her dorm room door when she was in college. "I suppose we could at least take a look at the place." She turned to Elizabeth. "Do you know where it is?"

"He pointed it out when we went by," Elizabeth admitted, her curiosity piqued. "But I haven't been inside."

"It's a start," Lucy coaxed. "Have you got any thumb-tacks? I want to hang this on the door."

"Right here." Elizabeth opened a kitchen drawer and extracted a plastic box of tacks. "Of course, I don't know if he was telling the truth or not. He might not really live there at all."

"There's only one way to find out," Miss Tilley said.

Lucy hung the wreath, smiling at the effect, then closed the door. "It's better than sitting around here with Miss Marple."

"I'm not deaf, you know," Miss Tilley said, clicking away on the keyboard.

Lucy busied herself unpacking and took a long bath while Elizabeth put fresh sheets on the bed. She only had two sets of sheets, and a few towels, so the arrival of her guests meant she needed to do the laundry if they were going to have fresh linen. When she got back from the apartment complex's laundry room, she found the bedroom door was closed and only one lamp was burning, indicating her mother and Miss Tilley had retired for the night. It was only a little past nine but in Tinker's Cove people went to bed early and got up early.

She put the fresh towels in the bathroom and made up the futon for herself, but she wasn't ready to sleep. She set up the coffeepot for the morning, then settled down with a book. Her eyes followed the printed words and she turned the pages but she couldn't have said what the story was about, as her mind was too busy working on her problems. Her last thought, before she finally turned out the light, was the realization that she had nothing in the house for breakfast.

*   *   *

When she woke next morning she smelled coffee and the unmistakable scent of bacon.

"I popped out and bought some things," Lucy said, waving the fork she was using to turn the bacon. She was washed and dressed, as was Miss Tilley, who was sitting at the table on the deck with a cup of coffee and the morning paper. "Breakfast will be ready in a jif."

When Elizabeth emerged from the bathroom, freshly showered and dressed, she found a plate with bacon, eggs, and toast waiting for her.

"The best thing about Florida is the orange juice," Lucy said, pouring herself a second glass. "So fresh."

"I certainly don't think much of the newspapers here." Miss Tilley folded the big sheets of paper with a snap. "There isn't a word about the jewel theft."

"Be grateful for small mercies," Lucy said. "Imagine if they'd named Elizabeth."

The thought took away Elizabeth's appetite; she put down her fork and picked up her coffee mug.

"The sooner we start investigating, the better," Lucy said. "Besides, they say rain is on the way."

Miss Tilley popped the last bit of toast into her mouth. "And while you're out and about you could pick up a bottle of sherry. Tio Pepe, if you can find it."

"We better go, before she thinks of something else," Lucy said, grabbing her handbag.

Elizabeth gave her mother a tour of the neighborhood, making a stop at a liquor store to buy Miss Tilley's favorite dry sherry. Chris Kennedy's alleged apartment complex was just around the corner, and was similar in layout to Elizabeth's, with a scattering of buildings set in landscaped grounds. A recreation area included a pool, tennis courts, and a fitness center.

"Which is his apartment?" Lucy asked as Elizabeth pulled into a guest parking spot.

"I don't know. We'll just have to check the mailboxes," Elizabeth replied, with a nod toward the gray metal cluster unit where a white postal service truck was parked. They waited and after a few minutes the truck moved off. The two women strolled over and studied the names affixed to each mailbox; Chris Kennedy's name was on the box marked C-4.

"He was telling the truth after all," Lucy said.

Elizabeth scowled, unimpressed. "This doesn't prove anything."

A glance at the neat white brick buildings revealed that each was identified with a large letter. Building C was only a short distance away. When they approached it, they had no problem identifying apartment 4.

It was the one with yellow police tape over the door.

"I expected as much," Lucy said, turning to go.

"Not so fast." Elizabeth found she was suddenly determined to discover as much as she could about the mysterious Chris Kennedy. "This is a ground floor apartment. I bet there's a patio door around back."

They followed the paved path that ran around the building, noting the Christmas decorations that some people had put in their windows. One twinkling snowman winked at them and waved his arm. "I hope he's the only one who sees us," Elizabeth said.

Chris's patio was the only one completely devoid of plants or furniture. "A typical bachelor," Lucy remarked, cupping her hands and peering through the uncurtained sliding door.

Elizabeth studied the patio area, trying to think where Chris might have hidden an extra key. There was no furniture, so that was out. The trim around the door and windows was narrow—no place to tuck a key there—and there was no doormat. Checking out the plantings, she noticed a scattering of conch shells, and when she examined them she discovered one had a key taped inside.

"Good work!" Lucy exclaimed as Elizabeth unlocked the door. "Are you sure you haven't been here before?"

"Never," Elizabeth declared, stepping inside the largely empty living-dining room where a bicycle suspended on large orange hooks screwed into the ceiling provided the only decoration. A saggy old sofa, clearly secondhand, faced a large flat-screen TV that perched on a plank stretched between two concrete blocks. A row of books, mostly paperbacks, was lined up on the floor against a wall.

"Definitely needs a woman's touch," Lucy observed, heading straight for the kitchen and opening the refrigerator. "Very interesting," she said, pointing out a package of fish that was dated the day of the robbery.

"Very smelly," Elizabeth added.

"And from that I deduce that Chris Kennedy was not planning to leave town. Look, there's even a bag of salad in the crisper. You wouldn't buy fish and salad if you were planning to abscond with stolen jewels."

"That's an interesting point," Elizabeth said, peeking into the single bedroom. The comforter on the double bed had been smoothed and there were clothes in the closet as well as a carry-on size suitcase. "It's weird, isn't it?" she said, when Lucy joined her. "It all looks like he just left to go out for a loaf of bread or something."

"If he isn't a lawyer, like he said, I wonder what he does do," Lucy mused.

"Whatever he does, he doesn't keep regular hours."

Elizabeth was thoughtful. "Maybe he's unemployed. Or maybe he's a jewel thief."

"There's no computer," Lucy said.

"I guess he took it with him—it could have been in the bag he was carrying in the video."

"There's also no phone," Lucy observed.

"He has a cell phone. Nobody bothers with landlines anymore."

"Right," Lucy said, feeling like a dinosaur, unable to keep up with a changing world. "Check the bathroom. See if his toothbrush is there."

"Good idea. Nobody travels without their toothbrush."

"Unless they forget it," said Lucy.

Elizabeth stepped into the small, utilitarian bathroom that could be a clone of her own. The tiny vanity sink was clean, a neatly folded towel hung on the rail, and a University of Florida mug contained a half-used tube of whitening toothpaste and a very worn toothbrush. "I guess he either forgot it, or he left town suddenly."

"Like somebody on the run," said Lucy.

Elizabeth nodded, wishing she hadn't come. Until now she had believed that Chris was just avoiding her, wary of entanglement and commitment. That was what guys did. The women's magazines were full of advice on how to turn casual love affairs into meaningful relationships. But now it seemed the police were right about him. Why would he leave town so suddenly—unless he had stolen the jewels?

Observing her daughter's crestfallen expression, Lucy tried to offer a positive slant. "Maybe he had to leave in a hurry because his mother was in an accident," she suggested. "Something like that. When people go home, they don't have to take stuff with them. He's probably got plenty of clothes and stuff at his parents' house."

Elizabeth brightened at this idea, but froze when she heard voices on the other side of the apartment door. "Somebody's coming," she whispered.

"Time to go," Lucy said, leading the way. They hurried outside and closed the sliding door behind them, then stepped to the side, where they couldn't be seen from inside the apartment, and waited. A slight breeze stirred the branches of a hibiscus bush, a bird sang, a lizard froze on a rock. Nobody entered the apartment; whoever had been outside had gone on their way.

Lucy exhaled and said, "I could use some of that sherry."

"Me, too."

Lucy studied her daughter's expression, noticing how depressed she seemed. "Cheer up, sweetie," she said. "I know just the thing. We'll stop and get a Christmas tree on the way home. What do you think of that?"

"Whatever," Elizabeth replied with a shrug.

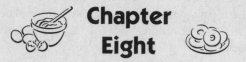

Chapter Eight

When they got back to the apartment, however, Miss Tilley was waiting for them impatiently. "What took you so long?" she demanded, picking up her purse and slipping on a light jacket.

"We stopped to get a Christmas tree," Lucy said as Elizabeth entered carrying a tabletop-sized balsam.

"It smells so nice," Elizabeth said, sounding almost cheery. "Christmasy."

"Besides, we haven't been gone all that long," Lucy protested. "And what are you up to? Where do you think you're going?"

"I am going out," Miss Tilley said. "Do you have a problem with that?"

"No," Lucy began, putting the bottle of sherry on the kitchen counter, "but I was thinking we could trim this tree. Elizabeth could use a distraction."

"There'll be plenty of time for that later," Miss Tilley

said. "You make hay when the sun is shining—that's what my dear mother used to say. Right now is the time for gathering evidence. We need to pick up the pieces of the puzzle. I'm feeling as if I've got a box of pieces but the top of the box, the part with the picture, is missing." She paused for a moment, clicking her dentures. "I need to see the hotel, need to get the big picture."

"That's a good idea," Elizabeth said. "You and Mom should take a look at the place."

"Your mother wants to play Mrs. Santa Claus," Miss Tilley said, pursing her lips. "And besides, I want the behind the scenes tour. I'll need you to be my guide, Elizabeth."

Elizabeth's jaw dropped. "I can't go. I'm on probation. I'm banned from the property."

"That's ridiculous," Miss Tilley said with a sniff.

"It is kind of high school," Elizabeth admitted, "but if I want to get my job back I have to play by the rules."

Miss Tilley's jaw was set and Lucy and Elizabeth could practically hear the wheels grinding away in her grizzled old head. "I've got it," she finally said. "You can wear a disguise."

"It's Christmas, not Halloween," Lucy said.

"And I'm not an elf," Elizabeth added.

"I wasn't suggesting you should dress as an elf," Miss Tilley said. "That would attract too much attention, which is exactly what we don't want. You should go as a maid—nobody looks at the maids."

"She has a point," Lucy said, who had opened Elizabeth's laptop and was soon scrolling through a list of uniform supply companies. "There's a place not far from here that says they provide uniforms for all major local employers."

"Come to think of it, I could use a little rest." Miss Tilley was taking off her jacket. "I think I'll take a short nap while you get your disguise together," she said, with a nod to Elizabeth. "And don't forget a wig. I'd suggest blond. Nothing changes a woman's look as much as a different hair color."

"She's right," Lucy said, writing down the address of the uniform supply store. "And you're in luck. There's a costume shop on the same block."

"Lucky me," Elizabeth said, realizing that resistance was futile. She didn't doubt that Miss Tilley and her mother meant well, but she doubted that their cockamamie efforts would actually help her. In truth, she suspected they would only make things worse and she would probably spend the remainder of her fleeting youth in jail. These were her best years and she would be behind bars, wearing unflattering jumpsuits and a bad haircut.

Her GPS took her into an unfamiliar area of West Palm Beach, where small stores jostled for space with dodgy-looking bars and churches belonging to unfamiliar denominations. When she reached the uniform shop, she was surprised to see it was decorated to the hilt for Christmas. Colored lights were twinkling in the plate glass window, a couple of mannequins in hospital scrubs had wreaths around their necks, and inside a huge Christmas tree took up most of the floor space and Christmas carols were playing. The woman behind the counter, who could have been Mrs. Claus, was plump and twinkly and dressed in a red dress, white apron, and mobcap.

"Merry Christmas!" she exclaimed. "And what can I do for you?"

It suddenly occurred to Elizabeth that she was on a fool's errand. The Cavendish housekeepers all wore lavender shirtwaist dresses that the company supplied, so there was no reason for the store to stock them. "I know it's unlikely, but do you have anything at all resembling a Cavendish maid's uniform?" she asked.

"I've got the real thing," Mrs. Claus replied. "What size?"

"Four," Elizabeth responded.

"No problem, I'll be back in a tick."

When she reappeared with a neatly folded uniform with lace collar and embroidered Cavendish logo on the breast pocket, Elizabeth could hardly believe her luck. "How on earth did you get this?" she asked. "The hotel supplies them and the girls have to turn them in when they leave. Who needs to buy them?"

"Well, you're buying one." Mrs. Claus raised an inquiring eyebrow. "I bet you spoiled yours and don't want to pay for the replacement, which is the Cavendish policy. My price is a lot cheaper than what Cavendish wants from the girls—a hundred fifty bucks, I think it is. Something like that. They're made in Italy, by nuns or something."

This was news to Elizabeth. "The maids have to pay for the uniforms?"

"Sure they do, if it's torn or stained and becomes unwearable." Mrs. Claus gave her a funny look. "I would've thought you'd know that. What do you want it for, anyway?"

Elizabeth blushed. "My boyfriend has this fantasy. . . ."

Mrs. Claus grinned naughtily. "Ah! Turn-down service."

One hurdle cleared, Elizabeth thought with relief. "But

I still don't understand how you get the uniforms if the girls have to turn them in when they leave."

Mrs. Claus chuckled. "They're leaving the country, dearie. They're going back to Indonesia or Slovenia or wherever and they want to take as much money with them as they can, so they sell the uniforms to me. They know the hotel isn't going to track them down in Outer Slobovia for a worn-out uniform."

"Right." Elizabeth realized she'd gotten more insight about how the Cavendish chain operated from Mrs. Claus than she had from hours of training sessions. "So, what is the price?"

"Twenty-nine ninety-five."

Elizabeth paid and left, humming along to "Frosty the Snowman."

As her mother had informed her, the costume shop was just a few doors down, next to the Reformed Chinese-American Church of the First Light. Inside the shop, Christmas and Halloween were fighting for space, the Bride of Dracula was sitting on Santa's lap, and a sexy little elf was clearly wild about the Wolf Man. There was no music; the chubby man behind the counter was listening to Rush Limbaugh.

"What can I do for you?" he asked, looking at her through thick glasses and scratching the wispy beard growing on his chin.

"I need a blond wig," she said. "And a pair of fake eyeglasses."

"Going undercover?" he asked, bouncing on the balls of his feet.

"Kind of," Elizabeth said. "It's just a joke, really."

"Like the ACORN thing?" he asked, eagerly.

"Sure," Elizabeth said, unwilling to give him too much information. "So where are the wigs?"

"In the back, behind Rudolph."

The reindeer's red nose was alight, illuminating a rack of variously colored wigs. Elizabeth chose the most realistic-looking blond one, a short, pageboy style, and also chose a pair of tortoiseshell eyeglasses with plain glass. The bill came close to forty dollars, using up most of her cash. On the way home she stopped at a drugstore and bought a bottle of cheap foundation, choosing the darkest shade she thought she could get away with. A display of Christmas tree lights caught her eye at the checkout and she impulsively picked up a box, breaking her last twenty-dollar bill. Going undercover was an expensive proposition.

Returning home with her purchases, she found her mother busy making origami crane Christmas tree ornaments out of colorful pages she'd ripped from Elizabeth's collection of fashion magazines. "Just what we need," Lucy exclaimed happily, when Elizabeth gave her the lights.

"I thought you were a sleuth of sorts, Lucy," Miss Tilley said, her voice dripping with disapproval. "What exactly are you contributing to this investigation?"

"This may look like busywork," Lucy said, waving the scissors, "but I'm actually freeing my subconscious to make connections and solve the theft. You'll see: the solution will pop into my head any moment."

Miss Tilley did not look convinced. "Come on, Elizabeth," she said. "Chop chop. I want to see the scene of the crime."

"Not until you have lunch." Lucy was already spreading tuna fish on huge slabs of whole wheat bread. "I don't know what to do for supper," she muttered. "I refuse to eat one of those microwave meals again."

Thirty minutes later Miss Tilley was seated beside Elizabeth in the Corolla, wearing her usual wool tweed skirt and cashmere sweater set along with thick support stockings on her scrawny legs.

"Aren't you too warm?" Elizabeth asked, sweating in the afternoon heat.

"Not a bit. Now what is our best plan of attack?" she inquired, as they proceeded down the long drive lined with royal palms that led to the hotel.

Elizabeth hesitated before answering, as she came up with a plan. As a pretend maid she had to park in the employee parking lot, but that was some distance from the entrance and she wasn't sure Miss Tilley could walk that far.

"I think it would be best if I dropped you off at the spa entrance," Elizabeth said. "There's no doorman there, so chances are nobody will see you getting out of a car driven by a maid. Once you're inside, you can ask the way to the lobby."

"If anyone sees me I'll just pretend I'm a dotty old lady," Miss Tilley chirped.

Not actually that far from the truth, Elizabeth thought, biting her tongue. "I'll meet you in the lobby. We'll pretend that you're lost and I'm showing you the way back to your room."

"Got it," Miss Tilley said as Elizabeth slowed the car and approached the canopied entrance to the spa. As she predicted, nobody was around and Miss Tilley was able to enter unobserved.

Driving onto the employee parking lot, Elizabeth was

strongly tempted to speed off and head for the Mexican border, then remembered that although Florida was in the southern part of the country it was a peninsula surrounded by water and didn't share a border with Mexico. No, she'd have to go to the airport and board a plane to somewhere. Anywhere, as long as it was far away. Australia, maybe. But since she had no money and only had a thousand-dollar limit on her one credit card, that wasn't really an option. And she certainly wasn't dressed for travel in this stupid maid's uniform.

Sliding into a parking spot, she braked and turned off the ignition, then flipped down the visor to check her appearance in the mirror. The blond wig was itchy, but it really did change her appearance. When she slipped on the fake eyeglasses she hardly recognized herself. She took a deep breath to steady her nerves, climbed out of the car, squared her shoulders and, once again, took the familiar route she had followed every working day to the employees' entrance. This time, she feared, would probably be the last.

Suddenly suspicious that she might be observed by a hidden camera, she paused at the time clock and pretended to clock in, snagging a name tag from the adjacent rack and fastening it just above the breast pocket of her uniform. Then she popped into a supply cabinet and got a squeeze bottle of cleaner and a rag; thus armed she was confident she would fade into the background, somebody nobody wanted to see.

Her next problem was getting access to the secure areas of the hotel, which required a key pass. Mr. Dimitri had confiscated hers and without it she wouldn't be able to give Miss Tillcy much of a tour. She decided to try the women's locker room on the off chance that somebody had dropped one. When she entered she found she was alone except for one middle-aged woman who was just unbuttoning her lavender shirtwaist.

"Hi!" she said, greeting her. "You haven't seen a key card, have you?"

"Did you lose yours?" the woman asked. She had big brown eyes that expressed concern.

"I must have. I thought it was in my pocket but now it's gone."

"You're in big trouble," the woman said.

"I know," Elizabeth wailed. "I can't afford to lose this job."

The woman's face softened. "Take mine," she said, offering a Cavendish-green rectangle of plastic.

"Are you sure?" Elizabeth was genuinely shocked at the woman's generosity.

"Just slip it through the vent in my locker when you're done—number thirty-four."

"I can't thank you enough," Elizabeth said, impulsively hugging her.

She patted Elizabeth on her back. "Just don't forget to return it."

"I won't," Elizabeth promised, watching the woman pick up her tote bag and leave, walking slowly as if her feet hurt.

Then she herself left the locker room and followed the service hallway, receiving nods and smiles from the few employees she met. So far, so good, but the lobby would be more of a challenge. For one thing, Toni might be on duty, and you never knew when Mr. Dimitri was going to pop out of his office. Reaching the unobtrusive doorway to the lobby, she nudged it open, relieved to see a large party of Asian tourists was checking in at the front desk.

Seizing the moment, she slipped into the lobby and began polishing the first thing she saw, which happened to be a lamp. Glancing around, she noticed Miss Tilley, who had seated herself on a plump sofa beneath a twinkling wreath.

Elizabeth made her way around the room, flicking her rag at imaginary bits of dust, until she reached the seating arrangement where Miss Tilley was making a show of admiring a handsome pink and white amaryllis plant that was on the coffee table. Elizabeth bent down and began dusting the table.

"What a beautiful plant," Miss Tilley said. "I believe this variety is called Apple Blossom."

"It's nice," Elizabeth muttered.

"I guess I really ought to go up to my room and get ready for dinner. My son is taking me out," she said, rising with effort and then plunking back down, as if she hadn't enough strength to stand.

"Let me help you." Elizabeth offered, playing along. She took the old woman's arm and helped her to her feet.

"Goodness, I don't feel very steady on my feet," Miss Tilley said with a big wink, just in case Elizabeth didn't realize she was playacting.

"I'll help you to your room," Elizabeth said, taking her by the arm and intending to lead her to the elevator. She was planning to give Miss Tilley a quick peek of a hallway, maybe a glimpse of an empty room, and then get her out of there. They were almost at the bank of elevators when Elizabeth spotted Mr. Kronenberg crossing the lobby in the same direction, clearly also headed for the elevators. Elizabeth's heart was pounding. She knew that she could kiss her job good-bye if she was discovered. She quickly decided to make a detour to the ballroom, confident they could slip in unnoticed while staff members were occupied with the large group of newly arrived Asian guests.

Much to Elizabeth's surprise, the decorations for the Blingle Bells Ball were still in place, though the Patience roses were wilting.

"Goodness me!" Miss Tilley exclaimed. "I didn't expect anything like this!"

"The party favors were diamonds," Elizabeth said. "Money clips for the men, pendants for the women."

"So unnecessary," Miss Tilley said, clucking her tongue. "Such extravagance."

"What next?" Elizabeth asked. "Did you see the pool?"

"I walked through, on my way from the spa," Miss Tilley said. "They have some lovely succulents. So exotic-looking! And birds of paradise."

"Did you see the tea room?" Elizabeth asked.

"I glanced in while I was waiting for you. I took a peek at the gift shop and the bar, too."

Elizabeth thought she might be granted a reprieve. "So do you have the big picture?"

"I'd really like to see the Grubers' suite," she said.

Elizabeth had a vivid mental picture of a jail door banging shut behind her, locking her in a tiny cell. "Really?" she asked, in a small voice.

"Let's go." Miss Tilley sounded like a nursery school teacher rounding up her small charges. "Don't dawdle."

"Take my arm and hobble," Elizabeth ordered, patting her pocket and extracting the key card.

Together they left the ballroom and made their slow way across the lobby to the restricted elevator, which they shared with a swarthy man wearing tennis whites. He ignored them and got off at the junior suite level, leaving them to ascend alone to the penthouse level. They stepped out, into a very white foyer, facing four sets of paneled doors, one for each of the hotel's most luxurious and most expensive suites.

"What now? Do we just go in?" Elizabeth asked. "What if they're here?"

"Knock and say 'housekeeping.' That's what maids do," Miss Tilley urged. "If there's no answer, just go in. You can always say you were checking to make sure they have enough towels."

"And how do I explain your presence?"

"I won't go in unless the suite is empty," Miss Tilley said. "I'll wait here. If anybody comes I'll just pretend I'm one of those foolish old people who go wandering off and get themselves lost."

"Okey-dokey," Elizabeth muttered, tapping on the door and getting no response. "What exactly is the penalty if you're convicted of breaking and entering?" she asked, slipping her key card into the slot.

"In Florida? Probably death by lethal injection."

"Not funny," Elizabeth growled, stepping inside the suite and closing the door behind her. A moment later she came back and admitted Miss Tilley.

It was clear at a glance that the Grubers were still in residence, at least Noelle was, judging from the numerous bags and boxes bearing the logos of exclusive shops that were strewn about the expansive living area with ocean views. The floor was dotted with shoes, and the furniture was piled with heaps of clothing: mountains of white satin and clouds of frothy tulle. The white fur coat was balled up in a heap on the floor outside the bedroom door.

Miss Tilley merely shook her head, clearly horrified at the mess. "Not a very ladylike way to live," she finally said.

Elizabeth was amused at Miss Tilley's old-fashioned word choice. "My women's studies professor insisted that the concept of ladylike behavior is a form of bondage that kept women from expressing their true selves."

Miss Tilley waved an arm at the mess. "Perhaps it's an old-fashioned term, but the concept remains valid, even today. There are still standards of decent behavior," she said, "and this is not any way to live."

Elizabeth was about to agree when she heard voices outside the door and the beep that signaled the door had been unlocked by a key card. "Quick!" she hissed, grabbing Miss Tilley and shoving her into the bedroom. Once inside she glanced around frantically, but the only place to hide was either under the bed or in the roomy closet. There was no way Miss Tilley was going to crawl under the bed, so Elizabeth chose the closet. "Quick, in here," she said, opening the louvered door.

Chapter Nine

As closets went, it was really top of the line, Elizabeth noted. It was huge, for one thing, amply ventilated and well lit, thanks to the louvered doors that admitted plenty of air and light. Noticing there was a bench to sit on to put on shoes, Elizabeth helped Miss Tilley lower herself onto it. It was really quite a comfortable hiding place, except for the fact that it didn't offer much in the way of concealment. There were only a few pieces of clothing hanging from the rod, probably put there when the maid unpacked. Noelle certainly didn't bother to hang up her clothes after she wore them; she simply pulled them off and dropped them wherever she happened to be when she undressed.

If anyone opened the door, which made the light turn on automatically, Elizabeth and Miss Tilley would be immediately discovered. But what were the chances of that? There was no need for Noelle to open the closet since the larger part of her wardrobe was scattered about the suite, tossed on the furniture and floor. The few garments left in the closet seemed to Elizabeth to be rejects: a simple gray tweed suit, a tan pantsuit, and a couple of conservative knit dresses in muted, solid colors. Not at all the sort of clingy, revealing thing that Noelle usually wore.

Feeling somewhat relieved, she concentrated on listening to what the two women were saying. The closet was located just inside the master bedroom door, only feet away from the wet bar in the living room.

"Jonah is furious with me," Noelle said, plunking some ice into a glass and following with a few splashes of liquid. "He thinks I was careless with the jewels."

He'd be right, Elizabeth thought, remembering the way Noelle ripped off the necklace and tiara after the photo shoot and tossed them on the bed. Elizabeth had actually needed to crawl around on the floor to recover the emerald ring. How could people be so careless? she wondered. Noelle seemed completely oblivious to the jewels' incredible value, didn't have any respect for the money they represented, or the talent and effort that enabled her husband to afford them. Gruber, as everyone knew, was a college dropout from an average, middle-class family who had built his fortune from the bottom up by developing a computer program that spotted developing market trends, which he then applied to build his astonishing fortune.

"What's the big deal?" Layla asked. Her voice was fainter than Noelle's, so Elizabeth figured she must be standing by the door to the terrace. Good idea, she thought, concentrating hard and willing the two women to step outside. If they went out to the terrace, it might give her and Miss Tilley an opportunity to make a quick escape.

But no—now Layla's voice was louder, which meant she was coming closer. "They're insured, aren't they?"

"You don't understand," Noelle replied. Elizabeth heard the slight sucking sound that meant the fridge was being opened, and there was more clinking of ice, which undoubtedly meant Noelle was fixing herself another drink. Elizabeth thought it must be alcohol of some kind that she was splashing into the glass.

"So tell me, what don't I understand?" Layla asked. "And since you're pouring, I'll have a Scotch, too, while there's still some left in the bottle."

"Oh, sorry. It's just I'm so distracted," Noelle said. "Jonah's been so mean to me lately. We haven't had sex for two whole days and now he's gone off to Seattle, leaving me to cope with the cops and everything. I know it's because he blames me."

"I still don't get it," Layla said. "If they're insured, what's the big deal? He'll get the money and he can buy more jewels."

"But not those jewels," Noelle said. There was the sound of a glass being set down on a table and Elizabeth winced, thinking of the flawless French polish finish, laboriously applied by hand to all the furniture in the suite. "He was batty about them. Like they made him some sort of emperor. An Internet emperor! He did all this research, and he'd go on and on about the empress, who was Napoleon's second wife. Did you know he divorced Josephine? I thought they were big lovers, like Cleopatra and that Roman guy, or Liz Taylor and Richard Burton."

"They got divorced, too," Layla pointed out.

"You're right!" There was more clinking of ice, and this time the glugging from the bottle went on longer than before; Noelle was pouring herself a generous drink.

"You know, Richard Burton gave Liz a lot of jewels. Do you think that jewels are unlucky? Bad for relationships, I mean?"

"Well, things certainly didn't work out for them, or for Napoleon," Layla said.

"Really? What happened?"

Elizabeth glanced at Miss Tilley, whose wide eyes and pursed lips seemed to express both disbelief and disapproval. She knew how the former librarian detested misinformation.

"He was killed at the Battle of Waterloo," Layla said.

Elizabeth made eye contact with Miss Tilley, who she knew was dying to rush out and correct this false statement. "No, no," she mouthed, and Miss Tilley rolled her eyes and expelled a long sigh.

"That's just tragic," Noelle said. "And he invented champagne, too."

"I don't think that's right," Layla said. Her voice was growing louder, which Elizabeth figured meant she was coming closer to the closet. "I think it was a monk."

"A monk!" Noelle exclaimed, also sounding closer. "That's crazy."

Elizabeth found herself tensing, crossing her fingers and willing the two women to go in the other direction, back to the terrace or the bar. Anywhere except the closet.

"So," Layla asked, "what are you going to wear for dinner tonight?"

When she heard Noelle's reply Elizabeth thought her heart would stop. She instinctively stepped closer to Miss Tilley.

"Jonah wants me to wear that ugly green dress, the one he chose because it set off the jewels. He said I need to watch my image, that I need to appear more conservative now that I'm the focus of so much attention. But if you ask me, I think he's punishing me."

Elizabeth and Miss Tilley both turned to stare at the demure green sheath suspended from a padded satin hanger. It was long-sleeved and high-necked, with a slight gathering of fabric that emphasized the waist.

"So where is it?" Layla asked. "I don't see it anywhere."

"I guess it's in the closet." Noelle's voice rose, as if she'd had a sudden inspiration. "I'm tempted not to wear it. He's not here after all."

Good idea, Elizabeth thought. You don't like it, wear something else. Like those skinny black pants you left on the sofa, and that silky halter top that was draped across a lamp shade.

"I wouldn't do that," Layla advised. "There's bound to be a photo of you on *Page Six* and he's already pretty pissed at you. Why make it worse?"

"Oh, all right." Noelle sounded exasperated.

Darn. This was it, Elizabeth thought, her heart thudding in her chest. The game was up. Miss Tilley stood up and Elizabeth took her hand, as if they were facing a firing squad.

"I'll get it for you," Layla said, opening the door.

You had to hand it to Layla. She was cool as a cucumber when she spotted Elizabeth and Miss Tilley. It was Noelle who was shrieking her head off.

"What are you doing here?" Layla demanded.

"Checking towels?" Elizabeth said. "Just making sure you had enough."

"Very funny," Layla said. "And who's your little wrinkled friend? The towel elf?"

Noelle had quieted down and was staring at Elizabeth.

"She's the one who stole the jewels!" she declared, snatching the wig off her head. "I'd recognize you anywhere," she snarled. "I saw you on the video."

"That's utter nonsense," Miss Tilley said. "Elizabeth is completely innocent and, for your information, Napoleon did not die at Waterloo. He died in exile on the island of Saint Helena. The cause is in dispute; some historians believe he was poisoned."

"Big deal," Layla said. "I'm calling security."

"I wouldn't do that if I were you, Lois," Miss Tilley warned, seating herself primly on the foot of the bed. Elizabeth remained standing protectively by her side.

"Lois?" Noelle demanded in a know-it-all voice. "There's no Lois here. You think you're so smart but you haven't even got Layla's name right."

"Oh, I think I have." Miss Tilley turned to Layla. "You're actually Lois Feinstein, aren't you?"

"Don't be ridiculous," Layla declared. "I don't know where you got an idea like that. Everybody knows me, I'm famous. I'm the party planner everybody wants. You can read about me in the *New York Times*, in *Vogue*, even *Vanity Fair*." She laughed. "And I'm pretty sure you can't afford me."

"Journalism simply isn't what it used to be," Miss Tilley said. "Whatever happened to investigative reporting? It only took me a few clicks of the mouse to discover your true identity." She opened her large purse with a click and extracted a printout of a mug shot picturing a younger but clearly recognizable version of Layla. The name beneath the sullen face was Lois Feinstein. "You were convicted of drunk driving and vehicular manslaughter, for running down three club-goers in Long Island in 2003. One died, one remains in a coma, and the third is confined to a wheelchair."

"Is this true?" Noelle demanded.

"Everybody has a bad day now and then," Layla/Lois said. "It was a long time ago and I've paid my debt to society. I went to jail for five years, and when I came out I started my business and it took off like gangbusters. I think I deserve some credit for making a new start."

"New start!" Miss Tilley scoffed. "Is that what you call stealing your client's jewels?"

"You didn't!" Noelle hissed.

"Of course I didn't," Lois insisted, picking up the Birkin bag she'd left on a chair. "She's all wrong. I didn't have anything to do with the theft."

"I think you did," Elizabeth said, remembering the confusion after the photo shoot. "You pretended to lose the key to the case—that's when the jewels were taken, when we were all scrambling around, looking for the key."

"That's enough!" Lois said, reaching into her bag and producing a small pink handgun. "All of you, get out on the terrace."

"Not me!" Noelle protested.

"You, too," Lois snarled.

"But I thought we were friends," Noelle whined.

"Friends? Is this what you call being a friend? Nattering on endlessly about your problems, about how Jonah doesn't love you? Do you have any idea how self-centered you are? Do you?"

Noelle's face crumpled. "You're the rat! You're the one who stole my jewels!"

"Shut up! Now, out, all of you." She waved the gun,

and Noelle darted across the room and out onto the terrace. Elizabeth followed, more slowly, helping Miss Tilley. Once they were outside, Lois slammed the door shut and locked it, leaving them to face the elements.

"We can call for help," Noelle suggested, leaning over the edge. "Yoo-hoo," she screamed. "Help!"

"Save your breath," Miss Tilley advised. "We're too high up, and it's too breezy."

In fact, Elizabeth noted with dismay, the sky had clouded over and the wind was kicking up, signs that a tropical downpour was coming. She was looking for a means of escape, looking for a way to cross the gap to the neighboring terrace, when she heard a shriek from inside the suite. Peering inside, she recognized Dan Wrayburn and—could it be?—Chris Kennedy.

Noelle immediately began banging on the glass and yelling, to get their attention. Wrayburn busied himself cuffing Lois and Chris unlocked the door.

"What are you doing here?" Elizabeth asked, confronting him.

"Yeah!" Lois exclaimed, pointing at Chris. "He's the thief! And they're his accomplices," she added, swinging around to indicate Elizabeth and Miss Tilley. "You've got this all wrong. They broke into the suite! They're the thieves, not me."

Noelle's face was a cold mask of fury. "I'm a thief? I don't think so. This is my suite. You took advantage of me, of my friendship, and you locked me out. Locked me out of my own room, left me to rot on that terrace." She started to move toward Lois, but Chris intervened.

"It's over. The jewels have been recovered," he said. "Your partner in crime, Sammie Wong, was arrested at Teterboro this morning, about to leave for Dubai."

"Sammie had the jewels?" Noelle asked.

"Most of them were hidden in his camera cases, but the Star of Bethlehem was concealed in a jar of Crème de la Mer."

Elizabeth's jaw dropped. "I got that for him," she said. "Maybe I am a conspirator after all."

Chapter Ten

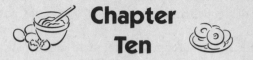

S uddenly the suite was filled with uniformed cops. Jonah Gruber had heard the news at the airport just as he was about to board and had returned to embrace a tearful Noelle. Chris Kennedy was explaining the situation to a police detective and Dan Wrayburn was talking on his cell phone, reporting to the hotel manager. Lois, handcuffed and sullen, was seated in a corner of a huge couch; her pink handgun was tagged and bagged and lay on the wet bar's polished pink granite counter.

"I don't think we need to linger," Miss Tilley said. "We're not needed here."

Wasn't that the truth, Elizabeth thought. Chris Kennedy hadn't given her a glance. It was obvious he didn't care a fig for her. He was some sort of investigator and he'd used her to get inside information. And besides, she wasn't eager to explain her presence in a Cavendish maid's uniform to Wrayburn. "Let's go," she whispered.

"I've got to get out of this uniform and return this pass before they figure out I shouldn't have it."

The two women worked their way through the crowded room to the open door, unnoticed in the confusion. The elevator was waiting for them and they descended without incident and made their way to the locker room where Elizabeth slipped the pass into locker thirty-four. They were making their way down the hallway and had almost reached the exit when Mr. Dimitri hailed Elizabeth.

"You know they caught the thieves!" he exclaimed.

"I heard," she said. "It's wonderful news." She stood awkwardly, unreasonably hoping he wouldn't notice the maid's uniform.

"Dan Wrayburn tells me you were instrumental in solving the case," he continued, speaking excitedly. "He said you went undercover, that the maid's uniform was a brilliant disguise and you will be able to testify against that awful party planner the Grubers hired." He shook his head and shuddered. "He said she is a convicted criminal and I don't doubt it. Those absolutely awful fake white Christmas trees were a crime! Talk about tacky."

Elizabeth found herself unable to speak, but Miss Tilley was only too happy to fill the void. "I'm proud to be Elizabeth's friend," she said. "Let me introduce myself. I'm Miss Julia Tilley, from Tinker's Cove, Maine."

Elizabeth blushed in embarrassment. "I'm so sorry. I should have introduced you. This is Mr. Dimitri, the hotel manager."

"Pleased to meet you." Miss Tilley extended a knobby hand and Mr. Dimitri took it in both of his, then bent down and kissed it. "My goodness," she said. "No one has ever kissed my hand before!"

"It was my privilege," Mr. Dimitri said, oozing the

charm he was known for. "And, Elizabeth, I hope you will return to work tomorrow?" His eyes twinkled. "In your green blazer at the concierge desk?"

Elizabeth was suddenly aware that quite a group of employees had gathered around them and were listening to every word. She recognized the faces of Kieran, Ada, Marketa, and so many others who had become her friends.

"Of course," Elizabeth replied.

"I'm not sure that's wise, dear," Miss Tilley said, patting her hand. She turned to Mr. Dimitri. "Elizabeth has been through a great deal lately and she needs some time to recover. Let's say she takes her scheduled vacation and starts her new position on January third."

"A much better idea," Mr. Dimitri agreed. "January third it is."

The group broke into spontaneous applause, causing Elizabeth to turn quite pink with pleasure. Mr. Dimitri leaned close and lowered his voice. "You'll be paid for the days you were on leave and you will find a generous bonus, too."

"Thank you, thank you so much," Elizabeth said.

And then, much to her surprise, Mr. Dimitri took her hand and kissed it, too. Over his sleek, oiled hair she caught sight of Toni, watching with an expression of shocked disbelief, and she smiled.

"*À bientôt,*" Mr. Dimitri said.

"*À bientôt,*" Elizabeth replied, taking Miss Tilley's elbow and walking out the door. It didn't feel like walking on stained and spotty concrete, she realized. She felt as if she were walking on a cloud.

* * *

Back at the apartment, they found Lucy putting the finishing touches on the Christmas tree. The origami cranes bobbed on their thread hangers and the little white lights twinkled and Christmas music was playing. "It's about time you got here!" she exclaimed. "I've been frantic with worry."

"We were stuck in a closet," Elizabeth said.

"And then we were discovered and Lois locked us out on the terrace," Miss Tilley added. "She locked Noelle out, too."

"It was scary. Lois had a gun, and the weather was turning nasty. We could have been stuck out there for hours until somebody noticed us."

"Chris Kennedy saved us," Miss Tilley said, seating herself on the futon. "He was on the case all along. They caught Sammie Wong trying to get to Dubai with the jewels."

"My goodness," Lucy said, blinking. "That's quite a tale."

"It was quite an exciting afternoon," Miss Tilley said, looking cool and collected with not a hair out of place. "I think I'd like a glass of that sherry now."

"I got my job back." Elizabeth reported the fact without any expression. "And a bonus, too."

"You don't sound very happy about it," Lucy observed, opening the bottle.

"I should be, shouldn't I?" she asked. "I don't know what's the matter with me. Thanks to Miss T I even got my Christmas vacation."

"That's great!" Lucy exclaimed, filling three glasses.

"You're probably feeling a bit let down after all the excitement," Miss Tilley speculated, taking the sherry glass from Lucy and tossing back most of the contents in one gulp.

"It's more than that." Elizabeth leaned her elbow on the dining table and rested her chin on her hand. "I feel used. Chris Kennedy didn't really like me, he just wanted to get information from me. And he got me in trouble at work. I was going crazy, worrying about paying the rent. And worse than that, wondering if I'd ever get another job with my reputation ruined."

Lucy gave her daughter a hug. "Well, all's well that ends well," she said, kissing her on the cheek. "Now, it's after six. What shall we do for dinner? There's nothing in the house and I was too anxious to go shopping."

Elizabeth knew that dinner was always at six in the Stone household; her father insisted on it.

Just then the doorbell rang.

"I bet it's Toni, come to apologize." Elizabeth opened the door and gasped, finding Chris standing there. He was holding a huge pizza box and an enormous bouquet of long-stemmed pink roses.

"I'm so sorry," he said. "Will you forgive me?"

Elizabeth thought about the sleepless night she'd spent, and how she'd worried she would never be able to get another job, but that wasn't what had really bothered her. It was the hurt she'd felt when Chris didn't call, when he seemed to lose interest and dropped her. She didn't want to go through that again, not with this guy, she decided, starting to shut the door in his face.

"Elizabeth," her mother said, "he's brought food." Then Lucy was pushing her aside, taking the pizza and flowers. "I think I smell pepperoni, my favorite," she said. "Do come in and have some with us. We're dying to hear all about how you tracked down Sammie Wong."

Chris didn't hesitate. He was inside the apartment and casting sad eyes in Elizabeth's direction. She wasn't moved, however, despite his contrite expression. It reminded her of the looks Libby, the Labrador back home in Maine, would make when she knew she'd done something wrong, like chewing up a favorite pair of shoes. It didn't mean she was actually sorry or that she wouldn't do it again, it was simply a manipulative tactic she used to avoid punishment.

"Put these flowers in water," her mother said, handing her the bouquet.

Elizabeth left Chris standing awkwardly in the living room with Lucy and Miss Tilley and went into the kitchen to get a vase for the roses. She supposed her mother was right and she shouldn't let the flowers die of thirst even if she didn't much like their giver.

When she returned with the vase of flowers she discovered her mother had found the place mats and set the table on the deck, and was opening the pizza box. The rich, spicy aroma filled the air. "Come on, everybody, sit down before it gets cold."

"Elizabeth," she instructed, in her bossy mother tone of voice, "I think there's a bottle of soda in the fridge. Could you get it, please? And some glasses?"

When Elizabeth returned with the soda she discovered the only free seat was opposite Chris, who was waiting politely for the others to serve themselves. She sat down but made a point of not looking at him.

"I assume you were working for the insurance company all along?" Miss Tilley inquired, attacking her piece of pizza with a knife and fork.

"That's right," Chris said, finally taking a piece that

was loaded with pepperoni. "When Gruber took out the policy I was assigned to keep tabs on the jewels. That's company policy when somebody insures an exceptionally valuable item. If it's a painting, we check out the security system, stuff like that. If they're going to loan it to a museum or something, they have to inform us. It's the same with jewelry. They have to agree to keep it in a safe that we've approved and they have to inform us whenever it's taken out of the safe. So when Gruber announced this Blingle Bells Ball I went undercover here at the hotel."

"So you're not a conservation lawyer after all?" Elizabeth asked, narrowing her eyes.

"I lied to you," he said, looking miserable. "I didn't want to but I had to. I was undercover. I couldn't risk being discovered."

Elizabeth, expressionless, chewed her pizza.

"When did you begin to suspect Sammie Wong and Lois Feinstein?" Miss Tilley asked.

"Pretty much right away," Chris replied. "We did background checks on everybody connected with the ball and they stood out like sore thumbs—both had criminal records."

"You'd think Jonah Gruber would have checked, too," Lucy said. "After all, he's supposed to be some sort of computer genius."

"We informed him and he was going to get rid of them but his wife put up a fuss. Noelle insisted on hiring Layla/Lois, said nobody else would do, and Lois insisted on Sammie Wong for the photos."

"And the switch took place at the photo shoot," Miss Tilley said.

"That's right." Chris was reaching for a second slice of

pizza. "The jewels were stashed in the photo equipment and Elizabeth took an empty case back to the safe."

"I can't believe I was that stupid," Elizabeth said, nibbling on the crust, her favorite part. "I should have checked the case. I just assumed they were inside when Layla locked it."

"It's a good thing you didn't question her," Chris said. "They might have harmed you." He looked into her eyes and reached across the table, covering her hand with his. "That's when I was most worried, when you were alone with them in that suite after the photo shoot. I was terrified something would happen to you."

Elizabeth snatched her hand away. "You could have told me. You played me for a fool. You even made it look like I was involved in the theft."

"That was for your safety," Chris explained. "We wanted you out of the way, safe at home. But it had the advantage of creating a smoke screen. As long as Sammie and Lois believed the police thought you and I were the thieves, they figured they'd gotten away with it. Sammie was headed off to Dubai with the jewels, on a private jet to avoid screening, and the New Jersey cops were able to nab him. Case closed."

"I guess you're pretty proud of yourself," Elizabeth said with a scowl.

Miss Tilley gave Lucy a significant look and stood up. "Lucy, dear, let me help you with the dishes."

"Oh, right," Lucy said, catching her drift. She picked up her plate and glass and followed Miss Tilley into the tiny kitchen, leaving Elizabeth alone with Chris.

It was warm on the balcony, the moon was rising and the air was fragrant with the sweet scent of Elizabeth's night-blooming nicotiana.

"Please understand," Chris pleaded. "I couldn't risk telling you, telling anybody. I had enough trouble with that friend of yours, that Toni."

"She was on to you right away," Elizabeth said. "She knew you were a Kennedy imposter."

"Imposter! I am a real Kennedy. My dad is Joe Kennedy from Dorchester, proud owner of Kennedy's Transmission Service."

For the first time since he'd arrived, Elizabeth smiled.

"Fake! That's something. Do you know how many Kennedys there are in Massachusetts?" he asked, cracking a grin.

"Quite a lot?"

"Yeah," he said, leaning across the table and taking her chin in his hand. "And I can't wait for you to meet the whole family." Then they were kissing, a hot, spicy, pepperoni-flavored kiss.

When it finally ended, Elizabeth came back for another. "I really, really like pizza," she said.

"Me, too," Chris said.

Dear Reader,

"I married him." No, that was a different book, different author (*Jane Eyre,* by Charlotte Bronte). So far we've had no weddings in Lucy's family, apart from Toby and Molly. Elizabeth does seem to have an active love life; her beau in *A Christmas Thief,* Chris, reappears in *French Pastry Murder,* when Lucy and Bill visit Elizabeth in Paris, where she works at the upscale Cavendish Hotel, but the sparks eventually fizzle out. Sorry.

It has been a great pleasure writing about Lucy Stone and her family, and I have to confess that Lucy's story roughly parallels my own. When I wrote the first book in the series, *Mistletoe Murder,* Zoe hadn't been born yet and the three older kids were very young, reflecting my own family. Now, more than twenty-five books later, my three kids are all grown and married, and I have five grandkids. Lucy is a bit behind, with only one grandchild, Toby, and Molly's son, Patrick, but he does seem to keep showing up in the books. A very young Patrick appears in *Easter Bunny Murder,* and a few years later reappears in *Yule Log Murder* with his parents, and also his aunt Elizabeth, who has returned to Tinker's Cove for Christmas. Now in second grade, Patrick has an extended visit with his grandparents in *Haunted House Murder.*

Lucy and Bill still have two daughters at home: Sara, who is a graduate student at Winchester College studying geology, and Zoe, the youngest, also at Winchester, where she keeps switching majors. The two girls can be difficult, they don't always get along, and their fluctuating dietary requirements—vegetarian, clean food, vegan—

are a trial for Lucy. Sara's been focused on her degree, but I predict she will soon move to Boston and a job at the Museum of Science, so I think she may finally have time for romance. Zoe, on the other hand, becomes very involved with a computer gamester in *Invitation Only Murder* (now in bookstores) but you will have to read the book to find out whether they live happily ever after.

Lucy has also evolved in the series. She's a lot more sophisticated these days than she was in the beginning. She's been to Europe three times (*French Pastry Murder, English Tea Murder,* and *British Manor Murder*) and has also visited New York, most recently in *Silver Anniversary Murder,* when she investigates the suicide of the dear friend who was the maid-of-honor at her wedding. She explores the lifestyle of the top one-tenth of one percent when she's invited to visit the island summer home of a hedge fund billionaire in *Invitation Only Murder.* But no matter where she is, or who she's investigating, Lucy is still very much Lucy. She loves her husband, her kids, and her friends Pam, Sue, and Rachel; and she loves her job at the *Pennysaver;* and she happily attempts to balance home and career. And as long as she's on the job in Tinker's Cove, I promise you that no crime will go unsolved in the quaint Maine town where nobody locks their doors. Maybe they should. . . .

I hope you enjoy reading more about my favorite sleuth and her family in the other books in the Lucy Stone Mystery Series.

Sincerely yours,

Leslie Meier